Praise for The First Formic War

"The story progresses nimbly, with plenty of tension and excitement and Card's usual well-developed characters."

—*Kirkus Reviews* on *Earth Unaware*

"Card's gift for strong, memorable characters combined with screenwriter Johnston's (*Invasive Procedures,* with Card) flair for vivid scene-building results in a standout tale of SF adventure that gives Ender series fans fascinating backstory to the classic *Ender's Game.* It should also please readers of military SF."

—*Library Journal* on *Earth Awakens*

Praise for *The Swarm*

"This time the invading alien Formics get serious. . . . Now the colossal mothership commanded by the Formics' Hive Queen, lurking beyond the solar system's Kuiper Belt, gears up for a real fight. It's a situation that fascinates."

—*Kirkus Reviews*

"To my delight, *The Swarm* mimics signature *Ender's Game* elements such as resistance against authority, creative problem solving, and childish wit."

—*Ender's Ansible*

BY ORSON SCOTT CARD
FROM TOM DOHERTY ASSOCIATES

THE HIVE

Volume Two of
THE SECOND FORMIC WAR

Orson Scott Card
and Aaron Johnston

TOR®

A TOM DOHERTY ASSOCIATES BOOK | NEW YORK

This is a work of fiction. All of the characters, organizations, and events portrayed in this novel are either products of the authors' imaginations or are used fictitiously.

THE HIVE

A Tor Book
Published by Tom Doherty Associates
120 Broadway
New York, NY 10271

www.tor-forge.com

Tor® is a registered trademark of Macmillan Publishing Group, LLC.

ISBN 978-0-7653-7565-0

Our books may be purchased in bulk for promotional, educational, or business use. Please contact your local bookseller or the Macmillan Corporate and Premium Sales Department at 1-800-221-7945, extension 5442, or by email at MacmillanSpecialMarkets@macmillan.com.

First Edition: June 2019
First Mass Market Edition: May 2020

Printed in the United States of America

0 9 8 7 6 5 4 3 2

*To the men and women
of the United States Armed Forces,
who sacrifice and serve to keep us free.*

CONTENTS

Deception was the Hive Queen's greatest weapon. A skilled and experienced architect of war, the Hive Queen, with the help of her distant sisters, devised an invasion strategy for the Second Formic War so unorthodox and alien, so contrary to the established conventions of human warfare, that the International Fleet, despite its years of preparation, was repeatedly deceived, demoralized, and divided.

It began with a swarm of Formic microships sent into our solar system from deep space, so small and slow-moving that they evaded detection as they attached themselves to thousands of our asteroids. Organisms genetically engineered by the Hive Queen then set to work, mining the asteroids for precious metals so that other worms and grubs and microweaving bugs under the Hive Queen's philotic control could use those harvested minerals to build warships within the hollowed-out centers of these asteroids.

The Hive Queen had not, as the IF had anticipated, brought her fleet with her. Rather, she manufactured it here, right under our noses, using the resources of our own solar system to do so. Then she mobilized these factories of war by moving the asteroids out of their normal orbits and into strategic locations of her choosing.

These movements sparked widespread panic within the highest ranks of the IF, as many feared that the enemy would send these asteroids hurtling toward Earth, initiating an extinction event unseen since the dinosaurs.

But the Hive Queen, as before, showed greater military acumen than the International Fleet gave her credit for. Rather than hurl her asteroids at her desired prize, she employed even greater measures of deception by concealing a small number of asteroids from human scans and scopes. Believing that these asteroids had been destroyed, the International Fleet failed to realize that the Hive Queen was bringing these asteroids together to build a superstructure for her and her army. This superstructure, identified later in IF ansible communiques simply as The Hive, proved to be another example of the true reason behind our innumerable losses and near extinction: the brilliant and cunning military mind of the Hive Queen.

—Demosthenes, *A History of the Formic Wars,* Vol. 3

CHAPTER 1

Commander

To: chin.li21%colonel@ifcom.gov
From: gerhard.dietrich%colonel@ifcom.gov/vgas
Subject: no place for children

Colonel Li,

It has been brought to my attention that you intend to bring a group of boys between ages twelve and fourteen to GravCamp for training in zero G combat and asteroid-tunnel warfare. I will respectfully remind you that GravCamp, known officially as Variable Gravity Acclimation School, is not a school for children. It is a training facility of the International Fleet for marines. As in, grown men and women. It's not an orphanage. Or a day care. Or a summer camp. Our facilities are not intended for the amusement of children.

Do not bring these boys here. Our position out near Jupiter puts us a good distance from the fighting in the Belt, but this is a combat zone. And war is no place for a child. The articles of the Geneva Conventions on this subject are clear. I have attached them to this message for your review. You'll note that special protections were articulated to orphaned children under the age of fifteen. Protocols were adopted to protect children from even helping combatants. You cannot discard international humanitarian law.

Do not board your transport bound for this facility. If you do, you will be denied entry upon arrival. I won't have a bunch of little boys scurrying around this facility like a swarm of rats. It is an affront to the dignity of men and women in uniform and a dangerous precedent within the IF. I have informed Rear Admiral Tennegard and Admiral Muffanosa of my strong objections.

Signed,
Colonel Gerhard Dietrich
Commanding Officer, VGAS

They found the captain's body drifting in his office with a slaser wound through the head and a mist of blood hovering in the air around him. The self-targeting laser weapon was still held loosely in his hand, and the suicide note on the terminal's display was brief and apologetic. It took the ship's doctor and officers over an hour to remove the body and document the scene, and by then word had spread throughout the ship and Bingwen had learned every detail.

The ship was a C-class troop transport that had left an International Fleet fuel depot in the outer rim of the Belt five weeks ago. It was bound for GravCamp out near Jupiter—the Fleet's special-ops training facility in zero G combat and asteroid-tunnel warfare. Bingwen and the other Chinese boys in his squad were the only real anomalous passengers on board. At ages twelve to fourteen, the boys stood out sharply among the 214 marines on board headed for GravCamp. A few marines had made quite a fuss about having a bunch of boys along for the ride, claiming that war was no place for children. But several of the marines on board knew Bingwen's squad well, having been with them when Bingwen had taken out a hive of Formics inside an asteroid and killed one of the Hive Queen's daughters. Upon learning that, the hostile marines had shut up, and everyone had left Bingwen and the boys alone.

But now, following the captain's death, the cargo hold where all the passengers were quartered was abuzz again with heated conversations. Everyone had a different theory on why the captain would take his own life. The prevailing—and unfounded—belief was that the captain had simply "space-cracked," that the isolation and emptiness of space, compounded by the daily depressing reports on the war coming in via laserline, were too much for the man to handle.

Bingwen didn't buy that theory. In his sleep capsule that evening, he hacked into the ship's database and accessed the incident report and autopsy, neither of which put his mind at ease. The medical examiner suggested that the captain had a hidden history of mental illness and perhaps suffered from an untreated case of PTSD stemming from a previous incident in the war. Bingwen's review of the captain's service records revealed that he had recently captained a warship in the Belt but had lost his commission after he had failed to aid another warship requesting assistance, resulting in the death of over two hundred crewmen. Based on what Bingwen read, the captain was lucky he hadn't been court-martialed for violation of Article 87 of the International Fleet Uniform Code of Military Justice, on wartime charges of acts of cowardice. Someone up the chain had given the captain a break and made him the captain of a transport rather than force him to face a tribunal.

Yet even that didn't sit well with Bingwen. Had the man killed himself out of guilt? Out of shame?

The following morning Bingwen gathered with the rest of the marines in the main corridor. A funeral march played over the speakers as a few members of the ship's permanent crew carried the body tube toward the airlock. Once the captain's remains were secured inside the airlock, one of the officers read a few verses from Christian scripture and offered a prayer. The ship's former XO, who was now the new captain, signaled for the loadmaster to open the exterior hatch. Bingwen watched as the body tube launched away silently with a burst of escaping air, spinning end over end until it was lost from view.

Slowly, as if not wanting to be the first to leave, the officers solemnly dispersed and returned to their posts. The passenger marines quickly followed suit. Bingwen and the boys in his squad lagged behind, watching the airlock as if they thought the captain might rematerialize.

"Good riddance, I say," said Chati.

Nak looked horrified. "Have you no respect for the dead? Or your elders? You shame yourself and China."

The boys, like Bingwen, were all orphans, recruited out of China by Colonel Li during the first war. They had each scored exceptionally high on tests designed to identify strong potential for military command. More impressive still, they had survived Colonel Li's aggressive combat and psychological training, or as Nak called it: Colonel Li's Totally Deranged and Borderline Psychotic Military School of Abuse for Orphans.

Chati rolled his eyes. "Spare me the sermon, Nak. This captain was a monster. You all disliked him as much as I did. Cruel to subordinates. Driven by ego. Plus, I hacked the guy's service records in the database. He was a total coward. Got all kinds of people killed."

Nak gave him a withering look. "You read his records? Those are private."

"He's dead," said Chati. "What does it matter?"

"You have no respect," said Nak. "He was a superior officer."

"Emphasis on *was*," said Chati. "He's spinning with the stars now."

Bingwen kept quiet.

"Whatever his motivations," said Micho, "it's still sad. I feel for the man's family."

"He was a total turd muffin," said Chati. "He exuded self-importance and treated everyone with contempt, criticizing everything the crew did, and yet all the while, he's the one with the biggest secret sin of all. The guy was a hypocrite and a scoundrel. You don't see me shedding any tears. I say the Fleet's better off without him."

"You marines okay?"

The boys turned around and found Mazer Rackham behind them. It was the first time Bingwen had even seen Mazer in a formal service uniform.

Chati smiled innocently. "We were just paying our final respects."

"Indeed," said Mazer, who gave Chati a disapproving look, suggesting that Mazer had heard their conversation. The boys quickly dispersed, but Bingwen stayed behind. Once he and Mazer were alone Bingwen said, "Something bothers me about the captain's death."

"Everything bothers me about the captain's death," said Mazer. "But I'm listening."

"The medical examiner's report. It said the captain was holding the weapon in his right hand when they found him. Autopsy report said the entry wound was on the right side as well. But the captain was left-handed."

"Do you always notice people's dominant hands?" Mazer asked.

Bingwen shrugged. "He saluted with his right, shook hands with his right, probably did a whole lot of things with his right hand because of military policy. But he signed every duty roster with his left hand. I watched him do it. And if I'm going to put a weapon to my temple and pull the trigger, I'm going to be very careful and deliberate about how I do it. I'm not going to want to have an unsteady hand and shoot at a poor angle and merely maim myself. I'm going to use the hand I write with, the hand I'm comfortable using. I want my grip to be sure."

"Your subtext here is that this isn't a suicide but a homicide. That's a serious accusation, Bingwen."

"His note was typed on his terminal," said Bingwen. "Not handwritten."

Mazer shrugged. "I never handwrite anything anymore. Paper is dead. As for the captain's hand use, he probably always fired with his right hand. Even if he was left-handed. His left eye might be his dominant eye, but all tactical formations and fighting positions rely on right-handed shooting. That's the training he received. Plus he was over forty, so he was probably trained with traditional ballistic weapons at some point in his youth or early in his career. Those rifles eject empty bullet casings to the right side, away from the soldier. If you're a lefty, you get hot casings ejected in your face or down your back if you hold it against your left shoulder. So you learn to shoot with your right. And keep in mind the first rule of weaponry: Every marine needs to be able to pick up any weapon on the battlefield and use it if necessary. Meaning, the military doesn't make left-handed rifles. Everyone uses the same rifle. It's the same reason why lefties during the twentieth century held grenades upside down when they pulled the pin. Military weapons are made for right-handed people."

"This was a handgun," said Bingwen. "Not a grenade or a rifle."

"Doesn't matter. If you're a lefty who has trained your right eye to be the dominant shooting eye, you're not going to change that up when the weapon is smaller. You're going to maintain whatever firing doctrine the military burned into your brain. That's the whole purpose of training, so weapon-handling becomes instinctual and second nature. You trained marines in China. Didn't you ever have a left-handed marine?"

"Sure. We trained with slasers, though. Never ballistics."

"But you trained left-handed marines to fire right-handed."

"I just wonder about the psychology of the moment," said Bingwen. "What would a man in that state of mind do? He's distraught, he's standing at a precipice. His life hangs in the balance. What hand would he use?"

"Why are you fixated on this? And more importantly, how did you get your hands on the incident report and the autopsy? Because those are both obviously highly confidential documents that a thirteen-year-old young man who is a mere passenger on this ship would know better than to read."

"The security on this ship isn't particularly strong," said Bingwen.

"Be smart, Bingwen. If someone were to catch you hacking this ship's databases, CentCom could inflict all kinds of punishments, including ones that might inhibit your training or participation at GravCamp. Or worse."

"Doesn't it strike you as odd, though? Did the captain seem like the kind of man who would take his own life?"

"I didn't know the man. And I don't pretend to understand suicide or what goes through a person's mind before they take that irreversible action. The man was universally disliked by his crew. That was obvious. He couldn't have been oblivious to that. His commission on a transport was a demotion from his previous assignment in the Belt."

"What do you know about that previous assignment?" said Bingwen.

"I've overheard some things," said Mazer. "It doesn't sound like his commission ended honorably."

"It didn't. It ended catastrophically, with two hundred marines losing their lives. Because of what the records called 'acts of cowardice' on the captain's part."

"I'm not going to ask how you know that," said Mazer.

"It doesn't matter," said Bingwen. "What does matter is that this guy's story proves several disturbing truths to me."

"Namely?"

"First, the incident that resulted in high casualties isn't something I had ever heard about, meaning the Fleet was keeping it quiet."

"The Fleet wouldn't want something like that widely reported," said Mazer. "Not among fellow marines and not on Earth. The IF is already highly criticized in the press. If the world knew that cowardice had killed two hundred marines, the IF would have a huge public-relations problem. I'm surprised you were even able to learn about it. I'd think the IF would scrub the man's records or at the very least classify the report."

"That file had an extra layer of encryption," said Bingwen. "Not a smart security stategy, really. That only drew attention to itself."

"Like I said, you need to tread carefully, Bingwen. Digging around where you shouldn't be digging is going to get you noticed. And not in a good way."

"Disturbing fact number two is that rather than burn this guy, they make him the captain of a transport. They give him another command position. You could argue that it's a less prestigious commission, but it's a command position all the same. The guy should have been sent packing. But he wasn't. He was kept in the game."

"A bad move," said Mazer. "I agree."

"More than a bad move," said Bingwen. "It's downright imbecilic. Why would the Fleet do that?"

Mazer shrugged. "Maybe he had a friend higher up the chain of command, someone willing to cut him a break, or someone who thought he was unfairly blamed for the incident. Maybe his uncle is a member of the Hegemony Congress. Maybe he had incriminating evidence on the people above him, and they couldn't risk burning him for fear that he would release it. Could be a hundred different reasons. I don't think we'll ever know."

"But that's my point," said Bingwen. "Whatever the reason, it's a bad one. It's not one that reflects well on the International Fleet, and it raises all kinds of suspicions."

"Like that the captain was murdered," said Mazer.

"You think I'm being ridiculously paranoid," said Bingwen.

"I think you're being inquisitive. I think that's only natural when something like this happens, particularly considering the captain's less-than-stellar personality and not-so-golden past. You might even begin to believe that people would want him dead."

"There are plenty of people who might," said Bingwen. "Those two hundred marines died because of this man's act of cowardice. Every single one of those dead marines is connected to other living marines in the Fleet. Buddies from basic training. Fellow enlistees. Friends from back home. Maybe even family members who took the blue. Siblings. That's a lot of people who would be angry at the captain for his actions and who might blame him for the death of a friend or a family member."

"Assuming these people know the captain was responsible," said Mazer. "Assuming they know where he is in the Fleet and can create a means to access him."

"There are over two hundred marines on this ship who are passengers to GravCamp," said Bingwen. "Any one of them could have volunteered for special-ops training solely because they knew that assignment would likely put them on this transport and in reach of the captain."

"You've given this a lot of thought," said Mazer. "And now what? You're going to trace the histories of every one of the marines on board to see if any one of them has a link to any of the marines who lost their lives because of the captain? That sounds like an investigative nightmare. Probably impossible, particularly with the records on this ship, which is all you'd have to work with and which aren't comprehensive enough to give you the connections you're looking for. This is a dead end, Bingwen."

"Which is what makes it the perfect setup for a homicide," said Bingwen.

"Maybe," said Mazer. "But I think it's more likely that this death is what it purports to be. A suicide. The deaths of two hundred marines is an unforgiveable tragedy. No question. But I think it far more likely that any marines affected by those deaths are focused on the real enemy. The Formics. I'm not convinced that marines would abandon their duties all in the pursuit of a personal vendetta. Not now. Not in the middle of war. We're trained to be killers, Bingwen. Not murderers."

"But there are murderers among us," said Bingwen. "You don't know Colonel Li like I do, Mazer. He's a killer. I've seen him shoot people at point-blank range."

"Because he considered the people criminals," said Mazer. "They were committing what he deemed treasonous acts against China. You've told me the story. I'm not saying he was justified. He wasn't. It *was* murder, plain and simple. But that was in China, under that regime. Do you think Li would try something like that now, in the Fleet?"

Bingwen shrugged. "I don't know. Probably not. But maybe. You didn't spend years with the man. You didn't see how he manipulates and controls and devalues people. A human life is nothing to him. He would put people in my path that he knew would try to kill me, not because he wanted them to harm me, but because he wanted to force me to harm *them*. He wanted to corner me like an animal, so I'd strike and become a killer just like he is. That's his mindset. A human life is a means to an end. Why do you think he took me and the other boys and started this whole initiative with the Chinese military? Why did he push the same initiative secretly with the Fleet? To make us into the commanders of the future? Because he wants to see bars on my shoulder someday? That's his stated purpose, but I know better. This is about him, Mazer. About elevating his career. My presence here gives him unique purpose within the International Fleet. This program is his baby. He knows that it protects his career and gets him recognized with top brass. That's all he cares about. And yes, I think he would kill again if it protected him, if he thought he could get away with it. And if there are murderers like him within the Fleet, there have to be others, too."

Mazer changed the setting on his magnetic greaves and took a knee in front of Bingwen so they were eye level. Bingwen might be thirteen years old, but he was still exceptionally small for his age. "We shouldn't be having this conversation in the open like this," said Mazer. "It's dangerous to have this conversation at all, anywhere. I'm sorry you've endured what you have, Bingwen. I can't undo that. Nor can I blame you for being skeptical or suspicious of an event like this. If I had experienced the years with Colonel Li that you have, I'd likely be equally skeptical and equally uneasy. If it were up to me, you'd never have to associate with the man again. Frankly, if it were up to me, you wouldn't be involved in this war at all. You'd be back on Earth going to school and doing all the things that thirteen-year-old boys should be doing. You certainly wouldn't be out here in a war zone, witnessing and experiencing the horrors of war."

Bingwen politely thanked him but didn't say more. He didn't want to reveal to Mazer how hurtful Mazer's words were. Well-intentioned words, yes. Kind, even. But hurtful, nonetheless. Because Bingwen had no home on Earth. That had ended the moment the Formic lander destroyed his village in China, the moment the Formic soldiers burned his parents to a crisp and left their corpses smoking and charred in a field for Bingwen to find. How could China be his home now? And why should he be there in a school, doing what other boys his age "should be doing"? What did that mean, anyway? Playing stick-ball? Passing notes to girls? Skipping stones at a pond? Did Mazer think that little of him? Did Mazer think Bingwen belonged on Earth doing such pointless, stupid exercises? Accomplishing nothing? Didn't Mazer realize that this was all Bingwen had? That without this his life had no purpose? He was here to find and destroy the Hive Queen, to end all the suffering that she had poured into the world. That was his reason for being. His squad was not his family. Mazer was not his family. And Colonel Li definitely was not his family. He had none. He had only his purpose. And for Mazer to wish that away from him was beyond hurtful.

"I've said the wrong thing," said Mazer.

"No. I'm just unsettled. Death in any form bothers me. Saddens me. I'll be fine. Thank you."

He left because he didn't feel like talking anymore.

That evening Colonel Li called him to his office. As the highest-ranking officer on the ship, Li had been given accommodations equal to the captain's: a small, private room adjacent to the helm with a sleep sack and terminal.

"I wanted to see how you were handling this," said Li. "The death, I mean. Very troubling."

"Yes, sir. Very troubling."

"At ease, Bingwen. Don't stand there like a Greco statue."

Bingwen visibly relaxed.

"You think I did it," said Colonel Li. "Killed the cap-tain, I mean. You think I went into his office, put a laser through his brain, and then made it look like a suicide."

For a microsecond Bingwen wondered if Mazer had

spoken with Li, but of course Mazer would never do so. This was simply Li being Li.

"I'd be lying if I said the thought hadn't crossed my mind," said Bingwen.

Colonel Li smiled. "Your candor, Bingwen. I'm not sure if it's what I love most about you or hate most about you."

"I can't lie to you, Colonel. I learned that a long time ago."

"Yes. And a critical lesson to learn. Anyone who lies, whether to me or to his subordinates, is not fit for command."

It was one of the colonel's favorite phrases: fit for command. He is fit for command. She is not fit for command. Everyone and anyone could be measured by whether or not he or she was fit for command. And in Colonel Li's mind, the list of those who were fit was a very short list indeed.

"The thought may have crossed my mind, sir, but of course you have no motive. Not unless you were connected to someone killed by the captain's cowardice. And even if you had been, you wouldn't risk your standing or command simply to commit an act of vengeance. You're smarter than that."

He explained to Li what he had learned about the captain's previous service and the many deaths attributed to his command.

"Yes," said Li. "I did some digging of my own. The captain was a fool and a coward and had no business commanding this ship. Also, I'm flattered that you would think me too smart to kill him myself. Such high praise for my intellect."

Bingwen said nothing.

"But I must admit," said Colonel Li, "your murder theory intrigues me. It creates an interesting hypothetical in my mind. Suppose this captain had kept his original post and still commanded a warship. And let's further suppose that you are an officer at the helm of his warship, and he is about to make another decision that will result in the death of two hundred more marines. Do you kill him to prevent him from making that decision?"

"You're asking me if I would commit murder," said Bingwen.

"Call it whatever you want to call it," said Li. "My question is: Is such an act justified in times of war? Would it not be better to kill that man and allow a more competent commander to take his place, than to allow a crew of several hundred to be killed needlessly?"

"Murder is murder," said Bingwen.

"That's not an answer," said Li. "If by taking this man's life, you knew that you would save the life of two hundred marines, would you do it?"

It was another of Colonel Li's tests. The game he always played.

"I would pursue another option," said Bingwen. "I would have him removed from office another way."

Colonel Li waved a dismissive hand, getting agitated. "There is no other way in this hypothetical, Bingwen, or in the heat of battle when decisions have to be made that will either save people's lives or condemn them to death. Do you kill the man or not?"

"Yes," said Bingwen. "If it would save the lives of two hundred marines."

Colonel Li smiled. "There. For a moment I didn't think you'd see reason."

"But then I would surrender myself to a military tribunal to stand trial for the murder of the captain."

Colonel Li's smile faded. "Just when I think you show promise, Bingwen. You demonstrate shortsightedness."

"Without respect for laws, sir, there can be no order. Without order, the entire command structure would crumble. Authority would no longer exist. And who would you command then?"

Colonel Li smiled again and shook a playful finger. "You save yourself with that tongue of yours." He handed Bingwen a data cube. "Here."

"What's this?"

"Whenever an IF officer is promoted or a senior officer is transferred, the requests go through a series of approvals. Some of those approvals are done by algorithms, some are done by real living human beings. If this incident with the late captain has taught me anything, it's that within the International Fleet, men and women hold command who have no business holding it. They are unfit for command. And yet the IF, to its great peril, continues to promote these people. I want you and your squad to tell me why. What you're holding in that data cube is the service records and full files of every marine that has received a new duty assignment or been promoted in the last six months. I made the request of CentCom immediately after the captain's unfortunate demise, and they responded swiftly. You and your squad are to identify not only who didn't deserve the promotions they received, but why you believe they were given the promotion in the first place. There are men and women in this fleet rising in authority to the detriment of us all. I'd like to at least inform CentCom why it's happening, how it's happening, and what can be done to keep it from happening. Without the proper leadership, we lose this war."

Bingwen looked down at the data cube now in his hand and then back up at Colonel Li. "Are there no privacy concerns here, sir? The squad and I aren't authorized to review service records."

"You're also not authorized to review autopsy records or incident reports, but that didn't stop you."

Bingwen said nothing.

"I'm granting you authorization to review these files," said Li, "and since I know you'll ask for it, I will send you that authorization in writing. This is an academic exercise, Bingwen. And considering all the excellent instruction I've given you over the years, it should be a fairly easy assignment. Tell me why people are getting promoted and being given command who don't deserve either. Help the IF identify the flaws in its current rank-advancement practices. You want to help with the war while being stuck on a transport? Here's how."

"Yes, sir. We'll get on this immediately."

"Also, I'll forewarn you. The current commanding officer at GravCamp is Colonel Dietrich, a German. You should know that he is strongly opposed to your presence at GravCamp. He finds a thirteen-year-old in uniform offensive to the extreme. He is insisting that you and the other boys in your squad not be allowed to train at GravCamp or, for that matter, to be permitted to leave this transport. It's a battle he will lose, and I'm taking care of it. I simply wanted to inform you that you will not be well received once we arrive. I'll forward you a copy of his email, to give you a more accurate idea of his vehemence."

"Thank you for the forewarning, sir."

"As a result, you'll no longer refer to yourselves as a squad. That will give Dietrich the ammunition he needs to claim we're now enlisting children into the International Fleet, which of course we are not. That would be illegal. Therefore, to protect the Fleet from accusations of unlawful child soldiering, you and the other boys are now officially enrolled in what CentCom is calling Commander Candidates Academy. You are a student, not a soldier. A citizen, not a marine. I want to be absolutely clear in this regard. You are technically not a member of the Fleet. You hold no rank. Nor have you ever since you were issued a blue uniform. The rank you held in the Chinese army did not translate once you took the blue.

You know this, of course, but I'm stressing these facts again for emphasis. The school is official. I am its superintendent. You will report to me. You will not be under Dietrich's chain of command. He has no control over you. Are we clear?"

"Understood, sir. What about Captain Rackham?"

"Mazer is going to GravCamp as an instructor of marines trained there. Therefore he will be under Dietrich's command. However, I am securing authorization for him to help with the academy as well. What is an academy if it doesn't have any teachers?"

"Agreed, sir."

"This means, of course, that Mazer will be placed in the uncomfortable position of reporting to two diametrically opposed colonels. I assure you I will try hard not to make his life difficult."

"For which he'll be grateful, I'm sure," said Bingwen.

"Lastly," said Li. "If this is indeed Commander Candidates Academy, as we have now officially called it, we must train you to become a commander. From this moment forward, therefore, you will not think of yourselves as a squad, but rather as an army. And since every army must have a commander, I am officially assigning you command over your army."

"Me, sir? Why not Nak or Chati?"

"That is not the response of a commander. The response of a commander is yes, sir."

"Yes, sir."

"Why should *you* be the commander?" said Chati. "I'm older than you."

Bingwen was gathered with the other boys in one of the ship's storage closets.

"Command isn't awarded by age," said Nak. "Ever heard of Alexander the Great?"

Chati scoffed. "Bingwen's no Alexander. And he's nearly a head shorter than me."

"Height isn't how we determine command either," said Nak. "This is rudimentary knowledge, Chati. Are you sure you took the same tests we did?"

Chati scowled. "Keep talking, fartface. See if I don't send you out the airlock with the dead captain."

"That's enough," said Bingwen. "You think Li is going to give you a shot at command if you constantly denigrate fellow soldiers?"

"I won't take orders from you," said Chati. "You're not *my* commander."

"Yes, that's a brilliant strategy," said Nak. "Demonstrate to the colonel how fit you are for command by being insubordinate."

Jianjun said, "Bingwen is the only one of us that's actually had command before. He led marines back home in China. It makes sense for him to be the commander."

"It doesn't have to make sense," said Bingwen. "It's the reality we've been given. Chati, if you want to take it up with Colonel Li, no one here will stop you. But you know him as well as I do. Do you really think you're going to convince him with any argument about your age and your height?"

Chati scoffed. "There are plenty of reasons why I should be commander."

"Really?" said Nak. "Because at the moment all I see is a glaring reason why you shouldn't be."

"Shut up," said Chati.

Bingwen took a softer approach. "Chati is right. There *are* plenty of reasons why he should have command. There are plenty of reasons for each of us. The colonel wouldn't have brought us all the way out here if that wasn't the case. But this isn't about who deserves it the most. This is about us playing along with Colonel Li.

This is simply another one of his games for us. And we all play along because it keeps us in the war. We may despise Colonel Li, but right now he's our link to the IF. He wants us here, and that, as much as I hate to admit it, makes him our ally. Because not everyone thinks we should be here."

Bingwen read them the email from Colonel Dietrich that Li had forwarded.

"Wonderful," said Chati. "Now we'll have two nightmarish colonels in our lives."

"Assuming we even get to stay at GravCamp," said Jianjun. "This Dietrich character sounds like he'd rather send us all home."

"He's involved an admiral and rear admiral in this," said Nak. "I don't like that. What if they take his side? They outrank Colonel Li. We could be screwed here."

"Did this guy say we'll scurry around like rats?" said Micho. "How short does he think we are?"

"We're kids," said Nak. "Kids get underfoot. Like rats."

"I wish I *was* a rat," said Jianjun. "I'd scratch the báichi's eyes out."

Bingwen said, "The point is, the guy has gone to war with Li. And Nak is right, with an admiral involved, Dietrich will be desperate to prove he was right. He can't lose face with an admiral. So Dietrich will be looking for any excuse to justify his assessment of us as goof-off punks and get rid of us. Which means we need to be better than any platoon that's training there. We need to be smarter and faster and more unified than every group of marines that man knows. We have to show him we belong in this army because he'll be gathering all the evidence he can to prove to his superiors that we don't. And if he wins, we go home. Is that what any of you want? Do you want to go home, Nak?"

"Me? No."

"What about you, Jianjun?"

"What home? This is my home. You guys are my home."

"What about you, Chati? You want to go home?"

Chati didn't answer.

"It's a game, Chati," said Bingwen. "I'm not your real commander. I'm your pretend commander. We're role-playing. Make-believe. You just need to pretend along with us. Because the people out there who are against us, those people *are* real. And if we aren't the best and most unified unit in everything we do, they'll win. Not us."

"Every army needs a name," said Chati. "A secret name. That only we know. We'll play Colonel's Li's game, but the name will be our own."

"What name?" said Bingwen.

"Isn't it obvious?" said Chati. "We're Rat Army."

CHAPTER 2

Ghost Ship

To: gerhard.dietrich%colonel@ifcom.gov/vgas
From: chin.li21%colonel@ifcom.gov
Subject: Re: no place for children

Colonel Dietrich,

I am delighted to learn that you have taken such a tremendous interest in the young men of the Commander Candidates Academy, an officially sanctioned school of the International Fleet. I fear perhaps that you may have been given some inaccurate information, however, and my hope is that I can clarify a few matters and put your mind at ease. My superiors at CentCom have already communicated with Rear Admiral Tennegard and Admiral Muffanosa and answered the concerns that you so dutifully raised with them. Admiral Muffanosa has since drafted his endorsement of the school, which I have attached for your records.

GravCamp is the International Fleet's premier special-ops training facility, and the young men of CCA and I consider it a great honor to have access to the facilities. We assure you that we will not interrupt your training programs, as our intent is for the young men of CCA to be segregated from adults in all activities.

This academy is a grand experiment, to determine if the commanders of tomorrow can be prepared from a young age to one day lead the armies that will preserve and defend the human race, should the need ever arise again. We appreciate your full cooperation and look forward to meeting you in person when we arrive.

Respectfully,
Colonel Chin Li
Superintendent, CCA

There was little for Mazer to do all day on the transport other than read the reports coming in about the war. None of it was good: more ships destroyed, more lives lost, more operations failed, more squadrons decimated. Occasionally news of a victory would provide a brief flicker of hope, but then several days of more losses would extinguish the hope before it gained any momentum. The Fleet was losing the war. That was obvious. Not by a small margin. Not even by a wide margin. But by an ocean's width. It wasn't even close.

Mazer had never felt more useless and antsy. Marines were dying all over the system, and here he was stuck on a transport, twiddling his thumbs, doing nothing—neither with his combat skills nor with his mind. He had created a forum on the IF intranet where junior officers could share ideas and tactics and give updates not seen in the official sanctioned reports, but he didn't have net access while on the transport, which meant he could neither learn from nor contribute to the forum's contents. Several marines, sensing his frustration, suggested he pass the time reading from the transport's digital library. But Mazer had no interest in crime novels or biographies. He wanted in-the-moment intel on the war: ship movements, seized asteroids, Formic anatomical studies, weapons advancements and challenges, anything that would give him a more comprehensive perspective on the state of the war. The meager daily reports that came in weren't cutting it. They read like truncated telegram messages: casualty counts, ships engaged, coordinates. Just a string of hard numbers. Like a stock market ticker. No in-depth analysis. No academic observations of Formic tactics or strategies. Just unadorned raw data. To Mazer it felt like someone describing a painting simply by listing off the colors used.

In past conflicts, Mazer could turn to physical exercise to take his mind off the bad news and tedium. But the cramped confines of the transport denied him that as well. The exercise room was always crowded to capacity, and there was no wide-open space to practice zero G maneuvers. Worse still was the unwelcome fact that he was heading toward a training facility to fulfill a teaching commission. The IF was making him a teacher. Him. Someone who had trained his entire career for combat. War was what he was made for. He was as a Maori. The warrior mindset was as much a part of him as were his arms or his legs. And yet rather than using those skills in combat, he'd be stuffed in a classroom a few hundred million klicks away from any fighting.

It was maddening.

Kim was delighted, of course. Mazer's status as an officer allotted him a small bit of data space every month to send home a brief message via laserline. It forced him to write painfully short emails. All he could communicate in the few words allotted was that he was still alive and moving away from the fighting, which was precisely what Kim wanted to hear. She would never forgive him if he somehow worked the system to put himself back in the fight, especially if anything happened to him. If he were killed after voluntarily diving into combat, she wouldn't despise him, per se, but she would feel something harsh and ugly. Anger. Resentment. Pain that might not heal.

And yet, Mazer couldn't shake the drive to get back into the field.

Could he somehow convince Colonel Li that Grav-Camp was the wrong fit for him? That he belonged on a warship?

It wouldn't be a difficult argument to make. Mazer was not teacher material. He didn't have the patience or the academic demeanor. That should be obvious to anyone. Nor did he have any interest in listening to himself drone on for hours on any subject, especially considering that there was no subject he felt especially qualified to teach. He was a marine. He was qualified to do marine things.

Which is why he was the first to volunteer to leave the ship when the opportunity unexpectedly arose.

It was nearly a month after the captain's death, and the new captain, a Belgian woman named De Meyer, received word from CentCom that a destroyed IF warship in the outer rim needed investigating.

"You can't go," said Colonel Li when Mazer floated the idea. "The wreckage is six weeks away. You'd have to divert from the ship in a secondary vessel and catch up with us at GravCamp later. This is grunt work. We have over two hundred marines on this ship who have absolutely nothing better to do. The captain should send them."

"The marines on this ship are mostly fresh out of basic," said Mazer. "They're young and inexperienced. That's why they're going to GravCamp. They don't have the training for a mission like this."

"You don't even know what the mission is," said Colonel Li.

"I can guess," said Mazer. "An IF warship was attacked. But it clearly wasn't completely destroyed or there wouldn't be anything for us to investigate. I can also assume that it's damaged beyond repair, or we'd be going to recover it. No one has mentioned the possibility of survivors, so I'm guessing it's been wrecked for some time. Which means this isn't a rescue operation. And yet this wrecked warship, for whatever reason, is deemed critical to the Fleet. Which leads me to believe that there's intel or equipment on that ship that the Fleet feels is too valuable to abandon. Am I getting warm?"

"It's both," said Colonel Li. "Equipment *and* intel. Or better stated, equipment that collects intel. A recon drone. The ship is called the Kandahar. It was sent to the outer rim of the Belt five months ago to investigate the sudden disappearance of a few asteroids. Upon reaching a predetermined point in space, the ship sent the recon drone ahead to investigate. The ship was subsequently attacked by Formics. No survivors are expected. Two months later, the recon drone returned to and docked with the ship as programmed."

"And now the Fleet wants to know what the drone learned," said Mazer.

"There's a data cube inside the drone," said Colonel Li. "It contains all the data the drone collected on its reconnaissance. That's the mission. Bring in the data."

"We can't access this drone remotely?" Mazer asked.

"A serious design flaw," said Li. "Nor can we order the drone to come to us. It responds to a signature unique to the Kandahar. Like a homing pigeon."

"If the drone found the ship," said Mazer, "then the ship was emitting its homing beacon, which means it had some power after the attack. Did the Fleet receive any distress signals?"

"Not after the attack. The Kandahar got off a brief laserline claiming that they were under attack, but they went silent immediately thereafter."

"Strange," said Mazer. "Why didn't they send a message when the Formics were on approach? The Kandahar should have seen the Formics coming well in advance. Why did they wait until the Formics were attacking to get a message off?"

"I've asked that same question," said Li. "No one knows. CentCom is hoping the detachment can shed some light on that."

"Whose mission is this exactly?" said Mazer. "Yours or the captain's?"

"I have certain contacts at CentCom that keep me informed," said Li. "But this is Captain De Meyer's mission."

"She'll heed your recommendation if you give one," said Mazer.

"I'm not going to send off my only other teacher," said Li.

"There are very few permanent crewmen on this ship," said Mazer. "All of them are support marines. Cooks, mechanics, flight assistants. They're not ideal for a mission like this. Everyone else is green."

"This mission doesn't need a special-ops commando," said Li. "It's straightforward. Get to the Kandahar. Retrieve a data cube. Get back in the ship. Leave. A child could do it."

"If this ship was attacked and catastrophically damaged, it's unstable and unsafe," said Mazer. "If Formics attacked it, they might still be in the vicinity. Plus, the ship may be filled with dead marines. We need to recover ankle tags. That needs to be someone used to the sight of death."

"All marines should be used to the sight of death," said Li. "Any marine who can't take it shouldn't be in the

Fleet. And anyway, we have a crew manifest. We know who was on the ship. We know who died."

"This isn't about making a casualty report," said Mazer. "It's about respecting the dead. We collect the ankle tags to return to the families of those lost, if we can."

"That's not the mission," said Li.

"No, sir, but it's the decent thing to do if we're there."

"Fine," said Li. "But you'll take Bingwen and Nak with you. They'll help you collect the ankle tags."

Mazer stiffened. "Sir, I don't think that's a good idea."

"You're wrong. It's a brilliant idea. This Colonel Dietrich at GravCamp is adamantly opposed to having young boys witness firsthand the atrocities of war. When he learns how Bingwen and Nak respectfully tended to the fallen, that frozen heart of his may soften."

"Or he'll be horrified that we made minors handle corpses."

"As I said, every marine should have the fortitude to do so. And it's important for a commander to understand that his mistakes have consequences. In war, poor leadership results in death, often in great numbers. Those are good lessons for future commanders to learn."

"Bingwen has already seen too much death, sir," said Mazer. "As has Nak."

"You're only reinforcing my belief that they're ready for this assignment. I'll inform the captain and begin preparations. I suggest you prepare as well."

Bingwen and Nak were not disappointed by the news. But the other boys were.

"Why can't we all go?" said Chati.

"Because one, your commanding officer has ordered you to hold your position on this transport," said Mazer. "Two, the mission only requires a few people. Three, more marines on the selenop means more mass and thus more fuel. Four, the selenop can only fit a handful of people."

The selenop, or flying spider, was technically known as a TRAC, or Tender Rescue Assault Craft, a small vessel that could rush into a firefight to extract marines in need of quick rescue. The TRAC earned its nickname because it resembled a spider when its six anchor arms were fully extended and grabbing on to a landing surface, like a giant mechanical spider clinging to a wall.

The interior of the selenop had to be modified for the mission, as it wasn't designed for long-distance flights. But the ship's engineers worked around the clock to retrofit it with the equipment and accommodations the mission required. A week later, Mazer, Bingwen, and Nak climbed inside, detached from the transport, and diverted. The initial acceleration was a hard kick in the gut, but it wasn't as bad as it would have been if Mazer had gone with other adults. Bingwen's and Nak's age and size required the navigational officer to design a flight that would put less strain on the passengers. The result was that Mazer and the boys would reach the Kandahar more slowly, but better that than kill them on the flight.

The first few weeks of the flight were tolerable, but by week six, flying in the selenop felt like the cruelest form of solitary confinement. Mazer had never been on such a confined flight for so long, and the boredom and tedium were beyond overwhelming. The exercise equipment was at least available whenever Mazer wanted it, and he and the boys worked out for several hours every day. Mazer hated not knowing what was happening in the war. The brief reports that had come in to the transport, short as they were, now seemed like an encyclopedia of information. Here he had nothing.

Besides exercise, his only other diversion was the volumes of intel he had brought with him. Before setting out, he had downloaded everything that the Fleet had reported widely since the start of the war. All the many bits of intelligence pulled together. With this, Mazer built a model of the system and plotted where Formic attacks had taken place. He had known roughly what that map might look like, but it wasn't until he had built the model and projected it in his helmet that he saw how comprehensive the Formic assault was. Traditional armies normally amassed large numbers of troops and vehicles before rolling across a landscape toward some military objective. But the Formics were spread out all over the system. Like seeds tossed in the wind.

That was the brilliance of the Hive Queen. She hadn't swept into the solar system with a massive fleet, like a swarm of descending hornets or a volley of fired arrows. She had secretly sent tiny detachments of her soldiers—inside microships so small that no one had even detected them—to asteroids throughout the system. Then she had released her grubs and mined the rocks and built the warships right there in the asteroids. Plus, she had sent these microships with dozens of her eggs, which would grow and hatch in a hive inside the asteroid and then become the crews that would pilot the warships. In that sense, her army was *exactly* like seeds tossed into the wind, except instead of growing into plants, the seeds had grown into a fleet.

To Mazer's surprise, Bingwen and Nak gave Mazer his space on the flight, allowing him to exercise and study his war notes without interruption. The selenop had a few small rooms, and Nak and Bingwen remained in their cabin and rarely came out. It was only at meals that they actually spoke.

"Colonel Li has an ansible," said Bingwen when they were several weeks into the flight and gathered for dinner.

"I find that hard to believe," said Mazer. "Maybe an admiral has an ansible. The Strategos and the Polemarch have an ansible. The Hegemon has an ansible. There's probably one for every thirty ships in the Fleet. Probably less than twenty in existence. Why would Colonel Li have one?"

"Because he reports to someone who has an ansible," said Bingwen.

"Who?" Mazer asked.

"I have no idea," said Bingwen. "But it's someone or a collection of someones who want to remain hidden. That's why they gave him an ansible. So they could speak to him directly and instantly and not have to rely on the traditional laserline links, which are passed up the chain from CentCom and rely on relay operators throughout the system. Li's superiors don't want people to hear what they have to say and the intelligence they share. Nor do they want anyone knowing that they're speaking to Li or that he is speaking to him. That's the beauty of the ansible. You get a direct link to someone without normal IF lines of communication knowing about it. It's a secret back channel, far more private than email, which can easily be intercepted."

Mazer smiled. "And pray tell, why would Colonel Li need a secret back channel to a secret group of unnamed secret somebodies? Li is the superintendent of a school for twelve boys. He doesn't command a fleet of ships."

"I think he knew about the Kandahar before Captain De Meyer did," said Bingwen. "Before the laserline came in with the instructions from CentCom."

"You're sure about that?" said Mazer.

"Not entirely sure, no," said Bingwen.

"And do you have any additional non-evidence for your speculation?" Mazer asked.

"Colonel Li gave us an assignment," said Nak. "That's what Bingwen and I have been working on in our cabin all this time. He ordered us to investigate how the Fleet was promoting its officers and what criteria was being used to give men and women command. He said a large portion of commanders within the Fleet were not fit to hold the command positions they have. He said the Fleet was making grave leadership mistakes throughout the system that could lose us the war."

"He's right," said Mazer. "I've seen plenty of commanders who fit that description."

Bingwen said, "Nak and I believe that Colonel Li's superiors gave him this assignment to give to us. We think we're being used as analysts in a study this secret group is conducting."

"With what purpose?" asked Mazer.

"To stop the Fleet from promoting unqualified commanders," said Bingwen. "To prevent authority being given to the incompetent, the cowardly, and the naive. To remove the idiot commanders and put in the ones who actually belong in positions of command."

"Good," said Mazer. "That's an effort I wholeheartedly applaud."

"But doesn't it bother you?" said Bingwen. "That there may be a secret group within the IF conducting this type of research and pursuing this thinking?"

"Why would it?" said Mazer. "You think they're acting outside their authority?"

"Aren't they?" said Bingwen.

"Maybe not," said Mazer. "Maybe this is a group assigned and created by the Hegemon for this precise purpose. It's no secret that Ukko Jukes has serious issues with IF leadership. It wouldn't surprise me to learn that he's examining how the Fleet promotes people and makes them commanders."

"But maybe it's not the Hegemon," said Nak. "Maybe it's a rogue group of commanders. Maybe it's a coup."

"It doesn't sound like a coup," said Mazer. "Coups are quick and violent. No one is seizing the Hegemony here. Whoever these people are, they're putting the Fleet under a microscope and looking for the bacteria. That's a good thing as far as I'm concerned."

"Except that we don't know who they are," said Bingwen. "Nor do we know what their ultimate goal might be. Maybe identifying bad commanders and bad practices is only phase one of their objective. That bothers me. I don't like not knowing who I'm working for."

"You've obviously given this a lot of thought," said Mazer.

"We've been crammed in this bucket for over a month," said Bingwen. "Time to think is all we have."

Nak said, "All the records that Colonel Li gave us to study came to him almost instantly after the captain's death. No way he could have gotten all those by laserline that fast. He has to have an ansible."

"And consider this," said Bingwen. "Someone greenlighted Colonel Li's program of turning orphaned boys into future commanders. There are those in the Fleet like Colonel Dietrich who are opposed to the initiative. And yet Colonel Li was confident that Dietrich wouldn't stand in his way. That means powerful people in the Fleet are willing to come to Li's defense and safeguard our program."

"Every military and government have an intelligence organization," said Mazer. "Maybe Li reports to the intelligence arm of the Hegemony. Maybe those are his superiors."

"What's the organization called?" said Bingwen.

"No idea," said Mazer. "But the Hegemony almost certainly has one."

"Isn't that a conflict of interest, though," said Bingwen, "to have an IF officer secretly part of an intelligence agency reporting to the Hegemony, possibly in direct conflict with his chain of command in the IF?"

"That's a question for Colonel Li," said Mazer. "Though, if true, I doubt he'd give you an honest answer. That's the secret of intelligence agencies: They prefer to remain secret."

They reached the Kandahar two weeks later. The selenop spread its anchor arms and gripped the Kandahar near the helm, where a large hole had been cut into the ship's hull, exposing the helm to the vacuum of space.

"That hole doesn't go through to the other side," said Bingwen. "So it wasn't a weapon's blast. It's too clean for that." He directed the selenop's spotlight toward the hole. "Look at the edges of the cut. How precise they are. How straight. And cut to the precise depth of the hull's thickness. That's an access hole, Mazer. The Formics didn't blast this ship into smithereens. They cut their way inside."

"Why would they board the ship?" asked Nak. "Have we seen them do that before?"

"Not that I'm aware of," said Mazer. "Maybe it wasn't the Formics. Maybe pirates came after the ship was scuttled and cleaned it out."

"If you were a pirate, would you venture into Formic-infested space to scavenge a dead ship?" said Bingwen.

"If I was hungry enough, I might," said Mazer. "If I thought the ship had valuable equipment that I could sell on the black market or keep for myself and make me more lethal in future raids."

"You think too easily like a pirate," said Bingwen, grinning. "I'm sensing a sinister side."

"It's called survival," said Mazer. "This far out, this isolated from everything, if you're a pirate you can't afford not to take risks."

"Check this out," said Nak, who had taken control of the spotlight and was moving the beam around the surface of the Kandahar. "Look at the hull."

"What about it?" said Bingwen.

"No markings," said Nak. "No IF insignia, no hull

numbers, no hull classification symbols, no painted shark teeth or bombardier maidens. There's nothing. The hull is solid black and completely clean. Like the ship doesn't exist."

"Ghost ship," said Bingwen. "Made to blend in with the black of space." He turned to Mazer. "If the Hegemony had a secret intelligence organization, would they have their own ships?"

"Depends on how big the organization is and what their mission is," said Mazer. "But if I had to guess, I'd say almost certainly. Space is vast. You can't expect scopes or satellites to gather all the intelligence you need."

They suited up into pressure suits and moved into the selenop's tiny airlock where the tether cables and winches were housed. Bingwen's and Nak's pressure suits and helmets had been custom made to fit their diminutive sizes. They spent an hour double-checking all their seals and life support before hooking the tether cables onto the rings on the back of their suits and moving outside the airlock. It was a short spacewalk from where the selenop was anchored to the hole cut into the Kandahar. Mazer led the way, moving gingerly along the surface of the Kandahar, relying on the NanoGoo on the soles of his boots to grip the surface and allow him to stand. Each step was slow and laborious as he had to wait for the NanoGoo to seep into and grip the tiny surface scratches on the hull. The distance to the hole was only twenty meters, but it took them nearly half an hour to reach it and swing down into the ship.

The helm of the Kandahar was dark and empty. No sign of the crew. A few tiny red lights blinked on the consoles.

"No bodies," said Nak.

"The corpses might have drifted out the hole," said Bingwen. "Or maybe they retreated further into the ship once they heard the Formics cutting their way inside."

They turned on their helmet lights and started their camera feeds to record everything. Mazer detached the slaser rifle secured to his leg but kept it on safety.

"Decouple your tether lines and hook them on to something in here," said Mazer. "The recon drone should be down in the cargo hold, assuming it docked correctly. We don't have enough tether line to reach it."

They unclipped their tether cables from the backs of their suits and then tied their tether cables together and anchored them to one of the flight chairs. Then they crossed the helm and Mazer banged on the sealed hatch that led to the corridor.

"Are you expecting someone to knock back?" said Bingwen. "There can't be survivors. The ship ran out of life support a while ago."

"Doesn't hurt to check," said Mazer.

"What do we do if someone knocks back?" said Nak.

"Pray it isn't a Formic," said Mazer.

No one knocked back.

Mazer opened the hatch and gusts of air were sucked out as the corridor beyond lost all pressure. When the air calmed and the corridor was a vacuum, Mazer and the others cautiously left the helm and drifted into the corridor. There were no blinking lights here. The corridor was pitch black and crowded with floating debris. Wall tiles, cables, cargo boxes, items that had shaken loose and bounced about in the battle, perhaps. Mazer swept the space with his helmet beam. The debris and bulkheads and structural braces along the walls created all kinds of shadows.

Mazer turned on his magnetic greaves and anchored his feet to the metal-grated floor. Bingwen and Nak behind him did the same. Pushing debris gently out of the way to create a path, Mazer advanced down the corridor. He took the slaser off safety as a precaution.

They hit a T junction and Mazer went left. Colonel Li

had supplied them with a map of the ship, which was projected on Mazer's HUD inside his visor. They found their first corpse shortly thereafter. A male, early twenties, drifting among the debris in a pressure suit. Mazer turned him over but he didn't find any visible punctures in the suit, suggesting that the man had died of asphyxiation once his suit ran out of oxygen. The man's wrist pad was blinking. Mazer rotated the man's wrist to get a better view. Words were flashing on the tiny screen:

Formics took three crew members alive. Others died in attack. See pouch. Full report <u>here</u>.

Mazer read the screen aloud.

"Why would Formics take people alive?" said Bingwen. "I've not heard of them doing that before."

"Me neither," said Mazer. "But it explains why they cut into the ship instead of destroying it outright. They came for people. That hole wasn't made by pirates."

"But why?" said Nak. "Why take POWs?"

"I'm not certain they are prisoners of war," said Mazer. "We might see them as such, but I'm not convinced the Formics would. Humans take prisoners because we don't like killing. It's the last and most brutal course of action we pursue. War is an instrument of change. If we can achieve that change without killing the enemy, all the better. Formics don't follow the same morality. A human life means nothing to them."

"Then why take people?" Nak asked.

"I don't know," said Mazer.

He rotated the body again and found a pouch at the man's waist. Mazer opened it and found a collection of ankle tags. Maybe fifteen total.

"Taken off the dead," said Nak.

"He must have collected the casualties after the attack,"

said Mazer. "Maybe gave them a ceremonial burial, releasing them into space."

Mazer deposited the ankle tags into his own cargo pouch. Then he took a pocket laser and cut the man's wrist pad free and tucked that away as well. Then he delicately cut the man's pressure suit open at the foot until he accessed the ankle tag. Mazer freed it and read the engraving. "He's French. A lieutenant. We've got his serial number. We'll get his history later. Let's keep moving."

They followed the corridor toward the cargo hold. There was evidence of violence everywhere.

"I see blood on the walls and plenty of damage from slaser fire," said Bingwen. "But no bodies."

"More evidence that the Frenchman took care of the dead," said Nak. "For which I'm grateful. If I don't see another dead person, I'll be perfectly content."

They found the cargo hold. Mazer opened the hatch, and they drifted inside. The recon drone was in its cradle by the bay doors and powered down, having self-docked upon returning to the Kandahar. It was about the size of a refrigerator and somewhat pyramidal in shape on one side. Mazer got to work, following the instructions Colonel Li had given him. It was a simple task to remove the designated hull plate and access the drive, which slid out easily. Mazer released the hatch and freed the data cube.

"All this way for that tiny thing?" said Nak. "Seems like a whole lot of trouble for a measly cube."

"We should check the helm," said Bingwen. "Maybe we can access the ship's main drives. If this is part of some Hegemony intelligence operation, I'd like to learn what we can while we're here. We saw lights on the consoles. Maybe some systems still have power."

"If we're taking votes," said Nak, "I say we get back to the selenop and get out of here. This place gives me the—"

He didn't finish. The ship spun violently to one side, and Mazer's magnetic grip on the floor was broken. He flew backward into the wall behind him and crashed into solid metal, the wind knocked out of him. Bingwen's body crashed on top of him, with Bingwen's oxygen tanks hitting Mazer in the chest like a runaway train. Pain exploded in Mazer's chest, and he thought for an instant that something had burst inside him. An object struck the wall above him. Nak's limp body. Something else struck the wall to his right. A crate. Debris. Objects were flying all around them. Everything had shaken loose in the room. Mazer grabbed Bingwen, pulled him close, and then rotated his own body over Bingwen as a shield. The move proved unnecessary, as nothing struck Mazer's back and the violence all around them began to settle as objects drifted and spun around the room, having ricocheted off the wall. Whatever had caused everything to shift suddenly was over as quickly as it had begun.

"What was that?" said Bingwen.

Mazer was breathing again, but the pain in his chest was unrelenting. At the very least he had cracked a rib. "Nak?"

"Here," said a voice.

They found Nak nearby, banged up but okay.

"Check your suits for leaks," said Mazer.

"Something hit the ship," said Bingwen.

"Something landed on it," said Mazer. "And then emitted propulsion once it landed to stabilize the ship. Otherwise we'd still be spinning." He checked his suit. "I've got no leaks."

"Me either," said Bingwen.

"My suit's tight too," said Nak. "You think it's Formics?"

"It's not the Fleet," said Mazer. "We were the closest ship. No one else from the IF was coming."

"Maybe it's pirates," said Bingwen.

"Pirates would wait for us to leave," said Mazer. "They wouldn't attack with an IF selenop anchored outside. That would put them in a firefight against trained marines. Pirates wouldn't take that risk."

"You sure it wasn't a meteorite?" said Nak.

"Chances of a meteorite that big striking the ship with that kind of force and velocity are remote. Chances of that meteorite then magically stabilizing us after striking us are nonexistent. No, Formics came precisely because we're here. They saw us come in."

"To take us alive," said Bingwen. "Like the crew."

"We don't have a prayer against a Formic warship," said Nak. "Even if we make it to the selenop, we can't outrun them. Nor do we have the firepower to destroy one. Especially if they have hullmat."

Mazer thought the same. Hullmat, short for hull material, was a silicon-based alien alloy that made the hulls of Formic warships near indestructible. A selenop against a warship was like a soda can against a freight train.

"It might not be a warship," said Mazer. "A warship wouldn't try to land on the Kandahar."

"Then what?" said Bingwen. "A microship?"

"Or something like it," said Mazer. He launched to a nearby weapons cabinet and found a row of slaser rifles inside. Older models, but better than nothing. He pulled two free. They would be awkwardly long for Bingwen and Nak, so Mazer gave Bingwen his shorter slaser and kept the longer one for himself. "Nak, you know how to use one of these?" Mazer asked.

"Point at the bad guy, pull the trigger."

"If you hold the trigger down, the beam stays constant," said Mazer. "Better to fire short bursts as needed or you might penetrate the hull."

"What's the plan?" said Bingwen. "We hunker down in here?"

"We need to get these cargo bay doors open," said Mazer. "Not enough to attract attention, but just enough to allow us to squeeze through and get outside."

"Why not go back the way we came?" said Nak.

"Because if it is Formics," said Mazer, "they'll enter through the hole, same as us. Then we'll have to push past them to reach the selenop."

"The bay doors don't have power," said Bingwen. "How do we open them?"

"We're looking for an emergency override. A big crank. Lots of warning decals."

They found it at the rear of the cargo bay, covered in a yellow cage to protect it from accidental access. Mazer sliced the lock with his laser and swung the cage door open. The crank for the bay doors had a safety latch. Mazer removed it, but the crank still wouldn't budge. Bingwen discovered a locking mechanism below the crank that first had to be pumped several times to manually release the locks on the bay door. Mazer pumped the lever, and the bay doors spun open easily.

"Kill your helmet lights," said Mazer.

Everyone did so.

Mazer watched as the bay doors began to separate. He stopped turning the crank when the doors were a meter apart. They found new tether cables on a winch anchored to the wall. Mazer pulled as much slack free as he could and rewound it around his arm. Then he turned Bingwen around and hooked the locking mechanism at the end of the tether cable to the back of Bingwen's suit. Mazer opened Bingwen's cargo pouch and moved the data cube, the ankle tags, and the Frenchman's wrist pad from Mazer's own cargo pouch and into Bingwen's. Then he turned Bingwen around again and handed him the excess cable. "Move outside and anchor your feet to the surface on the other side of the doors. Stay low."

Bingwen moved for the door, releasing cable as he went, then pulled himself through the opening in the bay doors and was gone.

Mazer repeated the process with Nak, using a second tether cable. When the cable was secured to Nak's back, he tapped Nak on the helmet, signaling him to go. Nak moved through the opening in the bay doors and disappeared from sight. The tether cables floated high above Mazer's head and would be easily visible to anyone who came into the cargo bay. Mazer grabbed them and pulled them down toward the floor where they would be more inconspicuous. He looped them around a pipe near the floor to anchor them in place, then hustled back to the crank and turned it in the opposite direction. At once the doors began to close.

"Mazer," said Bingwen over the radio, suddenly panicked, "what are you doing? Get out here."

"The Formics don't know how many of us there are," said Mazer. "So here's the plan. Bingwen, you get visual contact on their ship. We need to know what it is and what it's made of. If it's hullmat, there's nothing we can do, and you stay put until they leave and hope they don't scuttle the selenop. Nak, you watch the perimeter. Scan as much of space around us as you can see. Find out if there are others in the area, or if this Formic vessel is here alone. If their ship is not covered in hullmat, if it's vulnerable, and if it is alone, both of you sneak up on it and scuttle it. Find the retros and damage those first. If it can't turn, it can't chase us. Thrusters in the back are next. It won't take much to disable them. Then get to the selenop."

"We're not leaving you," said Bingwen.

"I certainly hope not," said Mazer. "My job is to keep them busy inside to give you the time you need to scuttle the ship. The one exception is if I'm dead. I'm sending you a link to my biometrics. If I flatline, follow orders, then get to GravCamp. All the data's in your pouch."

Mazer then switched on his dark-vision tech, put the slaser to his shoulder, and moved into the corridor.

CHAPTER 3

Saboteurs

Ansible transmission between Colonel Chin Li and Oliver Crowe, director of ASH. File #487766 Office of Hegemony Sealed Archives, Imbrium, Luna, 2119

CROWE: Your students are surprisingly thorough in their analysis. They've identified fifty-three commanders who don't deserve their posts. Most of these names match what my own analysts had already identified, but there are some new ones here we hadn't considered.

LI: That might not even be a complete list. I have yet to receive reports from two of my finest students, who are currently investigating the Kandahar.

CROWE: Sending them on that mission wasn't wise. If we lose two of our candidates now, we may lose support from the Hegemon.

LI: We will only lose his support if he learns of their loss.

CROWE: Believe me, if anything happens, Ukko Jukes will learn of it.

LI: Then we will take every precaution.

CROWE: See that you do. If we don't control these boys, we don't control the future.

Bingwen stayed low as he crept forward along the surface of the Kandahar, taking one deliberate step after another as the tether cable slowly extended behind him. In the near total darkness, he could see very little ahead of him. The black surface of the ship stretched out before him, like a giant metal hill he had to summit, ending at a distant horizon line high above his head, beyond which was even more blackness dotted with stars. He couldn't see any Formic ship or, for that matter, the selenop. The curvature of the ship made that impossible from his current position. He was on the opposite side, assuming the Formics had landed near the hole, which seemed likely.

Bingwen glanced behind him, where Nak had anchored himself flat against the hull of the ship on his back, gripping the surface with his NanoGoo boots and turning his helmet slowly from side to side as he scanned space around them. It wouldn't be a thorough scan. There could be an armada of Formic ships on the other side of the Kandahar and Nak wouldn't see them from his current position. He'd need to circumnavigate the ship to scan in every direction.

Bingwen glanced into the upper right-hand corner of his visor where Mazer's biometrics were projected. Mazer had an elevated heart rate, but that was to be expected. His body would be pumping adrenaline and all kinds of survival-based neurotransmitters. Bingwen only wished he could see Mazer's camera feed.

Bingwen was moving too slowly. Each step of his boots with the goo felt like slogging through the muddy rice paddies back home, like he had buckets of cement on his soles. He needed to pick up the pace. If there were Formics, they might be harming the selenop. Maybe they had the same battle plan that Mazer did: take out the enemies' transport, cut off their escape, isolate, and kill.

"NanoGoo command override," he said. "Toes only."

"Warning," a woman's voice said. "The full surface of the sole is recommended to—"

"Warning received. Override and execute."

At once his boot grip on the surface of the ship lessened. His heels were suddenly free, while the front third of his soles still clung to the ship like flypaper. He moved nearly twice as fast now. No longer did he have to wait for the full sole to lock. But the risk of the goo not gripping tight enough or not finding enough surface scratches to hold on to was exponentially higher. He could easily slip off and drift away from the ship. Then he would have to climb up the tether cable to reach the ship again, and it would put him back where he had started at the cargo bay.

He found a seam in the surface of the ship where two hull plates met, stretching out before him in the direction he was heading. He moved to it and tightrope-walked the seam forward, which relaxed him a bit. The goo easily seeped into the seam at each step and secured a firm hold.

Twice he released his foot too soon, causing his heart to skip a beat in panic, but in both instances he slammed his second foot down and reattached himself before he could drift away. Moving up the seam, he got into a rhythm, moving about half the speed of a belly crawl, which still felt painfully slow, but much faster than he was moving before.

"Status, Nak?"

"No birds in the sky that I can see. But I need to move around to the other side of the ship to make sure. Any sign of the uglies?"

"Nothing," said Bingwen. "But I'm not close enough. Check the far side and tell me what you see. Mazer? what's your status?"

"I got visual on three Formics ahead of me in the corridor," came back the quiet reply. "Maybe twenty yards away. Pressure suits, jar weapons. They're checking the Frenchman. There's a lot of debris between them and me, so my view is somewhat obstructed. I can't tell if there are more behind them or not."

Formics, thought Bingwen. Confirmed. The Frenchman's wrist pad flashed in his mind: *took three crewmen alive.*

"You got a visual on their ship?"

"Negative," said Bingwen. "But advancing. Mazer, you need to get out if they have jar weapons."

Jar weapons fired doilies, which were flat, bioluminescent webbed creatures encased in a thick tarlike substance that exploded violently almost instantly after striking a target.

"The debris in the corridor is working in my favor," said Mazer. "The obstructions will make it hard for them to get a shot to my position, whereas I can pick them off. Let's keep chatter to a minimum. We both need to concentrate."

Bingwen remained silent and advanced up the seam. The slaser rifle was held tight in his hands and anchored to his arm via the anchor strap, but his arm was so thin that the strap set to its tightest position still felt awkward and loose. The gun was no better. The grip felt far too fat for Bingwen's small gloved fingers.

A bump became visible above the horizon line. As Bingwen neared, the bump rose and came into full view. A microship, maybe half the size of the selenop. Bingwen couldn't make out much definition from this distance, though he doubted it was covered in hullmat. Every microship the Fleet had discovered was covered in crudely processed metal and looked like a piece of untreated iron that had been left to rust for years out in the rain.

"Microship," said Bingwen. "Anchored near the hole. No hullmat. No Formics. I'm moving in closer."

He would be in the open now, completely exposed, without any shielding whatsoever. He stayed low. The microship continued to rise above the horizon line as it came more into view. And then Bingwen saw the selenop as well. A Formic was crawling over its surface, perhaps looking for a way inside.

"Formic on the selenop. Mazer, I'm taking the shot. You ready to engage?"

"Don't take that shot," said Mazer. "They'll know you're out there. If I engage them, the one on the selenop might leave it and join his buddies. I want both of you unseen. Stand by. Engaging."

The radio went silent, but Mazer had obviously opened fire in the corridor because the Formic on the selenop whipped his head around toward the hole and immediately began crawling off the selenop and then across the surface of the ship toward the hole, like a roach scurrying away from a bright light.

Bingwen didn't move. If the Formic looked in his direction, he would be spotted.

The Formic disappeared down the hole, and Bingwen picked up his pace. He so desperately wished he could run forward. To move so slowly was maddening.

"Nak, what do you see?"

"A lot of empty space."

"Watch close. If there's something out there, they'll be moving in now. Mazer has engaged them inside, which means every Formic in the system probably knows we're here."

He checked Mazer's biometrics again. Heart rate steady. Still alive. Come on, Mazer. Stay with us.

"Three dead, but more coming," said Mazer. "Retreating back toward the cargo bay."

"Almost to the microship," said Bingwen.

He didn't have to wait further. He could see the thrusters in the back from here. Maybe twenty meters away. He brought the slaser up and targeted the center of a thruster. Mazer had said to take out the retros first, but Bingwen couldn't see those.

He fired.

A steady beam of red heat bore into the thruster. Bingwen didn't know what he was hitting exactly, but he was causing all kinds of damage. He could see metal turning red hot and liquefying. He moved the beam around, cutting one way and then another. Then shifted the beam to the thruster beside it. There were six thrusters total. Did he need to take them all out?

A shape flashed above him, soaring overhead, trailed by a thin cable tether. Nak's cable went taut and he swung downward fast toward the surface of the ship. He somehow got his feet under him at the last moment and landed in a squatting position about ten meters to the left of the microship. "Okay. That was either brilliant or incredibly stupid."

"You pendulum swung from the other side the ship?" said Bingwen.

"I figured I'd get here a lot faster. A miracle I landed that. I hope my helmet was recording."

"Take out the retros on that side," said Bingwen.

"On it."

Nak raised the slaser. "Oof, this thing feels like an elephant gun. Apologies in advance if I shoot you."

"Just don't hit the selenop. Come in closer if you need to."

Bingwen continued slicing the thrusters. He burned through another one, then a fourth. A hatch opened on the microship, and a Formic emerged. It moved faster than Bingwen thought possible, scurrying toward the back of the microship and leaping in Bingwen's direction.

Bingwen brought up the beam and caught the Formic midflight, slicing him through the center of his abdomen up through his head. But the Formic already had momentum, and it had executed its launch perfectly. Its dead body slammed into Bingwen, ripping him away from the surface of the ship and launching him backward into space.

Bingwen spun end over end, his head ringing, his chest throbbing with pain. The ship spun by his field of vision, then spun by again, but farther away. He couldn't stop himself, his orientation was gone. He felt like a rag doll. "Warning," said the women's voice. "Suit breach, chest area. Warning. Suit breach, chest area." Alarms were going off in his helmet.

His body snapped in half, or so it seemed, as his helmet slammed into his knees and his violent spin and motion came to a sudden and more violent stop. Pain, like a blanket, covered him all at once. His tether line had grown taut and reached its full extension, he realized. He was spinning again, but slower, moving back toward the ship in a slow rotation, stars whirring past his visor. The dead Formic was nowhere in sight.

"Warning. Suit breach, chest area."

He was leaking air, he realized. His head was ringing. He felt like vomiting. He tried looking down at his chest, but the metal ring in his suit where his helmet attached made it hard for him to look directly at the top half of his chest.

"Warning. Suit breach, chest area."

If he had a leak, he couldn't see it. He could see his suit from the sternum down. Everything above that was beyond his field of view.

"Warning. Suit breach, chest area."

"Where specifically? I can't see it." He fumbled for his cargo pouch. No, not that one; the data cube and wrist pad were in that one. Couldn't lose that. His hands found the other pouch, the one with the sealant tape.

"Warning. Suit breach, chest area."

"Yes, I know. Warning end. Siren off."

His helmet went quiet. "Where is the breach exactly?"

"Chest area."

"Where on the chest area?"

"Chest area."

Bingwen was screaming. "That doesn't help." He pulled the tape dispenser from the pouch. Could he feel the escaping air with his hand? He brought up a gloved hand to the area beneath the metal ring but felt nothing. His oxygen indicator on his visor was flashing. He was down to 17 percent. He was at 40 percent only a minute ago. He was leaking fast.

He brought the tape dispenser to his chest and began applying the sealant tape strips in random lines high on his chest. He moved quickly, applying multiple layers at the base of the ring. Perhaps the impact had separated the ring from the fabric.

The flashing leak warning stopped. Whatever he had done had sealed it, though how well Bingwen didn't know. Oxygen was now at 13 percent.

Stars around him continued to spin, and his tether cable was now bunched up all around him in a knotted mess.

"Bingwen, you all right?"

Nak's voice.

"Focus on the microship," said Bingwen. "I'll reel myself in."

He gingerly grabbed at the tether cable in front of him, worried that any big movements might break whatever tenuous seal he had placed over his suit breach. But it didn't matter anyway, because the cable was out of reach, and he had no means of stopping his spin.

He reached behind him instead until he found the place

where the cable's end anchored to his back. He gripped
the line and quickly began sliding his hand up the cable
to bring in the slack. A moment later the line suddenly
went taut and his body snapped forward, bending at the
waist. Bingwen lost his grip on the cable, but he soon realized it didn't matter. Someone was pulling him back
toward the ship.

"It's me," said Mazer. "You all right?"

The bay doors were open by several meters, and Bingwen could see Mazer inside anchored to the floor, pulling the cable in hand over hand.

"The Formics?" Bingwen asked.

"Dead. Five of them. What about the microship?"

"Not going anywhere, even if there is another Formic
inside it, which I doubt. Thrusters disabled. Nak took out
some retros. I've got a breach in my suit. I've covered it
with tape, but I don't know how long it will hold."

"We're getting out of here," said Mazer. "Nak, get to
the selenop."

"Already on my way. You okay, Bingwen?"

"I will be once we're inside."

Mazer reeled him in, and they ditched the tether cable
and quickly maneuvered back through the corridors. They
passed the dead Formics drifting in the corridor, and Bingwen hurried around them, fearful that they weren't quite
dead and might spring back to life and attack.

They didn't.

When Bingwen and Mazer reached the hull, Bingwen
moved to the blinking console.

"We're not hanging around to dig for data," said Mazer. "We're leaving. Now. We were spotted, which means
the Hive Queen knows we're here and may send reinforcements."

Bingwen didn't argue. They untied their original tether
lines from the flight chair and hooked them back into the
rear of their suits.

"If we walk, it will take forever," said Mazer. "You willing to launch to the selenop?"

"I'm willing to try."

They climbed up out of the hole. Bingwen positioned himself on the far side of the hole, then pushed off toward the selenop. The curvature of the ship worked against him, as the selenop wasn't directly in his path. He overshot, but he reached downward as he passed over the selenop's roof. His fingers scraped across the surface, desperate for purchase. Then his hand hit a handhold, and Bingwen gripped tight, stopping his forward motion. Mazer had an easier time of it and was back in the airlock before Bingwen crawled along the hull from one handhold to the next. When he finally swung down into the airlock, he found Mazer and Nak waiting for him. Mazer sealed the airlock door, and in ten minutes, the room was pressurized again. Bingwen had three percent oxygen when he finally removed his helmet and breathed in the cool stale air.

Mazer moved instantly toward the flight controls and detached the selenop from the Kandahar by reeling in the anchor arms. Bingwen and Nak braced themselves against the wall as Mazer pulled the craft up and away from the wrecked ship.

"Strap in," said Mazer. "We're punching out of here."

Bingwen and Nak climbed up into their flight seats and began attaching the oxygen and vitals-monitoring equipment. Mazer climbed into the seat between them and did the same.

"That data from the recon drone better be worth it," said Nak.

Bingwen smiled. "That cushy quiet teaching position at GravCamp isn't looking so bad after all, eh, Mazer?"

"I'll admit it has a sudden appeal," said Mazer. "Hold on to your breakfast."

He hit the launch button, and Bingwen was slammed back hard into his flight seat as they accelerated away from the Kandahar, the most wonderful and glorious feeling Bingwen had had all day.

In the Flood, Victum, and Ping wen. But Mazen
had held the line from son to son, generation to generation, from the Kumhachem to the beautiful and riotous
racing prince of a

CHAPTER 4

Zipship

One of the Hive Queen's most successful military
tactics at the outset of the Second Invasion was in
creating multiple military targets for the International
Fleet to investigate and pursue, some of which were
true targets but many of which were feints. These targets were positioned at strategically placed locations
within and outside the plane of the ecliptic and forced
the International Fleet to divide its ships and forces
into three smaller fleets to investigate all potential targets simultaneously.

Fleet One, or F1, was tasked with targeting the Formic motherships positioned well below the plane of
the ecliptic out in deep space. Known as Operation
Deep Dive, F1 included fifty-seven different combat
vessels, including thirteen asteroid-mining vessels
retrofitted with IF munitions and shielding. Total combat personnel exceeded seven thousand. Among
these ships were two ships equipped with ansibles.

Fleet Two (F2) was assigned to attack the Formic
motherships holding a position in the opposite direction, high above the ecliptic. Known as Operation Sky
Siege, the ships of Fleet Two were led by the Revenor, which carried the Polemarch, Ishmerai Averbach.

The total number of vessels that left with the fleet was initially tallied at forty-two, though this proved inaccurate in what came to be known as the Battle of False Faces.

Fleet Three (F3) remained within the plane of the ecliptic to confront the Formic warships built inside the hollowed-out centers of asteroids and the many superstructures the Hive Queen built throughout the Asteroid and Kuiper Belts. These structures, many of which proved to be hollow Potemkin constructions designed to draw Fleet ships into a trap or distract them from true targets placed elsewhere, proved especially damaging to Fleet morale and resulted in high casualties.

The decision to divide the Fleet into three smaller fleets, thereby weakening the forces within the ecliptic, would prove to be grossly ill-advised. History can only speculate how many thousands of human lives might not have been lost had the commanders within the highest ranks of the International Fleet dared to consider the Hive Queen not as an ignorant insect, but rather as a master of military deception.

This failure on the part of IF leadership to consider the Hive Queen as an intellectually superior organism is yet another example of how human arrogance nearly cost us the war. Our mental advantage as a species had never once been challenged, and thus IF command was slow to acknowledge that human intelligence would ever prove lesser than that of an enemy. In truth, no human military commander, ancient or modern, has proven to be the Hive Queen's equal in terms of creativity, craftiness, or strategic sleight of hand, with perhaps one possible and obvious exception: Andrew "Ender" Wiggin.

—Demosthenes, *A History of the Formic Wars,* Vol. 3

Victor Delgado awoke from his most recent flight coma to discover that the International Fleet had abandoned him. It was day 217 of the flight, and after seven months of travel, Victor's zipship, a cramped, single-passenger spacecraft, was finally approaching the rendezvous—a point in deep space high above the plane of the ecliptic, where the Vandalorum, a warship of the International Fleet, was scheduled to intercept him and nurse him back to health. The star charts projected inside Victor's helmet, however, showed nothing but vast stretches of empty space in all directions. No IF destroyers, no warships, no support vessels, no Vandalorum.

The fleet, apparently, hadn't bothered to show up.

"This can't be right," Victor said, his voice weak and raspy from lack of use. He blinked several times, trying to rouse himself further and shake the sleep drugs that still fogged his mind. "We're only four days away from the rendezvous. We should see someone by now. Are you sure we're in the right place? Could we have deviated? We've been going for seven months. If we were off by even the tiniest fraction of a degree, we could be billions of klicks off course. Please tell me we're where we're supposed to be. Scan again."

"One moment," said the zipship's computer, using a woman's voice that Victor found far too chipper considering the circumstances. "Scanning. Please stand by."

Victor felt a rising sense of panic. The fleet should be out there. Dozens of ships should be blinking and registering on the scans. One-third of the entire International Fleet had come in this direction. How many ships would that be? Fifty? Seventy-five? How could the scans not detect a single one? Why was space before him an empty sea of black?

The scan would take several hours, Victor knew. And if the zipship was indeed off course, it would only deviate further in that time. Should he order the zipship to decelerate? No, decelerating now might use fuel Victor couldn't spare. Better to wait and act once he had twice-checked the intel.

How long had he been asleep this time, he wondered. Five days? Six?

Victor tried reaching up to remove his helmet and rub his eyes, but he discovered to his surprise that his arms wouldn't move. He remembered at once that he was submerged completely in impact goo, a thick NanoGoo-like substance that filled the cockpit and suspended Victor in the center like a piece of fruit in a gelatin mold. During moments of intense acceleration, the goo would cushion Victor's body against the unrelenting G-forces. Victor still felt as if his stomach were dropping into his ankles every time it happened, but that level of discomfort was far less painful than enduring G-forces while strapped into a flight chair.

The downside of impact goo was that the body remained immobile, causing the muscles to atrophy. Victor's flight suit was designed to electrically stimulate his muscles while suspended in the goo, but the suit didn't work as well as the Fleet engineers had intended.

"Retract goo," he said.

At once, the impact goo around him began to soften, like stiff caramel growing more viscous in a heated pan. In moments it was soft enough for Victor to slowly move his arms and legs again, a painful ordeal that Victor dreaded every time he woke from a flight coma. The first movements were always the worst. After days of immobility, his body was like a rusted, unbending machine, stiff and achy and rigid with pain. He winced as he worked his elbows and knees, his joints screaming in opposition. After several minutes the agony had lessened to a dull ache throughout his body, and the goo was as thin as water.

He moved his arm about blindly through the liquid

until it brushed against a handhold. His muscles had atrophied terribly over the past seven months, and each flight coma had only worsened their condition. Some of the muscles were so thin and weak and nonresponsive that it felt wrong to classify them as muscles anymore. They had devolved into sad little lumps of pain tissue that resisted his every tweak, turn, bend, and reach.

Weak though his grip was, Victor held tight to the handhold and steadied himself. He knew no liquid could seep into his helmet or flight suit, but the fear of it happening was always there anyway. Having grown up on an asteroid mining ship, he had never experienced the sensation of being underwater. But he had seen movies where peopled drowned, and as a non-swimmer, the fear of being trapped underwater was as consuming and absolute as he imagined fear could be. He waited, uneasy, until the goo was sucked back up into the holding tubes just outside the cockpit.

"Goo retracted," said the computer.

Victor's body drifted freely now, anchored only by his grip on the handhold. He reached up, and with a hiss of escaping air, detached his helmet. The air in the now-pressurized cockpit smelled pungent, an unpleasant mix of body odor, soil, and dirty laundry.

Marines in the Fleet called zipships "coffin rockets." Not only because of their oblong shape and narrow cockpit that resembled a large sarcophagus, but also because of the risk anyone took whenever they climbed inside one. Zipships were fast, efficient, and inexpensive, but they were also the most dangerous spacecraft in the Fleet, largely because they avoided typical shipping lanes and flew more isolated routes instead. That generally put them at extreme distances from any other ship, which meant no one could come to the zipship's rescue if anything went wrong. And if there was one principle of spaceflight that

Victor knew with absolute certainty, it was that something always went wrong.

Then there was the issue of comfort, or more accurately, the lack thereof. The engineers who had designed the zipship had intended for the passenger to be suspended in the impact goo for the duration of the flight. They had therefore made few accommodations for the passenger without the goo. Which left Victor to float in a cockpit without a flight seat or a reasonable place to sleep. Victor had jury-rigged a sleep-sack by stitching together a towel and pieces of his second wardrobe. It felt like a warped version of Robinson Crusoe, except he was stuck inside a metal box instead of on a deserted island.

But that was the military. No consideration for comfort. Ships were functional, utilitarian, nothing wasted, zero frills.

Victor removed his flight suit and all the catheters that carried waste away from his body as well as the tubes that hooked into his IV port. The whole process took nearly thirty minutes, and he felt far more awake when he was done. He gripped the handhold again and floated there in his undergarments until he realized his undergarments smelled worse than the air. He stripped those off as well and stuffed them into the washing machine.

His head had cleared now. He was nearly himself.

The plan, as it had been explained to him seven months ago before launching from the Kuiper Belt, was that once he was aboard the Vandalorum, he would join its crew and continue moving upward away from the plane of the ecliptic toward a cluster of Formic motherships out in deep space. Attacking the motherships struck Victor as a suicide mission, but if the Vandalorum didn't pick him up, taking on the Formics was the least of his concerns.

Had the zipship overshot? he wondered. Maybe he had gone too far? Maybe he had passed the rendezvous point days ago? Or weeks ago? If so, he was a dead man. He would shoot off into nothing and either asphyxiate once his oxygen depleted or starve to death, whichever came first.

"Show life-support," he said.

He had rigged a screen on the wall and connected it to the projection feed in his helmet. Charts and numbers appeared on the screen, and Victor quickly scanned them.

As expected, he had food, water, and oxygen for only a few more weeks, which was hardly enough to get him to the closest IF depot, five to six months away. And that flight schedule was only possible if he accelerated for weeks on end, which he couldn't do with his current fuel supply. He'd run out of fuel long before he reached the necessary velocity, and then he'd have no fuel to decelerate once he reached the destination. Which meant his only chance of survival was finding the Fleet. If the Vandalorum didn't pick him up, this coffin rocket would literally become his coffin.

Victor felt angry then. He had suffered for seven months in a cockpit no bigger than a broom closet. All for nothing. He had left Imala in the Kuiper Belt for this. He had embraced his wife of only four months, promised to return to her, and then flown off into oblivion only to be forgotten by the military he had committed to serve. What a waste. What a meaningless, fruitless death. It was the ultimate sacrifice, and it had accomplished absolutely nothing. He never should have agreed to these ridiculous orders. He should have stayed aboard the Gagak with Imala and Mother and told the Fleet thanks but no thanks. What could they have done? Court-martialed him? Thrown him in prison? Either of those fates was better than what he faced now.

He had been told that the Polemarch had issued the orders himself and requested that Victor be a mechanic and engineer aboard the Polemarch's ship. What Victor couldn't figure out, though, was why. Why him? Why go to all this trouble for one man? Why spend a fortune to bring Victor halfway across the solar system to a ship he had never heard of, working with a crew he had never met? He was a mechanic. The Fleet no doubt had hundreds of mechanics, maybe thousands. And he was barely a soldier. He had a uniform, but he hadn't gone through basic training. He didn't even have a weapon or know how to use one. Nor was he particularly versed in military culture. He wasn't even sure what the rank order was, except that his own rank, Ensign, a junior officer, was more than he deserved. He was a man entirely out of his element in a uniform, and yet the Fleet had thought him so important that they had shoved him in a flying coffin and launched him to the rendezvous.

Unless this was all some cruel execution. Unless some big admirals at CentCom were all having a good laugh at his expense at the moment. But, no. He had no enemies in the Fleet, and if they had wanted to kill him, a laser through the head was much cheaper than a zipship.

"Show the asteroid files."

A list of files appeared on the screen, and Victor felt relieved to see that everything was still in order. Nothing had been corrupted or lost. The computer drive hadn't failed. All the intelligence he had gathered on the flight over the last seven months was still there.

The files were all observations that Victor had ordered the zipship to make as Victor soared higher and higher above the plane of the ecliptic, giving him an unobstructed view of wide swaths of the solar system. The focus of his research was the movement of asteroids outside their normal and projected orbits. The zipship had the same database that all spacecraft had, which was the orbital patterns of all known celestial objects in the solar system, basically a starmap that showed where every object was supposed to be located at any given time and in what direction and velocity it was supposed to be moving.

With that data, navigational experts could chart a course through the system without fear of flying their ship directly into an asteroid.

But the scans that Victor had ordered the zipship to make showed a slightly different story. Asteroids all over the system were deviating from their projected courses. Each one of these asteroids had obviously been seized by the Formics for some military purpose. Victor had looked for patterns in the asteroid movements in an attempt to identify a larger military strategy, and he was fairly certain that he had found one. A large number of asteroids had moved out beyond the Belt and congregated together at a concentrated point, suggesting that the Formics were intending to build something enormous. And since Victor had made that discovery five months ago, whatever the Formics intended to build might already be under construction or nearing completion, which meant Victor had to get this information to the Fleet as soon as possible. The problem was, he had no means of doing so. He was moving far too fast and was at too great a distance to send or receive any laserlines. His only hope of informing the Fleet was hand delivering the data cube to whatever ship received him.

There was the possibility, of course, that the Fleet already knew about the asteroid cluster. Perhaps Fleet cartographers had seen the same pattern and alerted CentCom. But Victor doubted it. The zipship's position high above the ecliptic gave it a vast unobstructed view of the system. Fleet observers within the plane of the ecliptic had no such advantage. Their scans were limited and filled with obstructions. They could see the trees. Victor could see the forest.

His reflection in the mirror on the wall to his left caught his eye, and Victor turned to it. He had been declining for several months now, and his appearance still horrified him. He was little more than skin and bone. How much weight had he lost? he wondered. Fifteen kilos? It was hard to tell in a weightless environment. Whatever the amount, he was a shell of what he was when Imala saw him last. Would she even recognize him now? He barely recognized himself.

Victor looked down at his hands: knobby and skinny and weak, no longer hands like his father's—strong and callused and reliable, hands that could work tools and bend metals and take abuse as they fixed whatever was broken on the family's asteroid-mining ship. Now they were like the hands of a frail old man. Fragile and thin.

Self-pity accomplishes nothing, he told himself. Move.

He gave himself a sponge bath and dressed in fresh clothes. Then he unlocked the garden bins, pulled out the drawers, and checked the seedlings. He had lost half of his crop a few months ago, though he wasn't entirely sure why. A fungus perhaps. From too much water, or too little. Victor was no botanist. He had tried changing the plants' feeding and watering schedule as he had seen Mother do before, but that seemed only to hasten the plants' demise. They had wilted and died days later, which meant he now had fewer plants producing oxygen. Victor had immediately planted seeds to restore what was lost, but the plants were slow coming. As a precaution, he had changed his sleep and exercise schedule to decrease his oxygen intake. It was a necessary move, but minimizing his movements added to his muscle atrophy and decline.

Hello, little seedlings. I'm glad to see you coming into the world. Too bad we're all about to die.

He closed the plant bins and evaluated his situation. If the zipship was right where it was supposed to be, where was the Fleet? Had the Formics destroyed the Vandalorum and all the other ships participating in the operation? It was possible. Or, less severely, had the Fleet merely been delayed? Maybe they were simply behind schedule and would have sent Victor a message if they could have:

Hey, Victor. Sorry to keep you waiting. We're running behind. Be there in a jiffy. Don't die. Love, the Fleet.

The truth was, anything could've happened in the seven months since the Vandalorum got its flight orders and the mission was put into motion. Maybe there was a change in command, and the new commander gave the Vandalorum a new mission entirely, one that didn't put it anywhere near the rendezvous. Or maybe the Vandalorum was pulled into a rescue mission elsewhere. Or delayed by an unsuspected battle. Or maybe it experienced mechanical or fuel problems and was forced to turn around and abandon the operation. Or maybe the Formic motherships were no longer just sitting there in space, waiting for someone to attack them. Maybe they had moved toward the system or toward Earth, and the entire mission had changed in an instant. Maybe there was no longer a military need for the Vandalorum to come in this direction. There was Victor to recover, yes, but he would be collateral damage. The Vandalorum couldn't abandon its new objectives and the war to travel all these months to save one person.

"Your heart rate is elevating," said the ship's computer.

"Because I'm considering the very real possibility that I'm screwed and will never see my wife again."

"An elevated heart rate can cause distress. Shall I sedate you?"

"Stick me with a needle right now, and I'll break your drive, you understand? Back off."

"I will not sedate you at this time."

"How kind of you to refrain from being a monster. Have you finished the scan?"

"Still scanning," said the computer.

Victor closed his eyes and tried to calm down. If only he could talk to Imala. Perhaps she could make sense of it all. She could see things he couldn't, propose explanations that he hadn't considered, find meaning where Victor saw none.

Imala. Did she know about his current predicament? Could she see his zipship on some chart? Was she tracking his movements? Did she know that the Fleet had abandoned him? Was she watching her husband fly farther and farther into the Black, knowing that he wouldn't find anything once he reached his destination?

He hoped not. That would be excruciating.

Of course, not knowing would be excruciating also, as Victor knew all too well. He didn't know Imala's location. He knew she was onboard the Gagak, the family's asteroid mining ship that the IF was now leasing, but where the Gagak had gone remained a mystery. Victor knew only this: The IF had detected something out in deep space that it wanted Imala and Mother and the Gagak's new crew of IF soldiers to investigate. But where in deep space? Victor had no idea. That intel was classified.

The more troubling mystery was what they were being asked to investigate. Was Imala going toward a Formic outpost? A Formic weapon? The Hive Queen's ship? And why would the IF choose to keep that a secret?

Because whatever it was would cause a panic, Victor thought. Because the secret the IF had uncovered out in deep space showed how weak and ill-prepared we are. Because the IF didn't want to squash people's hopes by revealing something that it knew would dash those hopes in an instant. Because the IF and the Hegemony wanted to preserve the idea that the human race could accomplish anything, that there was no force in the universe that could silence the human spirit. Which was a dangerous falsehood, as Victor knew all too well. He had seen, perhaps more than anyone, that the Formics could destroy far more than our belief in ourselves.

"Scanning complete," said the computer.

"And?" said Victor. "Are we in the right place?"

"Our coordinates and flight schedule are correct."

Victor wasn't sure if he should be relieved or disappointed. "If your nav system is broken, though, we might be off, and you would only think we're right."

"Navigation is fully operational."

"Fine. All I can do is take your word for it. So we're in the right place, moving in the right direction, toward the right destination. And the Fleet?"

"I cannot detect any Fleet ships nearby."

Victor swore under his breath.

"I'm sorry," said the computer. "I didn't catch that. Could you repeat your instructions?"

"It wasn't instructions. Again, you've got nothing in the scans? Zero? No ships. Nada."

"I can detect the Formic motherships," said the computer. "They're still holding a position high above us."

"That does little to put my mind at ease."

And yet . . . if the motherships were still there . . .

"You say you can detect the motherships?" said Victor.

"I assume the objects in the scans are the motherships," said the computer. "They are still at too great a distance for the scans to identify definitively. But something is out there."

"So what does the computer show you? A blob in space? A mass of something too far away to make out clearly?"

"I detect a large mass. Or perhaps several large masses clustered together. Far more powerful scopes from the Fleet have previously identified this mass as the motherships. But my scopes can only detect a mass."

"Could the Fleet already be there?" Victor asked. "At the motherships, I mean. Is it possible that the ships of the Fleet were ahead of schedule and already passed by and are positioned up near the mass? If that were the case, would you know it? Or would the ships of the Fleet just be part of the blobby mass?"

"I cannot detect individual ships from this distance. After a certain distance, only large celestial objects appear in my scans."

Victor knew that was true from his work tracking asteroids throughout the flight. The computer could see the asteroids down in the ecliptic, but the warships down there never appeared in the scans. The ships were too small; the distance too great.

"But it's possible," said Victor. "It's conceivable that the ships of the Fleet are already there, up at the motherships, correct?"

"It's possible."

"On the other hand, it's just as possible that the ships are way behind schedule and haven't reached us yet."

"Also possible."

"How far away would they need to be to be out of range of your scans?"

"Impossible to know. If I can see them, I see them. If I don't, I don't."

Whatever the distance was, Victor knew, it had to be great. Which meant, in either case, whether the Fleet was ahead of schedule or behind it, if they existed they were extremely far away.

"How much longer can I last with my current oxygen supply?" Victor asked.

"That depends on how much you use."

"Assuming I'm not moving. Assuming I'm asleep."

"These calculations are mere speculations and imprecise."

"How many days?"

"Perhaps twenty-four."

Victor winced. Twenty-four. So few.

"What about food?" he asked. "Assuming I'm given nutrients intravenously?"

"Thirty-two days."

"So I'll run out of oxygen before I run out of food.

Okay. We've got twenty-four days. We need a Fleet ship that may or may not exist to take us in within the next three weeks, give or take a few days, or we're dead. What about fuel?"

The computer gave him the amounts still in storage.

"I know how much we have," said Victor. "I need to know what that means in terms of maneuvers, in terms of how fast we can go and how quickly we can change course. Do we, for example, have enough to change course now and get on the flight path of the Vandalorum? Technically that flight path is four days directly in front of us, but I want to divert now and get on the path elsewhere and head directly toward it. My hope is that they'll see us coming, catch us, and bring us in."

"What direction do you want to divert?" asked the computer.

"That's the question. Should we assume the Fleet is above us and go up, or assume the Fleet is behind schedule, and go down?"

"I'm sorry. I do not know the answer."

"It's rhetorical," said Victor. "Thinking out loud here. But you can answer me this: If we did divert and go upward, how long would it take us to reach the Formic motherships?"

"Roughly sixty-four days."

"So if the Fleet is already at the motherships then I'm dead already because I won't last that long. I don't have enough life support to get there. But if they're above us and heading toward the motherships, I could potentially catch up to them. Assuming I could reach a speed so far above their own that I could close the distance within twenty-four days. No, scratch that. I have to do it faster than twenty-four days, because I'll need time to decelerate and match their speed so that they can grab me. Which means I would need to take that into consideration with my fuel supply. I need to save enough for the intercept. Otherwise, I would blow right by them, and my corpse would rocket into the Formic motherships like a kamikaze pilot in a spectacular but unappreciated show of fireworks. But, since I don't know if they are in fact ahead of us, I can't calculate what my speed needs to be to reach them. I'd be guessing. So I'd punch it, pray I guessed right, and hope I'm even going in the right direction. And pray I don't run out of fuel before I reach them. Or oxygen. Which is a lot of guessing and praying and risk-taking. I'm not liking those odds.

"But if they're below us, it won't matter what speed I choose if I go upward because I'll be rocketing in the wrong direction anyway and getting farther from rescue. In which case, another instance of corpse kamikaze fireworks. So going upward is a gamble on top of a gamble.

"If I go downward, I also need to guess at my velocity because I have no idea how fast they're coming. And since we're going in opposite directions, our velocities are compounded, and the chance of me rocketing past them is incredibly high. Even if I'm at a dead stop when I reach them—which is impossible in space, but never mind that for a moment—even if I'm at a dead stop and the Vandalorum is coming upward, the intercept would be a catastrophic disaster. That much kinetic energy would rip the zipship to shreds. Probably the Vandalorum as well. So if I go down, my only option would be to punch it, race downward, then decelerate, then change direction and start going upward again, matching the speed of the Vandalorum all at the right time and place so the Vandalorum could make the intercept without ripping us all into itty bitty pieces. But again, since I don't know where the Vandalorum is or how fast it's moving, I'm doing a lot of guesswork and flying maneuvers so complex I deserve to be an IF fighter pilot. Which I'm not. And for good reason. So going down is a gamble, on top of a gamble, on top of a gamble, wrapped in a miracle.

"Then there's option C. I curve upward into the flight path, but with the assumption that the Vandalorum is below us and coming. And then, when we see her coming, I accelerate just enough to match her speed and conduct the intercept. But, for that to work, the Vandalorum has to be close. It can't be too far behind schedule. It has to be just outside the range of your scans and yet moving fast enough to catch us within the next three weeks. Which is a lot of factors that may not align with reality. Going downward now may be my only chance of reaching the Vandalorum before my oxygen depletes. Three options, all of them stupid. All of them awful."

There was of course an option D, but Victor didn't want to give it voice. He could simply arc upward toward the Formic ship and turn himself into a missile, accelerate as fast as he could, so much so that he'd pass out and die in moments, and then crash into a Formic mothership at so great a velocity that he'd hopefully do massive damage. Of course, if the mothership was covered in hullmat, he wouldn't do any damage, no matter how fast he was going. He'd simply disintegrate.

Option C was the only option that seemed like a maneuver the zipship could feasibly conduct. And Victor figured that it was more likely that the Fleet was behind schedule than ahead of it. This was the military. The assault included dozens of ships. That would take coordination, logistics. Delays and problems were almost a foregone conclusion. And since the Formic motherships were still in space where they were positioned at the start of this mission, Victor had to assume that the mission was still a go.

"They're below us," he said. "And they're coming. We're going to divert and do option C and pray that they reach us within the next twenty-four days. But I need your help calculating our speed and position to determine if this is even possible. If we start off too fast, they may never catch us. So I'd rather err on the side of slow and then punch it when we can actually see them and can accurately determine the intercept."

They ran the numbers and made a lot of guesses, and when they finished, Victor was even more disheartened than before. The likelihood of the Vandalorum reaching them within twenty-four days was remote, even if it was moving at an exceptionally high velocity and was closer than their best-case distance estimates predicted.

He hesitated then. Should he try one of the other maneuvers? If he chose wrong now, it was over.

He dressed back into his flight suit and helmet and ordered the goo back into the cockpit. As it oozed in around him, he dictated a message to Imala. In all likelihood, she would never receive it. But there was a small chance that someone in the Fleet would eventually grab the zipship and download its database.

When the flight goo was ready, Victor finished the message.

"As soon as I'm under, punch it," he said. "The instant you detect the Vandalorum, wake me up again. If it doesn't come, just let me sleep."

"Understood," said the computer.

Then Victor gave the order and slipped into unconsciousness as the sleep meds took him.

CHAPTER 5

GravCamp

**Encrypted laserline transmission from VGAS (GravCamp)
to Selenop #87F3**

Mazer, Bingwen, and Nak,

Whatever you saw and experienced and recovered
at the Kandahar is classified, designation: top secret.
You are not to speak of your experience or of any data
recovered from the site with anyone but me. This
includes Colonel Dietrich, who does not have the
necessary clearance to discuss or view classified materials. All materials recovered from the site are to be
delivered to me immediately upon arrival in a sealed
container that does not reveal its contents.

Please note, the mishandling of classified material or the
divulging of classified information to those unauthorized
to receive it is unlawful, will result in court-martial, and
carries severe penalties. As in decades of prison.

Glad you're not dead.

Li

Bingwen finished reading the laserline aloud, then turned to Mazer and Nak, who had joined him in the selenop's small cockpit to prepare for their arrival at GravCamp. "You still think Li is nothing but a school superintendent?" said Bingwen.

"He's definitely in intelligence," said Nak. "Question is, who's he working for? The Hegemony or the Fleet?"

Bingwen said, "I find it ironic that he's warning us to keep our mouths shut when we don't know anything anyway."

The data cube from the recon drone and the wrist pad from the Frenchman were both encrypted and required passwords. Despite Bingwen's persistent efforts to crack them on the long flight to GravCamp, the data had remained unopened.

"We may be better off not knowing what's on that cube," said Mazer. "If Li and Dietrich have locked horns in a power struggle, as the laserline seems to suggest, the last place we want to be is in the middle of that fight. I'd much rather know nothing and truthfully say so than know everything and have to lie repeatedly to conceal the fact. Lying to a superior officer never ends well."

"Aren't you curious, though?" said Bingwen. "An asteroid disappeared. We know that much. That's what the Kandahar's mission was from the get-go. Find out why an asteroid disappeared. The obvious explanation is that it disappeared because the Formics blew it apart to release the warship they had built inside it. But that happens all the time. Clearly the IF thought there was more to the story or they wouldn't have gone to the trouble of sending the Kandahar and a recon drone. And now this intel is classified. Which means one of two things. Either the Fleet knows that the asteroid didn't blow up and that it disappeared for an entirely different reason, and they suspect that the data cube confirms it. Or, they still don't know why the asteroid disappeared, but they're fairly confident that the Formics didn't blow it up. Bottom line, they expect to find strange data on the cube that they don't want widely known."

"Will you listen to yourself," said Nak. "You sound like a crazed conspiracy theorist. The more you speculate, the more trouble you're going to get yourself into. We don't know anything. We won't know anything. End of story."

"No, not end of story," said Bingwen. "An asteroid disappeared. Big giant rocks in space don't up and vanish. The Fleet knows something, and they're terrified of what will happen when everyone else knows."

"I respect your zealous pursuit of truth, Bingwen," said Mazer. "I applaud you. But I have to side with Nak on this one. Our involvement with the data is over. If we can pump Colonel Li for intelligence, we will, but I'm not holding my breath. Right now the only information I care about is what's going on with the war. We've been off the grid for nearly four months. I don't have a clue what's going on. Are we winning, losing? Do we still have a fleet? That's my priority at the moment. So let's strap in, relax, and prepare to finally get off this damn boat."

They buckled into their flight seats for the dock with GravCamp. Mazer projected the exterior camera feeds onto the interior wall in front of them, which made it appear as if the hull of the ship were glass and they were looking directly outside as GravCamp drew nearer. The space station had once served as a massive depot in the asteroid-mining trade, serving families, clans, and corporates brave enough to venture out to the Kuiper Belt with its billions of unmined rocks. But at the start of the Second Invasion, the IF commandeered the depot and tripled its size, turning it into the largest zero G combat training facility this side of Mars.

They were cleared to dock, and Mazer piloted them to the designated docking port. Fifteen minutes later they were drifting up the docking tube from the selenop and into the airlock where Colonel Li was waiting. A second man in a colonel's uniform with a shaved head and an austere expression was anchored to the floor beside Li, hands clasped behind his back, brow furrowed.

Bingwen saw at once that Mazer's supposition of a war between the colonels was accurate. Li wouldn't want Dietrich present for the data cube delivery, and yet Colonel Dietrich was here all the same.

Bingwen anchored himself in front of Colonel Li, snapped to attention, and saluted. Nak beside him did the same. First acknowledge your CO. Let him direct the introductions.

"Colonel Dietrich, I present to you two of my students, Bingwen and Nak. And this here is Captain Mazer Rackham, formerly of the New Zealand Special Air Service and a test pilot at WAMRED."

Dietrich said nothing.

In his peripheral vision, Bingwen could see Mazer salute both colonels.

"At ease, everyone," said Li. "You've been crammed in a tiny spacecraft for months. No need to make yourselves stiffer than you already are."

Bingwen relaxed, smiled good-naturedly at Colonel Dietrich, and saluted. "Colonel, it's an honor to meet you, sir."

Colonel Dietrich's expression stayed grim. "How old are you, boy?"

"Thirteen, sir."

"You don't look a day over ten."

Bingwen shrugged. "I'm small for my age, sir. Perhaps when I'm old, I'll appreciate this youthful appearance. At the moment, it's rather annoying."

"Thirteen-year-olds shouldn't wear the blue," said Colonel Dietrich. "This is where Colonel Li and I strongly disagree."

"You're not alone in your position, sir," said Bingwen. "Many people object to military academies."

"You're not a military academy," said Dietrich. "Military academies are quaint brick campuses in the Virginia mountains for the rebellious sons of U.S. senators. You're nothing more than a thinly veiled attempt by the Chinese to disrupt IF command and elevate your own countrymen into positions of authority, likely at the expense of commanders like myself from Europe. Were it up to me, you would get right back on that selenop and return to China."

Bingwen maintained a pleasant expression. "I had heard that you were a man who spoke his mind, sir. Now I see that it's true."

"Whatever secret operations you've conducted for Colonel Li in the past end here," said Dietrich. "This facility is under my supervision. Which means anyone here is in my chain of command. I will not tolerate clandestine activity, particularly any activity that seeks to question or undermine the authority of the Fleet. Are we clear?"

"Clear, sir," said Mazer.

Colonel Dietrich's gaze shifted to Mazer. "Captain Rackham, you're several months late to your post. You were ordered to arrive at GravCamp with the transport, and you failed to do so. If you'll kindly give me a full accounting of what you've been doing over the past four months, I might find it in my heart not to court-martial you for dereliction of duty."

"With all due respect, Colonel Dietrich," said Li, "as you and I have previously discussed, Captain Rackham was under orders from Captain De Meyer to conduct a secret operation—"

"De Meyer, my ass," interrupted Dietrich. "He was out there under your orders, Li. Under Chinese orders. Doing what, I'd like to know." He turned back to Mazer. "You're under orders to explain yourself, Captain."

"No, you're not under orders," said Colonel Li, "as you

are only obligated to comply with lawful orders, as Colonel Dietrich well knows."

"What were you doing out there, Captain?" demanded Colonel Dietrich. "You'll answer me or you'll answer to a tribunal of my creation. I'm not opening my arms to some Chinese operative unless I know what the hell is going on. You were sent to a ship. I know that much. What did you find? Why did you go?"

"Bingwen and Nak," said Colonel Li. "You are dismissed. Report to your barracks. Follow the green-yellow lines on the wall."

"They're not dismissed," said Colonel Dietrich. "I'm not done with them."

"You are, Colonel," said Li. "Now and always. These young men are in my chain of command, not yours. And if you continue to embarrass yourself, the only demands being made by a senior officer will be Admiral Muffanosa demanding that you remove yourself from your post."

Colonel Dietrich kept his eyes locked on Mazer. "I'm waiting for an answer, soldier."

"To your barracks," Li barked to Bingwen and Nak.

Bingwen reluctantly moved out of the airlock, with Nak at his heels. When they were in the corridor and out of earshot, Bingwen said, "This is a problem."

"Problem?" said Nak. "This is a hurricane. We've got two psycho colonels locked in all-out nuclear war vying for control of us in some ridiculous power play. I'm half tempted to go back to the Kandahar."

They hurried to the barracks, where they found the rest of Rat Army.

"You two should have stayed in your selenop and made for the hills," said Chati. "GravCamp is more like GravHell."

"Dietrich is an obstructionist," said Jianjun. "He tries to block our access to everything. We wanted to use the

Battle Room during the hours when it wasn't already scheduled for adult training sessions, but Dietrich denied us access, claiming that the adult marine trainees needed it then for their private practice sessions."

"He's convinced we're part of some secret Chinese conspiracy to fill the Fleet with Chinese commanders," said Micho.

"Well, we all *are* Chinese," said Nak. "You can't blame the man for jumping to conclusions."

"We're an experiment," said Chati. "If we do well, the Fleet will obviously get boys and girls from other countries."

"How do you know?" said Nak. "Because Colonel Li told us? When has he ever been forthright with us?"

"You're taking Dietrich's side here?" said Chati.

"I'm not taking anyone's side," said Nak. "Except ours. Bingwen and I have learned that there's more to Colonel Li than he lets on. He's in intelligence, connected with some top brass at CentCom, most likely. This op he sent us on is now classified. We're not even allowed to talk about it."

"Why?" said Chati. "What did you see?"

"We're not allowed to talk about it," said Nak. "Did you not catch that part?"

"Not even with us?" said Jianjun.

"The truth is," said Bingwen, "we don't know anything except what all of us knew before Nak and I left the transport. An asteroid disappeared, and the Fleet wants to know why and how."

"You didn't find answers to those questions?" asked Jianjun.

"We don't know," said Bingwen. "And if we did find the answers, we can't access them."

"Now you're being cryptic," said Jianjun.

"We're speaking honestly," said Bingwen, "and saying all we can say. Maybe more than we should say. The point is, something is going on with asteroids beyond what we already knew. The Hive Queen is somehow making asteroids disappear without blowing them up. Or at least that's the Fleet's suspicion."

"You can't say Hive Queen anymore," said Jianjun.

Bingwen wrinkled his brow. "What? Why not?"

"Because the dull bobs at CentCom have outlawed it," said Jianjun.

He grabbed his tablet. "It was a memo straight from CentCom a few weeks ago," said Jianjun. He read the text off the monitor. "'Effective immediately, all commanders, instructors of new recruits, and other personnel will cease to discuss the Hive Queen or perpetuate the unproven theory that a single organism controls the Formic masses. This theory, because of its spectacular nature and due to the strong strategic desire to comprehend the enemy, gained acceptance among many within the Fleet without it first being vetted by CentCom or the Fleet's scientific advisers. As a result, far-fetched speculation has been accepted as fact, and combat decisions and training practices have altered to accommodate an unproven hypothesis. Such deviations from established wartime practices and training regimes are now deemed reckless and unlawful and subject to military discipline and court-martial. Commanders must give, and soldiers must receive, clear orders based on proven, accurate intelligence. The unfounded theory of the Hive Queen, therefore, will no longer be permissible in private discourse or official Fleet communications. Instead, for all matters regarding Formic psychology, anatomy, or group dynamics, all personnel will use the information found in *Formic Anatomical Considerations in Space and Warfare, 3rd Edition,* International Fleet Press, sections 14, 15, 18, and 21.' Signed, all the bozos at CentCom."

Jianjun turned back to Bingwen and gave a helpless shrug.

Bingwen blinked. "Please tell me you're joking."

"You see anybody laughing?" said Chati.

"We can't mention the Hive Queen?" said Bingwen. "Are they out of their minds? Are the commanders at CentCom really this stupid?"

Jianjun motioned for Bingwen to keep his voice down. "Calling Fleet brass stupid in a voice loud enough to be heard all over the station probably isn't wise. Especially in a prepubescent voice as high-pitched and recognizable as yours."

"This says we're not to discuss the Hive Queen," said Bingwen. "That's asinine. She's the enemy. She's the reason we're having this war in the first place. Do you think Eisenhower forbade his subordinates from mentioning Hitler? I'm trying really hard to give the stupid idiots who wrote this memo the benefit of the doubt, but I'm failing miserably."

"Your insistence on calling them stupid idiots was my first clue," said Jianjun.

"This is insane, what are we doing about this?"

"What can we do?" said Chati. "You're not going to change CentCom's mind on this."

A voice from the door interrupted them. "Bingwen. A word."

It was Colonel Li.

Bingwen stepped out into the corridor. "I've just been informed that we can't discuss the Hive Queen."

"Follow me," said Li.

Colonel Li led him through the space station to a small unadorned office near the Battle Room. Colonel Li sealed the door and then faced Bingwen from across a small holodesk. "The items."

Bingwen produced the small container from his pocket and handed it over. Colonel Li opened it. The data cube, the wrist pad, the ankle tags.

"And there's this," said Bingwen, producing another

data cube. "All our camera feeds, images, and a full written report."

Colonel Li took it. "I trust this is your only copy?"

"Yes, sir. Mazer thought it best if I carried it all off the ship since he is under Colonel Dietrich's chain of command. He worried the colonel would demand he hand it over."

"His worries were well founded, considering that's precisely what Colonel Dietrich did after you left the airlock."

"Where's Mazer now?"

"Confined to his quarters while Dietrich considers an appropriate punishment."

"Dietrich can't accuse him of dereliction of duty. That's outrageous."

"Don't concern yourself with Captain Rackham. Leave that to me. You're dismissed. If I have questions regarding your report, I'll call for you."

He took Bingwen's data cube with the written report and slid it into his terminal. The files appeared above the holodesk. Li regarded Bingwen and frowned. "You're still here."

"Do you know what happened to the asteroid? The one that disappeared."

"Do you honestly think I'm going to answer any questions regarding the operation or what is known or not known?"

"As a courtesy, you might," said Bingwen. "For the people who nearly died bringing you that intel."

"You did your job," said Li. "That sense of satisfaction should be reward enough."

"And what's my job now?" said Bingwen. "We've come halfway across the system to a training facility that refuses to accommodate us. Let us examine the drone data. We can help."

"You don't have the necessary clearance."

"And you do?"

"We're done here," said Li.

"If you let us examine the data, we can give you a thorough analysis that you can then take to your superiors. That will ensure that you get answers, and it will reflect well on your capabilities."

Li smiled. "Bingwen, ever the salesman. I've already demonstrated my capabilities by acquiring the intel. For now, that will suffice. You're not an analyst."

"We've been intelligence analysts for months now. You've had us combing through service records and identifying ineffective commanders. I continued that study throughout my flight on the selenop. My conclusions are in a second report there on the cube. Perhaps that can help your superiors determine how qualified we are as analysts."

Bingwen saluted and left.

It took him nearly half an hour to find Mazer's quarters.

The room was miniscule, smaller even than the cockpit of the selenop. Mazer was at his terminal display, with a myriad of files open in front of him.

"So you go from one prison to another," said Bingwen, taking in the room.

Mazer kept his eyes on his terminal display. "The selenop was more comfortable."

"There's a sentence I never thought I'd hear. I'm assuming you're feverishly reading all the updates on the war since we've been gone. Have you read the memo on the Hive Queen?"

"It was the first one I opened," said Mazer.

"Then why aren't you as visibly bothered by it as I am? I want to punch somebody."

Mazer faced him. "Take a breath and consider the source. The authors of that memo are powerful men seated around some table in a war room at CentCom, each of them so heavily decorated with service medals that they can barely stand upright, even in Luna's decreased gravity. They come from every country that's committed troops to the IF because no nation was willing to join the fight unless it had some guaranteed voice in the overall war strategy and thus a piece of the credit when we win. Which means that every commander seated at that table is in a constant state of fear. Not of the Formics, mind you. Not of losing the war. Not of standing at the bow of the ship as the human race sinks into extinction. No, their fear is a much more personal, immediate one."

"The fear of being replaced," said Bingwen.

"Correct," said Mazer. "The fear of losing their status, position, and power. And since nothing says 'unfit for command' more than ignorance, no member of the war council wants to embrace a theory that might later be proven wrong. They'd look like fools."

"If they bury a theory that is later proven true, then they also look like fools," said Bingwen.

"Not necessarily," said Mazer. "It's more likely that they'll look like cautious, rational thinkers because they'll embrace the idea the instant it's validated and claim they couldn't do so prior to the intelligence. The safer course, politically speaking, is to do what they're doing and wait until they have irrefutable evidence that the Hive Queen exists."

"Do they not see the stupidity of that strategy?" said Bingwen. "We have evidence of a Hive Queen. Or at least evidence that suggests she exists. We can't ignore that. And we have to make assumptions based on the evidence we have. If we do nothing until we have irrefutable evidence, then we miss countless opportunities to find her and take her out. What do they think, that we'll luck out and hit her with a stray laser beam?"

"They're not pretending to be deaf to evidence," said Mazer. "They simply don't have the evidence they think they need to substantiate the theory."

"Of course they have enough evidence," said Bingwen. "Look at tapes from the First Invasion. The Formics attacked as one, maneuvered as one, reacted as one. They were obviously responding to unseen instructions from somebody."

"Maybe not," said Mazer. "Maybe they have a hive mind, a collective conscious. Maybe there is no one entity at the head, but a billion entities thinking as one."

"I killed one of the Hive Queen's daughters," said Bingwen. "I put a bolt through her head. The Formics around her went stupid for a moment as her mental control over them was broken. And then someone took control of them again. Who else but the Hive Queen?"

"CentCom would argue that you're making huge leaps in logic here," said Mazer. "They'd say you're interpreting the events extremely narrowly in an attempt to substantiate your premise, when in reality, there are all kinds of scenarios that could explain what happened inside that asteroid."

"Now it sounds like you're taking their side," said Bingwen.

"I'm playing the same game that Colonel Li plays," said Mazer. "I'm encouraging you to see every angle of this. That's how we navigate the bureaucracy, Bingwen, by understanding how it operates and thinks."

"It thinks like a bag of chimps," said Bingwen.

"How can you be certain that the Formic you saw and killed was a daughter of the Hive Queen? What makes you so certain it was the Hive Queen's offspring? How do you know it was even female? Maybe it was another male in a different stage of the Formic life cycle. Like a caterpillar before it becomes a butterfly. Anatomical differences are not necessarily evidence of a second gender. We're not even certain that the Formics *have* multiple genders. They might be genderless. Or hermaphroditic, or have nine genders, for all we know. To assume that there are only two and that we can identify them without any concrete understanding of their anatomy and reproduction is speculation, not fact."

"Are you saying you don't believe in the theory of the Hive Queen anymore?"

"I'm saying *they* don't believe anymore," said Mazer. "And that's what matters because it makes it extremely difficult for us to do our job."

"So you *do* believe in the Hive Queen?"

"Until someone gives me a more logical explanation for what we've witnessed," said Mazer. "Or until I see evidence to the contrary. I'm not certain, of course, just as you're not. But I'd be an idiot if I abandoned the idea simply because CentCom told me to."

Bingwen nodded, relieved. "For a second there, I thought you were losing your mind."

"I lost that a long time ago. The question we have to ask ourselves now is what do we do about this memo?"

"We ignore it," said Bingwen. "Obviously. We pretend it never reached us."

Mazer shook his head. "Colonel Dietrich is a landmine waiting to be stepped on. He'd be delighted to have reason to indict us. We're Li's minions in his mind, and attacking us would be a swipe at Li. One hour ago I would have said a frivolous charge like this would never lead to a court-martial. Then I met Dietrich."

"We can't let the pursuit of the Hive Queen die because of blind stupidity."

"Agreed," said Mazer. "So how do we keep it alive?" He nodded toward his terminal display as if to prompt Bingwen. On screen was the forum Mazer had created on the IF intranet for the sharing of information among junior officers. A sort of digital think tank for tactics, strategies, maneuvers, and tech that might aid in the war effort.

"We create anonymous usernames on the forum," said Bingwen, "ones that the Fleet can't trace back to us, and we attack this memo. We write counterarguments and stress the importance of considering every viable possibility of the Formic command structure, including the idea of a Hive Queen."

Mazer smiled. "As a superior officer, I strictly forbid you from doing any such thing."

Bingwen squinted at him. "You've already done so, haven't you? Built an anonymous account, I mean."

"Don't play innocent," said Mazer. "You've been posting anonymously to the forum for a long time. At least, I'm 95 percent certain that one of the usernames I follow is you. And I'm pretty certain another username is you as well. Don't give me that innocent look. Both of these anonymous individuals stopped posting about seven months ago, right around the time we boarded the transport and lost net access. Coincidence?"

"Actually, I have three usernames," said Bingwen. "But they're long neglected, so I should probably create a new one anyway. If you can trace them back to me, maybe someone else can, too."

"Don't tell me what your new username is or when you post. Never mention it again. In fact, the last word on the subject is that you will not pursue this and neither will I. Understood?"

"Understood," said Bingwen.

"Good." Mazer turned back to the forum on his display. "Now, sadly, this Hive Queen memo is only the beginning of our problems. We've been out of the loop for seven months, and most of it isn't good. Take this, for instance." He tapped a post and it opened on screen. "A month ago an IF warship fired on a Formic-seized asteroid in the Belt. Typically this is a relatively easy strike for us. The cocoons the Formics build around the asteroids are filled with hydrogen gas. Ignite them, and the whole thing blows up in spectacular fashion, as you know all too well. The asteroid breaks apart. The unfinished Formic

warship being built inside is released prematurely, exposing all the builder grubs and Formic larvae to the vacuum
of space and killing everything instantly. The IF gives
itself a high five and moves on to the next target."

"Why do I get the sense a big 'but' is coming?" said
Bingwen.

"Because it is," said Mazer. "The igniting of the hydrogen gas in this case wasn't nearly as explosive as the
IF expected. The cocoon vaporized, but the rock didn't
break apart, and no warship was released."

Bingwen shrugged, unconcerned. "They blew the
cocoon early in the mining process, before the tunnels
had been dug and the asteroid had lost its structural integrity. Probably before construction on the warship had
started, too."

"That's what the Fleet ship assumed," said Mazer.
"And believing their work done, they went on their merry
way."

"I sense another 'but' coming."

"Fast-forward to one week ago," said Mazer. "To the
IF's head-scratching surprise, they discover another cocoon around the same asteroid. Replacing the one they
had already destroyed."

"Weird. That would be surprising," said Bingwen.
"But I see two possibilities. A different crew of Formics,
freshly arrived, orchestrated the construction of this new
cocoon. Or, option two, the explosion didn't completely
kill the first crew of Formics and grubs. Maybe they were
in the Formic miniship and protected from the explosion."

"The IF ship made the same assumptions. But to make
sure, they sent a team of commandos into the tunnels,
only to discover that the tunnels had been sealed off with
hullmat."

"The Hive Queen is blocking access to the ship," said
Bingwen.

"And protecting her mining and builder worms and her larvae," said Mazer. "She's changing her strategy. She's seen us blow up her asteroids, so now she's instituting countermeasures to ensure that we don't do it again."

"That's why the asteroid didn't break apart when the Fleet first shot it," said Bingwen. "The Hive Queen made the interior of the asteroid airtight. All the IF blew up was the cocoon and the hydrogen gas between it and the surface of the asteroid."

"And everything beneath the hullmat was protected," said Mazer. "Basically, this means our entire strategy to stop Formic ship construction is out the window. Because now we can't simply fire on the asteroids, blow them up, and walk away. We have to send people into the tunnels to penetrate hullmat roadblocks. And then, once we're through the barrier, *then* we blow the asteroid."

"The only substance that penetrates hullmat is the NanoCloud that Lem Jukes developed," said Bingwen.

The NanoCloud was a swarm of nanobots that supposedly "unzipped" the hullmat molecules by breaking apart their ionic bonds. In practice it looked like magic, like the hullmat was dissolving into nothing.

"NanoCloud is the answer," said Mazer. "No question. But it's not designed to be handled by marines in narrow Formic tunnels. It's designed as a projectile. The current delivery system is a missile that fires pellets of NanoCloud at the surface of a ship. Like a shotgun blast. The individual pellets adhere to hullmat and create a type of mini-dome beneath which the NanoCloud is released on the hull. Then it essentially dissolves the hullmat by breaking it apart."

"So what are the marines in these tunnels doing now?" Bingwen asked.

"They're asking for help," said Mazer. "They're posting on the forum and asking for ideas on how an individual marine might safely carry and use NanoCloud to penetrate the Hive Queen's roadblock countermeasures."

"Has anyone suggested anything worthwhile?"

"A few proposals are trickling in, but nothing that shows great promise. The problem with NanoCloud is that it doesn't discriminate. It will unzip anything made with silicon, including a pressure suit or the visor of a marine's helmet."

"Do those things have silicon?" Bingwen asked.

"I don't know," said Mazer, "but that's the first thing I'd wonder if I were a marine being asked to handle the stuff out in the vacuum of space."

"How can we help?" said Bingwen.

"We can't until we understand how NanoCloud works. That's our first objective. I've checked our stock records here at GravCamp. There are eight canisters of Nano-Cloud shot capsules in the armory."

"What are you suggesting?" said Bingwen. "That we stroll into the armory and ask the quartermaster to give us a barrel of NanoCloud capsules to play with? No chance of that working."

"Agreed," said Mazer. "We'll need to acquire them a different way. Do you have a backpack or a bag in your quarters that you can carry them in?"

"You want me to steal from the armory?" said Bingwen.

"Not steal," said Mazer. "Borrow. Surreptitiously. I'd do it myself, but I'm confined to quarters, and I suspect this is a job better suited for Rat Army."

"You're not supposed to know our secret name."

"We were crammed in the selenop for a long time. You and Nak don't always talk quietly."

"Assuming I'm able to acquire a few capsules of Nano-Cloud," said Bingwen. "Then what? This stuff could be volatile. If it eats through silicon and we unleash it in the space station, it could eat a hole in the wall."

"NanoCloud isn't a chemical," said Mazer. "They're nanobots. They turn off and on. We learn to control them before we handle them. Borrowing NanoCloud is probably one of the last steps here. The first being learning how to manipulate it and what the delivery system should be for an individual marine. This is involved. Lots of steps. You're going to need all of Rat."

"This is insane," said Bingwen. "We haven't even been here half a day, and already we're robbing the place and planning to buck orders from CentCom."

"We're fighting a war, Bingwen. Just because we're essentially in prison doesn't mean we stop fighting."

CHAPTER 6

Imala

Of the hundreds of technological advances achieved immediately prior to and during the Second Invasion, the greatest of these from a military and sociological perspective was, without question, the creation of the ansible. Developed in secret by a team of engineers gathered by Ukko Jukes, the Hegemon of Earth, the ansible was based on principles of philotic theory, which, prior to the First Invasion, were given little serious consideration within the scientific community. The central hypothesis is that all objects in the universe, regardless of size, are interconnected by philotic strings, and that paired subatomic particles across vast reaches of space can influence each other instantaneously.

During the First Invasion, as theories regarding the Hive Queen gained wider acceptance, particularly the belief that she could communicate with all of her children instantaneously via philotic strings, efforts to develop a communication device based on those principles began in earnest.

The actual ansible took on a number of iterations throughout the war as engineers learned how to build smaller and more intricate systems to influence and track the paired particles. The number of ansibles in use, however, remained relatively low throughout the war. Only one in thirty ships had one. As a result, a ship fortunate enough to possess an ansible would typically serve as the communications vessel for the fleet to which it belonged, sending and receiving instant messages to and from CentCom.

Due to the secrecy surrounding the ansible and the Hegemon's desire to safeguard the technology solely for military use, each ansible was housed in its own room on a ship. Only one individual, known as the communications officer, was given access and allowed to operate the ansible. This policy proved to be a great frustration to many captains, who were unaccustomed to and bristled at being denied entry to any room on their vessel. Any captain who violated these regulations, however, was quickly removed from his or her post, and all infractions ceased.

The Hegemony was so protective of the technology that the very word "ansible" was classified. Instead, officers were ordered to refer to the ansible either as "the device" or "the quad," a fictitious name that falsely suggested an object of four equal parts. Despite these efforts at clandestine nomenclature, the term "ansible" was often used among senior staff.

—Demosthenes, *A History of the Formic Wars,* Vol. 3

Imala hovered in the ship's hydroponic garden, pruning dead leaves from the tomato plants and trying to ignore the discomfort in her abdomen. Pregnancy had proven far more agonizing than she had imagined, especially now in the third trimester, with her womb so big and rotund that every activity in zero G was an exercise in awkwardness.

Insomnia didn't help matters. Imala's body screamed

for sleep. And yet as soon as sleep shift rolled around, the baby would start kicking and shifting and pressing down on her cervix, as if the little stinker was determined to keep Imala up and moving. Tonight was no different. Imala had tossed and turned for a while down in the ship's fuge before finally giving up and coming to the garden, hoping that a little physical labor would tire her out so severely that she'd fall asleep despite the baby's movements.

Yet working alone in the garden while most of the ship's crew was asleep meant that Imala's mind was free to wander and worry. She couldn't help herself. The ship was five to six months away from the nearest medical facility, and Imala was keenly aware of the dangers of giving birth on an isolated warship this deep in the Kuiper Belt. What if something went wrong with the delivery? What if the baby had complications and needed special neonatal equipment to stay alive, equipment that wasn't on board the Gagak? What if the baby required an operation? What if, what if, what if.

A few weeks ago, she had mustered all her confidence and buried those fears, convincing herself that all would be well. The ship had an IF doctor among the crew, after all. Not an obstetrician, of course, but a doctor nonetheless, which counted for something. And Rena, Imala's mother-in-law, had helped deliver nearly two dozen babies over the years as a midwife among her asteroid mining crew. That too gave Imala extra comfort. And then there was Imala herself, who by virtue of some stubborn maternal protector instinct, was simply not going to allow anything to happen to her child.

But now, eight months into the pregnancy, with the delivery fast approaching, all the doubts she had entertained early in the pregnancy were once again surfacing and taking root in her mind. Her child, this innocent, fragile person inside her, this symbol of her love for and union with Victor, might not survive.

The worst part was that she couldn't share her concerns with Victor. She couldn't ask him to carry this burden with her. He likely didn't even know that she was pregnant.

She laughed quietly at that. A laugh that turned immediately to tears. It was so absurd. So ridiculous. Her husband didn't even know she was pregnant. She had watched him climb into a zipship and rocket away without either of them aware that something was growing inside her.

She reached over to the next plant and began searching for the dead leaves.

If only I could just crawl into a sleep sack, she thought, like everyone else and sleep in zero G.

But no, Imala had to sleep in the fuge, the spinning center of the ship where she could experience a full G of gravity. It was strange to sleep on a mattress again, to feel the weight of her body sink into the foam and springs. She had been sleeping in zero G in a sleep sack for so long that lying down on a mattress now felt foreign. Her arms, so accustomed to floating effortlessly beside her, now flopped about like limp eels—sometimes even striking her in the face when she adjusted her position. How did people sleep this way? How had *she* slept this way for so much of her life?

She had no choice, however. Gravity was good for the baby's growth and development. Necessary, even. Cells didn't divide as quickly and as regularly in a zero G environment. Humans had evolved with their feet on the ground, and thus the development and delivery of human offspring required gravity as well. Gravity was our friend. Birthing a baby in space disrupted the entire process.

Still, to go from zero G to a full G in a day, with a baby inside her, was like changing who she was. Shedding one skin and putting on another. One minute she was floating, the next minute she was like a stone balloon trying to get her feet under her. It was almost a blessing that Victor didn't see her this way: ankles swollen, chin thick, face plump; even her fingers felt chunky.

Rena often told Imala how beautiful she was, that there was nothing in the universe as lovely and perfect as a woman with child. But even though Rena was probably being genuine, it sounded to Imala like a lie, like pity.

Imala pulled a wilting leaf off the vine and stuffed the leaf into the compost pouch on the wall.

The garden was a tube-shaped space with plants rooted in the walls, their vines and leaves growing inward toward the center, as if reaching for Imala, begging for her attention. A pole traversed the room from end to end, like a fireman's pole through a cylindrical jungle. Imala gripped the pole to steady herself. Her other hand, when not plucking a leaf, rested on her stomach, as if cradling the baby and keeping it inside her, away from a world ill-equipped to receive it.

She wondered what the Formics would plant if they took Earth. Did they have a fruit like tomatoes? Their fauna was so unlike our own that the prospect seemed unlikely. Their plants had evolved using a different protein structure, perhaps even harnessing light in a way that no Earth-born plant ever could. An alien version of photosynthesis, maybe. That's why the Formics had scoured southeast China, burning away the landscape and peeling back all biota. Their plants couldn't thrive alongside ours. Earth had to be reborn, the old harmful biosphere burned away so a new one could emerge and take its place, one more accommodating to the Formic species. Otherwise the Formic young could not survive.

The young.

Imala smiled sadly to herself. There I go again. Try as I might to take my thoughts elsewhere, they somehow always return to children. Her child. The only child that mattered.

"Can't sleep?"

Imala started, releasing the tomato vine she had just grabbed, and turned toward the sound of the voice.

Rena hovered at the exit, steadying herself at a handhold, her baggy sleepwear rumpled and unkempt, her white hair unruly, as if she had just floated out of her sleep sack. "I don't want to be the annoying mother-in-law who nags you all the time, but you do need sleep, you know."

Imala smiled and tucked the dead leaves she was holding into the compost pouch. Rena was so much like her son Victor—or perhaps it was better to say that he was like her. So much of who he was he had learned from his mother. They both seemed to possess a sixth sense, some secret ability to detect whenever Imala was feeling particularly glum, even when it happened in the middle of the night.

"Believe me," said Imala, "if I could sleep I would. I tried for two hours before I came up here."

"The offer still stands," said Rena. "I can give you a mild sedative. It won't hurt the baby."

It was the third time in as many days that Rena had offered Imala a sleep aid, and for a moment Imala considered it. If Rena said it was innocuous it almost certainly was. And didn't Imala deserve to sleep? How glorious it would be to close her eyes for eight hours and not be awakened by every slight shift the baby made. What a gift that would be. Even the thought of it nearly brought Imala back to tears. Damn the tears that came so easily now. It seemed like everything invited them.

"I know you want to do this naturally," said Rena. "I know you're worried that a sleep aid might slow the baby's heart rate. But if you're utterly exhausted, that's not healthy for the baby either. Your body is one with hers.

Trust me, this is my granddaughter we're talking about. I wouldn't give you anything that might hurt her."

"We don't know that it's a girl," said Imala.

Rena got that twinkle in her eye again, like a giddy child on Christmas Eve. "It's a girl. I'm sure of it. A grandmother knows these things."

"How exactly?"

"Intuition." Rena tapped the side of her own nose, as if the explanation were hidden somewhere inside.

Imala pulled on the pole and drifted toward her. "You're setting yourself up for disappointment. It's just as likely to be a boy."

"We've got too many boys on this ship already," said Rena. "We could use another girl. Even the odds, girl power and all that." She winked. "Let a grandmother dream."

Imala smiled, but her heart wasn't in it. She was too tired to be amused.

"Take the pill," said Rena, her voice becoming gentle. "You look half dead. I've done this before, remember? I know what eight months of baby feels like, even in zero gravity. Your muscles throb, joints feel stiff, your lower back aches, to say nothing of the constant pressure on your cervix."

"You forgot headaches."

"Migraines like the end of the world," said Rena, reaching into her pocket and pulling out the bottle. "Here."

"You're carrying that around with you now?"

"You weren't in bed," said Rena. "I figured you need this now more than ever."

Imala took the bottle but didn't open it. "The baby's about forty-six centimeters now. On average."

"Bigger than a cabbage," Rena said with a smile.

Imala smiled back, and this time it was genuine. Up until now, during every week of the pregnancy, the size of the baby had been compared to some fruit or vegetable. At sixteen weeks, an avocado. Seventeen weeks, a turnip.

And on and on. It had become an inside joke between Rena and Imala.

"No fruit or vegetable this month," said Imala. "At least, the ship's health wiki didn't list one. At eight months, it's the size of a baby."

"A beautiful baby, no doubt," said Rena.

"Lungs may not be fully developed, though," said Imala. "Brain is still developing."

"Everyone's brain is still developing. Even mine, though some may doubt it. And anyway, this baby has your genes as well as Victor's. I'm guessing its brain is going to be just fine. It she still kicking?"

Imala put a hand on her abdomen. "Like a soccer star. That's partially why I can't sleep."

"And why you need to take something to help you sleep," said Rena.

Imala shrugged. "I don't know. The idea of taking something that I need and the baby doesn't feels . . ."

"Selfish?"

"Risky. I know it's silly, I just can't not be worried."

"It's not silly," said Rena. "You're being a loving and conscientious mother."

"Oh yes, what a mother I am, carrying my baby off to war."

Rena regarded her disapprovingly. "You didn't know you were pregnant when we set out, Imala. You can't beat yourself up about that."

"I absolutely can beat myself up about it," said Imala, "and have, on many occasions, but if we argue the point now, it will only end in you praising me in an attempt to lift my spirits, for which I would be grateful but which would also leave me feeling weak and needy. So let's just skip it."

Rena laughed. "I'm glad we could have that conversation without me actually ever saying anything. That makes my part so much easier."

"Why are you even up?" asked Imala. "Not to check on me, I hope."

"I got a beep from the Eye," said Rena. "I have to check it out."

The Eye was the ship's scanning computer, searching the Gagak's flight path for possible collision threats. Most objects were small pebbles and rock debris, fragments from some long-demolished asteroid or hunk of ice. The ship's pebble killers handled those easily, vaporizing them with lasers. But occasionally a bigger object would hit the scans, one too large for the PKs to tackle, and Rena would be notified so she could determine if the ship needed to alter course to avoid the danger. Beeps didn't happen often; the Kuiper Belt was home to billions of objects, but the space between them was so vast that serious collision threats were rare. In the eight months since setting out, Rena had altered course only three times, and in all instances the move had been only as a precaution. Most beeps were simply alarms that said, "Heads up, there's something in the neighborhood."

Imala rubbed the front of her stomach. "If there's a large object out there closing in on our position, it's probably my fault. I think my stomach has its own gravity well."

"Wait until you're nine months pregnant," said Rena. "It felt like the skin on my belly was ready to split open and dump out baby, guts, and all."

"I thought you were supposed to bury my anxiety, not inflame it."

Rena smiled and hooked her arm in Imala's. "Come on. You need a change of scenery, and I need to check this rock."

They moved out into the corridor and headed for the helm. Imala had a hard time of it. With the baby, Imala's center of mass was off, and flying through the ship now felt like a game of pinball, with Imala pushing herself back and forth off the walls as she moved down the corridors, taking short, slow-moving jumps so as not to put any undue stress on her stomach.

Rena's wrist pad beeped, and a voice came through. "The computer's getting impatient, Rena. You coming?" It was Owanu, the ship's doctor, a young female IF lieutenant who had never delivered a baby, but who had studied hard in her off hours and consulted regularly with IF doctors via ansible to better treat Imala. The strange part was that Imala, as the Gagak's communications officer, was the only person on board authorized to use the ansible. Even Captain Mangold, much to his frustration, couldn't enter the small ansible room. Only Imala had access. She wasn't even allowed to call it the ansible in front of the others. The name of it, like the tech itself, was classified. To everyone but Imala, it was known as "the device."

Which meant that whenever Lieutenant Owanu had a question for another doctor about Imala's pregnancy, Imala was the one who sent the question and received the response and then relayed that response to Lieutenant Owanu, who would then, out of due diligence as Imala's physician, share it right back with Imala.

Imala appreciated Lieutenant Owanu's efforts, but it bothered her that Owanu had no prior obstetrics experience. What if the baby was breach? Or stopped breathing mid-delivery? Could Owanu handle that? Could she keep Imala's child alive?

Rena tapped her wrist pad. "I'm on my way." She clicked off and smiled at Imala. "We've got a team of highly trained marines on this ship, and who goes to the helm to check for danger? The white-haired old lady and the exhausted pregnant woman."

"You're not old," said Imala. "And I'm more of a floating whale, really. Why don't you go ahead and I'll catch up?"

"Yes, how noble of me to leave the pregnant woman behind."

"We're in space," said Imala. "Floating in zero gravity. It's not like I'm trudging up a flight of stairs. I think I can float to the helm easily enough. Plus, I'm pretty sure a giant asteroid crushing us midflight takes precedence." She flicked her wrist in a shooing gesture. "Go. Before we're squished. I'll be fine."

After a moment's hesitation and more shooing motions from Imala, Rena finally pushed on to the helm.

Imala steadied herself against a wall, took a calming breath, and felt grateful to be alone again. The pressure on her cervix had intensified since moving out into the corridor, but she didn't want to make a scene of it. This was one of those unexpected pains that Rena had warned her about. At eight months, all the serious discomforts started piling on. This was simply one of them.

A stabbing pain in Imala's abdomen nearly took her breath away. She gasped and tightened her grip on the handhold. At first she thought the baby had kicked, as the little stinker was prone to do, but then the pain lingered a moment too long and rolled across Imala's abdomen like ripples on the surface of a pond.

A contraction?

No. She couldn't be in labor. Not now. Not this soon.

It occurred to her then that the pressure on her cervix that had bothered her for the past few hours, the discomfort that had nagged at her and kept her awake in the first place, might have been pre-labor pains. Mini-contractions. The body preparing. Imala hadn't even considered that a possibility, since the pain was so mild. But now it seemed obvious. Even likely.

I should've stayed down in the fuge and forced myself to sleep, she thought. Coming up to the garden, moving around, being active, that had exacerbated labor.

If it was labor. Which it probably wasn't. It might have

been a fluke ache, or a bout of gas, or a who-knows-what.

No, it couldn't be labor. It couldn't. The baby's lungs might not be ready, and there was no neonatal unit on board, no synthetic womb, no skilled surgeon with expert hands if Imala needed a C-section because of some complication. Lieutenant Owanu wasn't prepared for that.

I never should have come, thought Imala. I never should have agreed to this. The ship was heading farther into the Kuiper Belt than any sane person would ever attempt, moving toward a Formic ship that someone at CentCom believed *might* be harboring the Hive Queen. If the Gagak and its crew could reach that ship and assassinate the Hive Queen, it would be a major victory.

If there was a Hive Queen. And *if* she was on that ship. And *if* Imala and the others could reach it without being blown to smithereens. And *if* they could then board that ship and put a bolt through the queen's heart. Why then, the mission would be a success and Imala and her newborn-in-arms could mosey on back from deep space to receive their medals of commendation.

It had all made sense at the outset. Imala had seen the wisdom of it. Cut off the head, and the whole snake dies.

But that was before Imala knew she was pregnant.

Now, with a baby inside her, a baby that was possibly pushing to get out, the whole enterprise seemed ludicrous, not to mention grossly irresponsible. What kind of mother carries a child into war?

Another stabbing pain struck her abdomen.

She had to get back to the fuge and lie down.

She readied herself to launch in that direction, but then tightened her grip on the handhold and stopped herself. Going back to a full G might be the worst course of action. She needed the baby to stay up and not drop. Wasn't that why women went on bedrest on Earth, to take the weight off?

She turned and pushed gently off the wall toward the helm. Toward Owanu and Rena, toward help.

At the end of the corridor, a third contraction hit, the pain so sudden and stabbing that Imala buckled midflight and didn't catch herself in time. Her shoulder slammed into the wall and she spun away awkwardly, arms flailing. She hit the opposite wall and grabbed a handhold, now breathing heavily and in a panic.

Imala reached for her wrist pad and then realized she didn't have it. She had taken it off before trying to sleep and had left it down in the fuge. It was no good to shout for help; no one would hear her, not this far from the helm and so near the engine room.

She was having the baby. If she didn't stop the contractions, it would come and die in her arms. On Earth it would be fine, given the proper care. But not here.

She had five more contractions before she reached the helm. Captain Mangold was anchored to the floor near the holotable, with Rena and Lieutenant Owanu opposite him, their faces showing concern and uncertainty.

"Rena." Imala's voice came out strained, almost in a whisper, as if someone else had spoken—a dying version of Imala.

Rena launched and was beside Imala almost immediately, feet anchored to the floor, grabbing Imala gently and pulling her into the room. "What's wrong?"

"Contractions. I think I'm having the baby." Imala felt so hot. Her clothes were drenched in sweat. She hadn't noticed until now. Her face, her back. It felt as if she were wearing five layers of clothes. She would have torn them all off if Captain Mangold weren't hovering over her, his face concerned.

Rena rotated Imala in the air, leveling her out, until she was parallel with the floor, as if lying on some doctor's invisible exam table. "I'm easing you down."

Imala allowed herself to be lowered to the floor. Rena

pulled straps from the wall and secured Imala's torso to the anchor hooks.

Captain Mangold stared at her, mouth slightly agape, as if she were some alien being.

Imala wanted to yell at him to go away. She wasn't about to spread her legs with him staring at her.

Lieutenant Owanu suddenly had diagnostic tools out, checking Imala's vitals, one device over Imala's heart, another over her abdomen.

Words finally came to Captain Mangold. "She's not having the baby, is she?" He sounded incredulous, like the idea of one human birthing another was a feat never before achieved.

Rena ignored him, looking at Owanu. "Can you stop the labor?"

Owanu moved one of the devices toward Imala's cervix. "She's mostly dilated and already ninety percent effaced."

"What does that mean?" said Mangold. "I don't know what that means."

"It means this baby is coming," said Owanu. "Rena, help me get her up again, we can't do this here."

"Wait," said Captain Mangold. "You're saying you can't stop it?"

"We need to get her into the clinic," said Owanu. "No, I can't stop it."

"We're in the middle of a situation here," said Captain Mangold. "A baby complicates this."

Rena whirled on him. "We're talking about my grandchild. Now either help us *gently* get her to the clinic or get out of the way."

"What's happening?" said Imala. "What's the situation? A collision threat?"

"One thing at a time," said Rena.

"Tell me," said Imala, just as another contraction came on.

"First the baby," said Rena. "Captain, go ahead of us and get all the doors."

It was awkward moving her. Imala's body kept trying to float away, and Lieutenant Owanu didn't want her pushing off any walls. She was weightless, but maneuvering her through the corridor and doorways was cumbersome, especially since Imala kept having contractions, like explosions in her abdomen, worse than she had imagined they would be.

Her water broke as they were securing her to the clinic's table. Rena began cleaning it up immediately with a vacuum tube. Fortunately Imala's clothing soaked up most of it. Imala knew she should be humiliated, but the pain was so intense, she didn't care.

Owanu was moving quickly, grabbing equipment, strapping Imala down, shouting orders to Captain Mangold. "Wake Corporal Merryweather. Rena, start an IV."

Imala was looking up at the ceiling, but couldn't seem to focus on anything there. The panels blurred together. A light moved into view, bright, burning, like a white flame descending. The voices were slowly slipping away, silence pushing in. Her breathing was labored and yet slow, as if someone else's lungs were doing all the work. An oxygen mask covered her mouth, but she didn't remember anyone putting it there.

Had Owanu given her something? A sedative? She didn't want a sedative. That might hurt the baby.

The world seemed to be moving in slow-motion now. Or maybe it was hyper-motion and Imala was only catching brief snippets.

A blur of motion in her peripheral vision. Lieutenant Owanu maybe. Or Mother. No, not Mother. Mother was still on Earth, far from here. Imala's fist clenched, opened, shut again, calling for Victor. Victor, take my hand. Hold it, squeeze it tight.

"The baby's heart rate is dropping, blood pressure's dropping."

Imala heard the words. They hovered there in her mind, drifting at sea, as if they expected someone to reach out and grab them and give them meaning. The baby. The baby was hurting. Trouble.

Spots of black danced before Imala's eyes. The silence was stronger now, leaking in, flooding out the noise.

There was a situation, Imala remembered. Not just the baby. Something else. Something dangerous.

The ansible. No one could operate it but Imala. No one *knew* how to operate it but Imala. How would they speak with CentCom if she died?

Pain. Like a package of thunder opened inside her. Her arm. Her abdomen. Her lower back.

A hand gripped her own. Rena's face appeared, trying to smile, pretending there were no tears. She was looking directly into Imala's eyes, her face close, expression earnest, lips moving.

But the silence and the pain and the blackness closed in, and Imala blinked and tried to focus and to squeeze the hand back, but then darkness, like a stone dropped in deep water, settling, sinking, swallowed in ink, dragging her down with it, wrapped her in thick nothingness and snuffed out all the light.

Imala woke to a light beeping noise, not an alarm, but a machine. Life support. Her heart rate. Steady. Normal. She was on the bed, gently strapped down. A gown covered her now, not her clothes from before. Someone had changed her. The lights were dim.

Rena was beside her, her feet anchored to the floor. Imala focused on her, blinked again, her mind coming out of a cloud. "The baby."

"Is fine," said Rena. "A tiny thing. Arms, legs, fingers,

toes, all there and accounted for. I checked. Skin so pink and wrinkly. And a head of hair so thick and black that she looks like a duster. I've never seen a girl with that much hair."

Imala's eyes welled with tears. "A girl?"

Rena smiled. "Yes, yes. I won't say I told you so. She has her father's spunk, I think. I could never keep Victor still for a minute. This little one here will be no different."

"Where is she?"

"Lieutenant Owanu is feeding her and checking her out." Rena placed her hand gently on Imala's arm. "Owanu saved her life. And yours, I suspect. She had to do a C-section. The Med-Assist guided her, but it turns out Owanu was prepared. She's been studying for this."

Yes. Imala could feel it now. Stitches in her stomach. Pain, poking through the numbness.

"Owanu apologizes for the scar. It was her first go at it, and she wasn't too happy with her own work. But everything is back where it is supposed to be. You'll heal fine. You just need time."

"Why a C-section?"

"There was a true knot in the umbilical cord," said Rena. "We caught it in time, before the delivery. Had the baby come vaginally, she would've died. I've seen it before. You have Owanu to thank."

Imala closed her eyes. Owanu. Thank God.

The door opened. Lieutenant Owanu stepped in, wearing her magnetic greaves, a small bundle of blankets in her arms. She smiled and placed the bundle into Imala's arms. The baby was sleeping. Someone had cut a sock in half and placed it on the baby's head like a knit cap. Imala could see the black hairs poking out in the back. She was so small. Smaller than any baby Imala had ever seen.

"She's six pounds, two ounces," said Owanu. "Two point eight kilograms. Big for being as early as she is. If she had gone full term, she would have been enormous. Better still, her lungs check out. She's doing amazingly well."

The words caused a burst of relief inside of Imala, as if the dam holding back eight months of doubt and anxiety had given way and burst in an instant. Her eyes became thick with tears.

Cradling the baby, Imala reached out a weak hand and squeezed Owanu's own. "Thank you."

Owanu smiled.

Imala stared at the bundle in her arms. A living thing. A person. A tiny, breathing person, one part her and one part Victor. A girl. A daughter. She had made this. She and Victor together. This perfect creation. This new center of everything. This beginning of everything. No, this baby would not die. She had already beaten death once. She had already defiantly rejected that threat. She was a fighter like her father. Like her mother. Nothing would harm her. Imala wouldn't let it.

"Do you have a name?" Owanu asked.

"It feels wrong to name her without Victor," said Imala.

"You can't wait that long," said Rena. "You may not see him for years. A baby needs a name."

"Captain Mangold wants to see you, Imala," said Lieutenant Owanu.

"Give her five minutes with the child," said Rena. It came out harshly, and Imala realized that a debate had been raging while she was out. Something was wrong.

"I'm under orders," said Owanu.

Rena looked like she might object, but Imala spoke first.

"It's all right. I'll speak with him."

Rena sighed but said nothing more. Owanu stepped outside, and a moment later Captain Mangold entered. He was an American; young, clean-cut, and a little more self-confident than Imala thought he should be. She had learned to tolerate him, but Imala wasn't sure the feeling was mutual. He wasn't unintelligent or incapable, but Imala suspected that he had ties elsewhere, likely in the highest levels of the IF. A father perhaps. Or a powerful uncle. Someone who had helped maneuver him into this position. Their mission might very well be the most critical in all the Fleet, and yet it had been trusted to a relatively inexperienced young man.

Mangold nodded at the wrapped bundle in Imala's arms. "Lieutenant Bootstamp, allow me to congratulate you. I am delighted to hear that you and baby are doing well."

"I have you and Owanu and Rena to thank for that," said Imala. "Forgive me for the inconvenience. But let's move past the small talk. We have a situation."

Mangold nodded. "One that requires your attention, I'm afraid. You're the communications officer. We need to counsel with CentCom."

Imala could tell he was annoyed. He hated not having access to the ansible. But operating the anisble required biosecurity checks only Imala could meet.

"It's not a collision threat, is it?" said Imala.

"A distress signal," said Captain Mangold. "Outside our trajectory. A free-miner ship was attacked by pirates. There are eight survivors, three of them children. They have enough food and oxygen to last them seven more days. We could reach them within that time, but just barely. We'd have to divert and change course within the next few hours to intercept them. There are no other ships within a two-month flight vicinity. If we don't go to their aid, no one else will."

"We shouldn't go," said Rena sharply.

Mangold tensed immediately. They had obviously already had this argument while Imala was out.

"You'll abandon your own people?" said Mangold.

"My people?" said Rena, eyeing him with disdain. "Do

you think free miners are some different species from you?"

"They need our help," said Mangold.

"This is a classic pirate tactic," said Rena. "They've been doing it since before you were born. They raid a ship, release a distress signal, and then lie in wait for help to come. And when it arrives, they attack the rescue ship. I've seen it more times than I can count. This isn't safe."

"I went back through the scans," said Mangold. "Whoever attacked them went deeper into the Kuiper Belt. You can see the heat signatures yourself if you don't believe me. There's no other ship near them."

"That doesn't mean it's safe," said Rena. "The first ship leaves and some of the pirate crew stays behind on the scuttled ship. Or it's not scuttled at all and it's only pretending to be scuttled. It actually functions fine. Help arrives, with the pirates left behind posing as the helpless survivors. I think you can figure out what happens next. They seize the rescue ship and jettison the rescue party into space. The end."

"I've drilled them with questions via laserline," said Mangold. "I've run their answers through the charts and trade directories we have on file. Everything checks out. I don't think this is a trick."

"You don't think?" said Rena. "Well, I'm relieved that you've reached that conclusion after your brilliant detective work. Did it occur to you that they might be answering under duress, that someone is holding a gun to their head?"

Mangold's eyes darkened, and his voice began to rise. "I will remind you that you are an ensign in this fleet and under my command. I will not tolerate insubordination from anyone, including you."

"Please," said Imala.

But Rena ignored her. "And I will remind you that we

have a mission, one that we are not to deviate from. Those orders trump your own."

"You're only objecting because of what it might do to the baby," said Mangold.

Rena opened her mouth, but Imala was quicker. "Stop it, both of you. I am holding an infant in my arms, and the first conversation she hears in this life will not be the two of you squabbling."

Rena exhaled and turned away from Mangold. The captain ground his teeth and straightened his jacket.

"Will the baby survive?" Imala asked. "If we decelerate and change course? We all know what kind of stress that puts on the body. Can the baby safely endure that?"

Mangold sighed. "We wouldn't just decelerate. We'd have to accelerate again once we had a new course. And then decelerate again once we got there. It wouldn't be an easy ride for anyone."

"That doesn't answer my question," said Imala. "Rena, there were babies in your mining ship all the time. Victor was born in space. Did you ever accelerate with an infant? How could you not? A baby couldn't stop the work of the family."

"We avoided it," said Rena. "We gave the mother and child a few weeks, at a minimum. Or we planned our runs to be sure we were anchored at a rock and mining when we knew a baby was coming. We certainly wouldn't accelerate at the rates we'll need to to reach this ship."

"I see," said Imala.

"Then there's you," said Mangold. "Your C-section wound is new and wide. It's fine for the moment, but Owanu doesn't think it wise to put pressure on it. Changing course would be, at the very least, painful. At worst, fatal."

"I see," said Imala again.

"We need to talk to CentCom," said Mangold.

"What do we know about this ship?" said Imala. "I'm assuming it's in the database?"

"It's registered as a mining vessel, but its registration expired years ago," said Mangold.

"Another sign of alarm," said Rena.

"Maybe," said Imala. "Or maybe not. Rena, how many families kept up with their registrations before the war? I assume some of them did, but I also assume a lot of them didn't, especially those this far out and away from regulators. Or am I wrong?"

"You're not wrong," said Rena. "Registering is expensive, and the mining regulators don't offer that much protection anyway."

"Did El Cavador stay registered? Your own ship, did your crew stay up to date with that sort of thing before the war?"

Rena looked uncomfortable. "Not always."

"Meaning what?" said Imala. "How often?"

"Almost never," said Rena. "It wasn't worth it for how we operated. There are all kinds of taxes and fees involved."

"So an expired vessel registration doesn't tell us much," said Imala.

"It certainly doesn't tell us anything good," said Rena. "It doesn't put my mind at ease."

"Nor mine," said Imala. "But it sounds as if this could be a family no different from your own."

"Or it could be a band of pirates lying in wait for a naive crew of do-gooders to come along," said Rena. "We know pirates are out here. Even if this is legit we have evidence of attacks."

"So you're admitting this could be a legitimate distress signal?" said Imala. "You admit that possibility."

"You're turning my words against me," said Rena. "I'm trying to protect you."

"That's what I'm afraid of," said Imala. "You're making your assessment based on how it could affect me and the baby."

"Of course I'm making my assessment based on that. That's two lives I'm not willing to risk."

"We lose eight lives if we do nothing," said Captain Mangold.

"Wrong," said Rena. "Those eight lives aren't on us. That's not our doing. And anyway, this isn't a matter of simple mathematics. We have to weigh all the risks. Not just to us, but to the mission as well. If we don't reach our target, if we fail to take it out, what does that do to the war effort? To my son? To every other mother and wife waiting for loved ones to come home? Are we willing to risk all of that for eight lives?"

The question hung in the air.

"Rena, you know mining ships better than anyone," said Imala. "What kind of weaponry would this ship have?"

"That's my point," said Rena. "We don't know. It could have militarized itself, retrofitted all kinds of weapons."

"Let's assume it hasn't," said Imala. "If it's nothing more than a mining ship, how would it defend itself?"

"It would almost certainly have a mining laser or two," said Rena. "Plus a few pebble killers for collision threats."

"Which wouldn't do us much damage," said Mangold. "Not with our shielding. And we could take out their lasers the instant we arrive."

"Disable their weaponry?" Imala asked.

"Easily," said Mangold.

"Is that true?" Imala asked Rena.

"That doesn't remove all risk," said Rena. "If they're pirates, they'll have small arms inside their ship. They could attack us as soon as we board them."

"Then we won't board their ship," said Imala. "They'll board ours, coming through the hatch one at a time, but only after they've stripped naked so we can be certain that none of them are concealing a weapon. Our weapons will be on them the whole time, then we can interview them one by one until we've erased all doubt and are certain they are who they say they are."

"I don't particularly like that approach," said Rena.

"Nor do I," said Imala. "It's cruel and humiliating. But they use that tactic in prisons to ensure that no weapons get inside, and it works well."

"It will terrify the children," said Rena.

"Dying is far more terrifying to a child," said Imala, "and it gives us the assurance we need. And anyway, the children need not strip. They'll come through first. We'll scan them, move them elsewhere, and then bring in the adults. Captain Mangold, do you object?"

"No objections."

Imala turned to Rena. "I'm assuming you've seen the questions the captain asked these miners and the answers they gave."

"I've seen them," said Rena.

"Does it sound bogus?" said Imala. "Don't answer as a grandmother or a mother-in-law. Answer as a woman who's been out here longer than all of us combined and who knows what true desperation sounds like."

Rena sighed and considered a moment. "It might be legitimate, yes."

Imala turned back to Captain Mangold. "I will inform CentCom that we are diverting. They may of course object, and if they do, we'll reconvene. Otherwise, we'll make plans to safeguard the baby as much as we can."

Rena began to object, "Imala—"

"My child and I will not be responsible for the death of eight innocent people. We'll put me and the baby in an impact bubble, and we'll divert."

"This is not a good idea," said Rena.

"No, it isn't," said Imala. "But it's the idea where the fewest people die."

"Why an impact bubble?" said Mangold.

"Because you can't strap an infant into a flight chair," said Imala. "Diverting will take a few days. I will have to feed her. I can't do that if I'm strapped in somewhere else, and she can't be fed intravenously, at least not the way the ship feeds us. That equipment is designed for adults."

"I'm not sure that will work, Imala," said Rena.

"Nor am I," said Imala. "But if you've got a better idea, let's hear it."

They inflated the impact balloon in the helm and installed additional foam packs and concussion bags. Then came blankets and life support. A storage box became a bassinette.

Conferring with CentCom was a far more complicated matter. They refused. Flatly. Nothing should deter Imala and the others from the mission. Period. End of discussion. They should answer zero distress signals. Not even from desperate, abandoned asteroid miners with small helpless children. Do not divert. The Formic ship out in deep space was the only concern. The world could burn around them, but the Gagak should press on to the Formic ship.

An admiral at CentCom then began lecturing Imala on the importance of full and absolute devotion to the mission. It was clear from his tone that he hated that Imala was the communications officer and in control of the ansible. He didn't even try to hide his contempt. His slights weren't even subtle. He thought her an imbecile.

Imala dutifully recorded his rant. Her job was to relay every word verbatim to Captain Mangold, who would then relay the orders to the crew. Imala didn't try to argue with the admiral. It wasn't her place. And it would only infuriate him. Instead, she patiently waited for him to finish and didn't interrupt.

When the lecture finally concluded, another admiral

thought it necessary to give the Gagak a similar lecture. Stick to the mission, do not divert. Apparently the admirals at CentCom couldn't stand the idea of one of them speaking for the group. They each had to assert their authority and have a say in the matter. Imala could almost imagine them sitting around a table, with chests puffed out, each one pretending to be the most wise and senior among them.

After the third mini lecture, Imala's eyes were glazing over. She had long since stopped taking notes. When the stream of text finally stopped, she sighed in relief and refocused her eyes, only to discover that the lecture wasn't over. The text had merely stopped mid-word, mid-sentence, as if the thread to CentCom had suddenly been cut.

This had never happened before. The ansible never paused. Something had gone wrong. Was the ansible broken? She could see no visible damage to it. Had the ansible broken on the other end? Had the person typing at CentCom merely become distracted? Or—and this thought frightened her—had something happened in that room that had killed the thread? An attack? An explosion? Or was it something less dramatic? Were Imala and the ship simply too far away now? Would there be a time delay from here on out, getting longer and longer?

No. The ansible's reach was enormous. Maybe infinite. But if so, what had happened?

Words appeared before her. But on a new thread, meaning it was within the same ansible network, but coming from a different ansible device. The text read:

Imala,
    Ignore them. Do the right thing, whatever you think that is. Humanity must win too.

                                            Regards, Ukko.

The text stopped.

Imala stared at the words. The only Ukko she knew was the same Ukko the whole world knew: Ukko Jukes, the Hegemon of Earth. He had interrupted the admirals at CentCom with his own, apparently superior, ansible device to send her a direct message. Go help these people in need, if that's what you think is necessary. He was giving Imala permission to disregard direct orders. Ignore Cent-Com. Do what you think is best.

Imala read the message again. Was this legit? Was Ukko Jukes literally speaking directly to her? Had the actual Hegemon of Earth listened in on the lectures from CentCom and then somehow severed that connection to address Imala directly? Why would the Hegemon concern himself with such a trifling matter?

And then there was the last sentence. *Humanity must win too.* Imala understood at once. The human race had to win the war, yes, no question, but if we lose our humanity in the process, we haven't really won. We can't lose who we are and what defines us as a species: our care for each other, our goodness. Because the instant we stop caring and turn a blind eye to those in distress, we stop being the thing that should be saved.

Was this the mind-set of Ukko Jukes? Imala had known him only to be selfish, cruel even. Had the weight of his office, or the horror of war, softened him? Had he experienced some change of heart? Some moral clarity? Was he really concerned with preserving humanity?

But yes, she realized. It had to be Ukko. Who else would have the ability to interrupt and disconnect CentCom?

And then another puzzle piece clicked into place in her mind. CentCom hadn't given her this assignment. Ukko Jukes had. The Hegemon of Earth had made her the communications officer. Her commission had happened at his insistence. Of course. That's why the admirals at

CentCom, who clearly despised her, hadn't already removed her from her post. They couldn't. The Hegemon was the commander in chief. His orders trumped their own. They would never have suggested that she be the communications officer. Were it up to them, Imala, a non-soldier, would never even be part of this mission. And yet here she was. Ukko didn't trust the Fleet. That was the issue. He couldn't stand the commanders. And he thought this mission too important to put entirely in their hands. Ukko wanted someone he could trust at the wheel, someone he could communicate with directly. Someone outside the military bureaucracy, who wouldn't feel beholden to that rigid chain of command. Someone who would challenge poor decisions and dumb thinking.

Imala laughed to herself. She had stood up to Ukko once. Defied him. Challenged him. She had thought at the time that it would ruin her, that a man of his power and influence would sweep her easily aside. Now it seemed that her defiance had affected him some other way.

Captain Mangold and Rena were waiting for Imala outside the ansible room. Imala grabbed a handhold and steadied herself. It hurt to move. Lieutenant Owanu had applied a wound-healing NanoSkin gauze and wrapped Imala's abdomen tightly to restrict her movements, but the decreased range of motion made it hard to get around.

Rena steadied her. "You can barely stay upright. How are you supposed to endure acceleration?"

"I'm fine."

"Hardly," said Rena.

"What did CentCom say?" said Mangold.

"We've been given permission to divert," said Imala. Which wasn't a lie. Ukko had given his blessing.

"There's something we haven't considered," said Captain Mangold. "We're heading toward a Formic ship. We can't exactly take these people with us into combat."

"Why not?" said Rena. "You're taking Imala and her baby into combat. Or do they not count?"

"Imala is a member of the Fleet," said Mangold. "These people aren't."

"The baby isn't either," said Rena.

Mangold opened his mouth to argue, but again Imala was faster. "Stop. We're wasting time we don't have. There's a depot station a few months ahead. We can drop any survivors off there after they're rescued."

"I ran the nav numbers and made some modifications," said Rena. "Our acceleration will be longer, but the G-forces will be less. I don't want us pushing too many Gs. That's not even open for debate. We do this gradually to minimize harm to Imala's wound and any harm to the baby."

"Does that affect our ETA?" said Mangold.

"That puts us dangerously close to the red line for the miners," said Rena. "By the time we get there, they'll be nearly out of oxygen or completely depleted. Not ideal, I know, but we're not accelerating to them any faster. We help them as best we can while protecting Imala as best we know how."

"Agreed," said Mangold.

"And I'm riding in the impact balloon with Imala and the baby," said Rena. "As is Lieutenant Owanu. This is not open for discussion, Imala. We've already made the arrangements. It will be close quarters in there, but you're going to be heavily monitored or we're not doing this."

The crew buckled themselves into their flight chairs. Imala climbed into the impact balloon with the baby in her arms, holding her close, cradling her, her blankets wrapped tight. Rena and Lieutenant Owanu climbed in next. Concussion bags were inflated around them, like they were porcelain or china being packed for rough shipment.

The baby's eyes were closed, and she looked at peace tucked snugly up against Imala's bosom. Imala could feel her little chest moving, taking in small delicate breaths. Her tiny hand gripped Imala's finger, clinging to her. Fragile, pink fingers that said, "I trust you, Mother. I am safe with you. I know you will protect me."

Imala's heart swelled with love then. This was her child. Half Navajo, half Venezuelan. The best of her and Victor's worlds. You have the strength of my family's tribe, little one. And the resilience of your father's people. That is why you survived. Because you knew how to fight from the instant you were born. And that is why you will have a warrior's name. A Navajo name. A name of purpose, truth, history.

The word and its meaning came to Imala then, like a message through time from her upbringing on the reservation. Like a gift being opened. A name that would make her father and tribe proud: Ch'íníbaa', meaning *She came out raiding*.

That is who you are, my warrior. Your father will stumble on the word, so we'll call you Chee for short. Now cling to me, little one. Go with me to war.

Imala pulled Chee close as she heard Mangold give the order.

The impact balloon squeezed, and the force of it, like a punch to Imala's wound, hit. It felt as if tissue in her gut was tearing, but she couldn't reach the wound to know for certain. The baby jerked slightly in her arms in the same instant and began to cry. Imala couldn't hear her screams, however, not over the roar of the engines. She cradled Chee close, pressing one tiny ear against Imala's chest and covering the other with her hand. Several hours of this, and then the pressure would decrease. Then in a few days, they would do it again. And a few days after that, yet again.

Imala bit her lip as another wave of pain beat like a drum upon her abdomen. She would not scream. She would hush little Chee and sing her a calming lullaby.

Even if the baby couldn't hear.

CHAPTER 7

Heist

The recent order from CentCom to remove—under penalty of court-martial—the theory of the Hive Queen from all trainings, tactical considerations, and even informal conversations within the International Fleet is a foolish, shortsighted error that will result in uninformed marines, unprepared tactical units, and, inevitably, higher casualties and losses. While it's true that we don't have irrefutable evidence of the Hive Queen's existence, it is also true that we don't have evidence that she does not exist. What we do have, however, is a great deal of evidence that suggests she (or it) COULD exist. MIGHT exist. Perhaps even LIKELY exists.

In fact, the more we learn about the Formics, the more logical the theory of the Hive Queen becomes, as everything we observe validates the theory and nothing we observe disproves it. I recognize that the absence of disproof is not the same as having proof, but the same logic can be applied to CentCom's decision. Where is the evidence that the theory of the Hive Queen is misdirecting our strategy, hindering our tactics, or harming our marines?

The first rule of war is to understand your enemy. Not just her supplies and weapons and objectives, everything that we can see and calculate. But also her psyche, her motivations, her fears. Everything that is in her mind. For it is only in the pursuit of that understanding that armies can identify the enemy's weakness and vulnerabilities. Why would we abandon a completely legitimate pursuit to understand our enemy? Do soldiers put blinders on their eyes before they charge into battle, or do they maintain a full view and consider every possible threat? If CentCom is so convinced that the Hive Queen does not exist, then what explanation can they give for what we've witnessed? If not the Hive Queen, then what? Or who?

Silencing our search for understanding cripples our thinking and makes us stupid. It leads us to believe that we DO have answers and we DO understand, when in fact we don't. CentCom would have us put on blinders. Don't look over there, they say. Ignore the thing behind the Formic curtain. What's really over there? We don't know. But it makes us look uninformed to not know, and we don't like people thinking we're uninformed. So we're creating our own reality to validate our desperate need to have the answers. Oh, and the sky isn't blue. And the grass isn't green. Go, fight, win! But don't forget your blinders.

Bingwen gathered Rat Army in the barracks during sleep shift and told them about the Hive Queen's countermeasures in the asteroids. He then mentioned the NanoCloud capsules in the armory, though he didn't tell them the information had come from Mazer."

"What are you suggesting?" said Micho. "That we steal from the armory? Please tell me you're joking."

"Nobody here wants to be court-martialed, Bingwen," said Jianjun.

Chati scoffed. "Court-martialed? If only. If we're caught stealing from the armory, we'll be shot on sight. Especially if we're caught lifting what is likely the most expensive weapon on this station."

"Acquiring NanoCloud capsules won't accomplish anything if we don't know how to control them," said Nak. "NanoCloud looks like tiny particles of dust, but every speck of that dust is actually a nanobot that must be programmed to complete a task. None of us are coders, Bingwen. Or nanoroboticists. Even if we had every Nano-Cloud capsule in the system, they would all be equally useless to us without the tools and programs required to put them into operation."

"What tools do we need?" said Bingwen.

"That's just it," said Nak. "I have no idea. None of us do. This isn't our expertise. We haven't the foggiest idea how to manipulate nanobots."

"I'm not saying this is easy," said Bingwen. "I'm saying the Hive Queen is winning in the asteroids. Tunnel commandos are dying because of her countermeasures. Meanwhile the Fleet has abandoned the very idea of a Hive Queen, which means they won't be approaching this problem, or any future problem, with her in mind. What are we going to do about it? Nothing? We spent the better part of a year on cramped boats to get here. And now that we're here, dull-bob-of-the-year Colonel Dietrich won't give us access to anything. Not the Battle Room, not the Tunnel Room. Not even a classroom. We can mope about that fact and shake our fists at the man, or we can do what we came here to do: find and kill the Hive Queen."

"It's complicated, Bingwen," said Nak. "There are huge obstacles here."

"Good," said Bingwen. "We're identifying obstacles. That's the first step to overcoming them."

"One," said Nak. "Communication. We've got basic net access here on our tablets, but if we undertake something like this, we're going to need more. We've got to rope in a lot of people to help. People back on Luna at Juke Limited, for example. Engineers. Roboticists. People who can write and send us code, maybe. That's a lot of net traffic coming out of this room. That will get noticed."

"Colonel Li has an ansible," said Michon. "What are the chances of us using that?"

Chati snorted. "Zero. We don't even know for certain that he has one. None of us have ever seen it. And even if he does have one he's not going to admit it. We're not even supposed to know that ansibles exist."

"The ansible isn't an option," said Bingwen. "Even if Li does in fact have one, it links to some intelligence agency, not to the people we need to connect with. And anyway, Li can't risk revealing to Colonel Dietrich that he has a secret back channel to an intelligence service. Dietrich would go nova. All of his conspiracy theories about us being part of some silent Chinese coup would feel validated."

"True," said Nak. "But an ansible sure would be nice in this situation."

"An ansible would be nice in every situation," said Bingwen. "But keep in mind that an ansible only communicates with another ansible. We can't email engineers at Juke Limited with it. It only connects with whoever is on the other end of Li's ansible."

"What's option B?" said Nak. "Laserline?"

"Which is slow," said Bingwen. "We would be relying on the series of relay stations that exist between here and

Luna. They would receive and then pass along our messages both ways up the chain."

"Bucket brigade," said Nak. "I hate that option."

"We're out near Jupiter," said Bingwen. "We don't have a lot of options."

"Even if we use the laserline option, there's still the issue of bandwidth," said Chati. "That will get noticed."

"I might be able to help there," said Jianjun. "The laserline array is actually not far from us on the exterior of the space station. Both the receiver and the transmitter. All the cabling runs through the ducts nearby."

"And you know this because?" said Bingwen.

"Because I accessed and studied the schematics of the space station when we arrived," said Jianjun. "I like knowing where all the emergency exits are."

"How did you get a copy of the schematics?" said Nak.

"Poking around in the service files. Security here is paper thin. At least for those kinds of files."

"How does this help us?" said Bingwen. "Knowing where the cables are?"

"The helm tracks all messages that go and come," said Jianjun. "They know who sends them and who receives them and how frequently. That tracking device is kept in the helm. It's called a switchbox. The lines from the laserline array outside feed directly into that switchbox. So all communication goes to the helm and then is networked out to the individual terminals. But, if we can access the cable between the laserline array outside and the switchbox at the helm, we could potentially send and receive messages without the helm knowing. We would have to hardwire that line, upload some instruction to the laserline array, and then tag all of our messages with a bit of code so the array knows to send them to us and not to the helm. We would also have to include code in our outgoing messages so that whoever responds to us has the code already embedded in the message when it comes back.

Otherwise the helm would start receiving messages intended for us and we'd be busted."

"This is legitimately possible?" said Bingwen.

"Theoretically possible," said Jianjun. "I would need equipment. The right cable at the right length; a switchbox not unlike what is found in the helm, though it doesn't have to be nearly that complicated; some tools; and a way to get into the ducts where the cables are located."

Bingwen tapped at his tablet.

"What are you writing?" said Nak.

"A list of all the things we need from the quartermaster."

"You mean all the things we need to *steal* from the quartermaster," said Nak.

"How long would it take you to set this up?" Bingwen asked.

Jianjun shrugged. "Not long once I have the equipment. But I'd want to test it before we actually put it into practice. There might be all kinds of security traps that I don't know about. We would need to tread carefully. If alarms go off in Dietrich's office, we're history."

"Assuming this even works," said Nak, "it doesn't do us any good if we're not connected to the right people. How are we supposed to link to the engineers and minds we need? The people most qualified to help us with the NanoCloud are the engineers who built it. We don't know who these people are or how to contact them. And even if we do connect to them, how do we convince them to help us? We're a bunch of kids."

Bingwen put a hand on Nak's shoulder and smiled. "This is why I love you, Nak. You're so good at pointing out next steps." He turned to the others. "Our first objective is to set up Jianjun's network. Jianjun, you said security protecting service files was paper thin. What about inventory? How do we find out if the space station has the equipment we need?"

"I can poke around and see," said Jianjun. "Inventory

data will likely have tighter security to discourage pilfering, though."

"See what you find," said Bingwen. "Chati, your job is to scope out the armory and the storage rooms. We need to case those locations without it being obvious that we're doing so. When are they watched, when are they not, how are they accessed? Including access points other than doors. Take whoever you need to help you."

"You mean like my own platoon?" said Chati.

"Sure," said Bingwen, "your own platoon."

"Nice. I'm a toon leader. You little rats are in my house now."

"Don't let authority go to your head, Chati," said Bingwen. "You're a toon leader, not toon dictator. You know the difference."

"What do I do?" said Nak.

"You and I are going to build our contact list," said Bingwen. "We'll identify the people we need to reach."

"I told you," said Nak. "I don't know who those people are."

"If you did," said Bingwen, "it wouldn't be an assignment. Victor Delgado should be the first person on our list, assuming we can track him down. We should also comb through Mazer's forum and identify those junior officers who are posting good ideas. I'll see if can I contact the people who designed the NanoCloud."

"And how do you propose to do that?"

"Colonel Li will help. For now, use our current net access to start building our list. But don't contact anyone yet. We should assume that Colonel Dietrich is monitoring our communication."

Once everyone was busy, Bingwen headed to Colonel Li's office. He knocked twice and waited.

"Identify," said the voice from inside.

"Bingwen, sir."

It was two minutes before Li opened the door, which

Bingwen figured was plenty of time for Li to clear files off his holodesk and tuck away his ansible, if he had one.

"Do you have so little to do that disturbing me is now a pastime?" said Li, once Bingwen was inside.

"There was a woman on the shuttle with us from Earth," said Bingwen. "A Buddhist monk. Wila, short for Wilasanee. I don't remember her last name. She was heading to Luna to take a job with Juke Limited. She's a biochemist and formicologist. She didn't self-identify as a formicologist, but that's what she is. She was the one who figured out what the Formic grubs were doing inside the seized asteroids. Now we have Formics introducing countermeasures. If we're going to overcome those countermeasures and stay ahead of the Formics, we should consult with someone who understands how the Hive Queen thinks."

"The theory of the Hive Queen has been dismissed by CentCom," said Li.

"You and I both know the Hive Queen is a viable, if not likely, scenario here. Someone or something engineered the grubs that are building Formic warships. Wila seems to believe that it's the Hive Queen. And even if it isn't, Wila understands the Formic species better than anyone."

"Wila would argue with that statement," said Li. "I've read some of her writings. She would tell you that she doesn't understand how the Hive Queen thinks any more than you do. She was able to speculate on the purpose of the grubs only after she was made aware of their existence. She can't speculate on what the Hive Queen will do next. No one can."

"Doesn't mean we shouldn't try," said Bingwen. "The Fleet certainly isn't. As far as they're concerned, a preoccupation with the Hive Queen is a dead end. Which means any efforts they may have made in the past to understand the Hive Queen have now been abandoned. You've said it yourself a hundred times, Colonel. We can't defeat an enemy we don't understand. If that's true, then we certainly can't defeat an enemy that we refuse to believe even exists."

"You're just as capable as I am of reaching out to Juke Limited's corporate site and requesting Wila's contact information."

"Which of course they won't give me," said Bingwen. "It might be easier if you ask your contacts. Perhaps they could assist us."

"My contacts?" said Li.

"Whoever requested that we analyze military commanders and recover data from the Kandahar. Whoever is secretly investigating the Formics' ability to make entire asteroids vanish into thin air. Or rather no air, since it's space. Whoever authorized this school, which incidentally doesn't feel much like a school at all."

Li smiled, but there was displeasure in it. "You don't like your school here?"

"I said it doesn't resemble a school, sir. At least not in the traditional sense. Our only teacher is confined to his quarters. We don't have a classroom. We aren't allowed in the Battle Room, or Game Room, or Tunnel Room, or any other room, for that matter, other than our barracks. Colonel Dietrich is determined to obstruct us at every turn."

"Do you think I brought you all the way out here to put you in a classroom?" said Li. "This may not be the school you envisioned, Bingwen. You may not have access to the Battle Room or the many other attractions here, but I assure you that school is in session. It began the instant we left Earth. This is a school of war. Of command. Your classroom is this solar system. From one tip to the other. This war is a much better course of study than anything I could put into a syllabus. If you haven't realized that by now, I am deeply disappointed. Colonel Dietrich is not an obstacle to your learning. He *is* what you're learning. Through his ineptitude and ego, he is teaching you what not to become. This memo from CentCom dismissing the Hive Queen, that too is a lesson in command. Your experience in the Kandahar was a lesson in command. Your study of incompetent commanders was a lesson in command. You're either learning or you aren't."

Bingwen considered a moment. "You're right. We have been learning. But we lack information and resources. A good commander assembles the right people and talent to accomplish his objectives. He gathers intelligence, and if he learns he doesn't have what he needs, he goes to people who can help him."

"You're wrong, Bingwen. If you think that a commander can always turn to others to rescue him from his problems, I haven't taught you anything. You don't get a lifeline here. You can't always turn to me or to Mazer or to anyone else and expect us to hand you the tools and people you need. I gave you an army. Those are your people. Those are your tools. If you want to accomplish something, I suggest you put them to work."

Bingwen saluted. "I apologize for wasting your time, sir." He turned and moved for the door.

"One more thing," said Colonel Li.

Bingwen turned back.

"The data you recovered from the Kandahar was examined by my . . . contacts. This war will get worse before it gets better, Bingwen. The Hive Queen, or whatever it is that's leading the Formics, is capable of far more than you or I or Wila or anyone can imagine. If I can get you clearance, you'll learn more. Be ready for it."

As soon as the lights in Rat Army barracks went out, signaling the start of the boys' sleep shift, Bingwen climbed out of his sleep sack, nodded to the others, grabbed his bag of supplies, and headed for the showers.

The row of shower tubes lined one wall in the restroom,

with each tube stretching from floor to ceiling so that no water escaped the tube during use. A shower in zero G was more of a sponge bath surrounded by floating globules of water, and Bingwen missed the days when he could turn on a faucet and let hot water rain down.

At the far end of the room in tube nine or ten he could hear someone whistling and operating a water vacuum. On Earth, gravity did all the work for you, pulling the water down the drain, but in zero G, there was no such luxury. You had to clean up the water when you were done. Space could be a pain sometimes.

Bingwen went to tube seven, slipped inside, and locked the door behind him. The tube would be cramped for an adult, but it was comfortable for Bingwen. He turned off his magnetic greaves, undressed, and waited.

Soon the vacuum shut off, but the whistling continued. Bingwen listened as the marine gathered his things, exited the shower tube, and left the restroom. Bingwen then opened his bag and pulled out his pressure suit and helmet. Once he was suited up and sealed tight, he turned on his oxygen, set his temperature, and drifted up to the ceiling. The metal ceiling tile had four screws. Bingwen removed them, slid the ceiling tile free, and pulled himself up into the narrow crawlspace. He tucked the screws into his pouch, pulled in his bag of supplies, then returned the ceiling tile back where it belonged, holding it in place with a few strips of suit-patch tape. The crawlspace was crowded with pipes and conduit, but it was wide enough for a small adult to maneuver through to conduct repairs, which made it plenty wide for Bingwen. The only discomfort was the cold, which didn't bother him in his suit.

Bingwen turned on his helmet lights and blinked a command to bring up the schematics on his HUD. Jianjun had laid out his path for him, but the walls weren't marked and Bingwen moved slower than he might have otherwise. He smiled to himself as he wiggled through an especially narrow grouping of pipes, remembering the months of training that Mazer had given him and the other boys on how best to maneuver the tunnels of an asteroid. He never imagined he'd be using those skills here.

It took him twenty minutes of moving through the labyrinth of the crawlspace until he turned a final corner and found Chati waiting for him in his pressure suit.

"What took you so long?" said Chati.

"Someone was using one of the showers. And then I went slow. Nice to see you, too."

Their first stop was one of the supply rooms. The hard part was accessing the room from the crawlspace since the screws to the ceiling tiles were only accessible from inside the room. Chati took a small laser and cut a circle around the metal where one of the screws was housed, slicing at a forty-five-degree angle to create an inverted cone shape. He repeated the process for the other three screws, then he and Bingwen used magnets to easily lift the ceiling tile up into the crawlspace.

The supply room had rows of shelves and cabinets that stretched floor to the ceiling, and it wasn't until they had removed the ceiling tile that they realized that their opening was half blocked by one of the cabinets.

"The schematics don't show where the cabinets are positioned," said Chati. "How was I supposed to know one was here?"

"Not your fault," said Bingwen. "And maybe this works to our advantage. The cabinet will hide two of the laser cuts we made when we put the tile back."

"I can't squeeze through a hole that small," said Chati. "Not with suit and gear on."

"I can," said Bingwen. "As soon as I'm down, replace the ceiling tile before we let all the cold air in."

Bingwen wiggled into the open hole and past the cabinet, reinitiating his magnetic greaves when he reached the floor.

The cable was on a spool on a lower shelf three shelves over, wrapped in plastic and unopened. Bingwen gingerly cut the plastic, then reached inside for the end of the cable. He couldn't find it. All he could feel were rows of cable tightly wound. He rotated the spool 180 degrees and cut the plastic a second time. He found the end of the cable easily, but it was glued onto the cable beneath it and Bingwen had to pull hard to release it.

The door to the storage room opened, and Bingwen could hear someone enter, walking in the stilted manner that magnetic greaves required. Bingwen froze. There were multiple shelving units between him and the door, but if the person walked far enough into the room, Bingwen would be visible.

The footsteps stopped. Someone coughed, tapped at a tablet. Then the footsteps started moving again, not back out the door, but down the row of shelves, toward Bingwen.

Bingwen looked to his left and right. There was an empty space on the top shelf to his left, maybe just big enough for him to squeeze into. He left the spool and silently pushed off the floor, drifting up toward the empty shelf. He gingerly caught himself on the lip of the shelf and swung his body up into the space just as a young ensign with his eyes on his tablet reached Bingwen's row and turned into it. The ensign walked within a meter of Bingwen, who could have reached out a hand and patted the soldier on the head.

The ensign read a series of numbers on his tablet that were so close that Bingwen could almost read them himself. Then the ensign turned away from Bingwen to the shelves opposite and grabbed a small box of supplies from a lower shelf, just above the spool of cable. The ensign tucked the box under his arm and, keeping his eyes on his tablet, exited the row and left the storage room.

Bingwen allowed himself to breathe. He lowered himself to the floor and pulled the spool of cable off the shelf. He didn't move slowly now. He pulled the plastic covering completely off the spool and hurriedly unwound forty meters of cable, which he and the boys had calculated was roughly equivalent to fifty-seven wraps of the cable from his palm to his elbow, along the length of his forearm. He then slid the spool back onto the shelf without the plastic and carried the torn plastic cover and cable back to the ceiling tile. A minute later he was in the crawlspace again, and Chati was putting the ceiling tile back into place and sealing it tight with a quick swipe of his welding rod.

"You were supposed to leave the plastic on the spool," said Chati.

"It was too damaged. It will be less suspicious if the plastic is gone. It will look like someone came in and got cable rather than someone stole cable and tried to conceal it."

The armory was next. They maneuvered through the crawlspace for another seventy meters, then Chati cut a hole into one of the ceiling tiles and slid in the camera feed line they had taken off Nak's helmet.

"Coast is clear," said Chati. "If you're facing the armory from the entrance, we're in the far-left corner. Equipment over here gets moved the least, if the inventory report is to be believed. We shouldn't see anyone."

"That's what you said about the storage room," said Bingwen.

"You do your job, I'll do mine."

Bingwen left Chati and continued through the crawlspace until he was past the armory and above a utility closet filled with cleaning supplies. He removed the ceiling tile, drifted into the closet, and changed from his pressure suit back into his jumpsuit. Then he hid his bag, initiated his greaves, and walked into the armory.

There were two quartermasters on duty near the front

desk, both of them sitting at their terminals, looking bored.

"Hello, there," said Bingwen, giving them his best smile.

The men eyed him curiously.

"This the armory?" Bingwen asked.

"And off limits to you boys," said the bigger of the two. He had a tattoo of some kind of animal peeking out of the collar of his jumpsuit.

"Off limits how?" said Bingwen. "Like I can't go back and see the weapons?"

Tattoo guy snorted. "Off limits like you need to turn your little Asian ass around and leave."

Bingwen smiled and nodded as if there were a hidden meaning in the words. "My dad, Admiral Cho, he told me quartermasters had to be tough. He says soldiers are always trying to rip off the quartermaster and steal the supplies." The two quartermasters exchanged a brief glance.

"Admiral Cho, you say?" one of them said cautiously.

"Do you know him?" said Bingwen, wide-eyed and hopeful. "He's in the Belt on the Chandigarh. That's the ship, not the city in India. I mean it *is* a city in India, but they named the ship after the city. Did you know the Fleet did that? My uncle, he's just a vice admiral. He's on the Seattle. That's a city in the United States. In California, I think. Or maybe Texas, I can't remember. Have either of you ever been to the United States?"

"You can't be in here, kid," tattoo guy said. "The colonel, he gave us strict instructions. He says you boys aren't allowed in here."

Bingwen laughed. "Yes, my father told Colonel Dietrich to be hard on us. Soft soldiers lose the day, he says. A soft soldier is a dead solider. But I told my father that he's wrong. *Unarmed* soldiers lose the day. Supplies is where the victory is. He told me to find Sergeant Bird when I got here, that he would show me the new TR-19."

The quartermasters exchanged another glance.

"Sergeant Bird works a different shift," said tattoo. "You'll have to come back when he's here. And I wouldn't get your hopes up on seeing the TR-19. That's a powerful weapon. We don't go around showing off stuff like that."

"Have either of you fired one?" said Bingwen.

"I have," said the other quartermaster. "Kicks like a cannon. Nearly tore my arm off."

"We don't do demonstrations or anything," said tattoo.

"My father has a platoon of commandos that carry TR-19s into the tunnels on asteroids. The platoon is called the Grave Diggers. Have you heard of them? Their patch is the head of a Formic on a pike with blood dripping from it, which is silly because blood wouldn't drip in space. It would just coagulate and drift away."

"Come back when Sergeant Bird is here," said tattoo. "You can tell him all about it."

"Can you tell me what time his shift starts two days from now?" said Bingwen. "That will be my next opportunity, and I'd like to be here when he arrives."

Tattoo sighed, annoyed.

"I'll email my father soon, and I want to tell him I saw a TR-19 in the armory."

Tattoo moved back to his terminal and tapped at the screen. Jianjun had apparently done his job because the quartermaster looked confused and tapped at the screen again.

"What's the problem?" said the other.

"Can't get on," said tattoo. "Give me your machine."

He moved to the other terminal and tapped at it as well, but nothing happened.

"System's down," said tattoo. "Sorry, kid. Wait. Here it is. Nope. Now it's gone again."

"Maybe reboot the terminal?" offered Bingwen.

They fiddled with the machines, which alternated

between functioning properly and crashing suddenly. Five minutes passed before they got them working again.

"There we are," said Bingwen. "Seems to be working now."

"Sergeant Bird is here at 1100 two days from now," said the other quartermaster.

"Very kind," said Bingwen. "Thanks."

One hour later, Bingwen and Chati were back at Rat Army barracks, taking stock of all the equipment they had taken.

"I can't believe that actually worked," said Nak, hefting a large capsule of NanoCloud pellets.

"This is more than enough cable," said Jianjun. He smiled at Bingwen. "Nice work with the quartermasters. You realize of course that you'll have to go there in two days and ask for Sergeant Bird."

Bingwen had worn a microphone under his jumpsuit so Jianjun could listen in and know when to scramble the terminals.

"According to Sergeant Bird's service record," said Bingwen, "he's a real hardnose. He'll kick me out immediately and that will be the end of it. Nice work with the computers."

"Don't give Bingwen all the praise," said Chati. "Distracting those dull bobs was the easy job. I had to fly around like a madman collecting everything."

"We'll get you a big giant medal," said Nak.

"How long will it take you to set this up?" Bingwen asked Jianjun.

"Couple hours, maybe."

Bingwen nodded. "Nak, how's that list coming?"

"You'd be proud. I've identified the chief engineer who oversaw the creation of the NanoCloud. Noloa Benyawe. I have her email."

"Good work. You think she'll help us?"

"She was quoted at a tech conference recently stating that it's foolish to abandon the theory of the Hive Queen."

"I like her already," said Bingwen. "Question is, will she help us immediately. Marines need answers now."

Chati tapped Bingwen lightly on the arm. "Don't be a downer, Bingwen. Let's take a moment and bask in our victory. Look at all this stuff we nabbed."

"This is hardly a victory," said Bingwen. "This is gathering supplies. We celebrate when the marines in the tunnels have what they need to do their job."

CHAPTER 8

Blinds

To: noloa.benyawe@juke.net
From: littlesoldier13@freebeltmail.net
Subject: Arming marines with NanoCloud

Dear Dr. Benyawe,

I wrote a rather convincing email to you pretending to be a captain of marines in the Belt in need of your assistance. I was afraid that if you knew my true identity you would dismiss me outright and delete this message. Then I reminded myself that you must be an enormously intelligent and open-minded person who is smarter than my first email gave you credit for. So I scrapped that email and started anew. Here goes.

My name is Bingwen. I am currently stationed at Grav-Camp in a secret IF initiative designed to train future commanders. I'm taking a risk in divulging that, but I need your help and trust. And trust is earned.

Formics are blocking asteroid tunnels with hullmat. I don't know if that's classified or not, but it shouldn't be because we need the best brains on this. The hullmat makes it impossible for marines to reach the

Formic warship and hive at the asteroid's center. The only weapon that penetrates hullmat is the Nano-Cloud. But there is no delivery mechanism for an individual marine to carry NanoCloud into the tunnels and physically apply it to hullmat. Will you please give this consideration and offer possible solutions? I recognize that I'm breaking protocol by beseeching your help directly, but every warship birthed from an asteroid leads to thousands of lives lost. Time is short.

Your prompt reply is appreciated.

Bingwen

PS: This is not a joke.
PPS: Lem Jukes can vouch for me.

Mazer was surprised by the alert on his wrist pad ordering him to immediately report to Airlock Three. His assumption was that Colonel Dietrich had arranged to get rid of him. Keeping Mazer sequestered in his quarters was costing the space station food and oxygen and getting Dietrich nothing in return. And since it was easier to throw Mazer onto the first transport out of GravCamp than to actually think up a use for him that didn't give Colonel Li a victory on the matter, Colonel Dietrich would simply send Mazer packing. Adios. Sayonara. Don't let the screen door hit you on the butt on the way out.

Mazer didn't have any personal items, so he left his quarters empty-handed and followed the directions on his wrist pad to the airlock. He considered going by Bingwen's barracks to say goodbye, but then thought better of it. That would create a scene. Bingwen didn't need a scene. Nor did he need another reason for Colonel Dietrich to despise him. Report to the airlock immediately, the order had said. And Mazer followed orders. He could write Bingwen a message once he was on the transport.

But there was no transport waiting at Airlock Three. Colonel Li was there instead, along with a small two-man service shuttle. "We're going for a ride," said Li. "Get in."

Li flew into the docking tube that led to the shuttle. Mazer followed. Li climbed into the passenger seat. "I assume you know how to pilot one of these."

"There's not much to it, really," said Mazer.

"I'll take that as a yes. Move us away from the space station."

Mazer climbed into the flight seat, decoupled the shuttle from the docking tube, and maneuvered the shuttle out into space.

"This is a repair shuttle, sir," said Mazer. "With a very short flight range. Dare I ask where we're headed?"

"Take us on a leisurely circle around the space station."

"All right."

Mazer eased the shuttle away from GravCamp and began a wide slow rotation. They flew in silence for a few minutes.

"Aren't you going to ask me why I brought you out here?" said Li.

"I figure you'll tell me when you're ready," said Mazer.

"This isn't why I brought you out here," said Li, "but I should start by offering you an apology."

Mazer glanced at him, surprised.

"What?" said Li. "You don't think I know how to apologize?"

"With all due respect, sir, you've never struck me as the apologizing type."

"You're making me rethink my apology."

"Sorry. Please continue."

"I knew Dietrich would be difficult. I didn't know he'd be a worm. I brought you all the way out here, away from the fighting, which I know you hate missing. And now you're locked in a room, not because of any infraction on your part, but because Colonel Dietrich can't punish me and he can't punish the boys. You're the only viable target. So he punishes you."

"I appreciate the apology," said Mazer. "Any chance of resolving this? Prison doesn't suit me."

"Sadly, no," said Li. "At least not at the moment. I'm waiting for the colonel to cool. As long as you stay confined, he allows himself to believe that he won. Though what he won exactly, I still don't understand. His belief that I'm some conspirator in a plot to replace him with Chinese officers is absurd."

"Dietrich is a man driven by fear," said Mazer. "Fear that you were sent here by CentCom to spy on him or replace him. Fear that CentCom believes him inadequate. Fear that his authority will be diminished by having another colonel at GravCamp."

"You think him that shallow?"

"I've seen worse," said Mazer. "CentCom is full of worse."

"Those are strong words," said Colonel Li. "Dietrich might even say treasonous words."

"To call our commanders incompetent isn't treason," said Mazer. "It's merely observational."

"I'm a commander," said Li. "Would you say the same about me?"

"You and I have very different philosophies, sir," said Mazer.

"You're avoiding the question, but I'll let it pass. How do our philosophies differ? And on what subject? Leadership?"

"Permission to speak freely," said Mazer.

"You're already speaking freely," said Colonel Li. "I haven't pulled a gun yet."

"You and I see differently on many subjects, sir," said Mazer. "How you treat the boys, for instance."

"They're not boys, Mazer. Their childhoods ended when the Formics slaughtered their parents in China. Bingwen found his parents burning in a field. That changes a person. That flips who someone is in an instant. Cruel, yes. Tragic, certainly. But that is what the Formics have done to all of us. They have robbed us of the life we were all intended to live. They have twisted the orientation of every single human being and given us a new path we did not deserve. Bingwen is no exception. His old self ended in that instant, and a new self emerged. Not a boy, but a soldier. Maybe not in training, maybe not in skills. But in his mind. You saw it. Why else would you have asked for his help in China?"

"I was alone and wounded," said Mazer. "I didn't know the language. Or the landscape."

"And Bingwen did," said Li. "You used his skills. You capitalized on a boy's abilities, meager though they were at the time, to accomplish a military objective. What I'm doing now is no different. These young men can offer the world a great deal once their training is complete."

"They don't have to be commanders to be great soldiers," said Mazer.

"Of course not," said Li. "I don't assume they'll all achieve command. Nak and Jianjun are followers, for example. Perhaps they might learn to be excellent intelligence officers one day. With some pushing they might even lead an intelligence agency."

"They can also be useful as loving husbands and fathers," said Mazer. "Contributors in their communities. There's greatness in that as well."

Li rolled his eyes. "Don't pretend to be sentimental, Mazer. Someone must always lead. If we don't control who receives that position of power, it will be someone we wish wasn't there. And then it won't matter how many good fathers and husbands the community has. When the seat of power is filled with a tyrant, everyone suffers."

"Is that your end game?" Mazer said. "Putting one of these boys on a throne?"

"The world no longer believes in kings and queens, Mazer. At least not as ruling governors. But we do have our share of leaders like them. What is the Hegemon, if not a king? What is the Strategos, if not a king? The Polemarch? Different names, different duties, all with checks and balances, but monarchs all the same. Colonel Dietrich fancies himself a king. GravCamp is his fiefdom. He rules with an iron fist because he's an imbecile and has no concept of command. Is that who you want leading us in the future, Mazer? Men like Dietrich? Men who know nothing of leadership? Whose only concern is self-preservation? Who will step on the back of anyone to ascend to a position of power? If that's what you want, then you're in luck, because the Fleet is flooded with such men. We have them by the hundreds, by the thousands, maybe."

"We have good commanders as well," said Mazer.

Colonel Li nodded. "Some, yes. But not nearly enough. You know I'm right. The only good apples are at the junior officer level. That's why you created the backchannel intranet, to give those junior officers a voice and a means for sharing decent ideas, rather than having their ideas beaten down, dismissed, or ignored by self-serving superiors. You've seen it your entire career. So have I. Vaganov treated you like trash for his own gain, and the Fleet made him a rear admiral. There are rumors that he's being considered as a replacement for the Polemarch. A horrifying thought, wouldn't you agree? And yet such horrifying considerations are bandied about every day in the halls of CentCom."

Mazer didn't respond. Vaganov as Polemarch? Horrifying was an understatement.

"There are people jockeying for positions, Mazer. Dangerous people. People who do not deserve to hold a mop, much less an admiralship, or the Hegemony. God preserve us if they get those positions. And while the rest of us sit back in shock at our misfortune at being led by such fools, the Formics will win this war. Then it won't matter who sits on any throne, because the Formics will wipe us all out. So you may disagree with my tactics, Mazer. You may shudder at my methods. But in the end, you know I'm right. Who would you rather have directing you in battle? Vaganov or Bingwen? And I don't mean Bingwen as an adult. I mean Bingwen now. As a thirteen-year-old. Hell, pick any commander in the Fleet against Bingwen. Who would you choose?"

"Bingwen is exceptional," said Mazer. "I can't argue that."

"He's more than exceptional. He has a better mind for war than most of our commanders in the field. Why? Because part of him is still a child. He has an unbridled imagination. He's not burdened by fear of what others may think of him, or of preserving his career, or of impressing his superiors, or even of failure. His strategic mind, like Nak's and Jianjun's, is not clouded with the emotional burdens of adulthood. Children create what the grown mind never can. Children see what few adults are capable of seeing. You may think my initiative of shaping child commanders irresponsible, but one day you're going to have to make a choice: follow these incompetent commanders into destruction or save the world from their stupidity."

Mazer didn't respond.

"That's why the world needs us, Mazer. Because the world keeps making idiots. It's up to people like you and me to shape and mold the real leaders who will save us from the fools."

"You and I have very different ideas on how to shape and mold," said Mazer.

"No question," said Li. "But both are needed. Bingwen follows you because he loves you, because you filled the vacancy left empty by his parents. But hate can be just as useful and influential as love. Sometimes even more so. Bingwen needs me as much as he needs you. My yin to your yang. I can tell from your expression that you disagree."

"Bingwen doesn't need hate. You see him as a tool. As a device. As a weapon to be wielded. Not as a human being. Not as a child unjustly thrown into war."

"You're wrong, Mazer. I see Bingwen for what he truly is far better than you ever will. And Bingwen would agree with me. You would wrap him in a blanket and send him somewhere safe. You would shield him, protect him, guard him, stop him from taking a single step into danger. When all Bingwen wants and needs is to burn the Formics down. To set a torch to their castle and watch it crumble to ashes. Yes, I see a weapon, but it's a weapon that chooses to be one. A weapon that needs to be hurled at the enemy, not sent off to his room. Did you ever stop to ask Bingwen what he wants, Mazer? Did that ever enter your consideration? Or did your adult arrogance make that decision for him? Oh yes, we adults are so wise. We have all the answers for the ignorant children. We know what's best. 'No, no, don't trouble yourself, child. These problems are for the adults to solve.' Do you have any idea how offensive that thinking is to Bingwen? How hurtful? How much he loathes being thought of as a victim, as a child? Spare me your sanctimony, Mazer. Bingwen may hate me, but at least I see him for what he really is."

Mazer said nothing. Because he realized for the first time that perhaps Li wasn't wrong. Not entirely. Not about Bingwen's mindset, at least. Not about what Bingwen wanted.

"But enough about Bingwen," said Li. "That's not why you're here. I didn't drag you into this shuttle to defend my training philosophy or to critique yours. You're here because my superiors need someone with an astute analytical mind.

Someone who sees things that others may not. Someone who knows what he knows and knows what he doesn't. As simple as that sounds, it's a rare skill in this army. My superiors believe that someone is you."

Mazer glanced at him, surprised. "Is this a recruitment conversation?"

Li didn't blink. "And what do you think I'd be recruiting you for?"

"We're speaking freely here, so I'll push on. You're an intelligence officer. Covert. That much is obvious. Either within the Fleet or, more likely, with the Hegemony."

"And why would you conclude that my association is with the Hegemony and not the Fleet?"

"You despise the Fleet and all the careerists who weaken it."

"You despise the Fleet for the same reason," said Li.

"I love the Fleet," said Mazer. "I despise the idiots."

"Can you separate the two?"

"If we can't, we lose this war."

Li smiled. "No argument there. This is not a recruitment conversation, Mazer. At least not yet. This is an assignment. A classified one."

"The last time you gave me a classified assignment, a team of Formics tried to blow me in half."

"And it was the most fun you'd had in months. This, I'm afraid, is far less dangerous fare. What do you know about Operation Deep Dive?"

"That it's a third of our fleet," said Mazer. "That their objective is to target and destroy the Formic motherships far below the ecliptic."

"What do you know of their day-to-day operations?"

"Next to nothing," said Mazer. "They're rarely included in the daily reports. I assume they're still moving toward their targets."

"They're not," said Li. "They haven't been for some time. They were essentially routed several months ago."

Mazer looked at him, shocked.

"Deep Dive consisted of fifty-seven vessels. Most of those were combat vessels, but there were a good number of support ships as well. They were attacked by a fleet of Formic ships over three months ago. Seven of our warships were destroyed almost instantly. Three more were chased down over the next couple of days and annihilated. The rest of our fleet was scattered and dispersed. They're still regrouping as we speak. As an organized military body, they're all but destroyed. The Strategos and Polemarch are torn on what orders to give them now. Bring them home or send them on to the motherships to complete their original mission."

"Why would the Fleet keep this a secret?" Mazer asked.

"Because it's a humiliating defeat in a time when the world desperately needs a victory. And because two of the ships that were destroyed were the only two ships equipped with ansibles. For the longest time we had no idea what had happened to the fleet. They're too far away for us to target accurately with laserline. All we knew from their ansible communications was that they were suddenly under attack, and then their ansibles went silent."

"How could they *suddenly* be under attack?" said Mazer. "Our fleet was out in open space. They didn't have any visible obstructions like we have in the Belt, asteroids and debris and whatnot. Our ships should have seen the Formics coming from way off."

"Sound familiar?" said Li.

"The Kandahar," said Mazer. "Same issue. They were suddenly attacked as well. They should have seen Formics coming but didn't."

"We believe the Formics are now building blinds," said Li, "or massive structures that are essentially invisible to scopes. Think of them as enormous, domed black shields dotted with stars. Huge pieces of camouflage. A surface so black that it somehow absorbs light rather than reflects it. Against the backdrop of space, these blinds are completely invisible. We believe the Formics placed some of these blinds along the path of our fleet. The Formic fleet then hid behind the blinds and waited. When our ships passed by, the Formics launched from their hiding places and attacked our ships from the rear, catching them completely by surprise. The only reason the Formics didn't obliterate our fleet entirely was because their fleet was smaller. If they had built more blinds and had more ships, we wouldn't be having this conversation because there wouldn't have been any human survivors to tell us what had happened."

"These blinds," said Mazer, "that's why an asteroid disappeared. That's what instigated the Kandahar's investigation. An asteroid vanished, and we didn't know why. You're saying the Formics may have hidden the asteroid behind a blind."

"Or built a blind around it," said Li. "We're not completely sure what happened to that asteroid. But we think whatever tech allowed it to vanish is the same tech the Formics used to sneak up on the Kandahar. And it's likely the same tech used to rout the ships of Deep Dive."

Mazer sat in silence. "If the Formics have the ability to camouflage their warships and hide their approach, the war has taken a drastic turn for the worse."

Colonel Li reached into his pocket and produced a data cube. "This contains an animation of the battles below the ecliptic. It has taken the Fleet this long to assemble the data from the surviving ships and piece together what likely happened. The animation was built based on the navigational data and scans taken immediately prior to, during, and following the attack." He then produced a small tablet and handed it to Mazer. "You'll connect the data cube to this tablet, which is encrypted and requires a password."

He told Mazer the password.

"Don't use the terminal in your quarters or access the network here at GravCamp for your analysis. Everything you need is on that tablet and cube. Analyze what's there and write me a report."

"You said this was classified," said Mazer. "I don't have clearance for this."

"We've increased your security clearance," said Li. "And Bingwen's as well. Once you've made your conclusions, you may show it to him."

"As another test?" said Mazer.

Colonel Li smiled. "You still don't understand, Mazer. Bingwen only has one test. It started a long time ago, and it won't stop until he's dead or sitting on a throne."

CHAPTER 9

Lem

Upon discovering that the Formics were building warships within the hollowed-out centers of asteroids and that the Formic threat was essentially all around them, asteroid-mining families and Fleet contractors throughout the solar system fled for the safety of Luna. The massive and sudden influx of refugees into the city of Imbrium reignited tense debate on existing immigration laws and introduced a multitude of economic and housing concerns for a city already burdened with overpopulation, dwindling food supplies, and an aging infrastructure.

Transporting refugees from Luna to Earth was, in most instances, not a viable option due to the high cost of fuel for any atmospheric entry or exit, the relatively low number of shuttles not already commandeered for use by the International Fleet, and the simple fact that most refugees were unable to withstand a full G of gravity. Even the relatively low gravity of Luna was more than some could endure, and hospitals on Luna quickly filled to capacity with those needing reconditioning treatment to build bone mass and muscle strength.

Since hospitals were already understaffed due to many medical practitioners on Luna having joined the

Fleet or returned to the greater safety of Earth, countless refugees received little or no medical treatment
whatsoever. The subsequent increases in homeless-
ness and crime incensed many longtime Luna resi-
dents, and protest marches and riots soon followed.

Many local charities organized assets and resources
to provide food and temporary housing for those in
need, but it was not until the Hegemony Council created the Department of Rehousing and Refugee Assistance (DORRA) that the plight of refugees received
significant financial attention.

—Demosthenes, *A History of the Formic Wars,* Vol. 3

Lem wove his way through the crowded lobby of the convention center on Luna, greeting guests warmly and acting
as if nothing pleased him more than to have them attend
the fundraiser. It was a lie, of course. Lem hated playing
host. He despised schmoozing and hobnobbing and pretending to be interested in other people's lives. "How are
the children?" he would ask, if the couple had any. Or,
"How is it that you look younger every time I see you,
Mrs. So-and-So? Whatever magic elixir you're drinking,
please share." Or he would grow somber and say, "Yes, I
read the latest laserline. Just awful news. We must pray
for our troops." And on and on, smiling and nodding and
forcing himself to laugh at other people's weak attempts at
humor.

They had come in numbers this evening: heads of in-
dustry, tech giants, dignitaries, entrepreneurs, wealthy
socialites, celebrities, the most elite citizens in all of
Luna, dressed in formal attire and fine jewelry and dec-
orative magnetic greaves to keep them anchored to the
floor in the Moon's lower gravity. Servers moved among
them, carrying trays of wine and shrimp flown up from
Earth. Lem peeled himself away from the Canadian lunar

ambassador and crossed to a corner of the room where Benyawe, his chief engineer and most trusted adviser, was standing in the shadow of a large plant, avoiding all conversation.

"You're trying to hide over here," said Lem. "It's not very inconspicuous."

"I was succeeding until you showed up," she said with a scowl. Benyawe wore a gown with a green and black pattern that nodded to her Nigerian heritage. And her long gray hair, normally in braids down her back, was now arranged in an elegant cone atop her head.

"You look lovely, by the way," said Lem. "I don't think I've ever seen you in an evening gown before. It's very . . ."

"African?" said Benyawe.

"I was going to say colorful," said Lem. "But yes, I suppose the pattern and cut have a uniquely cultural design about them. I think it's stunning. Especially all the green. Makes for good camouflage in these plants."

"*You* saw me easily enough," said Benyawe. "It's not working as well as I had hoped."

"Flying solo?" said Lem. "I thought you'd bring that new husband around."

"Mandu is not one for formal affairs," said Benyawe. "He finds them tedious."

"They *are* tedious," said Lem. "They're downright exhausting. I'm surprised you even came. I thought engineers preferred lab coats and takeout Chinese as they worked into the wee hours of the night."

"Call it morbid curiosity," said Benyawe. "I wanted to see if anyone actually showed up. I thought the protests would keep people away."

Lem had thought the same. Union workers and immigration hardliners had taken to the streets in Imbrium for two days now, denouncing the Hegemony's open-door policy on Luna for space refugees fleeing the war. The protesters claimed that refugees were taking jobs and inviting crime, which to some extent was true. Half-starved people had a tendency to get desperate, especially if children were involved. Lem wanted to punch the protesters in the teeth.

"It looks like I was mistaken," said Benyawe. "There's quite a crowd here. If anything, the protests have brought attention to the refugees. Maybe peoples' hearts are pricked. My faith in humanity is somewhat restored."

"Let's hope their hearts are pricked enough to open their bank accounts," said Lem. "Every shelter is full, and we've got hundreds of refugees arriving every day. The hospital is turning people away if they don't have a life-threatening injury."

Benyawe laughed quietly and shook her head.

"What?" said Lem. "You think the desperate cry of refugees is funny?"

"Not at all. I'm laughing at you. At this." She gestured at him and the crowd. "I never took you for a philanthropist."

"And what did you take me for? A cold-hearted rich boy consumed with self and leisure?"

"I've never known you to be leisurely," said Benyawe.

"I am not without a soul," said Lem. "It surfaces every now and again, and it isn't scared at the sight of its own shadow."

"Are you sure it's your soul that sparked all this?" said Benyawe. "Or is Wila wearing off on you?"

She meant Wilasanee Saowaluk, a biochemist the company had hired from Thailand because of her unconventional theories on the Hive Queen and her belief that the Formics used bioengineered organisms to mine asteroids, separate minerals, and build their warships—a theory that had turned out to be accurate.

Lem raised an eyebrow. "What are you insinuating?"

Benyawe shrugged innocently. "Precisely what I said,

that a beautiful woman determined to stop all suffering in the universe, and who has shown a particular interest in the refugees, and who seems to have your ear on all subjects, might be having a little sway over you. And that's not a bad thing. You could use a little reforming."

"Wila is a practicing Theravada Buddhist," said Lem. "She has sworn off any interest in men, including wealthy, handsome, brilliant, eligible ones like myself, so stop smirking like some middle-school gossip queen. Wila and I are not a thing and never will be."

"But you *wish* you were a thing," said Benyawe, smiling.

"Wow," said Lem. "I thought I grew out of conversations like this when I was seven."

"You're avoiding the question."

"The answer is no. I don't wish we were a thing."

"Shame," said Benyawe, shrugging again. "I happen to like Wila."

"I happen to like her as well," said Lem. "But not in the way your accusing eyes seem to suggest. She's not my type. Beautiful, no question, but far too devout. I prefer women who are unburdened by faith. Religion takes all the fun out of relationships."

Benyawe scoffed and made a face of disgust. "You're insufferable."

"And adorable. You can be both at the same time, you know. I looked it up. Any progress on the request from the kid at GravCamp?"

"The kid's name is Bingwen."

"Right, Bingwen. What's the update?"

"I've assembled a team and responded to him. We're looking at ways to arm marines with NanoCloud. Frankly, I'm surprised you're letting me pursue this. If we give tech to the Fleet, we don't get paid."

"I'm calling it our customer appreciation sale. Buy a fleet from us, and we'll throw in a few kitchen knives and maybe a NanoCloud device for free. Further evidence that I do have a soul." Lem scanned the crowd. "My father is a no-show, I see."

"Your father is the Hegemon of Earth. He keeps a busy schedule, what with the human race on the verge of extinction and all. Try not to take it personally. Besides, it's best if Ukko isn't here. His presence would only remind people of DORRA and dry up any hope of people opening their purses."

"DORRA is a good idea on paper," said Lem. "In practice, it's mired in bureaucracy and red tape and doesn't take unique circumstances into account. That lady that died near the shipyard, that wasn't DORRA's brightest day."

A young space-born mother, newly arrived on Luna and unaccustomed to any gravity, had registered for DORRA upon reaching the shipyard and then, unable to get immediate approval and assistance, had died in an alley nearby, holding her infant, the weight of her own body having put too much stress on her already strained heart. The baby was still in the hospital.

"It's a complex problem, Lem," said Benyawe. "Some of these refugees have never set foot on a moon, much less a planet. Their bodies haven't developed with gravity. They don't have the needed bone density to jump into the workforce here. They excel in space on mining vessels, but they're essentially handicapped from the moment they arrive on Luna. And we don't have the medical personnel or facilities to accommodate them."

"I should have *you* give the speech," said Lem. "You say it better than I do, and you're far more persuasive."

"You don't want me addressing the wealthy and elite," said Benyawe. "My contempt for pretentious haughtiness would be all too evident."

"Is that the look you're always giving me?" said Lem. "Contempt? And here I thought that was your resting face."

"Your father may not be here," said Benyawe, "but I see several of his cabinet members and plenty of Hegemony staff."

"Hegemony spies, is more like it," said Lem. "Father's eyes and ears, catching every conversation they can overhear."

"If your father uses spies," said Benyawe, "I hope he's a little more creative than parlor room eavesdropping or he won't last very long in office, not with enemies circling the Hegemony with claws out." She nodded discreetly to her right, and Lem followed her gaze to the opposite corner where Alexei Sokolov, the Russian minister for Lunar affairs, was chatting it up with the CEO of Minetek, a competitor.

"Sokolov," said Lem. "What a pleasant surprise. I'll need to fire whoever put him on the guest list."

"Not inviting him would have been a bigger mistake," said Benyawe. "He would have felt slighted. And his allies would have noticed his absence and taken offense. Plus this way your father's spies can catch his conversations."

Sokolov was Father's biggest critic, lambasting the Hegemon for every battle lost in the war—as if Father were the Strategos or Polemarch. Now Sokolov was building a back-room coalition against Father with the obvious intention of replacing him as Hegemon once Father's popularity waned. The press was all too eager to stir the pot and give Sokolov the pulpit, since political turmoil, ugly as it was, was a nice break from the demoralizing coverage of the war.

"Does he honestly think anyone would follow him if he were Hegemon?" said Lem. "The man oozes self-importance. The IF can't stand him. The Strategos, who's a fellow Russian, doesn't even hide his contempt. Sokolov has zero chance of unseating my father."

"I wouldn't say zero," said Benyawe. "Sokolov has the support of the Warsaw Pact and the rest of eastern

Europe. Even your native Finland has its share of Jukes haters. The war isn't helping. Your father's poll numbers have been abysmal."

"The unfortunate massacre of Fleet ships was not my father's doing. He's a politician, not a general. You would think people would know this."

"You're defending your father," said Benyawe. "That's not something I see often."

"I'm defending good sense," said Lem. "My father might be cruel and callous and a miserable excuse for a parent, but he's a halo-wearing Saint Peter compared to worms like Sokolov. If that clown was running the Hegemony, we'd be extinct already."

A few people nearby glanced in their direction.

"I'd keep your voice down," said Benyawe. "Making enemies with Sokolov isn't advisable. We can't afford to be a secondary target. Your father will take care of him. Let Sokolov be."

"Let him be?" Lem said. "Hardly. I'm tempted to go over there and bury a knee in his groin. Or maybe just insult him and avoid the lawsuit. How do you say, 'You have a stupid pig face' in Russian?"

"This is no joke, Lem. Sokolov has deep connections with Russian intelligence. Even from his position up here on Luna, Sokolov twists arms all over eastern Europe. Plus he has close ties with the Russian Shipbuilders Guild, many of whom we employ in our shipyards. Sokolov could easily agitate those people and make life hell for us. If our Russian guild workers were to strike or walk out, it would severely cripple our operations and delay our deliveries to the Fleet. We're in the middle of a war that we're losing, Lem. If we fail in our commitments to the Fleet, who do you think our stockholders are going to blame? Sokolov?"

"This is why I hate the guilds," said Lem. "They have leverage, and they know it, and so they exploit us. Did I mention that I hate them?"

"Spoken like a true capitalist," said Benyawe. "And you're right, it's 'guilds' plural, as in more than one. If the Russian shipbuilders strike, there's a strong chance that the other guilds follow suit: the Russian mining guild, and metal-processing guild, and safety inspection guild, and—"

"Yes, yes, and their hamburger guild and their toenail clippers guild," said Lem. "They have a guild for everything. I get it. I hate it."

"Again, spoken like a true capitalist. My point is, if we make an enemy of Sokolov, we make enemies with a lot of other people as well. Some of whom are our own people. That's not a hornets' nest we want to kick. Sokolov could make our lives very difficult very quickly. That would not only hurt the company, but also the war. Best strategy? Ignore the man."

"I don't like dancing around the devil," said Lem. "I like stabbing the devil in the heart."

"Sokolov isn't the devil. He's more like a first cousin. Besides, I know a few people who would say the same about you."

"That I'm the devil? Who says that? I'm as tender as a kitty cat."

"Leave the backroom battles to your father," Benyawe said, patting his arm. "Focus on the battles that will keep us all alive. The war. If the company falters, the Fleet will falter, and it won't matter who the Hegemon is. In the meantime, your father will keep an eye on Sokolov. You and I will just ignore him."

"That may be difficult," said Lem, "considering he's coming this way."

It was true. Sokolov had ended his conversation and was now moving toward Lem, with a smile as pleasant and innocent as a viper.

"I knew I should have stayed home," said Benyawe.

Sokolov reached them a moment later, shaking hands and bowing slightly in some courtly show of respect.

"Lem, how kind of you to arrange this. And Dr. Benyawe, you are even more lovely in person than I imagined."

"Since I don't know the extent of your imagination, Minister Sokolov," said Benyawe, "your words might not be much of a compliment." Benyawe took his proffered hand and gave it a tepid squeeze.

Sokolov laughed heartily, a deep baritone guffaw. He was a large man, a good ten to fifteen centimeters taller than Lem, with a generous double chin and a sculpted head of white hair that looked thicker in photos than it did in person. His trimmed white beard and jolly disposition gave him an air of innocence and gentility. Lem thought he looked more like the mascot for a Bavarian beer-drinking festival than a dangerous Russian bureaucrat.

Sokolov shook a playful finger at Benyawe. "A brilliant mind *and* a sharp tongue. Formidable traits. No wonder she is your chief engineer, Lem. I suspect she runs a very tight ship while she busies herself building them."

"Benyawe would defeat the Formics singlehandedly if we'd only give her the chance," said Lem.

"I believe it," said Sokolov, laughing again. "You are to be commended for your efforts, Dr. Benyawe. What Juke Limited has accomplished in a few short years is nothing short of remarkable. I never imagined that ships of such size and complexity and strength could be built and armed so quickly. And equipped with Formic tech, no less. Tech that had to be reverse-engineered, understood, and then redesigned to fit human vessels and our methods of warfare. It is, without question, the greatest achievement in human engineering. Ever. The Great Wall of China and the pyramids have been bumped from their lofty position in the history books to make room for you and your fleet."

Benyawe shook her head. "While I appreciate the kind words, Minister Sokolov—"

"Please, call me Alexei."

"While I appreciate the kind words, Alexei, the ships built by Juke Limited for the International Fleet are the handiwork of nearly three million Juke employees and contractors. Should the bricklayer who laid a dozen bricks get credit for the Great Wall?"

Sokolov laughed again. "I suspect you've laid more than twelve bricks, Dr. Benyawe. And now I must add humility to your growing list of attributes." Sokolov placed a hand over his heart. "I, shamefully, suffer from what you might call a scarcity of humility, as my critics will tell you. I'm a child of privilege, you see. Fed with a silver spoon all my life, leading me to believe that I can achieve anything I set my mind to. I'm sure you can relate, Lem, having had every privilege and opportunity laid conveniently in your lap. It makes men like you and me somewhat blind and naive to the threats around us, for we think ourselves indestructible."

Lem forced a smile and showed no reaction to the veiled slight. "If my father taught me anything, Minister Sokolov, it is to keep enemies close and that everyone is your enemy."

Sokolov frowned. "Too true. We must tread carefully. The Formics pose an existential threat, and yet if we survive their assault, I worry that the power struggle that will follow between the Hegemony, the Fleet, and the nations of Earth may tear us apart. I doubt that the Strategos or the Polemarch, for example, will be interested in relinquishing their authority should the International Fleet dissolve. That's why I was so intrigued to learn that your father, Lem, is considering resigning and calling for the Hegemony Council to elect a new Hegemon. But my goodness, I see from the look on your face that this is news to you."

Lem composed himself and smiled. "My father does not include me in his governing decisions, Minister Sokolov. We talk very little, to be honest. The demands of our responsibilities are great. As someone far more involved in the workings of government, you would know better about my father's plans than me."

"Perhaps I am mistaken," said Sokolov. "Rumors are not always delivered by truthful tongues. But if the rumors *are* true, we can only hope that the new Hegemon upholds your father's legacy and serves with as much wisdom and distinction as he has."

"I did not realize you thought so highly of my father."

"Oh, I have my criticisms. We all do. I have yet to meet the perfect leader who acts prudently in every circumstance. I don't think such a man or woman exists. The very idea of democracy makes it prohibitive. Abraham Lincoln, beloved by his fellow Americans, said it best. 'You can please some of the people all of the time, and all of the people some of the time, but you can't please all of the people, all of the time.'"

"I think it was also Mr. Lincoln who took a bullet to the back of the head," said Lem. "If I'm remembering American history correctly."

Sokolov nodded gravely. "That is precisely my point, my dear Lem. Even the noblest leader can be the victim of hate. Your father might be very wise to step aside. For his own safety. There are many who place the war's losses squarely on his shoulders. I would hate for some lunatic to take your Father's life in some senseless act of violence."

Lem let the words hang in the air a moment and kept his face a mask of politeness. "How kind of you to be concerned for my father's safety. If what you have heard is true, I hope the Hegemony Council elects someone who sincerely cares for the safety and well-being of all men and women, be they citizens of Earth, Luna, or space born."

Sokolov took a sealed glass of champagne from the magnetic tray of a passing server and sipped at the straw, smiling. "Well said, Lem. I could not agree more. I have even heard some suggest your name as a possible successor to your father. I think the idea splendid. You're young, but tenacious. Outspoken, but articulate. You've quadrupled your father's empire in only a few years, so you clearly understand markets and fiscal self-reliance. Your recent philanthropy work with the refugees shows that you possess sincere compassion toward the downtrodden, an attribute everyone will welcome. Your support for economic initiatives and work-placement programs for the refugees demonstrates an astute understanding of how social concerns can be addressed with sensible public programs. Plus you're devilishly handsome. Even my wife, who is old enough to be your mother, finds you attractive, though she would kill me for saying so. You are, in short, my dear man, bred for politics. I do sincerely hope that you will at least consider the prospect. Who else is more qualified than you?"

"I assure you, Minister Sokolov," said Lem. "I have no interest in serving as Hegemon or in any public office. My father is made for the task, not me. I'm far too impertinent. I think my life of privilege, as you say, makes me too sassy for politics."

"On the contrary, Lem. Sass is what defines a politician. The people hunger for it. Someone with a bit of flair, a gentle giant one moment, a pulpit-pounder the next. But I see that your mind is made up on the subject. Pity. I was rather excited about the prospect of your name being considered."

"I would think the Council would look to their own members for a possible replacement to my father," said Lem.

Sokolov shook his head. "The law prohibits it, I'm afraid. No member of Congress or of the Council can be elected Hegemon. If that were the case, they would all be constantly campaigning for the job, which would log-

jam the government. The emergency of our situation is so acute that humanity could not abide that. Only someone outside the Hegemony can be considered. That's why I was so hoping you would be open to the idea."

"I'm sorry to disappoint you," said Lem. "But clearly my ignorance of the Hegemony electoral process should convince you that I'm not the man for the job. I would think someone more experienced in politics and diplomacy better suited, someone with an understanding of the legislature and Hegemony law. Like yourself, for instance. You're a minister of the Russian Federation, not a member of the Hegemony. And yet you've interacted with the Hegemony enough to know how the system works. Could you be elected?"

Sokolov smiled. "You flatter me, Lem. While there is nothing in the law that would prohibit me from being elected by the Council, and while I would consider it the honor of my lifetime to serve in such a capacity, I fear there are members of the Council who would need a little convincing. Some think me too passionate for the job."

"Nonsense," said Lem. "We're at war. I would think the Hegemon must have fervor and fire."

"How kind of you to give me your endorsement," said Sokolov.

"Ah, but you misunderstand me, Minister. I am a businessman. The only endorsements I give are for my own products. And should we be fortunate enough to have you as Hegemon, I assure you, you would hear me endorse my products often. I'm quite the salesman."

Sokolov forced a polite laugh. "Indeed." He took a final sip of his champagne and said, "Well then, I seem to have drained my glass. If you'll excuse me." He bowed and walked off.

Lem and Benyawe watched him deposit his glass on the tray of a passing server and then join a cluster of dignitaries.

"You think he's lying?" said Benyawe.

"About my father resigning? I can't see why Sokolov would make that up."

"Why would your father forfeit the Hegemony in the middle of a war?"

"My father is a survivor. Perhaps he fears that his life is legitimately in jeopardy."

Benyawe regarded Lem with annoyance. "Have you ever known your father to be afraid of anything, especially of thugs threatening his life? If so, you don't know him half as well as I do."

"Then what's your theory?"

"Perhaps your father believes this is the only way to prevent Sokolov from taking the Hegemony, by having the Council vote now, before Sokolov can somehow manipulate each of the Consuls to vote in his favor."

"Maybe," said Lem. "But it still feels like defeat, and my father is not one to surrender."

"Your father is above politics," said Benyawe. "The human race is at stake here. I think he values that more than whatever place he may hold in the history books."

"But why would Sokolov be concerned about *me* being elected?" said Lem. "I'm not his political rival. There are a thousand reasons why the Council would never choose me to be Hegemon."

"I can think of a lot more than one thousand," said Benyawe.

"There we are," said Lem, smiling. "Different dress, but the same Benyawe I know and love. Always keeping me humble."

"No one can keep you humble. I've tried. But you ask a legitimate question. What game is Sokolov playing here?"

"Perhaps he's planting the thought in my mind in the hope that I'll pursue the idea, that I'll voice my desire to be Hegemon. Then Sokolov could attack my father with

accusations of nepotism and claim my father is acting
more like a king than a Hegemon."

"I've suddenly lost my appetite," said Benyawe.

"Well I hope you get it back because dinner, it appears,
is served."

Butlers had swung the dining-hall doors wide and were
now ushering people to their tables.

The dining hall was a massive space with an opaque
glass floor and glass ceiling, which meant everyone was
now moon-hopping to their tables as their magnetic
greaves no longer had purchase. The transition was a bit
alarming, but the citizens of Luna were accustomed to
reduced gravity, and they made their way to the tables
without incident.

The décor was bright and minimalist and elegant. Spot-
less white magnetic tablecloths with white china place
settings and white rose centerpieces. A string quartet on
the far end of the hall, also dressed in white, played a
soothing melody that kept the crowd quiet and whispering. Lem led Benyawe to their table near the platform at
the front and then waited until everyone had taken their
seats, the music had stopped, and the lights had dimmed.
Lem then bounded up onto the platform in a single leap,
a move that earned him a smattering of applause. Lem
smiled, then raised a hand for quiet. "Ladies and gentlemen," he said. "I want to thank each of you personally for
your attendance this evening and for your interest in this
cause."

An image appeared behind him on a large screen: a
refugee family deboarding a transport at the Luna shipyard, the eyes of the children wide and fearful, their faces
dirty, their little bodies thin and emaciated.

"Every day more than three hundred refugees fleeing
the horror of war arrive here on Luna," said Lem. "Many
with nothing but the clothes on their backs. They come

hungry, homeless, and in some cases helpless, unable to withstand a gravity environment. Their livelihoods have been taken from them. Many of these men and women enlist in the Fleet, leaving their children with spouses or other relatives so that some income can be earned. As a result, families in crisis are separated and strained. Wives without husbands, children without fathers. In other circumstances, one parent takes a position with a shipbuilding enterprise like my own because as free miners they possess unique skills that make them crucial to the war effort. In short, these refugees are crucial participants in the war effort, giving of themselves to preserve and protect us all. Tonight is our chance to return the favor."

Lem gestured to his right, where Wila was waiting beside the platform in the shadows, hands clasped demurely in front of her, head shaven, wearing her immaculate white mae-chee robe, the standard dress of priestly women in Theravada Buddhism. Lem couldn't help but smile at the sight of her, so free of adornments or jewelry or anything that might heighten her appearance, yet beautiful all the same. Pure and unrefined, with eyes full of empathy and understanding and calm.

She smiled at him, and Lem was certain that there was nothing in the expression other than sincere friendship, and yet the smile quickened Lem's heart all the same.

Lem said, "Ladies and gentlemen, I present to you one of our chemical engineers and a scholar of the Formic species, Wilasanee Saowaluk."

Polite applause echoed as Wila stepped onto the stage and Lem returned to the table with Benyawe.

Wila smiled at the applause, bowed slightly, and then began. "Here on Luna, far from the horrors of war, it can be difficult for us to fully comprehend the suffering of our brothers and sisters caught in the conflict. Go with me now as we board the Kotka, a transport vessel that has served as one of the many ships carrying refugees here to Luna."

The image on the screen winked out and the lights in the room extinguished. For a moment, there was only darkness. And then the holoprojectors hidden beneath the glass floor and above the glass ceiling turned on, creating a dim blue holofield that filled the dining hall. In a matter of seconds, the light seemed to organize into shapes as a room-sized holo materialized all around them. Walls formed, holos of people took shape, vague shapes increased in definition and become holographic objects. The dinner guests turned their heads to take in the scene that now surrounded them. They were no longer sitting in a white minimalist room; now they were in the cargo bay of the Kotka, surrounded by hundreds of people huddled together in the cramped space. Sleep sacks were attached to a series of ropes that crisscrossed the bay, floor to ceiling, like cluttered lines of hung laundry. The room was filled with families, crying children, mothers nursing infants. An elderly woman with her arm in a sling held a sleeping toddler wrapped in a ratty blanket. A group of teens maneuvered among the crowd passing out small pieces of flatbread, their expressions hopeless and empty.

"Over eight hundred refugees are crammed inside the Kotka," said Wila. "What you are seeing is actual footage from the cargo bay of that ship, now heading to Luna and scheduled to arrive in five months' time, if it survives the journey. Food and water are scarce. Meals are rationed. Families are frightened, not even certain if they will safely arrive at their destination." Wila paused and said nothing while the dinner guests took in the sight before them. Lem had told her before the event, "Let them soak it in. Give them a minute to process what they're seeing."

Wila waited, then glanced at Lem, who nodded for her to continue.

Wila broke the silence. "Formic warships have destroyed two transports just like this one in the last thirty days alone, killing over six hundred innocent civilians seeking safety here on Luna. The passengers aboard the Kotka are aware of these losses. They receive the reports just as we do. Can you imagine how they feel, knowing that their ship could be attacked at any moment? They live in constant fear. What will we as a people show them when they arrive at our port, desperate for relief? Kindness? Compassion? Understanding? Or will we shun them and push them into the streets, to fear once again for their lives and future?"

The holo of the cargo bay winked out, and the lights in the room returned.

"The Department of Rehousing and Refugee Assistance is doing great work," said Wila. "We applaud their efforts. However, the influx of refugees now exceeds the reach of DORRA, and the Hegemony is asking that corporate and private institutions assist in the rehousing effort. Generous tax incentives will be granted to those who help. It is on us, ladies and gentlemen, to welcome our brothers and sisters with open arms. The Juke Humanitarian Foundation, founded by Mr. Lem Jukes, is prepared to donate three billion credits along with the Formic scout ship currently in Earth's orbit. This structure, which has served as a research facility since the first war, will be converted into a vast housing facility for those refugees requiring low G or zero G housing."

The holofield projected schematics of the ship, a giant glowing teardrop-shaped monstrosity that split in half to reveal the proposed architecture inside.

"This is the Formic scout ship from the first war," said Wila. "Its exterior, as you know, is made of indestructible hullmat, an alien alloy of Formic design. The ship's interior architecture, however, is composed of more familiar alloys that Juke Limited has mostly removed to create space for refugee housing. Construction on that housing is already underway, with offices and workspaces to be built alongside the housing units, giving refugees work opportunities close to home and family. Areas for additional workspaces and housing, as you can see, are available to other entities and corporations who wish to build inside the ship and aid in the effort."

A voice from the back of the room interrupted her. "I thought this was a fundraiser. This sounds like a real-estate proposal."

Lem strained to see in the low light who had spoken and identified a junior minister from the Russian consulate, one of Sokolov's lackeys.

Wila maintained her poise and didn't miss a beat. "The issue at hand, sir, is one of housing for displaced free miners seeking refuge here on—"

"The issue at hand, madam, is one company's profiteering on the sympathies of these good people." The junior minister spread his arms, indicating the gathered crowd. "You're asking the distinguished members of this audience to invest in a real-estate scheme that will only benefit your corporation through massive tax write-offs, deplete our resources here on Luna, and in all likelihood end in financial disaster."

Lem was on his feet before he knew what was happening.

"Lem." A whispered voice to his right, Benyawe warning him, motioning him to sit down.

Lem ignored her, facing the junior minister. "You have every right to be skeptical," said Lem. "But I assure you this is completely legitimate and motivated by no other reason than to help those who need it. Each of you will receive a data cube of information showing this to be a humanitarian effort with only the interests of refugees in mind."

The junior minister scoffed. "Please, Mr. Jukes. You may be able to spread those untruths within your own company, but you'll find your audience here far less gullible. Juke Limited is preying upon the misfortune of displaced citizens who have no choice but to accept your housing, whereupon you use them for cheap labor because, again, what other choice do they have, while you profit off whatever they produce for you and sweep all of your expenses under the tax table. Did your father engineer this plan? It sounds like something the Hegemon would do."

"You are out of line, sir," said a second voice in the back.

Lem was shocked to see that it was Sokolov, standing at his table, actually coming to the Hegemon's defense.

"You will forgive my outburst," said the junior minister. "But I cannot sit here and listen to an obvious scheme to benefit one corporation at the expense of all the others. Especially not from a Formic sympathizer."

There were audible gasps from the crowd.

"How dare you, sir!" Again, it was Sokolov who spoke up, challenging his own subordinate.

The junior minister was on his feet now, unfazed, pointing a finger straight at Wila. "This woman prays to the Hive Queen!"

More gasps, and all eyes turned to Wila. She opened her mouth to speak, but the junior minister beat her to it.

"The Fleet has outlawed any discussion of the Hive Queen, and this woman not only mocks our commanders by ignoring their directive, but she also has the audacity to treat the enemy like it's our god!"

"Sir—" Wila began.

But the junior minister shouted over her. "She calls for

the preservation of the Formic species. She reveres the very creatures who slaughter our sons and daughters. She prays to the monsters who burned millions in China and who would have burned us all if we hadn't stopped them. There are no sides in this war, ladies and gentlemen. There is one side. And this woman before us, speaking on behalf of Juke Limited, is not on it."

"Now wait a minute—" Lem tried again, but the junior minister had pulled a piece of paper from his coat and was reading it aloud. "'Prayer for the Hive Queen,' by Wilasanee Saowaluk. It's on the nets. Do you deny it?"

"I have put nothing on the nets," said Wila, desperate.

"But you *did* write it," said the junior minister. "And you *still* practice it. While the world teeters on annihilation, you side with the enemy."

"It's true," said a new voice. Lem turned. The CEO of Minetek was holding up his wrist pad. "Someone sent it to me earlier. It's all about her."

"This can't be true," said Sokolov. "This is a mistake."

Lem held up his hands. "Everyone just calm down."

Sokolov continued as if Lem hadn't spoken, directing his words to the junior minister. "I would bet my reputation on the integrity of Lem Jukes. He would not fraternize with a Formic sympathizer."

Lem blinked. Suddenly this was about him?

He realized then what was happening. It was all theater. Sabotage. Sokolov and his minister had orchestrated the whole thing to discredit Lem, and they were using Wila and twisting her beliefs to do it.

"I regret to be the one to inform you otherwise," said the junior minister, handing the paper to Sokolov, who made a great show of pulling out his glasses to read it.

"This is a misunderstanding, Alexei," said Lem.

"And her submitted doctoral thesis," said the junior minister, shooting another pointed finger at Wila, "called for us to protect the Formics. To protect them! The very creatures who want to destroy us!"

Sokolov removed his glasses and regarded Wila with what looked like genuine heartbreak. "Tell me this isn't true."

"Sir, you must understand the doctrine of Theravada Buddhism—" said Wila.

"What I understand," said Sokolov, now with more volume, "is that we are at war, that our very species is at risk, and that I have neither the patience nor the stomach for what amounts to treason." He regarded Lem with a cold stare. "Shame on you, Lem. Shame."

Lem shook his head. "Everyone here sees what you're doing, Sokolov. Let's cut the charade."

"I'm leaving," said Sokolov. "And I will question the patriotism of anyone who remains." He grabbed his things and moved for the exit.

There was a momentary pause of confusion among the other guests as they looked at one another, surprised, unsure what to do.

"This is ridiculous," said Lem. "This is obviously sabotage. Everyone, please. He's trying to discredit me so that he can build alliances against my father."

But they weren't listening. The junior minister had grabbed his things. And the CEO of Minetek and his date were already halfway to the door.

"Treason!" the junior minister shouted as he moved for the exit. "A room of traitors!"

It was a calculated thing to say, because of course now everyone was getting to their feet, fearful of being labeled treasonous by association.

"This is political theater," said Lem. "Everyone, please. This was a setup. Surely you can see that."

But no one was stopping. The room filled with the commotion of a crowd hurrying for the exit.

Lem made a move to shout over them, but a gentle hand took his own. He turned to see that Benyawe had come up behind him.

"Let them go," she said.

Lem grimaced, his face a flurry of confusion and emotion. "That bastard."

"There's no good time to tell you this," said Benyawe, "but someone was filming the entire exchange on their wrist pad."

"Of course they were," said Lem.

"One of Sokolov's staff," said Benyawe. She pointed. "Seated at that table, to get the best angle on you and Wila. It's probably on the nets already and popping up in the press's inboxes."

"They'll no doubt edit out that part of me calling this whole display a carefully orchestrated work of political theater," said Lem.

"You should warn your father," said Benyawe. "He's going to be assaulted by the press, and he needs a heads up. Second, call legal and PR and prepare a statement. Get ahead of this. Silence the story before it becomes one."

"No statement from me is going to prevent this from becoming a story," said Lem. His head was swimming.

"Regarding Wila," said Benyawe. "You need a response to Wila."

"A response? You mean fire her? This was a sabotage, Benyawe. I'm not playing to their narrative."

"You may not have a choice, not unless you want to flush our stock down the toilet. I'm not speaking as an engineer, Lem. I'm speaking as a member of the board. I like Wila as much as you do, but I like the human race more."

He looked at her, not understanding.

She spoke calmly. "If the company falters, the war

falters. We are the largest defense contractor in the world. Weapons, ships, software, intelligence. We keep the Fleet operational. If we go south, people die. Maybe everyone dies."

Lem turned around to face Wila, to find meaning, to seek clarity, to say something.

But the platform was empty.

Wila was gone.

CHAPTER 10

Wila

To: littlesoldier13@freebeltmail.net
From: noloa.benyawe@juke.net
Subject: Re: Arming marines with NanoCloud

Dear Bingwen,

We did not know about the hullmat tunnel blocks in
the asteroids. The International Fleet is not always
forthcoming with this type of information. Or with any
information, to be honest. You would think that we
would be privy to intelligence regarding our tech's usefulness in the field and new applications of that tech
should it ever be needed. But no. Individual admirals
and commanders are needlessly protective of information. These people refuse to speak to each other.

But I digress. You need answers, not the rants of an angry old woman. I have assembled a team of engineers
to consider your problem. But you should know that
this is not the normal way of doing things. Normally,
the Fleet identifies a need. Like you have done. Hullmat blocks in the tunnels. Contractors like Juke Limited
learn of this need and then issue formal proposals to
the Fleet's acquisition department, which routes them

through a series of committees, which then authorize further development and the eventual construction of a prototype. That prototype is then tested repeatedly at WAMRED, the results of which are shown to a different series of committees, largely made up of people who shoot holes in such proposals simply to justify their jobs. Assuming the proposal has not yet been squashed, it is then greenlit for production and placed in a long line of other tech awaiting production. Once all the delays of production are weathered and manufacturing is finally completed, the tech is then distributed via zipship or other spacecraft to whatever far corner of the universe needs it. Meanwhile, the marines patiently awaiting these tools were killed eleven months ago because they didn't have the equipment when they needed it.

That's the normal course of action. But since I hate the normal course of action and despise the bureaucracy that I see obstructing common sense at every turn, we're going to do this your way and tradition be damned.

We will begin immediately on our end. Our challenge at the moment is this: We don't design the suits that tunnel marines wear. So we don't know if these suits contain any silicon. They may not, but if they do, putting NanoCloud in those marines' hands would obviously be disastrous. We are in contact with the German company who makes the suits and will hopefully get answers soon. Expect rough ideas in a few days.

Once we have a design, I will be relying on you to get it to the marines who need them. Lem has confidence that you can get it done, and thus so do I. More soon.

Regards,
Noloa Benyawe

Wila pushed her way through a series of curtains and exited the ballroom at the rear through the first door she found. To her surprise it led to the kitchen. The chefs and servers all paused in their work and looked up at her curiously. For a moment, Wila stood there frozen, staring back at them, uncertain, face flushed with shame. It horrified her to act so discourteously, to barge into a room so brusquely and uninvited, to invade these people's workspace so rudely. She opened her mouth to speak, to apologize, but just in that moment, a male server entered the kitchen briskly through another door, unaware of the awkward scene, and the loud bang of the swinging door striking the sink was like a gunshot at a race. Wila was off again, surging forward, weaving around the servers and stainless-steel countertops, apologizing as she went. Eventually she reached the opposite door and exit. She turned and gave a final bow of apology, but the servers and chefs were already back to work, no longer paying attention.

Wila exited and found herself in a dark corridor, obviously not being used for the evening's event. She paused and leaned against a wall, winded, catching her breath. She had ruined it. She had ruined everything. Lem had entrusted her with one simple task, and she had ruined it. And not just the evening, but Lem as well. She had embarrassed him. Embarrassed the company. They had twisted her prayer to the Hive Queen. They had made it something sinister, something evil, rather than what it was: a call for peace, a prayer for compassion, not toward the Hive Queen, not to make her an object of our compassion, but an appeal to the Hive Queen that she show compassion, that she end her assault, that she cease her fight. Isn't that what every human soul wanted? Peace? Wasn't that the prayer of every man, woman, and child alive?

But no, it didn't matter. Their objections were falsely

made. They cared nothing for Wila's prayer. Their true objective was clear: to humiliate Lem, to invalidate his efforts, to censure him before the world, to paint him as something the world should despise. Not because they saw him as a threat, or perhaps not entirely for that purpose, but because striking Lem was a strike against Lem's father, the Hegemon. That's what this was about: delegitimizing Ukko Jukes as Hegemon. It was a political attack. Wasn't that glaringly obvious to everyone?

Wila shook her head, ashamed at herself. She was throwing accusations and condemnations at Sokolov and his allies. That was not her way. That was not the path of enlightenment, to see corruption in others where corruption may not exist.

But Lem. She had humiliated Lem and Benyawe. She had ruined the evening, the fundraiser.

And then a new thought struck her, one that should have hit her first and shaken her the most. The fundraiser. In one stroke she had tainted the cause of the refugees. She had embraced a noble effort to relieve suffering among helpless people, including children, and spoiled the whole enterprise with her poisoned embrace. No one would donate now. Money would not come. Innocent people in desperate need would suffer without aid. The food they needed, the homes they needed, the jobs they needed now would not come. Because of her. Because of words on a page. Words that men had twisted and smeared and decried.

Wila closed her eyes, made fists with her hands. It was too much. Unthinkable. The faces of the refugees were suddenly before her. Pleading. Hungry. Abandoned. What a fool she had been. She had believed that she could make a difference here, that her skills and compassion, like stones and mortar, could help build a bridge for those looking to cross troubled waters. What arrogance. It was not a bridge that she had built, but a wall, so high and indestructible that no hungry child would ever climb over it.

She lifted the hem of her white mae-chee robe and bounded away, her eyes filling with tears. She should not have come, she realized. Not just tonight, but to Luna, to the company, to the job. She should not have left Thailand. That too had been arrogant. To presume that her knowledge, little though it was, would have some impact. Oh, what she would give to enter the teakwood temple now in Ubon Ratchathani and sit in prayer with Master Arjo, to meditate, to breathe in the incense, to bask in the silence, to escape, to forget.

She reached the building's exit and stopped, her hand on the bar to push it open. Her reflection in the glass of the door startled her. She looked a mess. Her face was streaked with tears, her robe bunched and wrinkled, her expression addled and desperate. She had lost herself, she realized. Everything she believed and embraced and stood for had been momentarily abandoned. Emotions were to be quelled and checked. They should not overtake her. How could she transform herself, liberate herself, and turn her attention outward toward others, if she allowed hysteria to consume her?

That was not the path to enlightenment.

She felt a new shame now. She had broken her control.

Her next thought struck her as odd: relief. Like a cool shower all over her. Relief that Lem had not seen her this way, that she had fled before she had lost control and experienced . . . what exactly? A panic attack? A burst of anxiety?

She focused on her face in the glass and took a few deep breaths until her visage began to soften and her posture began to change. She stood erect again and shook out an unwelcomed crease in her robe. She dried her cheeks, wiped at her eyes, and licked her lips. After two more calming breaths she was herself again. Not at peace, not settled. Sadness and shame still roiled inside her. But she could contain it now. It no longer controlled her.

She would find a place to pray and meditate. Peace would be her center. Calm would be her soul. Then she would apologize to Lem. And not with words alone. She would accompany them with actions that would attempt to restore what she had broken, if such a thing could be mended.

She left the building. The south side of the convention center was thankfully the least trafficked. People were all around her: couples moving arm and arm, men and women in suits, a mother pushing a stroller, all of them moving up or down the metal sidewalk with their magnetic greaves on their shins, like a scene from any bustling city on Earth. To Wila's relief none were formally dressed, as the guests at the fundraiser had been. No one here recognized her. If they looked in her direction, there was nothing more in their eyes than the mild curiosity most people showed when they saw a woman with a shaved head in a white mae-chee robe. Which meant they knew nothing of the firestorm she had just caused, the one that was likely already playing on the nets: the fall of Lem Jukes. The hypocrisy of Lem Jukes. The ignorance and arrogance and folly of Lem Jukes. Come, world, look and laugh and point and sneer at a man made to look like a clown.

Of course the truth of it would be printed as well, the harmless substance of the prayer, the true meaning. It was there and plain to see for anyone who cared to read it. Some people would come to Wila's defense. But not everyone would hear them, and more importantly, most people wouldn't care. News that embarrassed and shamed was the most quickly and delightfully consumed.

She tapped at her wrist pad and called for a car. She had no idea where she might go. She only knew she couldn't stay here. Her apartment was on the Rings, the manmade ringed structures that rotated around the Formic scout ship held in geosynchronous orbit above Earth, but the shuttle wasn't scheduled to return to the Rings until to-morrow. She had a hotel room that the company had pro-vided her here on Luna, but should she go there? What if there was press?

A man beside her was checking his wrist pad. He looked up at Wila with a curious expression, as if she were the final piece of an unsolved puzzle. He glanced at his wrist pad and then back up at Wila.

Was the news already covering the event? Wila won-dered. Had the press already pulled her photo and plas-tered it on the nets? Surely not. It had only just occurred.

Wila felt suddenly conspicuous. A female Buddhist on any street corner was an anomaly, even in a place as di-verse as Luna, but now Wila felt as if a spotlight from the city's domed ceiling high above was shining directly on her.

An autonomous taxi arrived, and Wila hurriedly climbed inside. The monitor before her asked for her des-tination, and Wila hesitated. Where should she go? She had no relatives on Luna. No friends outside of work. No acquaintances.

Out the window she saw the man with the puzzled ex-pression still watching her. Now he twisted his wrist pad in her direction as if preparing to take her photo.

"Docks," Wila said.

The taxi pulled into traffic, and Wila slumped down in her seat, grateful for the darkness of night. The dome lights of Imbrium were off now, projecting instead a beautiful swath of twinkling stars, which meant no one would likely see her inside the taxi or pay her any mind. Wila reached up and tapped at the glass to raise the tint to black and completely block out the world. Just in case.

The company shuttle that had brought her to Luna was still parked at the docks. Should she go to it? Or should she ride around the city until some course of action took shape in her mind?

Her wrist pad vibrated. Lem was trying to reach her. It was rude not to answer, discourteous to ignore.

Wila reached down to answer but hesitated. After several more vibrations, the call went to voicemail. A text message immediately followed: "Where are you? I'm worried."

At once she saw multiple meanings. Had her disappearance angered him? Was he asking in rage for her whereabouts? No, he had never lost his temper with her. Not once. Quite the contrary. His face and words and demeanor had always been kind, almost reverential, as if she were to be treated like some high priest, which was laughable, of course.

And what was he "worried" about? About her? About her feelings? About what the actions of the evening would do to the company? To him? To the plight of the refugees?

She tapped a quick response. Honest and brief. "I am horrified that I have caused you any embarrassment. Please accept my deepest and most sincere apology. I will of course—"

She paused. She will of course . . . do what? "Resign" was the word she was prepared to write, the word she *almost* wrote, the word she knew she *should* write. That was the only sensible course of action, was it not? To resign? To distance herself from the company as far as possible, to save Lem the further embarrassment of having to fire her. Wasn't that the kind thing? The right thing? And why was she even asking herself? She knew the answer. She had known it all along. Maybe it was the very thing she had run from, which made no sense to her and yet had the ring of rightness to it. But something else, some other emotion, had stopped her from entertaining the idea. Something else inside her had pushed the notion away and kept it hidden, even from herself. Until now.

She typed "resign" and pressed send. Watching the message disappear from her screen and move into the network, heading toward Lem's wrist pad and eyes, was like a blow to her stomach. Her life had found new meaning with her work. She had felt purpose, not just professionally, but spiritually as well. It was her path. Of that she had been certain. And now she was throwing it away. She knew it was right to resign, and yet it felt as if she were abandoning herself.

She couldn't stomach a response from him. She couldn't bear to think what he might write in return. She turned off her wrist pad. That too was discourteous, she knew. The kind thing to do was to wait and respond and do all in her power to alleviate any anxiety and suffering he might be enduring because of her. That was her duty now, not to wallow in self-pity, but to lighten his burden. That was the way of the path.

So why did it seem so impossible? Why couldn't she speak to him?

She rode in excruciating silence. She had promised to resign, and so it was done. That was her course now. She would write a formal letter once she could gather her thoughts and dictate the words. She would craft it as bluntly as possible to remove all blame from Lem and the company and the refugee program. She would place the blame entirely and squarely on her own shoulders. Then she would return to Thailand. How exactly, she didn't know. But Thailand was her path now.

She brought up her legs into the lotus position, which was awkward in the narrow seat of the taxi, and began to pray, not to any god, but as a statement of concern, as a demonstration of hope, as an act of faith, a plea to the universe, that the refugees wouldn't go hungry, that the children among them would be warm and loved and made to understand the value of their lives. She prayed for Benyawe. And for those on her team. She prayed for the people who had attended the fundraiser and whose hearts may have been pricked with compassion. She prayed for Lem, that his innocence would be evident to the world. She prayed for the men and women of the Fleet, that whatever damage the company would endure would not be so severe as to impair the work of the war. Wila was not one to pray for war, as conflict only compounded suffering. But she could pray that the hopes of those fighting it would not falter, for there was darkness and fear and discouragement down that path.

She prayed until the car stopped at the docks, and there were hundreds of prayers still inside her. But for the moment, the prayers had done their work and realigned her once again. She was centered now. She had uncharacteristically allowed her emotions to derail her from her path. But now she was back upon it.

Wila stepped out of the car and realized at once that there had been a mistake. She was not at the docks, or at least not at any part of the docks that she recognized. She was in a vacant parking garage, or what appeared to be a parking garage, except it was white and pristine and mostly tile. A thin, dark-skinned woman in a black suit was standing a short distance from the car, hands clasped behind her, facing Wila, almost as if waiting for her.

But no, that was silly. No one was expecting her. The car had misunderstood. It had misheard Wila's command. She had said docks, but it had processed something else entirely.

And yet something about the way the woman regarded Wila, her posture upright and stiff, her face free of any emotion, told Wila that this was no accident, that she was meant to come here. Someone had brought her here.

Wila moved to get back into the car, but the woman in the suit spoke and stopped her. "Ms. Saowaluk. If you will kindly accompany me, please." She gestured to her right, where an elevator waited a distance away.

Wila blinked. The woman knew her surname. And not just knew it, but knew how to pronounce it correctly, with all the accents in the right places, with every consonant struck and spoken as it should be, as if the name were as familiar to the woman as her own. Her accent was definitely east African, though where exactly Wila could only guess. The woman's skin was as dark as Wila had ever seen, as black as the fabric of her suit. The contrast between her and the bright white tile all around her was so distinct that the woman seemed to almost float in the air. She was perhaps the most beautiful woman Wila had ever seen. And yet there was an edge of danger about her. A gravity. A presence. Like a jaguar, lean and focused and lethal in an instant. Her head, like Wila's, was shaved to the scalp, and perhaps that was what relaxed Wila a bit. The sight of it created an instant kinship between them. A commonality. A connection. And yet this woman was clearly no Theravada Buddhist.

"Forgive me," said Wila. "You appear to know who I am, but I do not have the great pleasure of knowing you."

Wila did not feel fear. A jaguar should set off all kinds of alarms, but she felt nothing but calm. Was it the afterglow of her prayers, or something else? Because she should be afraid. Someone had brought her here, someone powerful enough to track her movements and then control the car that had carried her.

Lem, perhaps? He had said that he was worried. Had he taken matters into his own hands and returned her to company headquarters? Wila had visited headquarters before, but she had only seen a small portion of it. It was said that Juke Limited's facilities were larger than the city of Imbrium itself.

Was Lem that powerful? Could he control the cars of the city? Could he find her and bring her to him that easily? If so, perhaps Lem wouldn't be as adversely affected by Sokolov's attack as Wila had feared. Maybe the strength and size of the company would shield him.

And yet, if this woman worked for Lem—As what? Security detail?—then why had Wila never seen her before?

"My name is Nyalok," said the woman. She gestured again to the elevator. "If you would please accompany me."

Wila went with her, feeling completely at ease. As the elevator descended, Nyalok kept her eyes forward and remained as silent as stone.

"I am pleased to meet you, Nyalok," said Wila. "May I ask where you are taking me?"

"Everything will be explained," said Nyalok.

"But not by you," said Wila.

"No. Not by me." She faced Wila then. "You are not in danger, Wilasanee Saowaluk. You are safer here than you have ever been in your life."

There was no irony in the woman's voice, no hint of sarcasm, no veiled threat.

"I believe you," said Wila. "Thank you for the reassurance."

The elevator opened, and they stepped into a half-circle lobby with contemporary furniture and an unoccupied receptionist's desk, behind which there was no company logo. Instead, the walls displayed large gold-framed works of art. It was clearly a corporate environment, but it felt as welcoming as someone's home. Nyalok led Wila through a series of doors that unlocked and opened as they approached, triggered by something Nyalok had on her person, perhaps. The doors were thick and heavy and appeared indestructible. If this was a corporation, it was one that invested heavily in security.

They saw no one. The hallway was carpeted and quiet and empty. Nyalok, who was nearly a head taller than Wila, walked briskly and with purpose. Wila, falling behind, lifted the hem of her robe and quickened her pace to keep up. They passed doors to offices, but Wila heard nothing behind them. She glanced down side corridors, but those too were empty. Which was odd. The dome of Imbrium provided the appearance of day and night, but Imbrium was a city that did not sleep. Every place of business employed staff around the clock in one of several work shifts. The lights at Juke Limited were never off. The building never closed.

And yet this place appeared vacant.

Or, thought Wila, it was occupied by people who preferred not to be seen.

Wherever she was, it was not Juke Limited. The locks, the décor, the profound silence. At Juke, there were people everywhere, always, at every turn, hurrying somewhere, carrying something. There was a palpable energy to those halls. An urgency. To move down a corridor was to get swept into a current.

But this place was silent and empty. Immaculate, well lit, comfortable even. But completely devoid of people.

Nyalok reached a door and opened it, and the view before Wila nearly took her breath away. Before her stood Wat Thung Sri Muang, the ancient, tiny teakwood Buddhist temple in the park in Ubon Ratchathani. There it was, set atop stilts in the middle of a small pond. There were the lotus flowers, floating on the surface of the water, blooming, glistening in the sunlight, their pink and white petals reaching upward and out. There was the narrow bridge that Wila had crossed so many thousands of times in her youth, the bridge from the green grass of the park to the temple, the wood well worn and smooth from thousands of sandaled monks like herself. And there was the sky above the temple, blue and brilliant and clustered with clouds. And there were the high-rises beyond the park, reaching skyward.

All of it was there. An impossible reality.

Wila stepped through the door and onto the grass,

surprised to discover that the grass did not give beneath her feet. It was solid and flat, like glass or stone.

Because it *is* glass, she realized. Nothing before her was real. She was inside a holoroom, much like the one that Lem had adjacent to his office. But this was a holo unlike any she had ever seen. The level of detail, the dimension, the life of it, the realness of it, not like a trick of light, with obvious imperfections and translucence, not like something she could put her hand through, but something tangible, something of substance.

A man stepped out of the temple and crossed the bridge, coming toward her, his eyes fixed upon her, a light smile on his face. Wila did not recognize him. His black suit and shirt were like what Nyalok was wearing, not quite a uniform, but something that suggested order among them. Wila put the man in his mid-sixties, though there was nothing about his movements that suggested his age. Short white hair, parted to the side, not a strand out of place. He was trim, but with broad shoulders that gave him a commanding presence.

He stopped before her and his smile widened. "Hello, Wila. My name is Oliver Crowe." He spread his arms. "What do you think of our temple? None of it is real, of course, as you no doubt can see, but I thought you might appreciate it. A little taste of home. Call it our welcome gift to you. Shall we go inside?" He gestured back the way he had come.

He was English, his accent unmistakable. A gentleman, with a formal yet playful air about him.

"You will forgive me, Mr. Crowe," said Wila. "But where am I? Who are you exactly? And why did you bring me here?"

He smiled and cocked a finger at her. "That is why I like you, Wila. You demand answers. Come. I'll explain everything inside."

He turned on his heels and walked back toward the bridge, not waiting for her to approve. Wila followed. She glanced once behind her and saw Nyalock remain by the closed door, not coming with them.

The bridge, like the grass, did not give at all beneath Wila's feet as the bridge back in Thailand had. That bridge, the real bridge, constructed of teakwood centuries old, did not sway violently as if made of rope, but its planks had given slightly whenever Wila had hurried across them. The movement of the bridge had always been near imperceptible, a fraction of a micrometer, so slight that Wila had never noticed it. But she noticed it now. Because it was absent. Because this bridge, real though it appeared, moved not at all. This was not the temple, but a lie, a fabrication. Not because it wasn't real, but because it attempted to capture something so beautiful and holy and unique that no replica could ever do it justice. It suddenly felt profane.

"You don't like it," said Crowe.

Wila smiled at him. "I am enraptured by the realism of it," she said, which wasn't entirely a lie.

He grinned and motioned her to follow.

As she approached the walls of the temple, she saw how it was done. The walls had dimension and substance because they were actual walls. Wila reached out and touched one.

"Paneled monitors," said Crowe. "We can move them around however we want and create the appearance of a true wall. The monitor projects whatever we ask. Everything above the panel is projection. As is the floor, obviously."

"May I see the panels?" said Wila.

He looked somewhat disappointed to drop the charade. But he tapped at his wrist pad, and the world went gray. The temple was gone. The bridge was gone. The lotus flowers, the sky. They were in a gray room with gray paneled walls where the temple walls had been. The floor was opaque glass, as was the ceiling, which Wila was surprised to discover was closer to her than she had guessed. The sky, only a moment ago, had seemed a vast distance away.

"Impressive," said Wila. "I have never seen a holo so . . ."

"Realistic?" offered Crowe.

"Is this the work of your company?" Wila asked. "Holo creation? And why would you create one so intricate for me?"

"It's quite easy to assemble," said Crowe. "These panels took only a few moments to set up once we had the images from Thailand. And no, this is not the business we are in, Wila. I am in the same business you are. The business of understanding the Hive Queen."

He tapped at his wrist pad again, and the temple and flowers and sky reappeared. Crowe moved ahead, around one of the freestanding panels—now appearing as an exterior wall of the temple—and disappeared into the temple's interior. Wila followed, and like a page torn from her own memory, she stepped into the wihan, the great hall of the temple, where monks gathered to pray. In truth, there was nothing great about it, either in size or decoration. But perhaps that was its greatness: Like the pond and the bridge and the lotus flower, the wihan was beautiful in its simplicity, marvelous in its minimalism. Crowe had re-created it down to the grain of wood at her feet.

To Wila's surprise, Crowe sat down on the floor where so many monks had sat before him. The pillows on the floor that Wila had assumed were projections turned out to be real. Crowe set one down in front of him and motioned for Wila to sit. She found it offensive to do so, to plant herself so casually in a room dedicated to prayer. Again it felt like sacrilege. She didn't move.

Crowe stood. "I've made you uncomfortable. I've misjudged you. I thought you would enjoy a view of home, but I see now that I created something that perhaps I shouldn't have."

Wila bowed slightly. "Forgive me, Mr. Crowe. You have gone to a great effort to please me, and for that I am deeply grateful. You have shown me a tremendous kindness. This temple, this room, yes, are of great importance to me. Seeing them this way, it is an emotional experience that I did not anticipate this evening."

Crowe nodded. "You've had several emotional experiences you didn't anticipate this evening. You will forgive me if I added to your distress."

"Not at all," said Wila. "Forgive *me* if I gave any impression of ingratitude."

Crowe laughed. "Let's stop asking forgiveness of each other? I suspect you do that often, and only rarely is it warranted."

"I make mistakes, as all men and women do," said Wila. "Grave mistakes. Sometimes I hurt people deeply even when I do not intend to."

The words came out of Wila without her even giving them consideration. Her mind was on Lem, of course, and the refugees, and Benyawe, and everyone. And it appalled her that she would reveal her innermost feelings to a stranger. Was it the room, she wondered? She had come here countless times to speak to Master Arjo, to open up to him, to seek his counsel, to bare her soul to him in the hope of receiving comfort or wisdom.

"Mr. Crowe, would you be so kind to show me another of your holo creations?"

He seemed to sense her unease and tapped at his wrist pad.

The world became a field of yellow wildflowers. The sun, far behind Crowe, was half dipped below the horizon, blanketing the world in a warm amber glow. The freestanding panels that had served as the walls of the temple were now solid gray, like strange monoliths unexpectedly built in a field. Wila felt instantly more at ease, and sank down onto her pillow.

Crowe sat as well. "Better?" he asked.

"Beautiful. Thank you."

Crowe tapped at his wrist pad again, and a pair of men came in through a door that Wila hadn't seen and began removing the gray panels.

"It's cruel to keep you in the dark any longer, Wila. So let me explain. You're inside a facility owned and operated by a division of the Hegemony. I'm its director. My commission is to gather any and all intelligence that will aid the Hegemony and the Fleet in our fight against the Formics."

The two-man disassembly crew finished collecting the panels and carried them out the door as quickly as they had come, like the backstage hands of a well-rehearsed theatrical production. With the panels gone, the field of wildflowers stretched unobstructed in all directions. Wila now had a clear view of Nyalok as well, still holding her position near the door, lithe and poised and watchful.

"Nyalok helps with security," said Crowe, following Wila's gaze. "She's from South Sudan. Her father was a doctor in Pajok. Her mother a sanitation inspector. They shot her father in the street for having ideas and a degree. Her mother was raped and strangled for being the wife of such a man. Her brother was never heard of again. He was likely taken and given a rifle and made to shoot other doctors and mothers elsewhere. He was eleven. Nyalok was nine. She lived in the street for three years until a humanitarian organization found her."

Wila stared at him, suddenly feeling as if her heart had burned to ashes. Such horror. Such suffering. "Who would do such a thing to a family, to a child?"

"Much of the world is made of good people, Wila. But evil is thick as well. Nyalok reminds me of that. Not because you will find any evil in her—there is none. But because she stands to me as a testament of what humanity can overcome. Murderers will not stop us, massacres will not define us. We will be humans still, long after the Formics and their fire are gone."

"What is the name of your organization?" said Wila.

Crowe smiled. "There is no name. Because this organization does not exist."

"An agency that does not exist," said Wila. "So you are real but not real. Like the temple and this field of flowers."

Oliver Crowe smiled. "You understand perfectly."

"I understand not at all," said Wila. "While it is not surprising to discover an intelligence arm to the Hegemony, I still fail to see why the director of that nonexistent agency has any interest in speaking to me. Surely, with a war in progress that threatens the very survival of the human race, you have far more important matters that demand your attention than sitting in a field of fake flowers with a disgraced Theravada Buddhist."

"On the contrary," said Crowe. "This is an excellent use of my time. You're here, Wila, because you see what others can't. You unravel and reveal what remains hidden and inexplicable to the rest of the world. You discovered the secret to penetrating hullmat. You extrapolated the truth about the Formics mining and building with worms. You took a scant amount of intelligence that had left the world baffled, and you saw order and structure and meaning."

"You have misjudged me again," said Wila. "I am not as capable as you believe. There are many who can piece together the intricacies of Formic behavior. I have studied the writings of such men and women. I have analyzed and marveled at their conclusions and theories and considerations. If you seek to enlist the great minds on the subject, I can give you a lengthy list of names."

"Academics," said Crowe. "Theoreticians. Don't misunderstand me. I don't mean to minimize their contributions. But they are driven by their need to publish or to secure tenure. To them the Hive Queen is a theoretical construct. An anomaly to be examined and discussed at conferences in stagnant hotel ballrooms over stale refreshments. To them the Hive Queen is a puzzle, a challenge, an academic paper to be written. But to you, Wila, the Hive Queen is just that, a queen. A living thing of majesty and power and complexity. A biochemical wonder. A creature of vast intelligence. A being with a mind and a soul that we must try desperately to understand. To you, she is a creature of infinite depth and power, not only because of what she can do, but also because of what you believe she can become. The enlightened being."

"The theory of the Hive Queen has fallen out of favor," said Wila. "The Fleet now refuses to acknowledge her existence."

"I'm not prepared to allow the leadership at CentCom to determine what is and isn't true," said Crowe. "I don't think you are either."

Wila said nothing. She did not want to speak ill of anyone of CentCom.

"The Fleet pretends the Hive Queen doesn't exist because they fear what they don't understand," said Crowe. "Humans don't like fear. But sweeping it under the carpet doesn't make the thing we fear go away. I need people who will face what we fear, Wila. Who will seek to understand the Hive Queen. Or, if she doesn't exist, I need people who will seek to understand whatever it is that makes the Formics do what they do. You see things differently, Wila. The world judges the Hive Queen based on *our* moral compass, on human morality, what *we* perceive to be right and wrong. But you, you seek to understand the Hive Queen from her own alien perspective, from her own morality. Not because you fear her, but because you love her. Not in the sense that a mother loves a child, or a wife loves a husband, or a believer loves a god. But in the sense that a flower loves sunlight." He gestured to the flowers all around them. "That flower is drawn to a thing of power, whose reach and influence is so great that even from a distance it gives organisms life. I don't mean to suggest that the Hive Queen has influence or power over you. I merely mean that you see the Hive Queen as a creature with immense philotic power. I need someone who thinks that way. Who considers what others don't. The very future of the human race may depend on it."

Wila sat in stunned silence. He had read her dissertation, processed her beliefs, internalized her own careful considerations, and found—to her great astonishment—something to respect and admire.

But that of course was foolish. He did not know her. His was respect poorly placed. He knew only what the printed words and reports had told him. The elevated perception that people like Lem had for her.

"Mr. Crowe, I am deeply flattered by your kind words and consideration. But I fear that they are misplaced. I do not have the answers. I do not understand the Hive Queen. My fascination with her may be greater than that of most people, but it does not come by way of any confirmed comprehension. If you seek someone who can unfold the mind of the Hive Queen to you, someone who can provide some explanation for Formic behavior, or clarify and state unequivocally their motivations as a species, I am not that individual. I understand the Hive Queen as much as a dog understands calculus. I seek to understand her, yes, but desire is not knowledge. Curiosity is not mastery. I am not even certain that she exists. I hold to the belief more so than others, but that doesn't make me right. I can't help you."

"You helped Lem Jukes with the hullmat," said Crowe.

"I recognized a possibility," said Wila. "I imagined an explanation for how the hull had been created and what materials had been used."

"An explanation that proved accurate," said Crowe. "I'm not expecting you to have all the answers, Wila. I'm asking you to use your mind to help us see what no one else can. You're not an expert on the Hive Queen, no. But no one is. My job is to find the people whose best guesses are as close to the truth as anyone can get and then to pay them handsomely for their efforts."

"Money is of no concern to me," said Wila.

"Of course it isn't," said Crowe. "But your faith is. I need to find the Hive Queen, Wila. She's out there. Close. Probably in a hive somewhere. And I need you to find that hive for me. You want to stop human suffering? You want to follow your path? Then you'll help me stop the Hive Queen, the greatest source of human suffering the world has ever known."

It bothered Wila that he would use her own beliefs as a tool of manipulation. But had he said anything untrue? Perhaps he understood Theravada Buddhism better than she did.

Crowe said, "You can't possibly continue in Juke Limited's employ, Wila. Not after tonight. You know that as well as Lem does. I am offering all parties a solution. Lem can do PR cleanup, and you can do what you've wanted to do since you arrived on Luna: study Formic habitats. I wouldn't keep you at a desk. You're no good to us there. We have facilities in the Belt where you will find plenty to study and analyze, including mining worms and weaving worms."

A surge of excitement struck Wila. "Did you say *weaving* worms?"

"That's what we're calling them. Worms that consume

the mined pellets from the asteroids, and then weave alloys in their gut."

In an instant Wila's feelings flipped like a switch. She needed to see these worms, to handle them, examine them, understand them.

"There's more," said Crowe. "The Fleet has captured many Formics, but whenever a Formic realizes that escape is impossible, it dies. It's as if the Hive Queen is somehow discarding it, killing her own soldier so we don't extract information from it. However it's done, the fact is, we've never been able to study a live specimen. Until now."

Wila felt a second surge of excitement so sudden she nearly slipped off her pillow. "You have a live Formic?"

"It won't allow us to test it," said Crowe. "There were two of them at first. When we sedated one of them, it died. So we haven't sedated the other. We don't know how long it will live, but I need someone who can reach it, understand it, communicate with it, if such a thing is possible. I think that someone might be you."

For a moment Wila said nothing because no words would form. The idea of facing a Formic, of looking into its eyes, of being that close to the Hive Queen . . .

"Where is it?"

"In our facility in the Belt," said Crowe. "I have a shuttle standing by. It will take you to a transport outside Luna's gravity well, and you'll be on your way. Nyalok will accompany you. She'll assist you however she can and protect you. I assure you, she's very good at her job."

Wila glanced at Nyalok, who hadn't moved.

"I recognize that sending you to the Belt is extremely dangerous. But not enlisting you in this effort is the greater risk."

Wila lowered her gaze and stared at the false flowers around her. Only moments ago she had prayed for an escape. And now here it was. Coupled with an opportunity that she could not have dreamed of. A chance to find the Hive Queen.

But the shuttle was leaving now? How could she make a choice so quickly? What of Lem? What of the damage she had caused, the mess she had made? She could not simply walk away and leave it for others to resolve.

Crowe, sensing her hesitation, said, "Whatever you want to say to Lem Jukes you can say once you're on the transport. You'll have time to gather your thoughts and express yourself clearly. But know this: The greatest service you can do him right now is to disappear. That is what the company needs and what investors will insist upon. If you stay, Wila, you'll only do him greater harm."

She looked up at him, surprised.

He regarded her with a look of sympathy, almost pity, like an adult amused by the naiveté of a child. "Lem Jukes isn't kind to you because he's a good man, Wila. He's kind to you because he loves you. He wouldn't admit that if someone asked. I'm not even sure if he knows it himself. He may not be capable of knowing it, of allowing himself to be that vulnerable. But I do know that he will try to protect you if you stay. He will lash out at your critics. He will rise to your defense. Even if it hurts him and the company. That's what love does to a man. It blinds him to reason. You want to minimize the harm to Lem Jukes? Leave, Wila. And don't look back."

Wila stared at him. Love? How could he suggest such a thing? What did this man know of Lem Jukes? Or of her? Or of anything? She was a Buddhist. Lem was one of the most powerful and influential men alive. A man who could have his pick of women, should he seek them; a man who was smart enough to see that she had absolutely nothing to offer him. Not companionship, not beauty, not prestige, not power. She had nothing, was nothing.

And yet . . . there were moments when she had caught

Lem looking in her direction, moments when he seemed to give her more attention than others in the room, moments when his kindness to her exceeded the norm.

Was Crowe right? As backward as the idea seemed, as ridiculous as it was to consider, could such a thing be possible? Did Lem Jukes love her? As a husband loved his wife?

She almost laughed aloud at the notion.

Yet to Wila's surprise, she realized that a part of her wanted it to be true. A fact that suddenly alarmed her. Why should she long for such a thing? Why should she desire that his affection be directed toward her? Was she subconsciously trying to elevate herself? The companion of Lem Jukes would be a well-known woman. Did Wila subconsciously desire such attention? No. That meant nothing to her. Nor did his influence and wealth. Nor his standing, his ambition, his command over millions. All of that had no value to her. Then what exactly? Was she merely vain? Did she silently wish that a man would acknowledge her and find her beautiful? That idea disappointed her, because it had the ring of truth.

But what Wila wanted was irrelevant. Crowe had said Lem loved her only to strengthen his argument and give her another reason to go. He was tinkering with her emotions. It was a lie wrapped up and served to manipulate her and bend her to his will. Because it wasn't true. It couldn't be. Lem Jukes could not love her. Not in this world or in any other.

Wila stood.

Surprised, Crowe quickly got to his feet as well.

"You need not bring Mr. Jukes into this," Wila said simply. "I'll have that name now."

"Name?"

"Of the agency you direct, of which I am to become a member. The agency that does not exist."

"Agencia de la Seguridad de la Hegemonia."

"A Spanish name?"

"Our headquarters are in Argentina. We're known internally as ASH."

"ASH? Let us hope that ashes are not what we leave behind us through our service. Now, Mr. Crowe, if you would be so kind. Where might I find this shuttle?"

CHAPTER 11

Vandalorum

Ansible transmission from the Hegemon Ukko Jukes on Luna to the Polemarch Ishmerai Averbach aboard the Revenor, Operation Sky Siege. File #489950. Office of the Hegemony Sealed Archives, Imbrium, Luna, 2119

UKKO: Operation Deep Dive was a failure. I'll send you a full report momentarily. We believe the Formics built large camouflaged structures big enough to hide a fleet behind. They may be doing the same where you are. We're trying to identify a way for you to see these blinds before you reach them.

AVERBACH: Did F1 reach the motherships?

UKKO: Negative. Not even close. Ten of our ships were lost.

AVERBACH: And the remaining ships?

UKKO: We're bringing them home. They're needed in the ecliptic.

AVERBACH: You're abandoning the target?

UKKO: I'm salvaging a broken fleet before we lose the rest of it.

AVERBACH: And what of us?

UKKO: You are to press on. What you find at your

mothersships will help us determine if abandoning
the mothersships below the ecliptic was wise.

AVERBACH: So we're guinea pigs?

UKKO: You're marines. Charging into danger is what
you do. Just make sure you charge cautiously.
Expect an ambush not as a possibility but as a likelihood. Stand by for the report.

Victor woke to blurry vision and dim lights and a heavy
sluggish mind. He had hovered in a thick black fog of
sleep for so long that breaking free of it took some effort.
He tried opening his eyes, but the fog pulled back at him,
resisting, unwilling to release him. Yet he somehow knew
that his eyes needed to open, that he needed to wake, that
the drowsy blanket of sleep that enveloped him needed to
be tossed aside.

His eyes fluttered open, blinking, focusing. Sounds
reached his ears. The hum of equipment. The murmur of
voices. Soft, quiet, nearby. There were smells as well: an-
tiseptic, gauze, clean linen. His vision cleared, sharpened.

He was in a white, clinical room, devoid of any furniture, strapped to a padded floor and connected to various machines monitoring his vitals. His arms floated in
zero gravity in front of him, atrophied and thin, but they
moved when he sent them the mental impulse. He was
not dead. He was not in the zipship, either. Someone had
recovered him, grabbed the zipship, and pulled him in.
Saved him.

He looked down at himself. He wore blue cotton
scrubs. Plastic gray casts covered his legs and feet. Had
he broken his legs? He couldn't remember.

Victor pulled down the neck of his gown and found
sensors on his chest. He felt the side of his head and found
sensors at his temples as well. He ran a hand across the

top of his head and felt the soft fuzz of hair, buzzed to his scalp. One of the monitors to his right had a shiny aluminum surface. Victor looked at his reflection. He was thinner now. Gaunt. Sickly.

Beyond a large glass window to his right, nurses moved up and down a corridor, coming and going, all walking in the stiff, awkward gait that comes from wearing magnetic greaves. To Victor's surprise, the nurses' orientation matched his own. It was then that Victor realized that he was not lying down on the floor, but rather he was upright and against a padded wall.

One of the nurses noticed Victor and spoke into her wrist pad. Victor expected her to come in and tend to him, but she turned and disappeared down a side corridor.

Was he on the Vandalorum? Or another ship? How long had he been out?

"Hello?"

His voice was weak and hoarse.

He searched for a nurse call button but didn't find one. The straps across his chest, waist, and legs that kept him against the padded wall were not uncomfortably tight, but he couldn't easily wiggle out of them, either. He started pulling at the top strap to free himself.

"Don't you dare," said a woman's voice.

A young Hispanic marine wearing a blue jumpsuit and a disapproving expression hovered at the doorway. "Those straps are there to keep you still. If you remove them, you'll only detach your sensors, and then all these machines will start wailing and I'll have paperwork I didn't ask for. If the straps are too tight, we'll loosen them. Otherwise, hands off." The marine pushed off the doorway and floated into the room, a tablet in her hand.

"I'm Lieutenant Rivera. Your nurse. Major Tokonata is your physician. She'll probably come around tomorrow to check in on you now that you're awake. My orders are to keep you eating and downing your meds. Do you have any pain?"

"What happened to me?" Victor asked.

"Some idiots in the IF launched you in a coffin rocket. That's what happened to you. You're lucky to be alive, considering how long you were bottled up in that thing. I heard about a comms officer shot from Luna once who went six months in a zipship. When they opened the thing out near Saturn, they found him dead inside. Turns out, he'd been dead for months. The wound around his feeding tube had become infected, and his organs had all failed. I'm not sure you fared much better. Deep breath."

She had a device pressed against his chest. Victor breathed in multiple times while she listened.

She put the device back in her pocket. "Any pain?"

"Where am I?"

"The Vandalorum. The five-star luxury cruiser of the Fleet, with first-class accommodations for all passengers of any rank. What's your poison? Caviar and crackers, or the seared halibut? Just kidding, this ship's a rust bucket. The barracks *smell* like halibut, truth be told. Halibut or something else funky. Heaven knows why. Or what. But, hey, we're alive still, so I'm not complaining. Of course, that may not last."

"Why are there casts on my legs?"

"Those aren't casts. They emit high-energy electromagnetic waves and frequencies to help guide the bone-building medicines we've given you. The meds are delivered in nanostructures, and the waves somehow point the meds to areas of osteoporosis. Don't ask for a better explanation than that. I didn't build the things. I just put them on. You've lost a lot of bone density. Maybe fifteen, twenty percent. Months in a zipship will do that to you. Serious muscle atrophy, too. But you hardly need me to tell you that. But don't worry. You'll come around. Right now you look like kuso, but I've seen worse."

"You have?"

"Not really. I'm just trying to lift your spirits. You're by far the worst I've ever seen. But Tokonata is the best field doctor in the Fleet. We'll get you well again. It's going to take time, but we'll get there."

"How much time do we have?" asked Victor. "How close are we to the motherships?"

Lieutenant Rivera frowned. "Closer than I'd care to be, between you and me. Less than two months out."

"Is that enough time to get me well?"

"You won't be back to one hundred percent. Not even close. But you'll be a hell of a lot better than you are now. You can expect a bumpy road along the way, though. You've got kidney stones. Lots of them. From the calcium buildup brought on by the loss of bone density. We've blasted the stones, but to pass them they first have to move from your kidneys to your bladder. For that you need gravity. All of our exercise equipment is down in the ship's fuge. We'll move down there so you can start building back your muscle mass. The gravity will move those kidney stones but it's going to feel like a bear trap in your gut."

"I've had them before," said Victor.

"Then you know what a joy that experience will be."

"I need to speak to the Polemarch," said Victor. His head was clearing now. He was getting his bearings.

Lieutenant Rivera stared. "The Polemarch? Not a chance of that happening."

"This is his ship, isn't it?"

"No, the Polemarch is on the Revenor, another ship in our fleet, several hundred thousand klicks from us."

"I was told the Polemarch requested me for his ship, the Vandalorum," said Victor.

"Then you were misinformed," said Rivera. "The Polemarch has never touched this ship. And wouldn't. It's too old and small for his tastes. Nor has he made any request to transfer you to the Revenor that I'm aware of. Sounds to me like someone in the Fleet may have gotten their wires crossed on your orders."

"Wires crossed?" said Victor. "I've been flying for over seven months. Are you telling me I'm not even supposed to be here?"

"Relax," said Rivera. "You're supposed to be here. The Fleet wouldn't have put you on a zipship for that long unless they had a reason."

"I need to see the captain then," said Victor.

"I'd avoid Captain Hoebeck, if I were you," said Rivera. "He's not exactly thrilled to have you on board. We used a lot of fuel to pick you up, fuel that the captain didn't want to lose. Plus he wanted to be in the vanguard that attacks the motherships, but altering our speed and trajectory to pick you up took us out of that position. You basically wrecked the captain's plans."

"If he knew I would wreck his plans, why did he bother to pick me up?"

"He had to. The order came from the Polemarch."

"So the Polemarch does know I'm here," said Victor.

"Like I said," said Rivera. "You're precisely where you're supposed to be. Just relax and be grateful you're alive."

"Where's the zipship?"

"Your coffin rocket? In the cargo bay, I'm guessing. Why?"

"Can you tell me how to get there?"

Rivera laughed. "Your sleep drugs are still making you loopy, Ensign Delgado. You're not going anywhere. You're in recovery."

"I saw something when I was in the zipship," said Victor. "Something the Fleet needs to know about immediately. I couldn't broadcast it during the flight. I didn't have the capabilities. Now I do."

Rivera's smile faded. "What did you see?"

"As much as we can," said Rivera. "Little to no radio. Plus all the ships are spread out. We're not bunched up together. That would make us easier to detect. That was the Polemarch's orders: cover a wide swath of space, stay thousands of klicks apart. I suspect we'll close in before the attack."

"I need to get my intelligence to CentCom," said Victor.

"Why? What did you see out there?"

"A Formic superstructure," said Victor. "Or what I think is a superstructure."

"That isn't news," said Rivera. "The Formics have been building big structures all over the system. The Fleet has destroyed quite a few of them already. Most of them are Potemkin structures, though. Our ships reach them and discover that the structures are hollow inside. It's just deception. To waste our fuel, time, and resources."

"This isn't *a* superstructure," said Victor. "This is *the* superstructure. There's nothing else like it in the system."

"What do you think it is? A base?"

"I don't know," said Victor. "But whatever it is, it's of enormous value to the Hive Queen. She doesn't want us to find it. That's obvious. She's trying very hard to keep it a secret. That's why I'm certain it's a high-priority target."

"If you don't know what it is exactly, how do you know she's trying to keep it a secret?"

"Because she's making it invisible," said Victor.

Rivera stared back at him a moment. "Where are these data cubes?" she said. "I'll go get them for you myself."

CHAPTER 12

Analysis

To: littlesoldier13@freebeltmail.net
From: noloa.benyawe@juke.net
Subject: NanoCloud Paint

Dear Bingwen,

This will seem like an overly simplistic solution, but that's what we want: a solution that any marine can easily replicate. For a marine to apply NanoGoo onto the hullmat in the tunnels, he needs a small two-inch paintbrush, a metal bucket with a brush-holster lid, and a silicone paint of any color. All of these materials should be found on any IF warship in a maintenance closet. We checked with standard inventory files and confirmed this.

The marine pours one-fifth of a liter of NanoCloud dust per liter of paint and stirs. He then applies the NanoCloud paint to the hullmat impediment, seals the brush back in the bucket, steps back, and activates the NanoCloud.

Now, this is the part where we come in because activating the NanoCloud is the technical step that only

we can provide. My engineering team has created an app (attached below) that marines can download onto their wrist pads. The app turns the NanoCloud bots on and off. Once the NanoCloud has eaten through the hullmat, marines MUST TURN OFF THE BOTS BEFORE PASSING THROUGH THE HOLE to ensure that no NanoCloud bots get on other marine equipment and damage it.

This works. We tried it. Please forward this app to every marine who needs it.

Happy painting,
Noloa Benyawe

After twenty straight hours of staring at a screen and studying the battles that had ended Operation Deep Dive, Mazer was having a hard time staying awake. His eyes were bloodshot. His neck and back ached from hunching forward and crowding the screen. The words and images on the tablet kept going out of focus as sleep kept trying to take him. He had already dozed off twice. Not into a deep sleep, but into the ice-thin sleep that causes you to jerk violently awake when your head drifts too much to one side.

Common sense told him to go to bed. And yet just as he was ready to, he would discover something he hadn't seen or noticed before, some new thread of possibility that had to be explored. Those threads often went nowhere, but they had also led to what he believed were his most crucial observations.

Operation Deep Dive was a disaster. Mazer had reached that conclusion in moments. The individual battles that ended the operation were not all defeats; the IF destroyed more Formic ships than it lost. But since the Fleet's

casualties and losses were ones it could not afford, and since the operation was abandoned before the Fleet even reached the military target, to call it anything other than a total defeat would be inaccurate.

The Formic ambush was arguably the enemy's best executed stroke of the war. The blinds that the Formics built and hid behind defied reason in their size, stretching kilometers across in some instances. Even more impressive was the discovery that the blinds could move and position themselves closer to the approaching IF ships without the IF ships detecting their movement.

The animation of the battles showed the ships' movements prior to, during, and immediately after the battles. But since the battles all happened simultaneously across a vast stretch of space, moving through the model to analyze all the data points was painstaking and tedious. The ships of the IF had not traveled together, bunched up in a group, but rather spread out to minimize the risk of detection. The battles, therefore, were not a single ambush as Mazer had expected, but rather seven simultaneous ambushes from behind seven enormous domed blinds, each a great distance apart.

To Mazer's surprise, however, the data cube offered up no analysis. There were only facts, not what they meant. Most of the documents included on the cube were unhelpful—crew manifests, cargo manifests. But Mazer did unearth one collection of data that proved crucial: ship movements according to one lone observational satellite tens of millions of klicks away.

A knock at his door startled him.

Mazer opened it. Bingwen stood holding a paintbrush and sealed bucket of paint.

"You're either redecorating your barracks or vandalizing," said Mazer. "I'm afraid to ask which one."

Bingwen came in and explained how the engineers at

Juke Limited had found a solution to the hullmat obstacles in the tunnels.

"Have you forwarded the app?"

"It's on your forum and currently trending," said Bingwen. "There are already over two hundred downloads."

"That was fast. And Juke Limited just gave this away free of charge?"

"A win for humanity. A loss for capitalism."

"Well done. And the other countermeasures?"

"We're in communication with several other contractors. It's taking a little work because people are skeptical and not everyone wants to work for free, even if they're saving marines."

"So much for humanity. Who in Rat is working on this?"

"All of us."

"Welcome to modern warfare," said Mazer, "marines sitting at a computer terminal."

Bingwen glanced at the tablet in Mazer's hand. "Is that what you're doing? Fighting a war?"

"More like figuring out how not to lose one." Mazer pushed the tablet through the air to Bingwen, who caught it easily. "Colonel Li has given you clearance for this as well. I'm going to close my eyes. When I wake up, I expect you to have all the answers."

In his mind Mazer knew it was a dream. A dream and yet not a dream. He lay on his bed, staring up at the Hive Queen hovering above him, her face inches from his own. And yet despite her proximity, Mazer couldn't make out her features. Where her face should be was only darkness.

But he could feel her. She was a force, a presence, a weight pressing down. She was there and yet not there.

The ceiling behind her was the infinite canvas of space, dark and cold and dotted with stars. A black place, unforgiving and empty, and the Hive Queen, now a swirling black mass of smoke and tattered cloth, was almost invisible against the backdrop. Black on black forever.

Kim lay beside him, snuggled up tight, her chin near his shoulder, sleeping, oblivious to the thing floating above them. Mazer wanted to call to her, warn her, shield her, but the Hive Queen was a throbbing pressure in Mazer's mind, a constant thumping of mental power pushing through his brain, pressing him further into the mattress, smothering him, choking him, squeezing out what little life remained.

The Hive Queen called Mazer's name, but it was not his name. It was another word. A word unspoken. A word that could not be heard but felt. It was the name that she had given him. A small name. A name for something that had no worth. A name that demanded obedience.

She grabbed his arm, and Mazer jerked awake to find Bingwen recoiling from him.

"Hey, whoa, sorry," said Bingwen. "I just figured you'd want to be up by now. You've been out for eight hours."

Eight hours? Mazer hadn't slept that long since Luna.

"I've studied the battle," said Bingwen. "Not as extensively as you have. But I think I've reached the end of my mental patience on this. I don't understand fleet warfare."

"You do," said Mazer. "I was with you when you learned it."

Bingwen raised an eyebrow. "I think I would remember that."

Mazer anchored the tablet to the wall in front of them. "What ships do in zero G is not unlike what marines do in the Battle Room. In fact, learning maneuvers as a platoon in the Battle Room is akin to moving as a squadron of ships through space. Same principles. I'd go so far as

to say that mastering combat in the Battle Room is a good education in Fleet warfare."

"Good thing Rat Army is getting plenty of Battle Room practice," said Bingwen. "Oh wait, we're not."

"Are you going to be petulant, or are you going to listen?"

"I can't be both? You're right. Sorry. Go on."

"You're not getting Battle Room practice time now, but we practiced for months on our first transport out of Luna. The skills and lessons we learned then are the tools of analysis I'm using here. I think of each individual ship in a squadron as an individual marine in a Battle Room platoon. Master the Battle Room, and you understand Fleet dynamics."

"And what do you see?" said Bingwen.

"For starters, the Formics are relentless. They never stop. When the battle became fiercest, they didn't retreat. It's a standard military maxim to retreat so you can preserve your forces when the enemy demonstrates the advantage. Yet the Formics didn't, even when it made complete strategic sense to do so."

"I thought they ambushed us," said Bingwen.

"They did. We suffered instant heavy losses, and most of our fleet scattered. But a few of our ships made a counterstrike. The damage they inflicted was catastrophic. Look at this part of the animation." Mazer moved the model on screen until he reached a cluster of colored dots. "Here you have a large grouping of Formic ships that have emerged from behind this blind. This small group of our ships scrambled to counterstrike and pounded the Formics. I've got to give credit to some of our captains because their response was swift and lethal. It caught the Formics off guard."

Mazer fast-forwarded the animation and then paused it again. "Now, this is the moment of decision for the

remaining Formic forces. This is when any commander with half a mind would retreat. No, correction. This is the *last* possible moment. Anyone else would have retreated long ago. To stay is to die. Yet the Formics stayed. They continued to inflict some damage, but it was nothing compared to what we did to them. We annihilated this cluster."

"So they fought to the last man," said Bingwen. "Dumb, maybe, but they wouldn't be the first army to do so."

"But it's *all* they do, is my point," said Mazer. "They don't retreat. I experienced this inside the Formic scout ship at the end of the first war with individual Formics. Relentlessness. You experienced the same inside the hive in the asteroid. Even when it was obvious the Formics would die in their attack, they surged forward. Why?"

"Because they're under the Hive Queen's control," said Bingwen. "She tells them to fight, so they fight."

"So she doesn't care about her soldiers?"

"Apparently not," said Bingwen. "Or she believed that they would eventually win, despite all the evidence to the contrary."

"The Hive Queen is smart," said Mazer. "I think it's safe to assume she knew her soldiers would die and yet she made them stay and fight it out anyway."

Bingwen shrugged. "Maybe this isn't a big loss for her. She knows she can replenish her troops and ships easily. Maybe she sees these ships and crew as expendable."

"Maybe," said Mazer. "It still strikes me as wasteful. Now you tell me something *you* saw."

"Her ships were easily destroyed," said Bingwen. "Meaning they weren't covered in hullmat. They weren't shielded. We vaporized them without much effort. That surprised me because we also have evidence that the Formics moved asteroids down there long before we arrived. So they harvested asteroids and yet they didn't use those asteroids to make hullmat. Then I thought, they obviously

needed the asteroids for the raw materials required to build the blinds. These giant blinds would require more raw materials than the ships themselves."

"Then how did they build their ships?" asked Mazer.

Bingwen shrugged. "If I had to guess, I'd say the Formics cannibalized their motherships and built these smaller warships with scrap metal."

"That was my conclusion as well," said Mazer. "But why weren't these ships at least shielded? The Formics came here on a massive starship moving at a fraction of the speed of light. Without shielding, that ship would have instantly disintegrated as it came in contact with micrometeorites and particles in space. So we know they have shielding tech. Why not use it on these ships?"

Bingwen considered for a moment. "Okay, this is all speculation, but maybe they didn't shield their ships because they had to cannibalize their shielding tech for some other purpose. Or maybe they only know how to shield large vessels and not tiny ones. Or maybe small shields for small ships require far more energy than what they can produce on a small spacecraft. Or maybe they needed certain metals not found in our asteroids. Or maybe it was taco night, and they were too busy to bother."

"All good answers," said Mazer. "Except for taco night. It's a question that's been bothering me, and maybe we'll never know the answer. It just struck me as odd that for some reason the Hive Queen isn't using shielding tech when we know she's invented it. Which tells us what?"

"That she does have weaknesses," said Bingwen. "That she has some limitations here. That she isn't indestructible, that there are chinks in her armor."

"Maybe more than chinks," said Mazer. "Maybe gaping holes so big we can shove a lance inside. But before we get overconfident, we need to keep in mind that the Hive Queen learns and changes. She evolves her strategy. If she made a mistake here, she won't make it again."

"Her only mistake that I can see is that she kept her ships fighting when they should have retreated."

Mazer smiled. "Yes, but that, I believe, is the biggest surprise of all. It's not in the animation. I only discovered it by accident as I combed through satellite data. Here." He pointed to the animation. "The IF passes by the blinds. The Formic fleet leaps out from their hiding place and attacks us from the rear. Pandemonium follows. Most of our fleet scatters. But the blind rotates."

"How do you know it rotated? I thought the thing was invisible."

"Not invisible. Camouflaged. With stars on its surface. Which is what gave it away, because in the satellite scans, the stars all shifted to the right and got closer together. Meaning this domed surface, this camouflage, was turning."

"Why?"

"Because there was one ship hiding behind the blind that didn't leap out and attack like the others," said Mazer. "The biggest ship of all. So the blind rotated as the IF ships passed to keep the camouflage pointed at the IF so that the hidden ship remained hidden."

"Except by rotating the blind," Bingwen said, "the hiding ship exposed itself to this observational satellite it didn't know was watching."

"Not only that," said Mazer, "but when some of the IF ships fled, this hiding ship did as well. He moved back toward the ecliptic along with the fleeing IF ships. It did what Formics never do. It retreated from a fight. It ran for the hills. The biggest ship of all, the one that might prove most lethal in an ambush, bolted."

"Why didn't we go after it?" Bingwen said. "It would have left a heat signature."

"We didn't go after it," said Mazer, "because we didn't know it was one of theirs. It was chaos. It was every ship for itself. No one was scanning. Everyone was running.

None of our ships could really talk to each other, at least not in any cohesive manner, because of the time delay. None of the surviving ships had ansibles. And amidst all that chaos, the Formic ship slipped on by completely unnoticed."

"The Hive Queen," said Bingwen. "Has to be."

"I think that's a strong possibility," said Mazer. "Because it explains why these weak Formic fighters didn't retreat. Their objective wasn't to destroy us. Their objective was to engage our ships and hold them at the battlefield so that this one ship of theirs could slip away. A deception. If they had followed her to protect her, they would have drawn attention to her. So they kept the attention on themselves to allow her to escape unnoticed. A sacrifice with a strategic purpose."

"Has to be the Hive Queen," Bingwen repeated.

"Maybe," said Mazer. "Whatever it was, it was clearly of great importance to the Formics and we missed an opportunity. At the very least we know that there is a high-priority target somewhere in the plane of the ecliptic."

"Do you know the ship's trajectory?" said Bingwen. "Can we determine where it was headed?"

"Roughly," Mazer said, tapping at the tablet and bringing up a model of the solar system. "If her course was true, she was heading here, just beyond the outer rim of the Belt."

"That's near us," said Bingwen.

"Near in the relative sense," said Mazer. "But yes. Near us. Problem is, according to our scopes there isn't anything out there. There's no visible reason for the Hive Queen to go there."

"No *visible* reason?" said Bingwen. "You think there is something there, but we just can't see it."

"She made an asteroid disappear," said Mazer. "That was obviously the result of camouflage, the same tech she used to create these massive blinds. I think there's a

strong possibility that there's something out there hidden from our view, something she doesn't want us to see."

"Her hive," said Bingwen. "Her base, her headquarters, whatever you want to call it. It makes total sense, Mazer. She creates superstructures all over the system. She's done it many times. She makes a great show of bringing asteroids together. They're all very conspicuous, very visible. So we go there and check them out, and guess what, they're all hollow. They're Potemkin structures. She sends us on all these wild goose chases because she doesn't want us looking where she really is. Even the motherships. Those might be Potemkin ships too, for all we know. And all the while, her real hive is hidden out beyond the outer rim."

"There's one problem with this theory," said Mazer. "Her hive would have to be built. But we haven't seen asteroids move to that sector, and that's where she would get the raw materials to build any structure."

"The fact that we haven't seen asteroids move to that place should make us suspicious," said Bingwen. "She's moving asteroids all over the place. Except to there. Why? Because she doesn't want us going there to investigate an asteroid. She doesn't want to draw us toward her hive. She wants us looking everywhere *but* there."

"Possibly," said Mazer. "But it's speculation and not proof. And CentCom has already shown their aversion to theories and speculation. I doubt they'll investigate a hunch."

"Then remove CentCom from the conversation," said Bingwen. "Post your conclusions and all the data on the forum. Now. Today."

"Can't," said Mazer. "This is classified intel."

"So?" said Bingwen. "Who cares? We don't have to play by their rules. This is the Hive Queen, Mazer."

"This is *maybe* the Hive Queen. And if I post it, Intelligence will take it down immediately and shut me out of

any future intelligence findings. I think we should at least try traditional channels first. This intel didn't come from CentCom. It came from whatever intelligence organization Li belongs to. We should give our analysis to them."

"Through Li?" said Bingwen. "We can't trust Li with this."

"Why shouldn't we?" said Mazer. "Li has no reason to sit on the information. His people gave us authorization to review it. They're expecting a response."

"They're total unknowns to us," said Bingwen.

"This is the same organization that sent the Kandahar to investigate a disappearing asteroid. The same organization that has the data from the recon drone. The same organization that asked you and me to look at this highly classified battle. If anyone is going to believe us, it's them."

Bingwen frowned. "I know you're right, but I hate that you're right."

"I'll give my report to Li. We'll see what happens."

After Bingwen left, Mazer typed up his report and saved it to the cube. The question now was how to deliver it. Confinement to quarters meant he could visit the cafeteria and the restrooms. Otherwise, he was in his room. Li's office was on the other side of GravCamp, nowhere near any of those locations.

He considered ignoring his confinement and going directly to Li's office. Since the start of his confinement, Mazer had not once heard from or seen Colonel Dietrich. The suggestion from Dietrich that he "would figure out what to do with" Mazer had obviously been a lie. Dietrich was perfectly content to keep Mazer locked up indefinitely as a slight to Colonel Li.

At first, Mazer had found confinement agonizing. But then the forum had given him purpose. He wrote multiple posts condemning the decision to abolish the theory of the Hive Queen. He gave critical analyses of military

actions and commanders' decisions, praising what was done right and faulting what wasn't. He responded to requests from fellow junior officers on how to handle difficult problems with staff or command. He monitored closely the discussions on countermeasures the Hive Queen introduced and directed people to the conversation, namely engineers and anyone on the forum who might offer technical expertise. And now this: Li giving him classified intelligence that could potentially lead to military action in the outer rim. It was the most engaged he had felt in well over a year. And all within the tiny cramped confines of his quarters on GravCamp.

He could send Li a message telling him the report was ready, but if Dietrich was monitoring such communication, that would cause more problems than it solved.

In the end he decided to wait for Bingwen, who came around constantly, and who could easily courier it over to Li.

But Mazer never got that chance because MPs came to his room, asked him to step out into the corridor, and then did a thorough search of his quarters while he stood there watching. They found the tablet and the data cube, confiscated them, and then took Mazer into custody.

The MPs made Mazer wait for three hours in an anteroom outside Colonel Dietrich's office. One MP stood guard in the corridor, as if to ensure that Mazer didn't run for it, which Mazer found amusing. Where was he going to go? To one of the service shuttles? Top speed, five kilometers an hour? There was a brilliant plan. He'd reach Earth in about ten million years, give or take. Quite the getaway.

He suspected that Dietrich had employed one of his technicians to open the tablet and data cube, a suspicion that was confirmed when Mazer heard muffled shouting

from inside Dietrich's office, and then two young techs left in a hurry, looking defeated. They both glanced at Mazer as they left. One looked resentful, as if he blamed Mazer for his situation. The other one looked apologetic.

A lieutenant who looked far too young for his rank came out of the office and bid Mazer to follow him inside.

Mazer was not surprised to discover that Colonel Dietrich's office was a spacious shrine to himself. Framed commendations adorned the walls, along with photos of Dietrich throughout his naval career, posing with various German commanders, dignitaries, and politicians. Clearly a man who liked being seen with VIPs.

The young lieutenant maintained a flat expression and anchored himself to the left of Dietrich's desk at parade rest, like a statue that had enjoyed a brief moment of movement and was now settling back into its stone position.

Colonel Dietrich was anchored behind his holodesk with a fan of documents opened up in front of him, which he was pretending to read. He gave Mazer a quick once-over as if inspecting the state of Mazer's uniform and frowned disapprovingly, as if Mazer had just tracked mud into his office. Mazer kind of wished he had.

"Captain Rackham. I'm going to be perfectly honest with you. Your appointment to this space station is not one I would have approved. Instructor positions are filled by CentCom. I have no say in the matter. I had assumed that the Fleet vigorously vetted any marine being considered for a teaching position, as I would have, but I see from your records that I was mistaken."

Colonel Dietrich gestured to the documents in front of him. "I didn't have to look hard to find reports of insubordination and recklessness. Rear Admiral Zembassi gives you a strong recommendation, but Rear Admiral Vaganov gives you one of the most scathing evaluations I've ever read. Vaganov says you're a liar and a scoundrel and the

worst the Fleet has to offer. He calls you conniving and dangerous. He says it broke his heart to do so, but he had you court-martialed because he, quote, 'considered it my duty to remove Captain Rackham from the International Fleet to ensure that he didn't further tarnish the reputation of the military and further endanger the brave men and women under his command,' end quote."

Colonel Dietrich wiped a hand through the docs to make them disappear, then folded his arms. "I find those reports troubling, Captain. More than troubling. Disgraceful. I feel a great shame that I didn't review your records with greater attention when you arrived."

"It's worth noting, sir, that I was acquitted of all charges at the court-martial."

"Acquitted, yes," said Dietrich, "but the judge in the case, despite the acquittal, issued a letter of reprimand, which is unprecedented. A letter of reprimand is a form of punishment, issued only when the defendant is deemed guilty. I see that your attorney subsequently got the letter expunged, but I have to ask myself, why would an honorable judge break judicial precedent and threaten his own career to punish you? The only answer I can muster is that the judge knew you were guilty but the prosecutor, for whatever reason, couldn't deliver a conviction."

"The judge's actions were a disbarrable offense," said Mazer. "But I don't concern myself with the matter. My focus is the war, sir, the present. As for the evaluations by Rear Admiral Vaganov and others, I take great comfort in knowing that you, sir, are more than capable of making your own judgment of my character."

"On that we agree," said Dietrich. "But I doubt you'll find any comfort in my judgment. You were brought here, Captain, to be an instructor to the marines here and a teacher to these boys. So far you've done neither."

"No, sir. I am confined to quarters. By your orders, sir."

"Yes. By my orders. And yet you left your quarters to

have a secret meeting with Colonel Li. You violated my direct order. You broke military law. Don't deny it. Because I have all the physical evidence in the world. You then proceeded to steal a service shuttle and take it on a joyride around this facility, without any authorization from me or the docking officer on duty. More broken laws. You then colluded with Colonel Li to orchestrate a coup in this facility and forcefully remove me from command."

Mazer somehow kept his expression flat and avoided laughing. "With all due respect, sir, I think you've mischaracterized my interactions with Colonel Li."

"Have I now? Then explain these items." He produced the tablet and the data cube and anchored them to the holodesk.

"One of those items is a tablet, sir. The other is a data cube."

"Don't be a smartass," said Dietrich. "I want to know what's on them."

"Those items belong to Colonel Li, sir. He loaned them to me so that I might assist him with a matter that's classified. I'd recommend that you ask him for further clarification."

Dietrich's expression hardened. "Are you daring to tell me how to do my job, Mazer? Is that what they taught you in New Zealand? To disrespect your superiors by coaching them on their duties?"

"No, sir. I merely mean to suggest that this concern of yours can easily be resolved if you were to contact Colonel Li."

"Your co-conspirator?"

"There is no conspiracy, sir."

"Now you're calling me a liar?"

"I'm merely suggesting that you have reached inaccurate conclusions."

"This tablet and data cube are password-protected," said Dietrich. "Tell me the passwords."

"As I said, sir. The contents are classified."

"You're refusing to obey a lawful order?" said Colonel Dietrich.

"With all due respect, sir, the order is not lawful. The action you request is in fact unlawful. I can't share classified information with anyone who does not hold the necessary clearance. If you have top-secret clearance, sir, I'm certain Colonel Li will be more than willing to share the information with you."

"Colonel Li is not here," said Dietrich. "I'm not speaking to Colonel Li. I'm speaking to you, an officer under my direct command. Are you refusing my lawful order?"

"With all due respect, Colonel Dietrich, your concerns are valid. I want nothing more than for you to access the intelligence. But that is not in my power to grant. Might I suggest that you consider asking a higher authority to intervene?"

"I *am* the higher authority! This is *my* space station, Captain. Mine. Anything within these walls is my responsibility. Colonel Li is a guest here, as are these boys. I tolerated them when they arrived. But I'll be damned if I sit back and allow a traitor in our midst."

Mazer stiffened. "Sir?"

"Did you think me a fool, Captain? In all the time Colonel Li has been here, do you know how many messages we've received for him at the helm? Zero. Not one. No emails. No memorandums. No letters from home. Nothing. I've got marines here who haven't a friend in the world who get more mail than that damn colonel. Do you know why that is, Mazer?"

"No, sir, I don't."

"Don't lie to me. You know as well as I do that Colonel Li has his own quad."

"I don't, in fact, know that, sir. I've never seen a quad, either on a ship or in Colonel Li's possession. I have no idea what one looks like."

"Well, he has one," said Dietrich. "His own damn quad. I'm the commanding officer of the biggest training facility this side of Mars, and even I don't have one."

Mazer said nothing.

"So I began to investigate. I have contacts in the FIA, Mazer. That's the Fleet Intelligence Agency, the intelligence arm of this military. I connected with my contacts there and asked them for a favor. Could they tell me about Colonel Li, who is obviously one of their agents? But lo and behold, I was informed that they don't know who this man is. He's certainly not one of ours, they told me. Not with his record. Big empty holes in his record in China. Very strange, very shady, they said. Tread lightly. This is a man with a past that he's worked hard to conceal. So I'm going to ask you this only once. Fail to answer, and I'll have you arrested. Who do you and Colonel Li work for?"

"Sir, you've been misinformed. I am a captain of the International Fleet. That's my only association."

"Don't play stupid, Mazer. I've got three decades in the German navy. I've seen your type before. Maybe marital problems, bankruptcy, something not right in your life. And then you meet someone who tells you they can make all your problems go away. Give you all the money in the world. If you help them just a little bit."

"With all due respect, sir—"

"Save your respect, Mazer. I'm not a fool. You're an agent of the MSS. You and Li both."

Mazer couldn't help but smile then.

"You think this is funny, Mazer?"

"No, sir. You'll forgive me. But . . . I'm just caught off guard here. I assure you, I am not Chinese intelligence."

"And I'm to take you on your word?" said Colonel Dietrich. "When all the evidence suggests otherwise?"

"May I inquire what evidence you're referring to, sir?"

"The only reason someone at CentCom would put a

troublemaker like yourself at this school is because that someone at CentCom was *looking* for a troublemaker, someone who could disrupt operations from the inside, someone who could find fault with my command. That was your play with Vaganov as well, wasn't it? To ruin him? To take his command for yourself? Your plan with Vaganov may have failed, but Colonel Li's people clearly saw in you what they needed in an agent. So they made you a subordinate to Colonel Li, one of their most trusted agents. And they created this whole false school, filled with, surprise, Chinese nationals."

"You think the boys are Chinese intelligence as well?"

"They're up to something in their barracks, and you can be damn sure I'm going to find out what it is."

"I'll save you the trouble," said Mazer. "They're trying to win this war. Not for the Chinese, but for every living human alive, including you, sir, who suspects the worst of them. They are not Chinese intelligence. I am not Chinese intelligence. You may pursue whatever investigation of me you deem appropriate, sir, but I assure you, you're wasting your time."

"You're done, Mazer. I've tolerated your lies and insubordination enough. You're no longer confined to quarters. I think a cell would better serve you."

He nodded to the lieutenant, who went outside and returned with the MPs, who each took Mazer by an arm and escorted him out into the corridor. Mazer did laugh, finally. A small amused release of exasperation. This was Vaganov all over again. Except Dietrich wasn't unethical. He was simply ludicrously paranoid. How a man like that could rise to any level of command was baffling.

He wondered then if Colonel Dietrich would try to arrest Li as well. But no. Dietrich might be paranoid, but he wasn't foolish enough to apprehend a fellow colonel without probable cause and an assurance from CentCom that Dietrich's career would be safe if he made such a move.

For the time being Li was fine. But with Mazer, Colonel Dietrich could take all the liberties in the world.

The MPs took Mazer to the brig, locked him in a cell with a thick glass front, and left him there.

The humor was out of him now. His amusement at the absurdity of it all had dried up. This is why the Hive Queen will win, he thought. She knows no division. Her soldiers are never petty, or spiteful, or selfish. They never fight for position or prominence or more bars on their shoulders. They obey. They learn their duty and then fulfill it without deviation.

There was no free will, perhaps. No self, no identity. But her strategy had its advantages, including the only one that mattered: a clear path to victory, with Earth as her prize.

CHAPTER 13

Rescue

Ansible transmission between the Hegemon Ukko Jukes and Polemarch Ishmerai Averbach. File #474750. Office of the Hegemony Sealed Archives, Imbrium, Luna, 2119

UKKO: You're the military. You have the biggest guns. And yet you keep losing supply ships to thugs and pirates.

AVERBACH: Calling them thugs paints a false impression. These aren't bumbling thieves. They're highly sophisticated and well equipped.

UKKO: Yes, equipped with ships and tech that they stole from the Fleet.

AVERBACH: We've lined supply routes with escort vessels, but the Fleet is spread thin. We're fighting two wars at once here, and I'm more concerned about the Formics and the possible annihilation of the human race than I am about a few emboldened criminals.

UKKO: Then allow me to give you a lesson in economics. Wars are won with coin. Ships and supplies are not made from thin air. They are bought and paid for by the free citizens of Earth, who pay heavy taxes to the Hegemony to sustain your efforts. How long do you think they'll continue paying

those taxes if they believe their precious money
is being wasted on ships and supplies that never
reach their destinations or engage the enemy? And
how long do you think we can keep fighting once
our war chest is empty?

AVERBACH: I can only do so much. I'm high above
the ecliptic, leading an assault. Would you have me
pull our ships out of the war effort to run down pirates?

UKKO: You got this job because you're a brilliant
strategist. Be creative.

Imala was cradling her newborn in the airlock and trying
to ignore the pain in her abdomen when the final stage of
the rescue operation commenced. The Gagak had reached
the wrecked asteroid-mining ship deep in the Kuiper Belt
and was now extending a docking tube toward the ship's
emergency escape hatch. From what Imala could see, the
damage to the mining ship was catastrophic and beyond
repair. Its thrusters were either mangled pieces of shred-
ded metal or missing from the ship entirely, having been
blown off by devastating firepower. Long scorch marks
down the side of its hull from high-powered lasers had
taken out solar panels and various scanners with deadly
accuracy. The largest wound, however, was aft, where the
structure of the ship had twisted and caved inward, suggesting a collision so violent that whoever had hit the ship
could be accused of trying to break it in half. If pirates
had indeed orchestrated the attack, they had done so with
brutal savagery.

"Whoever hit that ship used military-grade weaponry,"
said Captain Mangold. He stood beside Imala, along with
Lieutenant Owanu and Rena, all of them watching the
feeds from the exterior cameras projected on the wall inside the airlock.

"See here?" said Mangold, pointing to scorch marks along the ship's exterior. "See how straight these cuts are? How accurately they hit all the scanning equipment? That's not good shooting. That's off-the-charts accurate, precision-guided shooting. Only IF targeting systems could have done that. No crew of two-bit pirates could have pulled it off."

"What are you saying?" said Imala. "That the Fleet did this?"

"It wasn't pirates," said Mangold. "Or not any pirates I've ever seen. This is *too* good, *too* strong."

"Then maybe these people are the pirates," said Lieutenant Owanu. "Maybe they're the bad guys. The Fleet tracked them down and took them out, and so they pretended to be miners and called for help."

"If the Fleet had hit a pirate crew, they would've taken everyone into custody," said Imala. "They wouldn't have left people on the ship to die."

Captain Mangold shrugged. "Maybe they did. Maybe the IF ship didn't have capacity for so many prisoners. Or maybe they didn't want the hassle of taking them into custody. Maybe that was too much trouble and too much paperwork. Maybe carting prisoners off to a holding station somewhere would have disrupted the IF ship's plans or mission. Maybe they couldn't spare the fuel. And rather than put a laser through the pirates' heads, which no marine would have the stomach for, the IF ship destroyed the pirate vessel as much as they thought was necessary and then left them here to die."

"No captain of the Fleet would do that," said Imala.

"I would," said Mangold. "If my superiors ordered it. Or if doing anything more than that might endanger my crew. This far out, this far from any outpost, you don't take stupid risks. And going inside a scuttled ship to arrest a bunch of savage pirates would be a risk. They're facing death or capture. You can be sure they would do all in their power to kill the marines and take the Fleet

ship. It's their last, desperate option. That's a battle no Fleet captain wants to fight. It would be much easier to cripple the ship and move on."

"I basically said all this before we came," said Rena. "That this could be a pirate trick. Now you're agreeing with me?"

"I'm saying what's possible," said Mangold, "based on this new intel. No one's saying you didn't warn us of this possibility."

"We don't know that they're pirates," said Imala. "We're making assumptions based on the damage to the ship's exterior."

"I'm telling you," said Mangold. "A Fleet ship did this damage."

"That may be," said Imala. "But it could've been a Fleet ship controlled by pirates. They've been hitting supply lines all over the Outer Rim. Maybe they've taken a Fleet ship or two in the process. We don't know. What we do know is that these people who asked for help sounded legit. We checked their creds."

Captain Mangold turned to Rena. "You've seen more pirate attacks than we have, Rena. Are we about to unleash a mob of pirates on our ship?"

"They claim to have children," said Rena. "And we've told them to send up the children first. We have the marines ready, and we see what happens. We came here to help them. If they are legit and we deny them rescue now, we're as monstrous as whoever hit them."

A team of marines was waiting outside the airlock. Mangold ordered them to come in and take position.

Owanu frowned at Imala. "You should be in the clinic, Imala. You had a C-section and then did several Gs with a surgical wound. Plus you've got a baby in your arms. We can handle this."

"I told her the same thing," said Captain Mangold. "But she won't listen to me, despite the fact that I'm her

commanding officer and practically ordered her to stay in the clinic."

"*Practically* ordered isn't the same as ordered," said Imala. "There's a narrow loophole in there. But I'm getting out of the way."

She carried Chee outside the airlock and watched from the corridor. The docking tube locked into place, and the buzzer announced that the seal between the two ships was secured and the tube was ready for use. That meant the airlock could remain open and pressurized, giving Imala a clear view of what happened inside.

Was this whole rescue a ruse? she wondered. Was she about to expose her newborn to murderous pirates?

"I want everyone on alert here," said Captain Mangold.

The marines had their weapons up and were down on one knee in a firing position.

"If there are children, you're going to terrify them," said Rena.

"I'd rather do that than be shot," said Mangold. "Sergeant, open the hatch."

The marine nearest the control pad punched in the order, and the airlock exterior hatch hissed and slid open. The long docking tube was empty, and Imala couldn't see beyond where it curved into the mining ship.

A moment later a child came into view, wide-eyed and haggard and dangerously thin. She flew up the docking tube and into the airlock, and Imala's heart broke at the sight of her. The girl was maybe four years old, with an old, threadbare jumpsuit at least a full size too small. A child's oxygen mask covered her mouth, and a supplemental tank of O_2 was at her hip. The little girl looked at the marines and their weapons pointed at her and she seemed on the verge of tears.

"Put your weapons down," said Rena.

Mangold nodded his agreement, and the marines lowered their guns.

Rena made herself small and approached the child at eye level, smiling. "Well, hello there. My name is Grandma Rena, and I am so happy to have you on our ship."

The girl glanced back down the docking tube, perhaps regretting having left the people she knew behind. They had told her not to worry, that these people were good and kind, but the look on her face revealed she didn't believe it.

"Don't you have the most beautiful hair," said Rena. "My goodness. I bet a girl with such beautiful hair will have a beautiful name to match it."

The girl's eyes wouldn't stop moving. She looked to Captain Mangold, then to Lieutenant Owanu and the marines, as if she feared any one of them might attack at any moment. It was only when the child's eyes fell upon Chee, wrapped in a blanket in Imala's arms, that Imala saw a change in the girl's expression. A subtle relaxing of the muscles. An easing of her fear.

That is the power of a baby, Imala thought. Its mere presence suggests peace and goodness and safety.

"I bet I can guess your name," said Rena. "I bet your name is, hmm, let me see. I'm going to guess . . . Cattywampus. No, no. That can't be right. Not Cattywampus. You look more like a Pumpernickle. Yes, that's it. Your name is Pumpernickle. Oh, and judging by that smile I see I must have guessed right. Nice to meet you, Pumpernickle. Welcome aboard."

"It's Lillianna," said the girl.

"Oh, Lillianna. That's a beautiful name," said Rena. "So much better than Pumpernickle. I'm happy to meet you. I bet they call you Lilly for short."

The girl's smile faded then, as if she were remembering the people who had called her Lilly, and the memory of them was fresh and hurtful.

Rena realized her mistake at once. "Well, you're safe with us, Lillianna. We even made cookies. Do you like

sugar cookies? I had to cheat on the recipe because we don't have all the ingredients, but they're yummy just the same."

Before the child could answer, another young girl came up through the docking tube and into the airlock. Smaller. Maybe three years old. Not as frightened as the first. She shielded her eyes from the bright lights and took in her surroundings with a slight look of wonder, as if she had never seen such a clean airlock before.

"Well, my goodness," said Rena, "here's someone else come to join us. Hello there. And who might this be?"

"This is my sister," said Lilliana. "Her name is Penny-Lu."

"Penny-Lu?" said Rena. "I love that name."

"Her real name is Penelope. But that's too long, so we call her Penny or Penny-Lu or Penny Lulu Bells, which is as long as Penelope but my mom uses it anyway."

"I like all of those options," said Rena. "It's going to be hard to use just one. Hello, Penny Lulu Bells. I'm Grandma Rena."

Child number three came next, but unlike the others this one was crying. Terrified. Screaming her lungs out at having been lightly but unceremoniously pushed up the docking tube by whatever adult she had been clinging to. She was about the same age as Penelope but was clearly no relation. Darker complexion, rounder features. Rena scooped her into her arms and instantly the child quieted, not because she was no longer frightened, but because Rena was such a curious surprise. A kindly old woman? That was unexpected.

Imala almost laughed then. Perhaps there was something instinctual bred into humans that old women were not warriors and thus not to be feared. To be in their arms was to be safe. Perhaps that had evolved in us, over tens of thousands of years and countless old women showing kindness in a tribe.

Whatever the reason, Captain Mangold spoiled it.

"Well, hello there," he said to the child. "You're all safe now."

The third child turned to him, remembered that she was in a strange, frightening place surrounded by strangers, and started wailing again.

"Nice move," said Lieutenant Owanu.

Mangold jumped to his own defense. "I said the same thing Rena did. Basically."

"I'm taking them into the kitchen," said Rena. "Come on, Penny-Lu. Come on, Lillianna. Let's get some cookies."

Imala watched her go, curious to see how Rena would handle taking a screaming child out of a room in zero gravity. On Earth, the parent would simply pick up the child, plant it on a hip, and march out, in control. But in space, to hold a child was to increase your mass and offset your balance and complicate the mechanics of your launches. You had to push off harder; but you also couldn't bend and rotate at will, for fear that you might sling the little person away from you and send it careening into a wall. It was like treading water while holding a watermelon, except the watermelon was made of fine china.

For Rena, handling screaming children was as natural as breathing. She deftly placed the crying child's arms around her neck and then gently swung the child up onto her back, like a mother orangutan gathering her newborn. Then she grabbed the child's ankles and pulled her in close, turning the girl into a wailing backpack. Then she pushed off the wall as graceful as always and drifted out of the airlock with the other two girls scrambling to keep up.

"I'll help you," said Imala as Rena reached her in the corrridor.

Rena caught herself and shook her head. "I can handle three children. You stay and make sure Mangold doesn't kill these people. They aren't pirates."

Then Rena pushed off again and led the children toward the kitchen.

Imala entered the airlock and caught Captain Mangold's notice.

"That accounts for the three children," said Mangold. "Next comes five adults. Are we going to make them strip naked and come in here with their hands up like you proposed? Or can we safely skip that part?"

"Pirates have children too," said Owanu. "We're not in the clear yet. I say we do this right and take every precaution."

"Have the adults come in wearing their undergarments," said Imala. "Rather than completely stripped. I'm sure these good marines can verify the miners are unarmed. Female marines patting down women, male marines patting down men."

"I know how a pat-down works," said Mangold.

"Of course," said Imala.

Captain Mangold relayed the request down the docking tube, and the adults came up one at a time in their undergarments. As each arrived, they were patted down and given an emergency blanket to stay warm. Imala knew at once that they weren't pirates. There was no edge to them, no appearance of evil, no deception. They were traumatized, terrified, thin and shivering, but otherwise normal, innocent people. Three women and two men. All young. Mid-twenties, early thirties. All wearing masks and breathing supplemental oxygen. They were gaunt and haggard and scared out of their minds.

Captain Mangold had obviously reached the same conclusion as Imala, because when he spoke he was kind and sympathetic. "I'm Captain Mangold. Welcome aboard the Gagak. You'll forgive us for taking such precautionary measures, but pirates use deceptive tactics, and my first responsibility is the safety of my crew."

"You don't have to apologize," said the shorter of the two men, who spoke with a slightly French accent. "We owe you our lives."

"They took my sister," said one of the women suddenly. "Her and three other women. We have to go after them. Please."

Captain Mangold glanced at Imala. This was news to them.

"It's true," said the short man. "They killed most of our crew. Lizbet, Dianne, and Marina here hid on the ship or the pirates would have taken them, too. We didn't tell you when we radioed because we feared you wouldn't come. Going after them would be dangerous, yes, but we can help you. These women, they are family."

"We have to find them," said the woman. "Please. My sister." The woman began to cry.

Captain Mangold held up his hands. "Everyone, please. I recognize you've been through an ordeal. My focus right now is tending to you and the children. This is Lieutenant Owanu, our crew physician. She needs to examine each of you so that we can provide appropriate care. Sergeant Lefevre here will then escort you to the showers, where you'll find fresh clothing and personal hygiene items. Following that, a hot meal."

"We shouldn't wait," said the crying woman. "The longer we wait, the harder it will be to find them. I beg you, please."

"Ma'am," said Mangold. "You've been through a harrowing ordeal, and you need medical attention. One thing at a time."

The short man spoke to her in French and the woman nodded, crying.

"We are thankful," said the short man to Mangold. "We hope you consider our plea. They have taken our family, people we love."

"I understand," said Mangold.

"Who were they?" said Imala. "The pirates, can you describe them?"

"It was Khalid," said the short man. "That was the pirate's name. Khalid. K-H-A-L-I-D. It was important to him that we remembered how to spell it. He had us practice doing so in front of him just to make sure we got it right. That's when I realized that he might not kill us. He wanted us to spread his name. He wanted everyone to know it was him."

Imala could see that Mangold recognized the name. "You've heard of him? This Khalid?"

"A Somali pirate," said Mangold. "The Fleet knows him well. High-priority target."

"He chased us for two days," said the short man. "It was a game to him. An amusement. Like a cat plays with a mouse. He would let us believe we were getting away, and then he would hit us. Literally. Ram us. He breached our hull. We lost three people instantly. We sealed off that portion of the ship and pushed on, but we knew it was no use. No one responded to our maydays. Which was another thing I didn't understand at the time. Khalid could have easily taken out our transmitter. He could have silenced us. But he didn't. He wanted us to call for help. He wanted everyone to know it was him."

The woman was crying harder now, and the other women were trying to comfort her.

"Sergeant Lefevre, escort these people to the clinic and assist Lieutenant Owanu."

"Yes, sir. This way, if you please." Lefevre repeated the instructions in French, and the miners and marines and Owanu exited the airlock, leaving Captain Mangold and Imala alone, with little Chee still in Imala's arms.

"This changes things," said Imala.

"This changes nothing," said Mangold. "We're not the Kuiper Belt Police, Imala. We can't go chasing after

Somali pirates. We have a mission to fulfill. CentCom may have allowed us to divert for this, but they sure as hell won't have us divert to track down pirates."

"Full disclosure," said Imala. "CentCom was against us coming here. They ordered us not to, in fact. But before you go nova, Ukko Jukes overrode their order and told me to do what I thought was best."

Mangold was furious. "You lied to me? You said Cent-Com gave us the go-ahead."

"No. I said we were authorized to go. Which was true. That authorization just happened to come from the Hegemon of Earth, whose authority trumps that of CentCom."

"You're telling me this now?"

"Would you rather not know?"

"I would rather you have been transparent and told me the truth before we launched."

"Coming to the aid of these people was your insistence. You wanted to come as much as I did."

"That was before I knew CentCom was against the idea. Do you have any idea what this does to my career? The leaders of the Fleet think I just disobeyed a direct order. This is insane."

"And that's why I didn't tell you," said Imala. "I knew you'd give too much consideration to CentCom's objections."

"You're damn right I would," said Mangold. "Because they're in charge."

"Unless their orders conflict with the Hegemon's," said Imala. "His orders are the ones we follow."

"How do I even know he gave you orders? You could be making that up. I have no way of verifying."

"Why would I lie?" said Imala. "If I was going to lie to you, I would have simply lied about CentCom and told you they gave us their blessing to proceed."

"That's essentially what you did before we launched," said Mangold. "You deceived me."

"When you fulfill this mission and kill the Hive Queen, I don't think anyone at CentCom will care much about any previous insubordination," said Imala. "They'll be too busy pinning medals to your chest. And if telling you before we launched would have made you change your mind and *not* come to rescue these people in some effort to preserve your career, then I see that I made the right choice in concealing it. I'd also be deeply disappointed to learn that you place a greater value on what stodgy old admirals think of you than on obeying the commander in chief or on the lives of innocent people."

"Don't take the moral high ground on this, Imala. You broke trust."

"Would you have come?" said Imala.

Mangold didn't answer.

"If you want to inflict some punishment, I'll gladly accept it," said Imala. "Court-martial me if you choose. But the Hegemon of Earth will come to my defense."

"You've never mentioned getting a message from the Hegemon before."

"Because I never had," said Imala. "I didn't realize he had an ansible. But of course he would have one, he's the Hegemon. And even if I had known that, I wouldn't have assumed he was on our network and would communicate with our ship. But he did. Nor would I have assumed that he would disagree with CentCom and veto their orders. But he did. Ask yourself, Captain. Who at CentCom wanted me to run the ansible? Answer: no one. Not a soul. And yet the position was given to me. Who has the authority to override them other than the Hegemon? The very fact that I have the position I do should be all the evidence you need to know that I'm not lying. It infuriates you that I'm the only person who can access the ansible, but just imagine how much more it infuriates CentCom. I'm barely a member of the Fleet. I have no military training. Or comms training. I have a baby in

my arms, for crying out loud. I am the last person in the world CentCom would want controlling the ansible, particularly on a military operation central to the mission of the Fleet. But that is precisely why Ukko Jukes gave the task to me. Because he doesn't trust CentCom. And he would much rather have a person loyal to him with the ansible than someone loyal to military commanders."

"So you're loyal to the Hegemon?"

"He seems to think so. Or it's less about loyalty to him personally and more about a mutually agreed-upon commitment to good sense first and the rule of CentCom second."

"We can't ignore CentCom," said Mangold.

"I'm not suggesting we do," said Imala. "They run this operation. But we also can't ignore good sense and human decency. We do what we must do, and we hope it aligns with the commands of CentCom."

"No, it can't work that way," said Captain Mangold. "This is a military operation. We can't go rogue and follow our own compass."

"It's not *our* compass," said Imala. "It's the Hegemon's, who is the commander in chief of all IF forces and the ultimate authority here."

Captain Mangold sighed and ran a hand through his hair. "This is not how it works."

"Then you are not a student of history," said Imala, "because men in congresses and parliaments and seated on thrones have been ordering generals around since war existed."

"From now on, you inform me, your commanding officer, of everything that's given to us via ansible, including and especially when that message is from the Hegemon of Earth. No filtering, no concealing."

"Of course," said Imala.

"The correct response is, 'Yes, sir.'"

"Yes, sir," said Imala. "And Chee here says, yes sir, as well."

Captain Mangold glanced down at the baby and sighed again, as if reminded that the mission was now writing its own script instead of following the one he had prepared.

"What do we do about the miners who were taken?" said Imala.

"I don't want to dehumanize the situation here," said Mangold, "but we're talking about four women. Wait, let me finish. Look outside again at the damage to that ship and remind yourself what we'd be up against. Khalid is a killer. I don't know what he's flying, but it's equipped with military hardware. Look at the dent in the side of that ship. He rammed them, intentionally, without any worry about inflicting damage to his own vessel, so we can safely assume it's got military-grade shield plating. A flying tank. A battering ram. We, on the other hand, are in an old mining ship retrofitted with a few weapons. Even if we were commanded to track this bastard down, we'd be in for the fight of our lives. What's more, we have already deviated from our mission, which takes precedence over everything. The Hive Queen may be in that ship out there, Imala, and if we take it out, we might end this war. If we don't take it out because we're playing constable and getting ourselves killed by a homicidal Somali pirate, we fail billions of people. So you do the math on that one."

"I'm glad to hear you still refer to the Hive Queen," said Imala. "You see? CentCom isn't always wise in their decisions."

He looked annoyed.

"I'm not suggesting we go after these pirates," said Imala. "But it does no harm to find out what we can and then pass that information on to the Fleet. That's intel the Fleet can use to conduct their strike or rescue mission."

"We'll interview them after they eat and shower," said Mangold.

"We?" asked Imala.

"You're the one who has to give the report to Cent-Com, so you're the one who should ask the questions and hear all the answers. Plus you're a . . ."

"Woman?"

"You have an infant and a, I don't know, a maternal disposition. These people will be talking about a traumatic experience. They'll see you as someone they can confide in. Your personality will play better than mine."

"Thank you," said Imala. "Though of course you're perfectly capable of doing it."

"That's my decision. And I want Owanu checking that wound of yours. You're the only person who can operate the ansible. I can't afford to have your condition worse than it already is."

"Yes, sir."

Later, when they gathered for dinner, the miners all looked more presentable in their IF-issued jumpsuits. Rena asked simple questions, keeping the conversation away from the attack and instead focusing on the miners and their history. The whole crew was from Montreal and surrounding cities. They had bought a ship after the first war and tried their hand at mining, believing that the Kuiper Belt was a much less saturated market and thus a land of opportunity. One of the surviving women, the one whose sister Khalid had taken, was the mother of Lillianna and Penny, which gladdened Imala's heart. The other girl, sadly, who had cried nonstop in Rena's arms, had lost both of her parents in the attack.

Imala left dinner early to nurse Chee, but in truth she needed an excuse to exit. Her abdomen was a hot cauldron of pain, after having moved around all day, and it was becoming more difficult to conceal the pain from the others.

She slipped into the ansible room, where she knew no one could follow her, and gave Chee her breast. The baby was a natural. Imala had read all variety of nursing nightmares leading up to the birth, but all of that breastfeeding anxiety had been for naught. Chee had no complications whatsoever. Even in the awkward, cramped confines of the impact bubble, Chee had taken to the practice without any problem when the ship wasn't accelerating. Upon realizing this, Imala had cried with relief. Sobbed, right there in front of Rena and Lieutenant Owanu. A big blubbery rush of relief.

A light tap at the door. "Imala?"

It was Owanu.

Chee had finished nursing and was sleeping again. Imala covered herself and moved out of the ansible room, cradling Chee in her arms.

"Hiding?" said Owanu.

"A big upside of nursing," said Imala. "It's a great get-out-of-any-situation card."

"Let's look at that wound."

They moved to the clinic and gently strapped Chee into the bassinet. Then Imala was strapped down on the examination table and Owanu removed the bandages. They had done this multiple times during the rescue flight, checking Imala's wound between each acceleration. The bruising around the incision was a wide, deep blotch of purple, as if someone had whacked Imala repeatedly with a canoe paddle. It was blood coagulating around the wound, brought on by the G-forces of acceleration, but Lieutenant Owanu thought it looked worse than it actually was. The pain had been terrible during the flight, and if not for the pain patches that Owanu had given her, Imala doubted she could have endured the flight.

Owanu used a few scanning devices and gently prodded with her fingers and ran a few tests. "Wound looks good," she said when she finished. "Better than expected,

to be honest. It was the healing strips." Nanosheets of synthetic skin had been applied to the wound to help re-build muscle structure and accelerate healing. "I'll apply some new nanosheets and give you another patch for the pain," said Owanu. "And no, don't object. It's localized and doesn't affect your milk. You're not doping up the baby. I've watched you wince all day long, and it's start-ing to hurt me to see it."

Owanu did her work delicately and well, and after the patch was administered, Imala immediately felt relief.

"We didn't have these nanosheets five years ago," said Owanu. "Without them, I'm not sure you would have made it. I know the bruising looks terrible, but you're not hemorrhaging internally, which was my concern. Every-thing looks good. If I hadn't done the stitching myself, I would have guessed that this incision was at least a month old. That's how fast it's healing."

"I owe you my life," said Imala.

"I'm doing my job," said Owanu, smiling. "Now let's take a look at this little pooper."

Owanu gently pulled back the blanket wrapped around Chee and placed a device near the infant's heart, head, and hands. The device flashed red and green and then Owanu said, "Blood pressure normal. Body temp normal. Oxygen normal. She's doing fine."

Imala visibly relaxed.

"The bad part is over," said Owanu. "She took a few Gs with no problem. It scared her to death, it stressed her little heart, but she did okay. Here." Owanu pulled a bundle of fabric from a cabinet. "It's a baby-wrap sling. Rena and I made it from some excess gowns and fabrics here in the clinic."

She helped Imala off the table and they placed Chee against Imala's chest. Owanu then showed Imala how to wrap the sling around her back and over her shoulders to create a little pocket where Chee was tightly held.

"Are you sure she can breathe in there?" said Imala.

"She's fine. Her head is to the side. Moms wear these all the time. And with her tucked into your little papoose here, your hands are now free to help stabilize you while you fly."

"I don't know what to say," said Imala. She could feel tears welling up inside her, so she said nothing more.

Owanu gave her a sideways hug. "You can name the next one after me."

With Chee tucked in her sling, Imala went looking for Captain Mangold, who had arranged for the interviews to take place inside his office.

They first met with the short man, whom they had learned was named Liam and who had become the group's de facto leader when the captain was killed in the raid.

"They took out our engines and retros using IF weaponry," said Liam. "Highly targeted lasers built by Juke Limited for IF warships. Khalid bragged about them. He claimed he had stolen the weapons from the Fleet. He said he had attacked an IF shipyard and stripped the ships under construction for parts. He said he'd killed over twenty shipbuilders and marines. He said it was the biggest news in the system, but the Fleet was too cowardly to put it in the press." Liam turned to Captain Mangold apologetically. "I mean no offense. I'm only telling you what he told us."

"None taken," said Mangold.

Imala turned to Mangold. "Is that true? Did Khalid hit a shipyard?"

Mangold shrugged. "Maybe. We don't get updates like that from CentCom. They tell us what they want us to know. Or they tell you, anyway. But if it's true, if Khalid did hit a shipyard, I can assure you it's not something the IF would want broadcast. It would be too embarrassing and wouldn't play well in the press."

"The press don't know about it," said Liam. "That's what angered him. He wanted the world to know what he had done. He was furious that the story wasn't all over the nets. That's why he made the vid."

"Vid?" said Imala.

"He and a few of his crew were wearing bodycams when they raided us. They recorded the whole attack. They kept recording until right before they left. They downloaded the video into our holotable and told us we were to give it to whoever rescued us, if we were lucky enough to survive. He said he was also putting the vid on his channel, that the world would soon know the name of Khalid."

"You still have this vid?" said Imala.

"At the helm," said Liam. "On our holotable. You don't want to watch it. He kills people."

"Does the vid show Khalid's face?" Imala asked.

"He was the star of the whole thing," said the miner. "He was performing for the cameras. It was all about him."

"Can this file be moved to a data cube?" asked Imala. "Can you show our marines where it's located and bring it on our ship?"

Captain Mangold called Sergeant Lefevre and ordered him to suit up with Liam and a few other marines and recover the vid.

As they waited, Imala relayed what she knew back to CentCom via ansible. The commanders ranted and cursed and called her irresponsible for conducting the rescue and disobeying orders. They told her she was removed from office and was to be confined to quarters and would endure a court-martial via ansible with them as the acting judicial body. They told her she was treasonous and undisciplined and her actions unconscionable. They told her Captain Mangold was now the only person authorized to use the ansible. They told her she would spend the rest of

her life in a cell, and that if the mission failed, the consequences to Earth, however great, would be squarely on her shoulders.

All things considered, Imala thought it went better than expected.

She wrote back that she would gladly leave her post if the commanders could produce an order from the Hegemon calling for her removal.

The commanders cursed her again and used even more colorful language and told her she was insubordinate and out of line and that they didn't need to bother the Hegemon with such a ridiculous and lowly matter as this and she should leave the ansible room immediately and have Captain Mangold take her place.

"Nice talk," wrote Imala. "I so look forward to our conversation tomorrow."

Then she and Chee left the ansible room because she had nothing further to say to them.

"Well?" asked Mangold. "What did they say?"

Imala told him. Every word. Even the colorful ones. When she finished, she said, "So now you have a choice, Captain Mangold. Follow CentCom and put yourself in that room. Or follow the Hegemon of Earth."

Mangold was quiet while he considered. "And you would stay out of the ansible room?" he said. "If I followed their orders and took over the ansible, you'd stay out?"

"What choice do I have?" said Imala. "You have twenty marines at your command on this ship. And I'm a recent mother with a killer birth wound. I couldn't beat you in a thumb-wrestling contest."

"So you'll follow my orders, but not CentCom's?"

"I follow the orders of the person who is the greatest superior to whom I have access. Unless the Hegemon of Earth gives me different orders, that superior is you."

"I don't want your job," said Captain Mangold. "As far as I'm concerned, I didn't hear this order from Cent-Com."

"They'll think I kept the order from you," said Imala.

"So what? You can't annoy them any further than you already have. So until they produce an order from the Hegemon, the ansible is your business."

Sergeant Lefevre returned with the data cube and said, "Sir, the vid. The miner said he'd rather not watch it with you, if you don't mind."

"Of course," said Mangold. "Thank you, Sergeant."

Lefevre left them, and Mangold called for Rena and Lieutenant Owanu.

"Are you sure you want to watch this?" said Rena once they were all gathered in Mangold's office. "I know this Khalid. He's chased this ship in the past. Before Imala and Victor joined the crew. He would've killed us if he had caught us. He had a reputation then, and it's far worse now. Whatever happened on that mining ship isn't something we want to witness."

"We're gathering intelligence," said Imala. "Anything that would assist the Fleet. The weapons Khalid has, the tactics he uses, the number of troops under his command, their weaknesses if they have any, the direction they may have gone, the defenses on their ship, his lieutenants."

"Can't we just forward the vid to the Fleet?" Rena said.

"We can't send video via ansible. Only text. Our description of this intelligence is all we can give."

"Why even bother with that?" said Owanu. "Let's be honest with ourselves. No one in the Fleet is going to come looking for this guy. You can give them a report with a full sequence of his DNA and a giant neon arrow pointing to his hideout, and that won't make any difference. The Fleet is not in any position to pirate-chase out

here. The reason the Gagak was commandeered for this mission is because there was no available IF ship even remotely close by. We're it. Out here, this far from Turris and every other outpost, we *are* the Fleet. Sending a report to CentCom is a waste of time."

"We know his ship moved deeper into the Kuiper Belt," said Imala. "But at some point, he'll likely move back toward the Belt, back toward the supply lines. That would be my guess. He's a grandstander. He wants his name in headlines. He wants to strike fear in the hearts of millions. He's not going to hide out here forever. He's going to keep hitting targets until he gets the press he wants, and then he's going to hit more targets once he gets a taste of fame and feels even more indestructible. The Fleet won't have to hunt for him. He will go to them. That's his MO."

No one argued the point, so Imala inserted the data cube into Captain Mangold's terminal and they watched the display.

A thin Somali man appeared on screen wearing an IF uniform with the sleeves removed. He stood before a nondescript metal background, perhaps an interior wall of his ship, and faced the camera. "A message to the Hegemon of Earth, the rapist of nations, the puppet of the West, he who robs from my people with his taxes and soldiers, he who rules but who was not elected, he who commands but who holds no authority, he who enslaves all people from atop his false throne with his policies of control. I am Khalid. The face of fear. The messenger of God, who sent the Formics to rid the world of you and your fellow oppressors. I take from you IF thieves because you have taken from my people. I kill your builders and miners and suppliers, the dogs of your tyranny. Blood for blood. Life for life."

The screen went momentarily black, and then the vid

returned, but now the camera was elsewhere and moving quickly through darkness, the image whipping one way and then another. Imala couldn't make out what she was seeing.

"The man's a nutcase," said Owanu.

"He's a terrorist," said Mangold.

On screen a hatch opened and chaos ensued. The two ships had docked, Imala realized: Khalid's and the mining vessel. Khalid and his crew were gathered at the hatch and trying to force their way inside. Fired bolts flew up toward the camera, shot from miners anchored behind crates. Most of the bolts were wide and poorly aimed, but one shot through the open hatch and struck the pirate next to whoever was holding the camera. The pirate screamed in agony at the bolt in his shoulder, but then rough hands grabbed him and pulled him away so that another man could take his place.

For a moment Imala thought the miners might hold them off, but then the pirates had rifles firing steady beams of lasers through the hatch into the mining ship like a column of searing wires. The pirates kept the lasers concentrated on their targets, burning into the crates shielding the miners and sending up tendrils of smoke that obstructed Imala's view. She feared for a moment that the lasers might punch straight through the ship and out the other side, breaching the hull and exposing the ship to the vacuum of space. But the lasers were not that powerful, and the pirates, like surgeons, turned off the beams as soon as the lasers had penetrated the crates and found the miners hiding behind them. Three dead bodies and then a fourth rose up from behind crates, each pierced with a scorched hole or line. One man spewed a steady stream of blood globules.

The bodies were like a green flag waved before revving engines. The camera-carrier and the men huddled

around him at the hatch surged forward, pouring through the opening and bursting into the mining ship in a roaring mass of fury. These were not disciplined soldiers, but a scrambling, raving mob, launching forward without any order or cohesion, jacked up on adrenaline.

The camera-carrier landed in the cargo bay, and his magnetic greaves anchored him to the metal-grated floor. Then he was off again, lumbering forward in big magnetized steps. A dead body floated into his path, but the corpse whipped by so quickly that Imala couldn't see if it was man or woman, miner or pirate. The mob reached the opposite end of the cargo bay, where several passages branched away in multiple directions. Without consulting with each other, the pirates divided to rush through all the passages at once.

The camera-carrier took the passage on the far left and pulled himself through a hatch and into a dark corridor. The beam of light from his helmet found a screaming woman. She fled before him, terrified, launching into a side room and slamming the door behind her. The camera-carrier pushed on, ignoring her, passing another corpse left drifting and unanchored. The passage turned left, then right. More rooms, all ignored. The camera was on a rig on the man's head. Wherever he looked, the camera followed. A miner popped out from a side room in front of him and raised a crossbow. The camera-carrier shot him without slowing down, then shouldered the corpse aside.

Imala reached into the holofield and sped up the video so it was four times its normal speed. They didn't need to watch every single kill. Plus the sight of it all made Imala want to vomit.

"I'm guessing fifty men," said Rena. "Hard to get an exact number in the chaos, but fifty at least. All armed with IF slasers."

"Robbed from a supply ship, no doubt," said Mangold.

"Fifty psychopaths, is more like it," said Owanu. "All of them on phencyclidine or some other crazy chem. That's obvious. That's not adrenaline fueling those people. Khalid has them lit up like Roman candles. We saw this all the time in the ER during my residency. Drugs that made you think you were indestructible. People punching through glass windows and not even feeling all the broken bones in their hand. They call it monster juice."

"Butchers," said Rena.

"How helpful is this?" said Owanu. "What are we learning exactly? They're killers. We knew that already. And we knew from the damage done to the mining ship that Khalid has his hands on Fleet tech. If we're hoping for some clue on his location, I think we're setting ourselves up for a disappointment. Khalid isn't going to step in front of the camera and announce his address."

"She's right," said Mangold. "The only thing this video is giving us is sleepless nights and images best forgotten."

Then, on screen, the camera-carrier reached the helm of the mining ship, where a few miners were gathered with their hands raised in surrender. Imala slowed the vid to normal speed and let it play. A large group of pirates was gathering around one man anchored at the center of the room, his back to the camera, his slaser rifle raised high above his head. The pirates cheered and raised their own weapons in reply, like spectators in some gladiatorial arena roaring for their champion. It was Khalid, of course. He turned toward the camera-carrier, his face lighting up at the sight of it. Then he turned back to his men, knowing the camera was on him now, ready to immortalize the moment. "They say that the Hegemon of Earth, the thief of the world, fears no man," shouted Khalid. "That he cowers from no man. That he bends to

no man." Khalid paused for effect and then opened his body to the camera before continuing. "But now the Hegemon will know *this* man." He slapped himself in the chest repeatedly, and the men roared. "He will fear *this* man. He will bend to *this* man."

"Khalid!" the men shouted. "Khalid!"

Khalid raised his rifle repeatedly in the air, egging them on.

"Khalid! Khalid!"

Imala froze the image and examined it.

"Thank you," said Mangold. "I think we're heard enough psychotic ramblings for one day. Can we agree this is a dead end?"

Imala gestured at the display. "These uniforms. The yellow ones that some of his men are wearing. What are those?"

Mangold shrugged. "I don't know. Yellow uniforms. What are you asking?"

"Look at Khalid," said Imala. "He's wearing the jacket of an IF officer."

"With lieutenant colonel bars," said Mangold. "So?"

"So he's ripped off the sleeves and cut up the uniform. Desecrated it. Several of the other men are wearing pieces of IF uniforms as well. Also ripped and mutilated. Like badges of honor. Like tokens of kills they've made in battle."

"We already knew they had killed marines," said Mangold. "What's your point?"

"These yellow uniforms," said Imala. "They're not from the Fleet. Look."

She tapped the display and used her fingertips to zoom forward on the frozen image, focusing it on the back of a man in a yellow jacket, where the word MINETEK was stenciled across his back.

"Minetek," said Mangold. "Defense contractor. One of Juke Limited's big competitors. So Khalid and his goons

raided a Minetek ship, killed the crew, and took their uniforms. So what?"

"There's a Minetek facility out here," said Imala. "An old shipbuilding depot. Not far. Couple weeks out. I saw it on Rena's nav charts."

"She's right," said Rena.

"But it's no longer in operation," said Imala. "Minetek moved all their shipbuilding efforts closer to Luna at the start of the war. They were too exposed out here, too much hazard pay for the union members. Even if the Fleet provided security, the company couldn't afford to keep the place in operation, not with so many other second-tier corporations and miners rushing for the Belt. For a shipyard to function, you need raw materials from asteroids. And a lot of them. Without the resources, you've got nothing to build with."

"So this Minetek facility is abandoned?" said Mangold.

"Completely," said Imala. "They couldn't sustain business this far out anymore, not without a robust supply chain feeding them building materials."

"And you know all this because?" said Mangold.

"I worked in shipping and trade before the first war," said Imala. "I was an auditor. Tracking corporate trends and financial models was part of my job. There are trade journals."

"That you still read?" said Mangold. "Voluntarily?"

"That's where Khalid is," said Imala. "Has to be. He'd have the entire structure to himself and all the equipment and tools he'd need to retrofit his ship with all the Fleet tech he's stolen. That's why he has such sophisticated weapons and powerful thrusters and heavy shielding on his ship. Because he's parked at an abandoned shipbuilding depot."

"And you've made all these elaborate assumptions because a few pirates are wearing old Minetek jumpsuits?"

said Mangold. "They could have gotten those jumpsuits from anywhere."

"Minetek's corporate colors are red and white," said Imala. "If those jumpsuits had come off a Minetek ship, they'd be red and white. Company branding guidelines would demand it. Yellow jumpsuits are a SOSA requirement for working around big dangerous bots and equipment."

"You lost me," said Mangold. "SOSA?"

"Space Occupational Safety Administration," said Imala. "Rules for corporations. Like you have to wear a hardhat at a construction site. Yellow Minetek jumpsuits would only be at that depot. Why else would Khalid, one of the most notorious pirates in the system, be all the way out here? To hit that ship?" She gestured at the mining ship on the display terminal. "A two-decade-old piece of junk? No, this was a stop on his way home. An easy kill. A gift to his crew. He stumbled upon this ship en route to his hideout, and he played cat and mouse with it for his amusement."

Captain Mangold considered and then nodded. "Okay. Fine. We pass this on to the Fleet and let them handle it."

"The Minetek facility isn't back toward the Fleet," said Imala. "It's in the other direction, farther out in the K Belt."

"In the direction we're already supposed to be going," said Rena. "More or less."

Mangold shook his head. "No. I made this clear. This isn't our op. We have a mission. I've got no problem gathering intel, but we're not infuriating CentCom further by going after Khalid and getting ourselves killed. Our war is with the Formics, not with some Somali butcher."

"Owanu is right," said Imala. "We are the Fleet out here. Us. No one else. If we don't do anything no one will."

"You have an infant, Imala," said Mangold. "Do you

really want to push this? Because do you know what someone like Khalid will do to a child?"

"Of course I know," said Imala. "This vid tells me everything." She tapped at the screen and it zoomed out again. "Look at this image. Look beyond the crazies with the rifles and instead at the people behind them, all holding their hands up in surrender. I haven't counted them, but I see at least twelve adults and eight children. Khalid took four women with him. The three women who survived aren't even in this image because they're hiding somewhere. My guess, the three children who survived are hiding somewhere else too. Because I don't see them here either. What I do see is about twenty innocent people, including women and children. The only faces I recognize are the two men we rescued, who are here on the end of this line. And I'm guessing the only reason they're alive is because of their position in this line. They were last. And Khalid let them live because he wanted his vid of violence porn broadcast to the world. So I can play this vid, but do we really need to watch it? Do we need to witness Khalid go down this line and murder these people one by one while his drugged-up cronies cheer him on? Because if we're going to do nothing, then we should at least watch these people be massacred so we know good and well what we're doing nothing about."

Captain Mangold was quiet for a long moment. Finally, he said, "I know all of you are angry. I'm angry too. But this man, if he is in fact at this shipbuilding depot, is in a fortified position, with weaponry greater than our own. With troops in greater numbers than our own. With hostages. That's a no-win situation. We don't come out of that with a victory. We don't come out of that at all."

"And the marines on this ship?" said Imala. "Sergeant Lefevre, the others. All special ops. All hardened, disciplined soldiers who believe in something greater than themselves. All the most elite and well trained the Fleet

has produced. If we show them this vid, what will *they* say?"

"They'll say whatever the hell I tell them to say," said Captain Mangold.

"You better be sure of that," said Imala. "Because whether they see this vid or not, they'll know what's on it. They've been helping the survivors all day. They know what they lost. They know what kind of man Khalid is. He is the opposite breed of man from them, the other end of the spectrum, the kind of man that made Lefevre put on a uniform in the first place. He is injustice and cruelty and evil. And if we roll over and do nothing, you can be sure Sergeant Lefevre and every other marine under your command will remember that. The fact that we let a man like that go, with female hostages, will burn in our marines' memories. And when we reach the Formic ship, and the lives of those marines are in your hands, awaiting your orders, that memory will bubble to the surface, right when you need their loyalty and trust and service the most. They'll remember."

"You're trying to blackmail me," said Mangold.

"Not at all," said Imala. "I'm doing what I told you I would do. I'm telling you the truth. If you don't believe me, call Sergeant Lefevre in here and put the question to him. Ask him if we should find this Khalid or not."

"Lefevre isn't the captain of this ship," said Mangold. "I am. For a reason. It is my job to consider these decisions strategically. To consider how they will affect the mission."

"And that's what I'm trying to articulate," said Imala. "Do nothing, and there are consequences to the mission. Help, and there are consequences to the mission. No, we can't deviate from the mission to answer every act of inhumanity. But we also can't ignore inhumanity, if we want marines to believe in the mission and in your com-

mand. I am not the captain, and I'm grateful for it. That burden is yours."

Captain Mangold closed his eyes and exhaled. Rena and Imala and Owanu watched him.

When he opened his eyes again, he turned to Rena. "Where exactly is this depot?"

CHAPTER 14

Hegemon

Prior to the creation of the Hegemony, most governments of Earth were hindered by partisanship, corruption, the blatant and selfish pursuit of power by those in office, or all of the above. These barriers to good government obstructed the passage of common-sense legislation and resulted in greater deficits, greater division, and greater suffering among the populace.

With the arrival of the Formics and the survival of the human race hanging in the balance, Earth could no longer abide deadlocked, corrupt governance. Hence, the Hegemony adopted a two-chambered legislature and executive branch to unify the nations of Earth and to govern more efficiently to better meet the demands of war.

The Hegemony Congress is the larger of the two legislative houses. It grants one seat per nation. The smaller house is the Hegemony Council, containing representatives from only nations with a population over 100 million. At its inception, the Council had nineteen seats.

Members of the Council are called Consuls. Acts of the Council are Consular. The Hegemon is elected by the Council. There is never a popular vote or election

for any of these offices. All are appointed by national governments.

Legislation originates in the Council, where it is debated and voted upon. Congress can veto a bill with a 55% vote, but only for three months while the Council reconsiders. After the Council passes a bill for the third time, it cannot be vetoed by Congress, but it can be vetoed by the Hegemon. The Council needs a 60% vote to override. If it is vitally needed legislation, then the Hegemon can break the Congress's veto and put the bill into effect. But only for a year, at which time Congress must approve it by simple majority or the law ceases to be valid.

The executive branch consists of the Hegemon and the ministries, headed by Ministers, who have sweeping powers under the control of the Hegemon, who appoints them with simple majority approval from the Council.

—Demosthenes, *A History of the Formic Wars,* Vol. 2

Lem followed the instructions on his wrist pad and flew his skimmer to a secluded private docking tower in the industrial district in Imbrium. A pair of Hegemony Secret Security agents greeted him at the gate and escorted him through a checkpoint, where Lem was scanned, frisked, and pronounced clear for entry. A second pair of agents escorted Lem down an escalator to where a subsurface tube car was waiting. "My instructions didn't say anything about a tube car," said Lem.

"I can't speak to your instructions, sir," said an agent. "I can only speak to mine. If you would be so kind, please." He gestured for Lem to board.

The agents remained on the platform as Lem stepped into the car, strapped in, and shot away. Ten minutes later, after multiple forks and sidetracks, the tube car arrived

at an underground platform adorned with the seal of the Hegemony. Lem had lost all sense of direction by now. He was clearly outside the city limits, but he had no idea where exactly.

The tube car slid open, and Lem stepped out. The station was simple in its design—gray concrete, exposed moon-rock walls. But the polished steel door into the facility opposite the platform looked like the entrance to some impenetrable fortress, the bunker to end all bunkers, capable of withstanding a nuclear blast. Father was clearly taking no chances, and if the Formics ever did invade Luna, this would be the place to be. It made Lem wonder how many secret facilities Father had built for himself. The tracks leading here had branched off in multiple directions, and each of those tracks led somewhere.

Nice work, Father. Even if the Formics win the war, perhaps some small segment of the human race could survive in your concrete box here.

Lem approached the door, where six armed IF marines in full battle suits were standing guard, their faces concealed behind IF-blue visorless helmets, daring anyone to enter. Lem noticed that each marine carried a Skalpell FG19 slaser rifle designed by a German arms manufacturer that had beat out Juke Limited for the contract. Lem had felt stung by the loss, but the Germans deserved the win. Their slaser had better suit integration, faster processing, more accurate targeting, and better heat control. You win some, you lose some.

A small section of the door slid open, and a woman in a conservative business suit stepped out and greeted Lem with a handshake. "Welcome, Mr. Jukes. If you would follow me, please. The Hegemon is ready to receive you."

Lem fell into step behind her and smiled to himself. *The Hegemon is ready to receive you.* As if Father were some grand sultan whom his people were forced to consider half mortal, half god. Careful, Father. Enemies al-

ready wait in the shadows with knives drawn. Don't give them another reason to strike.

Lem also thought it noteworthy that the woman hadn't said, "*Your father* is ready to receive you." It was the *Hegemon*. As if to remind Lem that there would be no air of informality here. No chumming it up with dear old dad. Ukko Jukes may be your blood relation, but here in these hallowed halls of government he is first and foremost the supreme ruler of Earth.

It amused Lem. Does this woman actually think I *enjoy* seeing my father? Or that he enjoys seeing me? She hardly needed to set any rules against nepotistic treatment. If there was one rule between Lem and Ukko Jukes it was that all stabbing must happen in full view of the other. As a familial courtesy. None of this behind-the-back business.

Like the platform, the interior of the compound was minimal in its design. White walls, bright lights, the occasional bust of someone important on a short column. A government building. Functional, traditional, with that new building smell, as if the construction crews had just gathered their tools and left the building. Lem and his escort saw no one as they moved through the halls, for which Lem was grateful. The main offices of the Hegemony in Imbrium were filled with diplomats and dignitaries, lobbyists and journalists, and Lem had worried that in coming to meet with Father he might be ambushed by some random journalist hungry for a sound bite for that night's broadcast. To see no one was bliss.

The woman led Lem to a small but ornate dining room with empty tables lit by lamplight. She assured Lem that the Hegemon would join him momentarily, but it was an hour before Father arrived with four security agents. Father sat opposite Lem and shook out his napkin while the agents took up positions around the room, each with a holstered weapon beneath his suitcoat.

"I've been waiting for an hour, Father," said Lem. "Is that standard for your guests, or am I getting the special treatment?"

"Never arrive when you're scheduled to," said Father. "That's the first rule of office. It throws off the plans of your would-be assassins."

"I'd laugh, but I'm not sure you're joking," said Lem.

"The Polemarch and Strategos take the threats made against my life very seriously. They insist I have constant security."

Lem gestured at the armed agents. "These aren't Fleet marines."

"I use my own people," said Father. "Safer that way. Bringing in marines might invite wolves into the sheepfold."

"You don't trust the Polemarch and Strategos?"

"I don't trust anyone," said Father. "And certainly not the Fleet. And especially not the admiralty at CentCom. Most of them would love to see my head on a platter."

"There's a pleasant image," said Lem.

"The war is going poorly, Lem. That makes the admiralty look like the buffoons they are. They need someone to blame. I'm an easy target."

"So fire them," said Lem. "You're the Hegemon. The commander in chief. Send the dirty admirals packing and elevate those who can actually lead."

"Think, Lem. If I fire an admiral, let's say a Russian admiral from CentCom, then I invite the ire and condemnation of the entire Russian people, who would accuse me of impeding their country's participation in strategic command. They'd claim I was favoring the West, and all the many simmering plans for a Hegemony coup would be set into motion. I'd be throwing liquid hydrogen onto an already fearsome fire."

"So replace the bad Russian admiral with a good Russian admiral," said Lem. "You can hardly be accused of

emasculating Russia if you fill the vacancy with someone else from their country."

"And what is a 'good' Russian admiral?" said Father. "One who has greater loyalty to the Hegemony than to his own country? Assuming I could find such a person—which I can't—but even if I could find such a person, he'd be labeled a Hegemony puppet the instant he accepted the appointment. And even if he were someone the Russian people and oligarchs and fellow Russian commanders would readily acknowledge as a good choice for the post, they would swiftly condemn him as soon as I made the announcement. They can't allow me that victory. It would disrupt the narrative they're promulgating."

"Which is?"

"That Ukko Jukes is unfit to continue as Hegemon and must be removed from office. That every decision I make is flawed. Every choice a mistake. That is their game, Lem. To ruin me. Particularly the Russians. They would gladly throw their finest general into the flames if it meant striking a political blow against me and turning public opinion in their favor, which would, in turn, increase their chances of seizing my post. Which is of course their ultimate goal. To put a Russian in as Hegemon. Thus, nothing I do, however beneficial it may be to Russia, will satisfy them. They can't afford to be satisfied."

"Sokolov informed me you were resigning," said Lem. "It sounds like he was mistaken."

"Of course I'm resigning," said Father. "I'm making the announcement in a matter of days. The Hegemony Council will choose my replacement as soon as possible."

"Then I'm confused," said Lem. "If you resign, aren't you giving the Russians, or whoever, the golden opportunity they've been waiting for? A chance to make one of their own the supreme ruler of Earth?"

"My appointment was always intended to be temporary,"

said Father. "Now that the Hegemony Congress is established, now that the Council is in place and writing legislation, the house is established. My work is done. I was given this office because the world needed to build a fleet. Who better to give it to them than me? I've done that. It's time for someone better suited for wartime leadership to take this role."

Lem kept his expression flat. "I see. Well, that is noble of you, Father, to recognize the limitations of your own abilities. Such humility will certainly be part of your legacy. I wonder if we might speak in private."

Ukko Jukes dismissed his security detail, and the armed men stepped from the room.

"Let's stop the charade, Father," said Lem. "What's the play here? You wouldn't forfeit a seat of power unless there was a bigger seat elsewhere."

"What could be bigger than the Hegemon?"

"Spare me, Father. I know you. What am I not seeing?"

"I'm doing what must be done, Lem. Even if we win this war with the Formics, which is unlikely, I'm not sure we will win the war that follows. My leaving the Hegemony will hopefully prevent that war from happening. Or at the very least, minimize the fallout and casualties."

"What war?" said Lem. "A war with Russia?"

"A war with everyone, Lem. A world war. Unlike any war we've seen before because the actors will have IF weapons from space that can send us back to the Stone Age. This should be obvious. This war is already brewing. It will be a conflict between those nations that wish to see us continue under Hegemony rule and those nations that will insist on a return of full national sovereignty. Consider the United States. They've seen their position of power and influence in the world diminish under Hegemony rule. While at the same time, second- and third-world nations have grown in strength and prominence. Brazil, Mexico, India, Egypt. We have the war to thank

for that, a global economic and technological boom. The strong have remained strong, but now the traditionally weak are gaining in strength as well. The United States doesn't particularly like progress that isn't their own. If anyone should be in charge, they say, it's us. Do you know how much it irks the Americans that the Hegemon of Earth is a Finn? It's a great injustice to them."

"You're a man of Luna," said Lem. "A man without a nation. That's why you were appointed."

"Finnish by birth and thus a Finn in the eyes of my critics. No one wants to see a Finn in charge, Lem. Especially not the Americans."

"The Americans have a seat in Congress and in the Council," said Lem. "They have far more power in the Hegemony than most nations."

"True," said Father. "But they aren't the king of the hill. A damn Finn is. Imagine their horror if a Russian became Hegemon."

"Like Sokolov," said Lem.

"Yes," said Father, "like Sokolov. Or some other autocrat like him. Because even if we were to dispose of Sokolov, there are ten thousand just like him who would rise up and take his place. And if such a man were to seize the office of Hegemon, it would be disastrous for the U.S. and Canada and all of Europe. I can't let that happen."

"But again," said Lem, "if you resign, isn't that the opportunity that Sokolov and the Russians want?"

"Sokolov doesn't have a prayer of being chosen by the Council," said Father. "I have the Council's assurance on that."

"Are you sure?" said Lem. "Sokolov isn't an idiot. He wouldn't be secretly campaigning for the post if he didn't think it attainable."

"Sokolov *is* an idiot, which is why I was so terribly disappointed to see him humiliate you in public. Really, Lem, you should have known better. Neither he nor his

deputy ministers should have been in that room. We keep our enemies close, but not that close."

"So this vote by the Council is a sham," said Lem. "You know who the Council will choose because you've secretly made it a stipulation of your resignation. They have to choose your man or you're not leaving."

"What makes you think it's a man?" said Father.

"A woman?" said Lem. "Who?"

"Sharon Solomon."

"The American president?"

"She'll resign as president to accept the role of Hegemon once she's chosen. I thought she'd be the obvious choice. An American, Jewish, and a former U.S. marine. Terminal rank: major. So she has military cred, not to mention an impeccable record as a former U.S. senator. Plus she has broad support across Europe, East Asia, and much of South America. Africa and the Middle East are problematic, as is Russia, but that would be the case with any American."

"Sokolov will hate the idea," said Lem.

"The Americans won't," said Father. "It would restore their standing as the leader of the free world. Plus, they're the largest financial contributor to the Hegemony and thus the country most invested in seeing it succeed. Most importantly, with an American as Hegemon, they'll be more likely to keep and maintain a global coalition of support for the Hegemony. That coalition is crucial. If alliances break down, war results."

"And you think Solomon has a better chance of preventing war than you do?" said Lem.

"She's a seasoned diplomat. Respected among world leaders. I'm an outsider. A businessman, brash and inflexible. As far as diplomats are concerned, I'm oil to their water. The alliance within the Hegemony exists because of the united effort to defeat the Formics. Not because of me. The instant the Formics are out of the picture, it will

be a power scramble. And besides, once this war is over, I'll be needed elsewhere."

"Where exactly?"

"We can't allow the Formics to return a third time," said Father. "If there's a third invasion, it must be us invading them, destroying them on their home planet, ensuring that they never threaten us again."

Lem scoffed. "Us go to the Formics? Father, we don't have the tech for interstellar flight. We're not even remotely close to their speeds and firepower. We barely have a fleet as is. We're getting our asses kicked in the Belt. Plus, we don't even know where the Formics come from. How could we possibly stage an invasion?"

Ukko Jukes leaned back in his chair and regarded Lem with a look of disappointment. "I gave you several years with the company, Lem. I left you with capable people. Some of the brightest minds in the world. My hope was that you would somehow develop vision, that you would break out of that finite way of thinking you've developed. That you would think and act like a CEO. In some ways you've done well. You've grown the company. You've built much of the fleet. But for all those successes, you still lack vision. There *will* be a third invasion, Lem. It will require a different fleet, one built for interstellar travel, with weapons of mass destruction the likes of which the world has never seen. Weapons that can wipe out an advanced civilization like the Formics. We haven't developed that tech yet. It will likely take decades before we do. But it won't happen if military contractors don't have vision, if they can't do what simple minds consider impossible."

It took a moment to realize what Father was saying. Then it all became clear. All of Father's planning, all of the political maneuvers. "You're taking back the company," Lem said. "You're leaving the Hegemony to oust me as CEO."

"You've made yourself a laughingstock, Lem. You allowed Sokolov, a half-witted toad of a man, to humiliate you before the world. You brought foolish designs to the Hegemony and lost on contracts that we should have easily won. You invested millions of credits in a charity that is leaking capital like a sieve and wasting our resources."

"*Our* resources?" said Lem. "The company is no longer yours, Father. You sold your stake. You have no say in whatever path the company pursues."

"It's already in motion, Lem. Solomon will see to it that Juke Limited will build the new fleet for the third invasion. That will guarantee the company's growth and prosperity for decades to come."

Lem was on his feet. "You made a deal with Sharon Solomon? You give her the office of Hegemon, and she gives you all the wealth in the world?"

"You will continue as a member of the board," said Father. "I'm not throwing you out. This isn't a coup. You'll graciously welcome me back as CEO once I leave the Hegemony. Global confidence in the company will be restored, and we'll go about saving the world together. That is, assuming we don't lose this war and all die anyway."

Lem shook his head. "Unbelievable. You think that's how this works, Father? Is that what the Hegemony has taught you? That you can simply make demands and have everyone around you rush to make it so? I have made the company what it is. We have grown more in three years than any other corporation in the history of the world."

"Yes, with contracts that the Hegemony awarded you," said Father. "My administration has built the company as much as you have, Lem. If not more so. Without me, you would be nothing. And without me in the company now, you are nothing as well."

"I'm the CEO, Father."

"Are you sure about that, Lem?"

Lem froze. The rest of Father's plan unfolded before

him like a giant map. Father had brought Lem out to this secluded facility, forced him to take transportation Lem didn't control. Lem was trapped here, locked here. He couldn't rush back to company headquarters even if he wanted to.

"The board just finished their emergency meeting," said Father. "I received the message from Norja Ramdakan before I came in here. You've been removed as CEO. None of that will be made public, of course. Once I make the announcement concerning my departure from the Hegemony, you'll give a press conference wherein you'll announce that you informed the board that you wish to voluntarily step aside so that I might return to lead the company. A gracious move the board will accept. You'll make the announcement joyfully, as nothing makes you happier than to have your father back where he belongs. Your speech at the press conference will be stipulated in the contract the legal team is now preparing. And before you storm out of here and resign in a fury, consider your future, Lem. This way, my way, is best for you. It allows you to save face and your stake in the company. You deserve that."

Lem said nothing.

"Or there's another option," said Father. "You could accept a gracious buyout offer from me and retire with more money than most people could ever dream of. You'd never have to see me again, which I know is an attractive proposition. You could buy an island somewhere, find a wife. I only ask that you don't pursue this Buddhist woman. You can do better than that."

Lem left without another word. He passed the security detail out in the corridor and wondered if Father had brought them along in case Lem tried something when Father revealed his plan. What a headline that would be: DISGRACED CEO STRANGLES HEGEMON IN SECRET LUNAR BUNKER.

The corridors were still empty. No one tried to stop him. Lem found his way back to the platform, but of course the tube car was gone. Father had no doubt arranged that as well. Lem looked around for a control box, something that might hold a switch, a button, a lever, some means to call the car back. There wasn't one. The platform was empty.

Lem moved to the edge of the platform and considered the track. Could he walk back? Was there enough room beside the track for him to fit between the tunnel wall and the tube car? Or would the tube car crush him if it came? And even if he could walk, would he know the way? He was more likely to get lost in the dark.

"Mr. Jukes?"

Lem turned around. One of the marines who had been standing at attention had removed his helmet and come up behind him. "Can I be of service, sir?" the marine asked. "You look like you're considering walking that track. That's not a good idea, sir."

Lem kept his rage in check and calmly asked for the car. The marine called it back easily by tapping a command on his wrist pad. It arrived a few minutes later. Lem asked how to program the car to return to the docking tower, and the marine typed in the command.

"It's strange that no one escorted you out, sir," said the marine. "Your father's aides normally do that with visitors. Sorry about the mix-up."

"There was no mix-up," said Lem. "Thanks for your help."

It took Lem over an hour to get back to his skimmer and fly to corporate headquarters. As the minutes passed and the scene played again and again in his mind, Lem's anger only intensified. Father had orchestrated the whole thing: the emergency meeting of the board when they knew Lem was indisposed, a handshake deal for a second fleet, the arrangement with the American president.

Even the company's lawyers were in on it, drafting Lem's speech for the press. It was all so . . . Father. So callously, predictably, deceitfully Father. Lem was angry at himself more than anyone, for being foolish enough to believe for an instant that Father would show genuine concern for him amid all the bad press. Come to the Hegemony, Lem. Let's strategize, Lem. I'm uneasy about all this, Lem. How had Lem allowed himself to believe it? He should have recognized instantly that Father had something damaging in mind, something cutting, something condescending, some slight. He should have known that Father would cut Lem off at the knees.

And not only Father, but the board as well. The people Lem had paid handsomely and trusted.

He could understand betrayal from the longtime board members, the ones Father had put on the board. Their loyalty was to Ukko more than to Lem. Except perhaps for Benyawe. She and Lem had no relationship outside of work, but Lem had considered her a friend. Or loyal, at least. Lem couldn't believe that she would toss him aside. Not after everything they had endured. Had the board given her false information? Maybe Benyawe hadn't been invited to the meeting. Maybe they suspected Benyawe would object, and so they had shut her out.

Lem went straight to the boardroom. It was late in the evening. If there had been an emergency meeting when Father had claimed, everyone would be long gone by now. But he had to see if there was evidence of a meeting. Or perhaps Lem had allies after all, and they had rejected his ouster and were still in the boardroom, debating their next move.

But if that were true, why hadn't Lem received any messages on his wrist pad? Warnings, condolences, reassurances, statements of loyalty?

Lem entered the boardroom. It wasn't empty. Across

the room a white-haired man sat alone at the head of the table where Lem normally sat. Lem didn't recognize him.

"Hello, Mr. Jukes. My name is Oliver Crowe."

Lem kept his distance, suddenly uneasy. "You'll forgive me, Mr. Crowe. But I believe you're sitting in my seat."

"It *was* your seat," said Crowe. "Two hours ago. I asked my contacts on the board not to send you any formal announcement just yet. I wanted us to talk first. But here, why don't you sit in this chair for old time's sake, and I'll sit somewhere else." He moved to get up.

"Keep the seat," said Lem, not moving.

Oliver Crowe smiled pleasantly and sat back down. "I was hoping you and I would meet under different circumstances, Lem, but your father has set things in motion now."

"Who are you?" said Lem.

"An ally," said Crowe. "I'm not a danger to you. You need not be afraid."

"Why should I be afraid?" said Lem. "A stranger has somehow bypassed our security and given orders to members of the board that they felt obligated to obey, suggesting leverage, power, and influence. Nothing strange about that at all."

Crowe smiled again, nonthreateningly, almost cheerily. "You won't take this as a compliment, Lem, but I do intend it as one: You're very much like your father. Not just in physical features, of course. But in temperament. You're not as taciturn, not as unyielding, but you still have that Jukes fire about you. Which I find admirable."

The man was playing with him. Dancing around the questions. Lem was tempted to call security, but curiosity won out.

"You know my father?" said Lem.

Crowe laughed good-naturedly. "Goodness, I've known Ukko Jukes for longer than you've been alive.

We fell out of contact, as acquaintances sometimes do. He went his way. I went mine. But I watched him closely over the years. Now the war has brought us together once again. I'm the director of ASH, the intelligence arm of the Hegemony. I report to your father."

"So members of my board are agents of ASH?" Lem said. "I'd ask you to tell me their names so I might take appropriate action, but I doubt you'll do so."

"If I told you all our secrets, Lem, we wouldn't be very good at intelligence, would we?"

"What do you want?" Lem asked.

"A formal alliance. I need your help and you need mine." Crowe pulled an index card from his pocket. "The thirteen names on this list are all employees of Juke Limited in your finance department who are guilty of criminal activity, including wire fraud, bank fraud, bribery, and money laundering. We have more than enough evidence for prosecutors to secure indictments and have police take every one of these individuals into custody. Can you picture that image in your mind, Mr. Jukes? Thirteen Juke employees in a line, hands cuffed behind their backs, heads hung low with shame, as they're led into prison? Can you imagine how that would play on the nets?"

"I can imagine some non-flattering headlines, yes."

"The press would eat it up," said Crowe. "Especially after all the fuss you've made in the news regarding Wila. This would be chapter two in the chronicles of your poor leadership. Confidence in the company would collapse. IF contracts might disappear. The people of Earth, whose taxes fund this company, would call for your head. Your stock would freefall."

"You're forgetting that I'm no longer CEO," said Lem. "The fate of this company is no longer my concern."

"Oh, you care very much about this company and its people," said Crowe. "You can't convince me otherwise."

"So you have dirt on some people in my accounting department," said Lem. "If your intent is to blackmail me, Mr. Crowe, you're wasting my time. Not my company, not my problem."

"You misunderstand me, Lem. I'm not here to threaten you. I don't care about the snakes in your finance department. What I *do* care about are the members of the Fleet who cooperate with your finance department and who use threats and extortion to make your employees silently comply. That's who I'm after, Lem, the bad guys in the International Fleet who are using their association with Juke Limited and other contractors to pocket all kinds of kickbacks. Admirals, commanders, undersecretaries. We don't need those bad apples in the Fleet."

"The International Fleet has a Judge Advocate General's Corps," said Lem. "If you have incriminating evidence about a member of the Fleet, I suggest you take it to JAG and let them do their job. I thought they would have taught you that in spy school."

"If JAG were not corrupt to the core, I might do just that," said Crowe. "But many of the judges are not the squeaky-clean white knights of justice we'd like to think they are. Your friend Mazer Rackham can attest to that."

"That breaks my heart to hear, Mr. Crowe," said Lem. "You have my condolences. I fail to see what that has to do with me."

"The International Fleet is full of bad apples," said Crowe. "Along the supply chains, commanding warships, sitting at big desks at CentCom. Officers who by their incompetence or their criminal activity endanger the good men and women under their command, and by so doing endanger us all. This is a war we can't afford to lose, Lem. And I fear these bad apples will lead us to ruin. You've seen it yourself. Admirals who have no business commanding a squad of marines, much less a fleet

of ships. These people need to be removed, Lem. And you're the man to help me remove them."

"You'll need to clarify, Mr. Crowe, because what you're suggesting sounds a lot like treason."

"I need funding, Lem. Secret funding. Funding that I can't account for on official government documents. Funding that a man of your enormous wealth and re- sources can provide."

Lem laughed. "This is a sales call? Mr. Crowe, I think you've been misinformed. I'm not in the habit of giving my wealth away to men plotting secret assassinations."

"Men can be removed a number of ways," said Crowe. "What matters is that they're removed." He took a round disc the size of a hockey puck from his pocket and slid it across the surface of the table. It stopped near Lem, and a small holoprojection of an IF warship appeared in the air above it.

"This is the IF Apache," said Crowe. "An A-class fast combat support vessel. Captained by a Harrison Poin- dexter. An American. Captain Poindexter won his ap- pointment because his father is an aluminum tycoon with friends in the Hegemony Congress. Daddy wanted little Harrison to captain a ship, and Daddy got what he wanted. Sadly, the crew of the Apache didn't get what they wanted, which was a captain with any sense of command and an ounce of courage. At the first sign of trouble, Poindexter abandoned two other warships in desperate need of his weaponry and support, assistance that Poindexter could have easily provided. Six hundred and fourteen crewmembers on those two other ships lost their lives as a result. Poindexter later abandoned three platoons of his asteroid commandos because he thought a Formic warship was nearing the asteroid where they were positioned. The object on approach proved to be an IF recon satellite, not a Formic ship. But Poindexter didn't

hang around long enough to find that out. The twenty-seven commandos he left on that asteroid all died of asphyxiation once their oxygen ran out."

Crowe tapped at his wrist pad, and the holoprojection above the puck disappeared. "I'll do the math for you, Lem. Six hundred and forty-one marines have lost their lives because of one idiotic, spineless, incompetent commander. Had someone like myself removed Poindexter from his post before the fact, all of those marines would still be alive. I can tell you twelve stories just like that one off the top of my head. Bad commanders who have needlessly lost lives. I have a list of other commanders who are equally ill-suited for their posts, and who will almost certainly lead their marines to ruin. That's our dilemma, Lem. The International Fleet is rotting from the inside out, and the entire world will pay the consequences. I need someone who can help me prune away the bad fruit and ensure the most competent men and women are leading this war. Not the nephews of senators and business leaders. Not the backstabbing sycophants, who claw their way to command. But the real leaders, like your friend Mazer Rackham, who are sidelined by careerist imbeciles and kept as far from command as possible. I need someone brave enough and smart enough to help us see this through."

Lem steepled his fingers together and nodded. "I see. Okay. Let me make sure I understand you clearly here. You want me to give you, a man I've never before met, a large portion of my personal fortune to fund your top-secret hit squad with a kill list of IF commanders that you, for whatever reason, don't deem worthy and up to snuff. And in return for my financing this treasonous endeavor, which would almost certainly lead to me being tried and executed, you graciously agree not to inform the press that I've got some bad apples in my accounting department? Am I catching the gist of your offer here,

Mr. Crowe? Because gosh, I've got to tell you, as much as that sounds like a humdinger of a sweet deal, I'm going to have to give you a hard pass and say thanks but no thanks."

Oliver Crowe stood and buttoned his blazer. "You've had a difficult day, Lem. I don't expect you to see clearly right now. I'm merely planting the seed in your mind. And in the meantime, I invite you to continue to watch the news about this war—and by that I mean the secret news, not what the Fleet press office is sugarcoating and broadcasting to the world. Not the propaganda. But the real events, the real defeats, the real injustices committed by dangerous people in power who are leading us to our extinction. When you hear those stories, Lem, you'll remember this conversation and that you did nothing to keep that tragedy from happening."

"I'll do my best to sleep at night," said Lem.

Crowe smiled. "Here's the rest of my offer, Lem. I'm not looking solely for a donation. I'm also looking for an agent, someone I can trust here inside the company now that your Father is returning."

Lem almost laughed. "You want me to spy on my own father?"

"Why not? Your father has been spying on you from the moment you took this job. His informants and saboteurs are all over this company."

"Saboteurs?" said Lem.

"People who have frustrated your efforts because your father ordered them to do so. Maybe you didn't win a contract you should have, or maybe production was delayed, or maybe HR problems leaked to the press. I'm not floating conspiracy theories here, Lem. I have evidence for every one of these claims. Your father may have resigned as CEO when he became Hegemon, but his control over this company never went away. He has people in every department, people who appear to report to you but who

in truth report to him. The board choosing to oust you is all the evidence you need."

"Then you don't want an alliance with me," said Lem. "You want an alliance with the man who has the real power and resources to help you. My father."

Crowe shook his head. "Wouldn't work. Your father is likely to continue the company's relationship with bad actors inside the International Fleet if it benefits the company financially. I can't trust him to be ethical in this matter."

"You think assassinations are more ethical?" said Lem.

"As I said, Lem, there are many ways to remove dangerous people from power. They don't all require a laser to the back of the head."

"But some of them might," said Lem. "That's what you're telling me."

"Your father has already made plans with the future Hegemon that will secure this company's dominance for decades to come. Ukko Jukes intends to build a new fleet and take the war to the Formics' home planet. For that your father will need to be married completely with the Fleet, working with both the good and the bad apples to design, test, and build the tech required. This effort will require more money than the world has ever gathered, more even than the price of this current war. Money on that scale breeds the worst in men. Your father can't help us clean up the International Fleet. He'll be too busy corrupting it. Not directly, perhaps. He's not foolish enough to openly engage bad actors. But he won't have to. They'll come to him."

"I thought you said you reported to my father. This is how you serve him, by enlisting his son to spy on him, by making back-alley deals to secure secret funding?"

"I serve the free people of Earth, Lem. Not your father. I'm giving you an opportunity to do the same."

Oliver Crowe tapped his wrist pad, and the puck slid back across the table to him. He picked it up and tucked it in his pocket. "I'll leave you with this, Lem. Four names. Colonel Dietrich, Captain Mangold, Captain Hoebeck, and Captain Wu. These names mean nothing to you. But each of them is a poor choice for his post. Each of them will likely lead the men and women under his command to their deaths. That fact also means nothing to you until I tell you who these men command. They're people you *do* know. Good people. People who deserve to survive this war. Mazer Rackham, Imala Bootstamp, Victor Delgado, and Wilasanee Saowaluk."

Lem tensed at hearing Wila's name.

"Yes, Lem. I know where Wila is. She's on a ship heading for the Belt. And her captain is an indignant fool and coward who will, in all likelihood, get Wila killed. When you hear of her death, and the death of these others, you'll know you did nothing to save them. I hope you can live with that."

Crowe moved for the door.

"Why is Wila going to the Belt?" said Lem.

Crowe turned back.

"She wouldn't have joined the Fleet," said Lem. "She doesn't believe in war."

"She's doing what she knows is necessary to save the human race," said Crowe. "I expect no less from you."

"And what's in it for me?" said Lem. "I give you an investment, and get nothing in return?"

"You're not investing," said Crowe. "You're donating. And once the donation is given, you don't have a right to anything. It doesn't buy you control, it doesn't buy you information. What it does buy you is victory."

"You make treason sound so noble," said Lem.

"To abandon marines on an asteroid to save your own skin is treason, Lem. To be paralyzed with indecision

when your fighter squadron is calling for additional support, that is treason. To send a junior officer with enormous potential to the front lines to die simply because you think him a threat to your position, that is treason. But don't take my word for it." He tapped his wrist pad, and Lem's own wrist pad vibrated. "I just sent you a link to a private forum on the IF intranet, where junior officers have detailed countless examples throughout the Fleet of incompetent leadership. Your friend Mazer Rackham has written anonymously about this very subject. He'll show you through his own observations what real treason looks like."

"I could turn you in to my father," said Lem. "I could have you arrested."

Crowe smiled. "You could, yes. But you won't. That's the advantage of working in intelligence, Lem. I know everything about you. I know precisely what you'll do when given an opportunity like this. I wouldn't risk revealing myself to you if I didn't. You'll give me the money I need. Have a good evening. I'm glad to have you on our side."

Crowe turned and was gone.

Lem tapped at his wrist pad and went to the IF forum. He tapped again and moved the content from his wrist pad to the projection wall. A popup included from Crowe directed Lem to several posts. Lem read them. He sat in the nearest chair and read others. He read posts from three anonymous officers, all of whom, according to Crowe's popup, were handles used by Mazer Rackham. He read rebuttals from the senior officers accused of incompetency, which only validated the accusations against them. They were fools; arrogant, blundering fools.

Lem read for hours. He had known that the IF had its share of careerists and toxic commanders, but he hadn't realized how rampant their rule had become. Crowe had

not exaggerated, if what Lem read represented the Fleet as a whole. The question was, what to do about it?

To do nothing was the safest course. At least for the time being. Father had been right. Lem could retire. With a buyout of his shares, he could live like a king somewhere. Not on an island. What was the appeal of that? But somewhere busy where money could be spent. London, perhaps. Paris. Hong Kong. The cities could be his. That is, until the Formics came.

And in that sense, doing nothing wasn't a safe course at all.

Lem checked his accounts. He could afford to liquidate some of his assets. And he had people he trusted who could move the funds through international accounts so as not to attract notice. It would be easy. And with that money he could do what needed to be done.

He turned off his wrist pad and left the boardroom. He was no longer CEO, but his security ring on his finger still gave him access to his office. The letter of resignation he wrote to the board was short. It simply stated that his father, Ukko Jukes, had informed Lem of Ukko's choice to resign as Hegemon. Upon learning of this decision, Lem was now asking that the board hold an emergency meeting to consider reinstating Father as CEO as soon as word of the Hegemon's resignation was announced. Nothing thrilled Lem more than to have his father return to the company he had built.

He pressed send.

He stood. There was nothing in his office that had any real sentimental value. And even if there were, he would leave it. Better that than to endure the humiliation of walking out with a cardboard box filled with office trinkets.

The staff that worked the late shift was waiting outside his office. Most of the women were crying. The men looked small and sheepish and embarrassed. There

would be no transition period, no passing of the torch. Lem tapped his wrist pad and gave everyone in the room a generous bonus that quickly dried the tears.

Yes, he thought. You *can* do anything with money.

Then he put his hands in his pockets and walked out the door.

CHAPTER 15

Khalid

Transcript: Special State of the Union Address to Congress; Sharon Solomon, President of the United States, Hegemon-elect, 2119

SOLOMON: Over centuries, through the might of the United States Armed Forces and through the compassion of our global humanitarian efforts, we as Americans have shown our fellow citizens of the world that our commitment to peace is not limited to our borders, that the cries of the innocent and the oppressed do not fall upon deaf ears. America has always been a nation of doers, men and women who rise up in times of peril and who rush forward in times of conflict, eager to ease suffering, ensure democracy, and preserve freedom throughout the world.

This resolve is what defines us as Americans. It is what built this nation.

I am honored that the Hegemony Council has chosen me to serve as Hegemon. I feel humbled by the kind words and support of Ukko Jukes, who has led us through these dark days of fear and sorrow. As president of the United States, I have made and kept promises to our people. Now I

make a solemn promise to all the free citizens of Earth, Luna, and throughout the solar system. I will bring to this new office the same steely resolve that defines me as an American, as well as a respect for all people of all nations, which defines me as a human being. [Applause] I give you my solemn vow, that I will do all in my power to preserve what is ours, to protect what we cherish, and to reclaim this solar system as our own. [Applause] We will not fall to the Formics. We will not yield. The human race will stand shoulder to shoulder, arm in arm, and we will crush those who threaten to take our world. [Applause]

In an abandoned Minetek shipbuilding facility deep in the Kuiper Belt, Khalid, the man of all men, the father of fear, the founder of New Somalia, brooded over the ansible. The machine had gone quiet. For months it had given Khalid immediate updates on the war. Casualty numbers, ships lost, asteroids destroyed, rear admirals promoted—information that had little relevance to Khalid, but which had made him feel important simply by having it. He had read its reports every day without fail, waiting for the IF to announce one of his conquests: a supply ship Khalid had destroyed, a shipyard he had attacked, an asteroid-mining crew he had killed. Surely the ansible would pass along such knowledge to all the other ships that were on this ansible's shared network. Surely the Fleet would acknowledge Khalid's power and presence. Surely. But the ansible had spoken of none of these things. The dogs of the Hegemony were too frightened to tell the truth of Khalid. They were too small to say his name, too weak to admit their defeat. And now, after all Khalid's waiting, the ansible had stopped saying anything at all.

"Perhaps the battery is dead," said Ibrahim. The room

they were in had once been a large break room, with vending machines and hologames and other minor entertainments. Now it was the private quarters of the ruler of New Somalia, filled with the tokens of Khalid's victories.

Khalid grunted and waved a dismissive hand. "What do you know? The ansible may not even have a battery. Perhaps it runs on a new kind of power."

Ibrahim shrugged and swiped through the screen on his tablet, a trinket he had taken off a dead Fleet navigational officer. "Perhaps. But what does it matter? Battery or not, you cannot fix it, brother. It is too complex of a machine for you."

"Do not presume to know the limits of my mind," said Khalid.

"You must explain what *presume* means," said Ibrahim. "Or use simpler words, brother. We stupid folk can't keep pace with you."

Khalid scowled. "Someday I will cut out that tongue of yours and feed it to you."

"That will be hard," said Ibrahim. "Without my tongue, how could I move the severed tongue around in my mouth to eat it properly?"

"Shut up and read your tablet," said Khalid. He leaned in close to the ansible and tried to imagine where a small battery might be housed. Behind the paneling here, perhaps? He dared not try to pull the paneling back for fear of breaking the machine. There were no screws he could see that might allow him entry anyway. But even if there was a battery there and Khalid could remove it, did he have extra batteries here on the station? The company, Minetek, which had so graciously left this facility unattended, had clearly left in a hurry. When Khalid and his men first discovered it, they had found food in the pantries and all manner of supplies and goods in the storage bins. If there were batteries, they would be in the cargo area. Somewhere.

"Why do you fuss over the device anyway?" said Ibrahim. "Let the dogs have their war. What is it to us? It gives us information we do not need. Messages for ships, reports, policy changes. This is the bark of the dogs. What use is it?"

"Someday we will do a DNA test, brother," said Khalid. "Because I cannot believe that you and I share a mother. Your intelligence came from a stone or a tree. The ansible is knowledge, Ibrahim. Knowledge is power. Power is rule."

"The slaser rifle is power," said Ibrahim. "The shields on our ship are power. The thrust of our engines is power."

"This is why you will die a fool," said Khalid. "Because you do not see and understand. The ansible is what has allowed us to identify and seize supply ships. You would not have that stupid tablet in your hands if the ansible had not informed us of vulnerable traffic lanes. We eat because of the ansible. We avoid capture because of the ansible. We survive because of the ansible."

"You are the man of men," said Ibrahim. "The ansible did not make you so. It is a tool, brother. You will rule fine without it."

Khalid wasn't so sure. Rulers only remained in power if the people under them ate well and lived free of fear. Could Khalid provide that without the ansible?

When Maja brought his supper later he told her about the ansible going silent.

"It's been upgraded," she said. "Do you not remember? The ship we took it from, the communications officer who gave it to us, he said the Fleet upgrades the ansibles every four or five months. It's been eight. The Fleet has made new ansibles now. With a new network. The network this ansible was on has been retired. It's like a knife without a blade now."

Khalid remembered now, yes. Upgrades. The IF marine *had* said that. Perhaps we should not have killed

him, thought Khalid. Perhaps he would be useful now. He could tell us how to acquire a new ansible. Or he could make some modification to this one to connect it to this new network.

"You are restless," said Maja. She was one of the few members of the crew he could speak with openly. She was his lover, his counselor, his most deadly enforcer. She had killed more marines than Ibrahim and Maydox and Breaker combined. Often with nothing more than her dagger, as she opened her victims' throats. And yet here alone with him, Khalid felt no danger from her. That had faded. She had seen what he was and the power in his rule.

She slid up next to him, embraced him, and placed her head on his shoulder.

"The ansible put me at ease," said Khalid. "It kept me confident."

"Why?" said Maja. "They were words on a screen. Words not even directed at you."

"Yes, but those words told me what the Fleet was doing, where they were focused, what they were saying."

"And you wished they had spoken of you?" said Maja.

"Yes," said Khalid. "Or so I thought. I think now perhaps not seeing my name is what put me at ease."

She lifted her head from his shoulder and looked at him. "Why?"

"Because it meant the Fleet was occupied elsewhere," said Khalid. "The words told me they were not looking for us, that we were not their concern, that we could do as we pleased."

"And now that you don't have an ansible, you worry that they are coming for us?" said Maja.

"Only a fool wouldn't worry," said Khalid.

"But the IF are deceivers," said Maja. "If they were coming for us, and they knew we had an ansible, they would send us misinformation. They would keep the

ansible active and feed us mundane intel so that we wouldn't become suspicious. They would not silence it. That would put us on alert. They would try to deceive us."

"Perhaps," said Khalid. "But I do not like it. When the Fleet chatters about supplies and ships and deaths, I think, they are not looking for Khalid. Now I am not sure what they speak of."

"They speak of the same things," said Maja. "Their talk is no different. No one is coming here for us, Khalid. The Fleet must focus on the Formics. We are safe here."

"Until the food runs out," said Khalid. "Until the men get hungry for more juice."

She frowned. "Why do you sour so? You rule this country."

He scoffed. "A country of less than sixty men. That is no country."

"I do not like this talk," said Maja. "You should not speak so. We are New Somalia. No one rules us here."

"They may not rule us," said Khalid. "But we must know our enemy. The Hegemon has resigned. Without the ansible, how am I to know who the new Hegemon is?"

"What difference does it make?" said Maja. "What is the Hegemony to us? We are not bound to their laws and taxes. We are not subjects of the Hegemon. They are several billion klicks away."

"Distance does not matter," said Khalid. "This war will not last forever, Maja. And when it ends, what hope is there for us? If the Formics win, there will be no world, no supplies. We will starve out here, or they will hunt us down. Either way, we die quickly. And if the Hegemon wins, the corporates will come back and drive us out. We cannot hold this place. And then where will we go?"

"Wherever we want," said Maja. "If the Fleet wins the war, we will continue to do what we do. There will always be supply lines to hit. We can live forever out here."

"You are wrong," said Khalid. "If the Formics are gone, then the Fleet will no longer be occupied. With nothing better to do, they will hunt us down. We would not last long."

She pushed away from him, angry. "This is not the Khalid I know. Khalid is the father of fear."

"Yes, but it is Khalid who is afraid. The future is not so clear."

"Is that why you took these four women from the mining ship? To give yourself a new future?"

She was scowling at him, and her question had completely thrown him. "The women? What do they have to do with this?"

"We have not taken women before," said Maja. "And now you take four. Why?"

Khalid shrugged. "Because Breaker cannot cook, because we have plenty of food supplies but no one who can prepare it well. Breaker nearly set this whole space station aflame. These women will cook for us, do laundry."

She folded her arms. "That is the worth of a woman to you? Cooking? Cleaning your filthy clothes?"

He sat up, startled. "Why are you harsh all of a sudden, woman?"

"You do not call me woman. I am Maja. I have a name. And I am more than the meals I prepare and the socks I scrub."

Khalid frowned, baffled. "What meals? You do not cook or scrub clothes at all."

"Perhaps because I do not want to be perceived as nothing but a scrubber of socks."

"You are speaking nonsense, woman," said Khalid.

"Maja! That is my name. Maja. Has your lust for these women made you forget already?"

Khalid stiffened and then laughed. "Is that what this is about? You think I lust for these women? Is that why you have such fire in you? You are jealous?"

"You took these women to take them as your wives, didn't you?"

Khalid shook his head. "That was not my intent."

"And yet you prohibit the men from lying with these women. You told them that any man who touches these women would answer to your slaser. I heard the words."

"And what of it?" said Khalid. "I will not have my men prey upon these women."

"And why not?" said Maja. "Because you want to prey upon them yourself?"

He slapped her. She had pushed and pushed, and he would not tolerate her attacks. "You forget your place, woman. You do not speak to me so. I am Khalid."

Her face darkened. "Yes. The mighty Khalid. The king of the universe. We all know your name, great one. I wonder if you can remember mine."

She pushed away from him and flew out of the room.

He had never struck her before, but she had been wild with her fury. What choice did he have? And why would Maja push him so? Why should she be jealous? Khalid had not touched these women. He had not even looked upon them other than to assess their usefulness in the kitchen and laundry. They were workers. He had given the men rules and kept them away from the women because he would not have the women harmed. That would diminish their usefulness.

He went to the kitchen and checked on the women. They were busy preparing the next meal, but they became stiff and shifty-eyed when they saw Khalid, as if a tiger had been let loose among them and they were all pretending it wasn't there. They focused on their work with the pots and food and ovens as Khalid watched them. They were like caged animals, jittery and uneasy. It looked as if they hadn't slept in days.

Khalid approached the one nearest him, and she averted her eyes.

"What do you think of our home here?" said Khalid. "This factory, all to ourselves. It is a prize, is it not?"

The woman didn't answer.

"Come, speak. What is your name?"

The woman stared down at the counter.

He left the kitchen. He did not want to speak to these women further. They left him feeling dark inside. Angry. He should have left them on their damaged ship.

He ate alone in his quarters that night, tinkering with the ansible, searching for some way to connect it to the network again. A commotion in the corridor stopped him. Shouting. Movement. The sounds of a struggle. Screams. Fired slasers. The banging of boots on the metal grated floors as a mob of people in magnetic greaves came closer.

Khalid flew to his chair and grabbed his slaser.

A moment later the door was kicked open and there stood Maydox with twenty men behind him. They were armed with slasers and swords and smaller blades. The sword in Maydox's right hand was red with blood. The slaser in his left hand was fired up and beeping green, ready to go.

I should have killed Maydox long ago, thought Khalid, for this was mutiny and Maydox was clearly the father of it.

"You have forgotten where you are, Maydox," said Khalid. "This is the private quarters of your ruler. To barge in with such violence is foolish, as I might mistake you for my enemy." Khalid held the slaser loosely by his side, but it was charged and purring and ready.

Maydox was a broad man, with scars upon his chest and back received from money fights with blades and whips in his home country of Afghanistan. Maydox wore the scars like badges of honor, and Khalid should have known that such a man would only be trouble and corrupt the hearts of others. Khalid never should have welcomed him into the crew.

Maydox raised the sword and pointed it at Khalid. "You take women as a prize and keep them only for yourself? This is how you lead?"

"There is blood on your sword, Maydox," said Khalid. "Any man who spills blood among my men must answer with blood of his own."

"Your rule is over, Khalid. It is time for a new man to stand and lead us."

"And who might this man be?" said Khalid. "You? A man who whispers lies to these fools who follow you? I have not touched these women. They are here to feed us and keep us from smelling like dead animals, though I don't think there is enough soap in the world to get that scent off you, Maydox."

Maydox scowled. "Put down the slaser."

"How can you lead New Somalia if you are not even Somali?" said Khalid.

Maydox laughed scornfully. "New Somalia? This is no country, Khalid. You live in a dream of your own making. The men laugh at you behind your back for such a dream. A country has land, resources, families, communities, laws, order. You have none of these things. All you have for a country is a madman who thinks himself a king."

"Where is my brother?" said Khalid, for he knew at once that Maydox would be smart about this mutiny, removing lieutenants before coming to the general.

"Ibrahim is dead," said Maydox. "This blood you see is his. Dead like your dream, Khalid. Dead like you and your rule."

Khalid had feared this day would come. Men like Maydox were restless, hungry, insatiable. They would not follow Khalid forever. They wanted their own rule, their own crew.

They had killed Ibrahim. The truth of that was like a knife inside him. His own brother. Dead. They had likely killed Maja as well.

"You wish to challenge me for the right to rule?" said Khalid.

"No challenge," said Maydox. "You die here. Now."

"This is not our way," said Khalid. "Any challenge to rule must be made in combat. You choose the weapon, and one of us lives or dies."

Maydox laughed. "You only prolong your death, Khalid. I have fought fifty men in such fights and never lost."

"Then you will make it fifty-one, if you are so skilled. You have twenty men with you there, Maydox. Which means there are others here in the facility who do not follow you."

"They will follow me when you're dead," said Maydox.

"Reluctantly," said Khalid. "They may follow you today. But they will hate you for showing cowardice and defying my call for combat. They will not call your name. They will not honor you. They will talk in whispers and plot against you and cut your throat in your sleep. Look at the faces of the men beside you now. Even they know how foolish it would be to deny my request for combat."

Maydox glanced at the men beside him, and that was when Khalid raised his slaser and shot Maydox through the chest. The beam passed right through him as if Maydox were nothing but paper and hit the men behind him, killing them as well. Khalid moved the beam to the left and right, using it like a knife to slice through the assembled mob. The men screamed and scattered and fled. They hadn't even bothered to return fire.

Khalid grabbed the microphone on the wall connected to the public address system, and his voice came through the speakers throughout the facility. "Brothers, this is Khalid. I have killed Maydox for treason. He was not alone. He and his mutineers killed Ibrāhīm and others. Find them and kill them. If they surrender, bring them to the yard."

The yard was the central shipbuilding site inside the

space station, a massive cube where large segments of ships were assembled. Upon completion, each segment was released out the big bay doors and into space, where it could be added to other completed segments. All of Khalid's village from Somalia could fit inside the yard, including the small fields where the crops had grown. That's how wide and immense the space was. Khalid had learned from the ansible about a Battle Room the Fleet had built outside a few of their ships using scaffolding to construct a giant caged cube. Platoons would fly about inside this cage and conduct mock battles. Khalid liked the idea of a Battle Room, but the yard here on the station was far better for such a game. Here there were obstacles, as in real battles: massive beams and hooks and welding arms and bots and tools, sharp corners, hiding places, and there in the middle, the biggest obstacle of all, a segment of a ship in its early phase of construction: a large steel skeletal structure like the carcass of some long-dead whale.

Khalid moved alone through the corridors until he found Ibrahim drifting outside the kitchen, his body limp, a mist of blood hovering around him. There were scorch marks all over the walls here from the cuts of the slasers, but it was a sword that had taken his brother's life.

Khalid closed his brother's eyes and pulled him to the nearest airlock. After he placed Ibrahim inside, Khalid thought perhaps he should offer a prayer. But no words came. He did not know how to pray. He jettisoned the corpse into space and wiped at his eyes and cursed himself. Maydox was right. Khalid was a fool to think he could make a country here with such men.

The fighting was over in an hour. Someone came to Khalid with news that only five had surrendered in the end and that they were tied up in the shipyard awaiting him. The rest of the mutineers were dead.

Khalid went to the yard to finish the business.

The five mutineers were bound and anchored to the floor on one of the tool decks, which was a narrow extension of flooring on the side of the shipyard's far wall. There were ten tool decks total, stacked on top of one other, like a giant fire escape on the side of a building. Khalid's heart sank when he saw the five mutineers. One of them was Maja. She would not look at him.

He anchored his feet to the floor in front of her and knelt down to face her.

"Why, Maja? Why would you have a hand in this?"

Her eyes met his then. "I did not think they would kill you. They said they would take the ship and go with the four miner women. They would leave us here to have our country. I did not want death, Khalid."

"Maydox was not a man to be trusted," said Khalid. "You have wounded me, Maja. Betrayed me."

"I wanted them to take the women away. You do not need other wives."

"Other?"

"Am I not your wife?"

"I suppose," said Khalid. "There was no ceremony, but in our country we make the rules. No ceremony is needed. You are my wife."

"And now you will kill your wife?" said Maja.

Khalid didn't answer.

"I did not resist these men who took me. I could have killed them. You know that. I stayed my hand and surrendered so that I might speak to you, to tell you the truth of it."

"What did you tell Maydox?"

"That if he wanted the women so badly he should take them. I did not know he would come for you as well."

"You told him to disobey me," said Khalid. "You put the fire of mutiny inside him."

"The fire was already there," said Maja. "We should have killed him a long time ago."

"Yes," said Khalid. "I should have killed him when I first met him. It seems we both have made mistakes."

"You cannot kill me," said Maja. "After all that I have done for you, all that I have given you."

"You sadden me, Maja. You have been a good wife. In Somalia we could have planted and had children and lived as one."

"We still can," said Maja. "This war will end. We need not stay out here in the frozen Black. And you need not wait for children. There is one already inside me."

Khalid stiffened and glanced down at her abdomen.

"I was waiting for the right time to tell you," said Maja. "I thought you would be angry, that you might not want a child, that you might order me to end it." Her expression hardened. "Then you go and take these other wives. The wives of dogs. Why shame me so?"

"You are lying," said Khalid.

"I am not lying," she said, still angry. "I have not had my woman's cycle for two months now. Kill me and you also kill your own child."

Khalid stood. She was not lying. Maja was not one to lie, and he had seen the face of liars countless times before among his men and victims. There was a child inside her. His child. A boy perhaps. To carry his name, to be strong like his father.

And yet . . . Maja was the cause of it all. She had given the boulder only the slightest of nudges, but it rolled down the mountain all the same, gaining momentum and strength and crushing everything in its path. Who was to blame? The boulder? Or the one who had unleashed it on the world?

Khalid reached down and powered up his slaser. It hummed with energy in his hand. The light on the side turned from red to green. He released the safety. She had fought for him, raided for him, killed for him. And now he would take her life. Wife and mother to his child.

I am a monster, thought Khalid. Soulless. Killer of women, children, men, and now my own blood. That is why the words of prayer do not come. God does not hear the prayers of the devil himself. God does not acknowledge a demon king.

He placed the end of the barrel against the back of her head. Her head bent forward slightly, surprised. But then she stiffened and became more erect. She would not cower from it. She would not plead. Not Maja. Khalid spread his feet shoulder-width to steady himself. He brought up his second hand and steadied the slaser. The trigger was tight against his finger. The squeeze would only need to be slight. Just a touch. An infant could do it.

Infant.

Not his infant. Because he would end that life now. His child who had pushed no boulder, started no mutiny, committed no crime.

The men around him waited. To wait was weakness. And he was not weak. He was Khalid, the men of men, the father of fear.

And the father of a dead child.

His finger tightened on the trigger, but before he pulled it back, there was a sudden noise, like the bending of metal, and then the world shifted hard to the right. Khalid was thrown to the side so violently that the hold of his magnetic greaves was torn away. He spun away in space, slung off the tool deck and out into the yard, spinning uncontrollably, the slaser no longer in his hand. And he was not alone. Everyone who had been positioned on the tool deck had been thrown as well.

The space station was moving, he realized. Something had struck the station. They were under attack. His body slammed into a beam, and pain exploded through his back. He ricocheted away but was able to grab another beam close by and stop himself.

A man spun by him, screaming in pain, his arm broken and bent at a strange angle.

It was the Fleet. Khalid was sure of it. They had tracked his ansible and killed its power and were coming for him. He had been a fool to take the device.

He shouted orders. Everyone needed to get to the ship. But no one heard him. There was screaming and the ear-piercing sound of metal bending and large objects breaking and snapping, as if the entire space station were buckling under the pressure of a mighty force. Tools and broken piece of machines and debris were flying past him. The yard was breaking apart.

Amid the chaos, there was a loud popping sound, like the firing of a gun. Khalid, clinging to a beam, looked upward and could see across the vast distance of the yard to the far opposite wall, past the ship segment under construction, past the beams and bots and lifts and welding arms and all the gear that filled the shipyard. And there on the opposite wall, a piece of the ceiling was floating away from where something had cut it free and pushed it inward. For a brief moment, Khalid feared that the Fleet had cut a hole in the hull and exposed the entire room to the vacuum of space and in an instant they would all be sucked toward the hole, striking the beams and bots and obstructions along the way, breaking their bodies again and again until they finally reached the hole where space was waiting.

But there was no mad rush of air, no pull of the vacuum, meaning the Fleet had created a seal around their point of entry, a docking tube perhaps, and cut a hole in the station to give themselves a place of entry. And he was right, because a moment later bodies poured through the hole and into the yard, launching downward in a mob, just as Khalid and his men had done so many times before when raiding. Twenty bodies, forty, fifty.

But they were not, Khalid realized, the bodies of men.

They were Formics, with jar weapons in their hands, rushing toward him like a wave, like a mass of insects swarming into a hive.

Khalid was shouting orders again. "To the ship! Move!" He did not wait to see if they followed. He launched downward, aiming for the bottom tool deck. If he could reach the door, he could get to the corridor. The Formics' ship was above him. His ship was below. He could make it. Men were following him. Some flew faster than him. Others fired upward with their slasers. Khalid could not see if they hit anything. His eyes were focused completely on the tool deck below, racing up to meet him. He realized too late that he got the angle wrong. He tried rotating midflight, but that only made it worse. He landed sloppily and crashed into the tool deck, his shoulder striking a metal box. He felt his collar-bone snap and screamed in agony. He spun and rolled and finally came to a stop. His left arm was dead and limp at his side. Blood from a gash in his head was oozing into his hair. His right hand touched it and his hand came back red.

He looked upward. The swarm of Formics was dividing as individual Formics split off and landed on beams and bots and other obstructions in the room. Then they launched downward again, not as a chaotic mob like Khalid's pirates would have done, but in an orderly and coordinated manner, like a swift and lethal dance.

"Come on," said a man. "Get up."

Khalid had not even known the man was there. A member of the crew. Bedjanzi was his name. He pulled on Khalid's left arm, and Khalid cried out in pain.

Something struck the man in the chest and he stopped, frozen, and stared at it. It was a doily, fired from the Formic jar weapons. The web-shaped organism glowed with a blue bioluminescence and was covered completely by a thick translucent gel adhesive. Bedjanzi grabbed at the sticky substance on his chest, perhaps in an effort to pull

it off and throw it to the side. But the motion only stuck his hand to his chest, like tar. A second later the doily exploded and Bedjanzi along with it.

Khalid was thrown backward from the blast. He slammed into a metal tool chest and again the pain at his broken collarbone was like a hatchet buried in his shoulder.

Khalid's face was wet, and his ears were ringing. There was screaming, but it seemed distant now, at the end of a long tunnel. There were more explosions, too, but Khalid couldn't make sense of it anymore. He felt as if he were falling, not physically, but in his mind, spinning inward, the world going dark and silent.

Hands grabbed him, and the pain in his shoulder ripped at him again. The hands turned him over, and Khalid realized that they were not human hands.

A Formic was over him, two hands pressing Khalid hard against the floor of the tool deck, holding him in place. The other hands wiped Khalid's face. The blood was not all his own. The Formic's hands were coarse and hard and covered in fur.

The Formic had brought Khalid back from whatever mental precipice he was falling from, but now he was too terrified to scream. The Formic's face came in closer, inches from his own, as if searching for a message written behind Khalid's eyes.

There were screams elsewhere in the yard. Men screaming like children. The Formics were grabbing them, Khalid knew, just as they had grabbed him.

Two more Formics came and joined the one holding Khalid, making it three before him now, all of them staring at him as if he were a fish they were considering keeping or throwing back. One of the Formics pulled a rope from a pouch at his hip. They wrapped the rope around Khalid's wrists, but it was not rope, he realized. It was a living thing. A worm, long and black and strong as rope.

It coiled around his hands and squeezed like a python, binding him. Horrified, Khalid bit his bottom lip so as not to scream. Another worm went around his ankles. A third went around his chest, pinning his arms to his side. And when this worm tightened, Khalid did scream, for the movement had further separated his broken collarbone.

Why were they binding him? Why were they not killing him?

The Formics grabbed him roughly and unceremoniously tossed him back the way they had come, slinging him into the air like a sack of grain thrown onto a truck. Khalid screamed again, despite himself. He spun through the air, bound, helpless, unable to stop or catch himself. But he didn't need to, he realized, because a Formic on a beam above him was waiting to catch him. The strong Formic hands stopped his momentum, spun him, and threw him upward again. They were positioned in a line, like a firemen's bucket brigade, throwing him from one Formic to another, passing him up the chain like cargo. He spun and screamed as he moved up the chain. They're taking me into their ship, he realized. They will eat me in their ship.

Then, at the top, where the Formics had cut a hole in the side of the yard, a pair of Formics caught him, rotated him, and tossed him up through the hole and into darkness.

CHAPTER 16

Superstructure

To: robert.hoebeck%captain@ifcom.gov/fleetcom/
vandalorum
From: maria.espinosa.rivera%lieutenant@ifcom.gov/
fleetcom/vandalorum
Subject: What Victor Delgado saw

Dear Captain Hoebeck,

I recognize that I am breaking protocol by emailing
you directly rather than my immediate commanding
officer, but I have already pursued those channels and
was informed that you would be unconcerned with
matters not directly affecting the specific mission in
which we are engaged. However, since I firmly believe that the intelligence I have received is of critical importance to the Fleet and should be shared with
CentCom immediately, I am setting protocol aside
and will suffer the consequences.

Victor Delgado has evidence to suggest that the Formics are building a structure of enormous size out
beyond the Belt. Please see the attached animation
and documents. He and I would appreciate a few min-

utes of your time to discuss this matter further and
seek your permission to send this data via laserline to
the Polemarch on the Revenor, so that an immediate
message via quad may be sent to CentCom and the
Hegemon.

Sincerely,
Lieutenant Maria Rivera
International Fleet Nurse Corps

To: maria.espinosa.rivera%lieutenant@ifcom.gov/fleet
com/vandalorum
From: robert.hoebeck%captain@ifcom.gov/fleetcom/
vandalorum
Subject: Re: What Victor Delgado saw

This is an automatic response. You are not authorized
to send communications directly to [officer's name
here]. Please see your immediate commanding officer
to resolve any concerns.

Respectfully,
International Fleet Office of Communications

Victor was anchored to a seat in the medical-wing break
room, across from Lieutenant Rivera. "The captain didn't
even read your email?"

"Doesn't look like it," said Rivera. She tucked her
tablet back into the front pocket of her nursing bib.

"This is laughable," said Victor. "Is the entire International
Fleet like this?"

"You mean mired in bureaucracy and stupid communication
policies? I'm hoping this ship is the exception and
not the norm, but I doubt it."

"I know this is going to sound radical and dangerously

unorthodox," said Victor, "but when we asteroid miners needed to communicate with the captain of our ship, we simply went and spoke to her."

"That's because there's no formal hierarchy of authority on an asteroid-mining ship," said Rivera. "You're a family. The military's different. You don't break chain of command here. That's the one unpardonable sin. I took an enormous risk sending him that email. If Captain Hoebeck *had* read it, and if word had gotten back to my direct CO that I went around him, I would have been castigated because every person up my chain of command from me to Hoebeck would think I had betrayed them. These people take that very seriously."

"I didn't realize you were taking that kind of risk," said Victor. "I don't understand the culture. I shouldn't have asked you to send it."

"I chose to send it," said Lieutenant Rivera. "It needed to be done. But it doesn't matter, because it obviously didn't get us anywhere. So now what? How do we get this intelligence to the Fleet?"

"I still don't see why I can't go straight to the helm and ask to see the captain. You have a chain of command you have to respect. I get that, but when does common sense prevail?"

"You can't reach the helm," said Rivera. "It's on Deck Three, which is inaccessible to little folk like you and me. Senior officers only."

"Inaccessible how?"

"Think big door guarded by a marine holding a slaser rifle."

Victor laughed scornfully. "Captain Hoebeck intentionally keeps his crew from reaching him? The International Fleet makes no sense to me."

"Again, it's all about chain of command," said Rivera. "This is how it works. The guard is there to remind us that there's a command structure that must be respected.

Captain Hoebeck is in the highest position. We're down here in slumville."

"I thought the military was supposed to homogenize us," said Victor. "Isn't that the point of the uniform? To convey that we're all the same, that we can stand shoulder to shoulder and fight together as equals, regardless of where we came from?"

"I can't tell if you're being naive or sarcastic," said Rivera.

"Naive, apparently," said Victor.

He sighed and rubbed at his eyes with the palms of his hands. "I don't understand. The International Fleet spends a fortune to bring me here, at great risk to my own life, and yet the instant I show up, I'm isolated and ignored."

"You're isolated and ignored because you're still in recovery. Your body's been through hell. It takes time to heal. You're not ready for an assignment."

"The Polemarch didn't ask for me," said Victor. "That much is clear. Otherwise I would have gone to his ship, or, at the very least, he would have made inquiries since my arrival. He hasn't. Why am I here?"

"I've been thinking about that," said Rivera. "It's obvious from his behavior that our Captain Hoebeck didn't ask for you either. He didn't want to grab your zipship, and he hasn't made any effort to check on you either. As far as he's concerned, you're an annoying inconvenience. Which means whoever *did* order you here is above Hoebeck. Someone higher up the chain. He only picked you up because a superior ordered him to do so. Now, there are dozens of ships out here with us on this mission, but only a handful of them have people above Hoebeck who could've initiated that order."

"Who specifically?"

"Four people other than the Polemarch. A rear admiral. Two vice admirals. And Admiral Rheine."

"I don't know any of those people," said Victor. "Why would any of them order me here?"

"I don't think they did," said Rivera. "And here's why. If any of them had initiated the order to bring you here to the fleet from the Kuiper Belt, why didn't they order you to their own ship? Why send you to the Vandalorum? Captain Hoebeck doesn't have a reputation for being especially accommodating. Quite the opposite, in fact. He's known for being gruff, unapproachable, and sometimes cruel. He especially doesn't like asteroid miners wearing the blue. That's why you won't find any space borns among his senior staff. This is the last place top brass would send you."

"You said the Vandalorum gives the best medical care," said Victor. "Maybe they sent me here because they knew the flight would nearly kill me."

"Our medical facilities are good," said Rivera, "but they're no better than any of the other Fleet ships out here that are our size or bigger, of which there are many. And we're certainly not the best. The Kennedy and Manchester have far superior medical facilities."

"You told me my doctor was the best in the Fleet."

"I say that to all my patients. It keeps their hopes high. And that's good for their recovery. And I didn't lie. Doctor Tokonata is an excellent doctor. But other ships have excellent doctors, too."

"Then I'm stumped," said Victor. "If Captain Hoebeck didn't order me here, and if none of the admirals or the Polemarch ordered me here, then who did?"

"This is my theory," said Rivera. "It has to be someone above all of them. Someone they couldn't refuse. Maybe someone they don't like taking orders from, but someone they must obey. So they followed the order to recover you, but in a small show of defiance, they sent you to the least accommodating captain in this fleet. It's a slight of

sorts to the person who gave the order without that person even knowing he was slighted."

"There's only one person above the Polemarch," said Victor. "And that's the Hegemon of Earth."

"That's the only explanation that makes sense to me," said Rivera. "Ukko Jukes ordered you here. So here you are. And now you're ignored because Fleet commanders don't particularly like being micromanaged by the Hegemon. At least that's what I've heard. There's friction there. The Hegemon is frustrated with CentCom, and vice versa."

"Because of the state of the war?"

"Because of a lot of things," said Rivera. "The fact that we're losing is a big part of it, but it's also the age-old problem between leaders and the armies they control. The military doesn't mind being told to go to war by their commander in chief, but they don't like being told *how* to go to war. Their attitude is: 'Give us the go order, and then get out of the way and let us do our job.' But that's not Ukko Jukes's style."

"You're making a huge supposition on circumstantial facts," said Victor. "Maybe the Vandalorum was simply the ship in the best position to pick me up."

"We were," said Rivera. "But only because we were forced to be there to get you. Most of the ships out here could have done it. The Vandalorum got the assignment the same time you got yours, eight months ago."

"But why would the Hegemon bring me here?"

"My guess? Because you're the only person in this fleet moving toward the motherships who has ever been inside a large Formic vessel. You've seen the enemy up close. You've interacted with their tech. You've maneuvered through the tunnel systems on their ships and dug through their asteroids. Maybe by virtue of your experience the Hegemon trusts you more than he trusts his own commanders."

"But why?" said Victor.

"For the same reason guys like Captain Hoebeck *don't* trust you. You're not military. You don't have an agenda or a career to protect. You only care about the mission at hand. And you have an excellent track record when it comes to these kinds of missions."

"It's not a track record. I just happened to be the person in the right place at the right time."

"That's not true," said Rivera. "In every circumstance, you learned information at the same time as a lot of other people. But you were the one who did something about it. You acted. You *put* yourself in the right place at the right time and did what needed to be done. Fluke coincidence or luck or whatever had nothing to do with it. And you didn't concern yourself with pleasing superiors and getting a commendation while doing it."

"You're describing every rank-and-file member of the military," said Victor. "Marines get things done. Marines go where they need to go."

"Of course," said Rivera. "But always at the mercy of their commanding officer. They can't go rogue. They have to follow the chain of command. That's the order of things. And when you have intelligent, noncareerist commanders, the chain of command works. But when you don't have excellent commanders then you're inefficient, poorly managed, and destined to fail. No one knows that better than Ukko Jukes because he sees the Fleet as a whole with the eyes of a businessman and a manufacturer. He understands models of efficiency. That's his expertise. If something is mucking up the system or slowing down the assembly line, you remove it. And right now he sees a lot of poor commanders, and it terrifies him. So what does he do? He calls upon someone who he knows will get things done despite the obstacles the Fleet creates. And it's a person unhindered by loyalty to any one side in the military. You're not American or Armenian or

Pakistani or whatever. You don't have a national agenda, or a personal one. You simply do what needs to be done."

"I'm not some secret weapon of the Hegemon," said Victor. "I barely know the guy."

"You don't have to know him," said Rivera. "You don't even have to communicate with him. He just has to drop you into the right situation, and he knows you'll get things done. In fact, maybe he worries that communicating with him, or taking specific direction from him, might even cripple you out here because your Fleet commanders will then be all the more resentful of you and hinder you at every turn out of spite."

"This is all speculation," said Victor. "And even if this theory of yours is right, my situation is different now. Because now I'm in the system. I'm beholden to a CO like everyone else."

"Then he expects you to find a way to get things done within the chain of command."

"First you tell me not to barge into the helm and demand to speak to the captain, and now you're telling me I should."

"I don't know what the approach is," said Rivera. "I only know that doing nothing isn't an option, and everything I've tried so far hasn't worked. So you tell me, now what?"

Victor unstrapped himself from the seat and drifted upward. "Where's this door to Deck Three?"

Ten minutes later Victor and Lieutenant Rivera approached a marine standing guard at the door to Deck Three.

"Excuse me, Corporal," said Victor. "Would you kindly call the helm and inform them that Victor Delgado requests a few minutes of the captain's time regarding a matter of grave importance?"

"That's your big plan?" said Rivera.

"Sometimes the direct approach is the best approach," said Victor. "Also, I'm testing my own theory."

"Shouldn't you at least tell the helm what this matter of grave importance is?" said Rivera.

Victor shook his head. "If I tell them there's a giant invisible Formic fortress out near Saturn, they'll think I'm high on hallucinogenic drugs that my nurse gave me."

"Good point," said Rivera. "Better keep it vague. Do as he says, Corporal."

The marine relayed the vague message, and the response came back almost immediately. "My apologies," said the marine. "I'm to inform you both that the captain is not to be disturbed for the duration of our flight."

"Did this denial come directly from the captain?" Victor asked.

"The message came from the second assistant helm officer," said the marine.

"The *second* assistant," said Victor. "Walking up the chain of command, how many people are between the second assistant helm officer and Captain Hoebeck, would you say?"

The marine looked to Rivera, the highest ranked among them, and gave his answer. "I'm not certain, ma'am. Maybe four or five?"

"Thank you, Corporal," said Rivera.

Victor stepped away a few paces down the corridor, out of earshot, and Rivera followed. "Welcome to chain of command," she said, keeping her voice low. "Now what?"

"What's a great honor given to a commander?" asked Victor. "A medal or award for meritorious service? Think big."

"The highest medal is the Hegemony Congressional Medal of Honor," said Rivera. "Awarded for valorous actions in direct contact with the enemy. Why?"

"That doesn't work," said Victor. "What's an award that you might give someone for an act that doesn't involve enemy contact?"

"If you're trying to dangle a carrot in front of Captain Hoebeck," said Lieutenant Rivera, "it would be the IF Commendation Medal. He may already have one of those, but if you're Hoebeck, you can't have too many ribbons on your jacket."

"Then we'll call the helm again and inform them that I wish to take a photo with the captain as part of the application I am submitting for the captain to be considered for the IF Commendation Medal for his heroic rescue of me and my zipship."

"That's not how it works," said Rivera, "having you submit the application, I mean. A commendation would come from Hoebeck's superiors."

"I'm new to the IF," said Victor. "I don't know the protocol. You explained to me the process, but I'm determined to inform Hoebeck's superiors of his actions as he is too humble to do so himself. Hoebeck will be all too happy to tell me who to contact to get it done."

"That isn't going to work," said Rivera. "Hoebeck is difficult, but he isn't that vain."

The captain saw them immediately.

An aide came to escort them, and a minute later, they were all posing for a photo in front of the holotable at the helm. Hoebeck was in his early fifties, bald, and with a touch of belly fat. He was flanked by his aides and helm officers, with Victor at his immediate right giving a thumbs-up as Lieutenant Rivera snapped the photo with her tablet.

"There you are, young man," said Hoebeck, patting Victor on the shoulder. "You have your photo. If we survive this assault, the world might actually see it."

One of Hoebeck's lieutenants leaned in and said, "It *was* a heroic act, sir. You certainly deserve a commendation of the highest order for that rescue. Well done."

Victor exhibited great restraint by not rolling his eyes. Hoebeck grinned at the praise. "Yes, well, all of us

deserve the credit. That is the value of having a properly trained crew. Every man can be a hero."

"You'll be a hero ten times over if you give me five minutes of your time," said Victor. "It's concerning a matter of utmost importance to the survival of the Fleet."

There was an awkward pause as everyone realized that Victor had come in under false pretenses. The aides and lieutenants looked warily to Captain Hoebeck, unsure how he'd respond. "Is that so?" said Hoebeck finally, without enthusiasm. "Well, if you have something of importance for the Fleet, I'd be wrong not to hear it, wouldn't I?" He gestured to his left. "Please. My office."

The helm officers glared at Victor as he and Lieutenant Rivera followed Hoebeck into his office, a small room adjacent to the helm with a holotable and a view of space projected on one wall. The suck-up lieutenant came in as well and stood off to the side.

Captain Hoebeck gestured to him. "This is my aide. First Lieutenant Al-Baradouni, from Yemen."

Al-Baradouni nodded an acknowledgment to Victor and Rivera.

Captain Hoebeck initiated his magnets on his back and rear and sat in his office chair. "I'm listening," he said, with a slight air of annoyance.

"Sir," said Victor, "I have reason to believe that the Formics are building a superstructure beyond the outer rim of the Belt and that they have the capability to conceal the structure from traditional scopes and infrared. Considering the number of asteroids the Formics have gathered at this place and the lengths they have gone to to hide them from the Fleet, I believe this superstructure could possibly represent a significant Formic target. Perhaps even the primary Formic target."

"And what primary target is that?" said Captain Hoebeck, raising an eyebrow.

"Sir, the Fleet may have discarded the idea of a Hive Queen, but there must be some command structure to their army. Some leadership. The idea of a collective hive mind gets no serious traction among formicologists."

Captain Hoebeck waved a dismissive hand. "I'm not interested in litigating theories on Formic command, Ensign Delgado. And frankly I don't care if you believe in the Hive Queen or the Formic General or some hokey Formic collective brain mumbo jumbo. I operate on corroborated facts. Hard evidence. Intelligence. And judging by your preface, you don't have facts. You used words like 'I believe' and 'could possibly' and 'perhaps,' which leads me to believe that you've got a whole lot of nothing that you're trying to make into a whole lot of something."

"I have facts," said Victor, "and I think you'll agree they are facts worthy of investigation, if you'll allow me to explain."

Hoebeck folded his arms and frowned but didn't object.

Victor placed the data cube in the holotable. A starmap appeared, showing a segment of the Asteroid Belt, with nine asteroids marked with small red flags. "I was in that zipship for nearly eight months," said Victor. "Every day I monitored and tracked asteroids seized by the Formics."

"The IF tracks asteroids as well," said Hoebeck. "We probably have an army of people on the task. You think you saw something they didn't?"

"I don't know, sir," said Victor. "I don't know what they've seen and reported."

"So you could be wasting my time?" said Captain Hoebeck.

"It's possible, yes," said Victor. "In fact, that's my hope. I would sleep much better knowing that the IF had already thoroughly investigated these. But I highly doubt that's the case for a number of reasons. My scans picked up what they did because of my position high above the

ecliptic, which afforded me an unobstructed view of vast areas of the system at once. Even this ship and others in this fleet don't have that advantage because of their direction of flight."

Captain Hoebeck considered in silence, then waved a hand for Victor to continue.

Victor pointed to one of the asteroids in the animation. "What first caught my eye, sir, was that the Formics seized this asteroid here, which is strange because it's a snowball."

"Snowball?"

"That's a term we asteroid miners use, sir. It means a rock that's mostly ice and frozen ammonia, mixed with gravel and small segments of rock. We usually avoid them because they're fragile and are dangerous to mine. The instant you start drilling into them, they shatter. A junk rock. Not worth flying to and digging."

"Okay. It's a snowball. So what?"

"Well, sir, we haven't seen Formics seize snowballs before. We've only seen them seize dense rocky asteroids, which they use to build their warships."

"I know what the Formics do with asteroids, Delgado. What's your point?"

"My point, sir, is that the Formics have no use for a snowball that we know of. They can't build a warship inside one. The asteroid would break apart the instant they started digging through it."

"Maybe they don't grab snowballs to build warships," said Hoebeck. "Maybe they grab them for the same reason we do. For the ice."

"That was my thinking as well, sir. Ice gives them oxygen for their ships and fuel for their thrusters. And with the ammonia they could make fertilizer for their gardens, which also produce oxygen on their ships. Ice would be a valuable resource. But here's where it gets weird. Sixty-

seven days after this snowball deviated and assumed a new trajectory it disappeared from my scopes."

"They blew it up," said Hoebeck. "This happens all the time. The Formics blow the asteroids, and the resultant fragments are too small to be seen by our scans. This is nothing new."

"*Sometimes* the debris is too small for our scans, yes," said Victor. "But not always. On the larger rocks, we usually detect a debris field whenever an asteroid is destroyed. Also, keep in mind *why* the Formics blow the asteroids. They're building a warship inside it. The explosion breaks apart the asteroid to release the ship. Except in this case, the asteroid in question is a snowball. There is no warship to release. Nor has the asteroid reached any destination for ice processing. So why would they blow it up?"

Hoebeck shrugged. "Logical answer is they *didn't* blow it up. It shattered on its own as they were moving it. You said these asteroids were fragile. The Formics move these suckers by attaching a mini-thruster to the rock. The G-forces from the thruster became too great, the ice cracked, the whole thing shattered. End of story. Your presentation is going nowhere."

"Yes, sir," said Victor. "That was also my conclusion. This asteroid appeared to be a dead end. But now I had some useful information. I knew the direction the asteroid was headed before it vanished. I had its new trajectory. And from that I could possibly determine where the ice rock was being taken for processing."

Victor made a series of finger gestures in the hologram, and a dotted red line extended from the asteroid and moved from its original position in the outer rim to just beyond the Belt.

"What I found," said Victor, "is that the snowball was basically going nowhere. There is no Formic structure in that direction that we know of."

"Another dead end," said Hoebeck. "I hope you actually have a point to all of this."

"I'll spare you the story of each of these other individual asteroids that I've flagged," said Victor. "Suffice it to say, each was seized by the Formics, each left its traditional trajectory, and each deviated toward the same point in space out beyond the outer rim."

Victor made another hand gesture, and dotted red lines from each of the remaining flagged asteroids arced upward and coalesced on the same point outside the Belt.

"Again," said Hoebeck. "None of this is new. The Formics have been doing this for the better part of a year. They move asteroids all over the place. Sometimes they build a ship inside them. Sometimes they move asteroids just to make us chase them down. Decoys. Deception. Sometimes they cluster the asteroids together and begin building a structure, which we reach and promptly destroy. You're giving me old news."

Victor gestured to the red lines and flags. "These asteroids are different. Unlike all the decoys and all the rocky asteroids we've seen captured and moved, these asteroids here all disappeared from view at roughly the same time. Right when the snowball did. From within sixty to ninety days after the asteroids altered course, they vanished. Stranger still, sometimes that vanishing took three days as the asteroid's albedo slowly dimmed. Also, each of these asteroids was moving at a unique velocity. When you take into consideration their distance from this destination point, you realize that they're all arriving at this rendezvous point out beyond the Belt at roughly the same time. Now, you can argue that this is simply another Formic deception, that they seized these asteroids and then blew them all up at once because they thought we were tracking them. But in each case, sir, my scans found no debris fields. Nothing. These asteroids literally vanished without a trace. And some of them are three to

five kilometers across, sir. With an asteroid that big, with that much rock, we would absolutely see a debris field. And yet with all nine of them we see nothing whatsoever. Which leads me to believe that the Formics *didn't* blow them up, sir. They made them invisible."

Captain Hoebeck, to Victor's surprise, did not laugh. Instead he glanced at First Lieutenant Al-Baradouni.

Victor read the brief look between them. "I take it from your lack of surprise that you've seen the Formics make an asteroid invisible before."

"An asteroid? No," said Hoebeck. "But we've been told that the Formics have built convincing camouflage. We received word from the Polemarch that Formics attacked F1 and routed their fleet after emerging from behind huge blinds that resembled the black of space, complete with twinkling stars."

"Those would have to be enormous blinds," said Victor.

"Impossibly large," said Hoebeck, "which is why I'm skeptical."

"You question the intelligence?" said Victor.

"I believe our boys were ambushed, but I have a hard time believing the Formics could create such a massive plane of camouflage. It would be the largest structure ever conceived. Bigger than the scout ship of the First Invasion. And there were six of them. Allegedly."

Victor's mind was racing. "It's not that farfetched of an idea, really. When the Formics seize a rocky asteroid, they completely cover it with a self-healing membranous material. Some formicologists believe this membrane is organic. If the Formics can engineer an anaerobic animal or plant that can withstand the cold vacuum of space, then they can theoretically engineer the membrane to be completely nonreflective. More even than a charcoal rock. I'm talking no albedo whatsoever. It reflects zero light. Maybe the filament could even absorb light. We have

materials that can do it, and if we can make them, why can't the Formics?"

"Even if that's possible," said Hoebeck, "this structure would only be invisible to our light scopes. There's always infrared. I'll entertain the prospect that this membranous nonreflective cocoon thing could absorb light, but it's still going to be on the electromagnetic spectrum. We'd see it with infrared scopes."

"Maybe not," said Victor. "What if the Formics could somehow hide or dampen the asteroid's electromagnetic radiation? Not just infrared, but gamma rays, X-rays, ultraviolet, the full spectrum. Everything normally detected by our scopes and scanners. What if the Formics know that radiation is a method of detection and they've designed a membrane to mask radiation from the sun and keep the surface of the membrane near absolute zero?"

"That would be impossible," said Hoebeck.

"Everything about the Formics is impossible, sir. Building a worm that can chew rock and poop out a pellet of silicon is impossible. Building an indestructible hull is impossible. Communicating mind to mind across the solar system is impossible. But that hasn't stopped the Formics from doing it. The Hive Queen is a master of deception, sir. She's bringing these asteroids together, and she doesn't want us to know about them. And remember, some of these asteroids are big. If the Formics can make them invisible, perhaps they can make this superstructure invisible as well. And what better place for Formic leadership to hide than in something we can't even see?"

"This isn't hard evidence," said Captain Hoebeck. "This is eighty percent guesswork and conspiracy theory. Just because a contractor dumps a load of bricks in a field doesn't mean there's a library there now. Or a house of congress. Or a mud hut. As I suspected, you've got bits of interesting data that you've molded into a flimsy narrative." He shook his head and leaned forward. "This is

what *I* see. You saw something before the First Invasion, and all the world got into a fuss, and that gave you a taste of fame. You were suddenly the guy who saw something, the big shot, as we say in America. So now you're seeing something else because you realize that you're nobody now, and that hurts your little rock-digger ego. Worse still, you've apparently fooled one of my own crew." He turned to Rivera. "What did you say your name was?"

"Lieutenant Maria Rivera, sir. Nursing Corps."

Hoebeck chuckled. "A nurse. Well, Victor Delgado must be quite the charmer to convince you to abandon your duty of tending to the sick. I'll be speaking with your direct supervisor, Lieutenant. You've let this man manipulate you, and you made a mockery of my heroic act to save him." Hoebeck rose from his chair and turned to Al-Baradouni. "Lieutenant, escort these people off the deck and instruct the guard on duty not to allow them reentry."

"Yes, sir."

Captain Hoebeck got to his feet and adjusted his jacket. "I'll take that data cube now," he said to Victor, holding out his hand. "I'd like to amuse myself later as I review the contents."

Surprised, Victor handed it to him.

Hoebeck tucked the cube in his jacket pocket and exited.

Victor waited for Al-Baradouni to escort them out. Instead, Al-Baradouni faced them, his expression more alert. He had seemed so obsequious when Hoebeck was in the room. Now he spoke with a quick and quiet urgency. "Do you have another copy of that data cube?"

Victor glanced at Rivera then back to Al-Baradouni. "That was the original. But I have a copy, yes."

"Good," said Al-Baradouni. "Make another copy for me. I'll come by the medical wing and pick it up. I'll see that it gets to the Polemarch."

"How?" said Rivera. "Laserline?"

Al-Baradouni shook his head. "By packet. A small rocket no bigger than your arm. We send them back and forth between the ships."

"Who's we?" said Victor.

"The packet isn't a secret," said Al-Baradouni. "Captains and commanders use them all the time. Documents, plans, data. It's largely how we communicate during radio silence. Orders come from CentCom via the quad to the Polemarch on the Revenor. He then distributes those orders to a few key cooperating ships via packet. The vast majority of the ships don't hear from him or us at all. They just follow. I'll include your data cube as well as instructions to my man on the Revenor, who will receive it. He'll make another copy. The copy I send will go to the Polemarch. The second copy goes to the quad operator, who will send it to our people at the Hegemony."

"Your people?" said Victor. "Meaning what exactly? This sounds like an organized group."

"Just make a copy as soon as you leave here. I'll do the rest."

"Two minutes ago I thought you were the captain's stooge," said Victor.

"I play a role," said Al-Baradouni. "My position with the captain gives me crucial access to information, but it's a position I have to work to maintain. You focus on getting well. The Hegemon wants you infiltrating the mothership when we arrive. We're to learn what we can and destroy what we find, including the Hive Queen, if she happens to be there. You'll get your orders soon."

"So it *was* the Hegemon who sent Victor here," said Rivera.

"He won't be the Hegemon for much longer," said Al-Baradouni. "But yes. The Hegemon is concerned about this mission and the people running it."

"Then why doesn't he make changes?" said Victor.

Al-Baradouni smiled. "On the eve of a major offensive? That makes him an easy scapegoat if anything goes wrong. Critics will claim we would have won, if not for the Hegemon's last-minute changes in command."

"If he's leaving the Hegemony," said Victor, "what does he care what critics will say?"

"It's not just him," said Al-Baradouni. "It's the whole political structure of the Hegemony that would be under attack. The Hegemon is trying to avoid a civil war within the Fleet and a global war if we win against the Formics."

"This organization," said Victor. "Does it have a name?"

Al-Baradouni smiled. "You worry about healing. Leave everything else to—"

A piercing alarm interrupted him.

Al-Baradouni rushed into the helm, where the officers and technicians were moving and shouting in a sudden flurry of activity. Victor and Rivera stayed against the wall, out of the way, trying to decipher what was happening. An attack was underway. That was clear. Three or four ships of the fleet were already damaged, possibly disabled, maybe even destroyed. It was hard to make out details. The siren continued to wail. Helm officers were yelling orders over each other via the comms lines to other officers and departments throughout the ship. At first, Victor assumed that whatever tactic the Formics had used below the ecliptic was being implemented here: the giant blinds, the undetectable camouflage, the swarming Formic fleet, waiting to spring forth at the right moment. But he didn't hear anything to suggest that was the case. Instead, based on what he could hear over all the chaos, the Fleet wasn't being attacked by the Formics at all.

"Get those people off my helm!" Captain Hoebeck shouted, pointing at Victor and Rivera.

Al-Baradouni rushed over and took them both by the arm and pulled them toward the exit. They paused and

braced themselves against the wall twice as the ship began to decelerate.

"What's happening?" Rivera shouted, when they were out in the corridor.

"Get to your flight seats and buckle in," said Al-Baradouni.

"Why?" said Victor. "What's going on?"

"Three ships of the Fleet just went rogue," said Al-Baradouni. "They're firing on every other ship near them."

CHAPTER 17

Fighters

To: littlesoldier13@freebeltmail.net
From: gregory.samuelson%corporal@ifcom.gov/fleetcom
Subject: Works like a charm

Bingwen,

All the boys in the squad had a good laugh when I told them about the paint with NanoCloud. They thought I was bananas, said it couldn't be that easy. But then I showed them the app and how the nanobots ate the paint, and the next thing I know we're all mixing up buckets of it in the barracks, and the captain is telling us to suit up and get down in that asteroid.

So we did, and the paint worked. We applied it to the hullmat roadblocks, fired up the app, and the nanobots ate through the hullmat like it was soft butter.

Turns out, there were multiple blocks, too. We'd get through one block, go twenty meters, and find another. One tunnel had five in a row. But the bots and the paint were like liquid magic, and we got through all the way to the Formic ship in the core. And since we had some paint left, we figured, hey, might as

well keep going. So we painted up the ship, burned a hole through, and stormed inside. And lo and behold, I'll bet you never guess why the Formics had put up so many obstacles. Inside we found a daughter of the Hive Queen. I mean, excuse me, I can't say Hive Queen anymore. We'll call her a High-Priority Target Formic. Or an HPTF. Well, that little target is up in Formic heaven now, or more likely, down in Formic hell.

Who knew paint could be so powerful? Keep those ideas coming.

Regards,
Corporal Gregory Samuelson

Third Fleet, 45th IF Expeditionary Combat Unit
Tiger Tails Red, Tactical Asteroid Guerrilla Assault Team (TAGAT)
Greenville, South Carolina
God Bless America
Semper primus, semper paratus.
"Always first, always prepared."

The wail of the alarm inside Mazer's cell in the brig was so loud and piercing and incessant that he pressed his hands against his ears to muffle the noise. The speaker broadcasting the alarm was positioned directly above him in the ceiling and was clearly intended for an open area on a ship instead of a tiny confined box where sound reverberated off walls to the point of being painful. Mazer was tempted to reach up, rip off the speaker cover, and yank the wires loose.

He moved to the front of the cell, a solid piece of thick glass. From here he could see the processing table in the other room, where the MPs on duty were normally

anchored and passing the time. The table was empty. The MPs were nowhere in sight. Mazer banged on the glass with the palm of his hand, but he doubted anyone in the other room could hear over the alarm.

The fact that no one came for him made him wonder if this was a drill. New trainees arrived at GravCamp every few weeks, making it necessary to conduct frequent trainings on what to do should the station ever come under attack. Mazer had not yet experienced such a drill, but he knew they happened periodically, and he figured the station was due one.

It struck him as odd, though, that none of the MPs had come in to reassure him that all was well. The alarm had been going for over a minute now, and Mazer was an officer. He might be locked in a cell; Colonel Dietrich might be trying to degrade and humiliate him; but MPs generally took their duties seriously and treated prisoners with dignity. Especially officers.

So why didn't anyone come?

Perhaps they thought *not* coming was the greater courtesy. Maybe they thought it would be humiliating for an incarcerated officer to have to engage in such a drill, for it would require him to leave his cell in cuffs and be frog marched by two MPs through corridors filled with marines. Maybe they thought Mazer would appreciate sitting this one out.

But the more likely explanation was that this wasn't a drill and that the MPs hadn't come because they had all been urgently pulled away. If the space station was breached or damaged, MPs would need to be placed in strategic locations throughout the station to direct people to escape pods and keep everyone calm.

Mazer's suspicions were confirmed a moment later when the alarm stopped and an officer from the helm got on the speaker and ordered all pilots to their fighters and all marines into their pressure suits and then to their

assigned escape pods. Everyone needed to be ready for a breach and to abandon the space station if necessary.

The sudden urgency of the message alarmed Mazer. GravCamp was in a stable orbit around Jupiter. There were plenty of Trojan asteroids in the sector to provide the enemy some cover, but they were all a great distance away from the space station. Formic warships couldn't sneak up on GravCamp undetected—we would see them coming. And yet Colonel Dietrich was scrambling fighters, which meant Formics must be relatively close. Mazer's mind went to the Kandahar. A ship investigating a vanishing asteroid. A ship attacked without warning. A ship that should have seen the enemy approach but didn't. Then there were the blinds used in the ambush of Operation Deep Dive. Had the Formics built blinds here? Had they used a blind to approach GravCamp without being seen? Were they right outside already?

Mazer banged on the glass, but no one came. The other two cells were empty. No one else was in the brig. He needed to get out and into a pressure suit. He moved around the room, looking for any structural weakness that he might exploit, but of course he didn't find any. The room was designed to incarcerate, to contain, to hold. The walls were metal. The front was thick glass, likely unbreakable. If he could've anchored himself to the floor or furniture, he might've been able to kick the glass forcefully. But the room was devoid of any furniture and the MPs had taken his magnetic greaves. In zero G there was no need for a bed or desk or anything. Even the toilet was a mere hole in the wall with a vacuum setting. Mazer didn't even have his wrist pad, so he couldn't contact anyone or call for help.

He was stuck in here until someone came for him.

And five minutes later, someone did.

Bingwen, already dressed in a pressure suit and hel-

met, flew into the brig and anchored his feet to the floor in front of the glass. A small bucket and brush were in his hand, and he started painting the glass with white glossy paint. The paint was speckled with dots of black, as if Bingwen had doused it with pepper. He slapped the paint on quickly in wide, long strokes that crudely resembled the shape of a door. Then he holstered the brush and tapped at his wrist pad. At once, the paint began to vibrate almost imperceptibly. Then small wafts of dust began to drift away from the paint as it disintegrated.

In seconds, the paint was gone, and for a brief moment Mazer thought that this would be the end of it, that the NanoCloud bots had unzipped all the paint but couldn't penetrate the glass. Or perhaps the glass wasn't glass at all but rather a petroleum-based nonsilicon material or composed of other elements the nanobots couldn't recognize.

But then the glass began to disappear in a flurry of activity, as if the nanobots had struggled through the bog of paint in slow motion but now sprinted as they found true glass. Silicate dust puffed away in all directions, making a cloud as the entire glass wall, end to end, disappeared. Bingwen quickly tapped at his wrist pad again, and the process suddenly halted. Mazer shielded his eyes from the dust and launched through the space where the glass had been, sending the dust swirling in every direction. He landed on the opposite wall and then pushed off again toward the exit.

"That worked better than expected," said Bingwen as they hurried from the brig, keeping their eyes half-closed and shielded from the dust. "When you didn't show up at your pod, I figured the MPs forgot about you."

"I'm sure you realize that helping someone escape from military custody is a serious crime," said Mazer. "As is destroying IF property."

"You're welcome," said Bingwen. His voice was broadcast from the external speakers in his helmet. "We need to get you in a suit."

They hurried up the corridor, back toward Mazer's quarters where his pressure suit was stored, passing crowds of marines as they went, some in their pressure suits, others frantically still dressing. One blond-haired kid was holding his helmet and blinking stupidly as if paralyzed by the panic.

Mazer grabbed him. "Marine, what's your name?"

The marine looked at him blankly. "Frandsen, sir. Ensign Frandsen."

He was Dutch. He'd probably lied about his age. He didn't look a day over sixteen.

Mazer grabbed one of the marines rushing past him, moving for the pods.

"Your oxygen," said Mazer, shaking the man's shoulder. "Your life support isn't on. Wake up."

Comprehension registered on the man's face, and he tapped at his wrist pad. The lights in his helmet winked to life. "Sorry, sir."

"This is Ensign Frandsen," said Mazer, gesturing to the young marine. "You're going to help him get into his suit, and then you're going to make sure it's all powered up, and then you're going to help him get to the pods. Grab five marines to help you look for stragglers along the way."

"Yes, sir."

The marine sprang into action and focused on Frandsen, and Mazer and Bingwen moved on, maneuvering through the tide of bodies hustling in the opposite direction.

"Bingwen, what do you know?"

"The ship attacking us is one of ours. It just obliterated the Antietam, a transport, several million klicks out. We don't yet know if there are any survivors on the Antietam. Colonel Dietrich is ordering all pilots to their fighters."

"You said it's one of ours?" said Mazer. "A ship of the Fleet?"

"That's what the helm is saying. D-class battleship. Jianjun has a direct link to the helm. He's feeding me intel."

"That doesn't make sense," said Mazer. "Are we certain this ship fired on the Antietam? There are no other ships in the vicinity?"

"None. We don't know what weaponry was used, but this ship caught the Antietam completely by surprise."

"Who's the captain?" said Mazer. "Do we have a hull number? Why would one of ours attack the Antietam?"

"No one knows who the captain is because we don't yet know which D-class battleship it is. We can't identify it at this distance, and neither could the Antietam. We only know its shape, and it's definitely one of ours."

"What's the distance? How much time do we have?"

Bingwen relayed the question to Jianjun via the radio in his helmet and waited for a response. "Considering the ship's velocity, Jianjun says it will reach GravCamp in ninety-three minutes."

"That's not a lot of time," said Mazer. "Have Jianjun find out which ship it is and who the captain is. Get a manifest of the crew. Check flight and traffic reports in and around Jupiter. It couldn't have popped out of nowhere. It belongs to a squad. My guess is escort or recon. If it's one of ours, there will be a record of its movements. A paper trail. Shipping reports, fuel stops, something."

"How is Jianjun supposed to figure that out?" said Bingwen. "Where does he begin? This ship could be from anywhere."

"Look at its current trajectory and go backwards," said Mazer. "It came from somewhere. Draw a line from its stern and put the starcharts in reverse. The instant that ship in reverse collides with something in the past, we'll know its origins. Tell him to call us the instant he has an answer."

Bingwen relayed Mazer's message.

By then they had reached Mazer's quarters. Mazer tried the door and found it locked.

"Bingwen, you got in any tools in that pouch?"

Bingwen extracted his pocket laser and made quick work of the lock. Mazer was inside an instant later and pulling his pressure suit down from the closet.

"Have you got a theory on this?" said Bingwen as Mazer climbed into his suit. "Why would a D-class battleship take out one of our transports? And why is it coming for GravCamp? Was it hijacked? Pirates?"

"I've heard stories of pirate crews bold enough to attack and steal an IF vessel," said Mazer. "But what pirate crew would be foolish enough to hijack an IF ship and then use it to brazenly attack a well-defended IF facility? What would that accomplish? That's strategically pointless."

"Maybe we have supplies here that pirates want."

"This is a training facility," said Mazer, "not a weapons cache or a supply depot. There's nothing here of value for pirates to seize and cash in on."

"We have the soldiers' individual battle suits and the training tech used here."

"That's hardly the motherlode," said Mazer. "No, this isn't pirates. Pirates might be bold, but they aren't stupid. They survive by avoiding risks and hitting easy targets full of valuable goods. GravCamp is the opposite: high risk, minimal spoils."

"Unless the pirates know something we don't," said Bingwen. "Maybe there are valuable supplies at Grav-Camp that Colonel Dietrich has kept hidden from us? Advanced weaponry? Or navigational data? Something that would allow pirates to raid supply ships elsewhere, information on their vulnerabilities?"

"Even if that were true," said Mazer, "attacking Grav-Camp is asking to be destroyed."

"Then who?" said Bingwen. "Terrorists?"

That seemed the likeliest explanation. Had an IF crew-man or team plotted mutiny? Had they seized control of the helm of that ship and killed the principal crew, with the intent of taking out an IF training facility? If so, who would have such a grievance against the Fleet? There were nations on Earth vying for control of the Hegemony and vilifying Ukko Jukes at every turn. It was all over the press and Mazer's forum. Russia was the most outspoken. But Turkey and Pakistan and others were equally com-bative. Had they staged this? Was this a coup within the IF? Was this part of a larger, coordinated mutiny happen-ing simultaneously throughout the system? Was this an isolated incident or civil war?

Mazer snapped on his helmet, sealed his suit tight, and initiated life support. "Jianjun, it's Mazer. Can you hear me?"

"Loud and clear, sir."

"Has the helm sent a message via laserline to Daver-oon? Do they know we're under attack?"

Daveroon was the closest IF outpost, positioned at the outer rim of the Belt.

"I don't know, sir."

Mazer switched his commlink and radioed the helm. "Helm, this is Captain Mazer Rackham. Connect me to the laserline operator."

The voice said, "One moment, sir."

There was a click and another voice answered.

"Laserline. Tech Assistant Gomez."

"This is Captain Mazer Rackham. I'm here at the facil-ity. Have we sent a message to Daveroon? Do they know we're under attack? Or have we heard if they're under at-tack?"

"Why would they be under attack?" the tech asked.

"Just find out," said Mazer. "Call me back on this chan-nel the instant you know."

"Yes, sir."

Mazer switched channels and tried for Colonel Li but got no response. If Li did have an ansible, now was the time to use it.

The number of soldiers hurrying past Mazer's quarters toward the pods was thinning now.

"Now what?" said Bingwen. "If we go to our pods, we're not helping. We're just sitting there, waiting for the order to eject. We're nothing but targets."

"Jianjun," said Mazer into the radio. "Where are the fighters docked?"

"Hangar D3."

Mazer turned to Bingwen. "You know how to get to Hangar D3 from here?"

"All the fighters are likely spoken for," said Bingwen.

"Let's find out," said Mazer.

Bingwen launched down the corridor and Mazer followed. They reached the deck shaft and dove downward several decks, with Bingwen landing and launching and moving like a jackrabbit. Mazer noticed how Bingwen's small size gave him the advantage in these narrow spaces, where he could twist and maneuver and land far easier than Mazer, who was struggling to keep up.

"Where are the other boys?" said Mazer.

"Jianjun's in the barracks. The others are at the pods."

"You abandoned your army?"

"My pretend army. To bust you out of prison. Which is probably where we're both headed after this is over. Especially if we steal a fighter. Incidentally, are we planning on stealing a fighter? Or is this another one of those instances in which we merely surreptitiously borrow?"

"Neither," said Mazer. "We need to assist a squadron, if we can, not disrupt them."

They reached the control room outside Hangar D3 moments later. Flight coordinators and assistants were gathered around a cluster of terminals.

"Who's the CO here?" Mazer asked.

A captain with the flag of Senegal on his country-designation patch stepped forward. His nameplate read Sarr. "Who are you?"

"A pilot, if you need one," said Mazer.

Captain Sarr appraised Mazer suspiciously. "A pilot of what exactly? Our squadron flies Tikari fighters."

The Tikari—Finnish for dagger, or Tik as it was commonly known—was a squat, two-seater Juke design that had proven especially nimble in the war, dodging in and out of combat like a pesky housefly. Mazer had test-flown it at WAMRED—the Fleet's testing grounds for all combat equipment and vessels—and given the Tik good marks for maneuverability and speed. Designed to hold nine guided breach missiles and two slasers, the Tik could pack a quick wallop.

"I test-flew Tiks at WAMRED," said Mazer. "I've got five hundred flight hours in them easy."

Captain Sarr gestured to Bingwen. "And who's this?"

"Co-pilot and gunner," said Bingwen. "I have zero hours in a real Tik, but about two hundred hours in the sim. The same sim pilots train with. We had them on the transports on the way out here."

Captain Sarr shook his head. "I can't put a stranger and a kid in with my squad. I don't know either of you. You don't know our maneuvers, our formations. You'll only get in the way."

"So you have a Tik available," said Mazer. "Maybe a couple. Otherwise that would have been your first excuse to get rid of us."

Captain Sarr considered. He read the nameplate on Mazer's suit. "Captain Rackham, huh? I'll have to clear this with Colonel Dietrich."

"No, you won't," said a new voice.

They all turned as Colonel Li landed beside them and anchored his feet to the floor. "Colonel Dietrich is

no longer the commanding officer of this station. I am. Captain Rackham and Bingwen are to be given access to whatever equipment or vessel they require. Those are my orders."

Captain Sarr looked at each of them in turn and hesitated, as if unsure what to believe.

"I recognize this all comes as a shock, Captain Sarr," said Colonel Li as he typed at his wrist pad, "but none of us have time for your dithering. I am sending you a copy of my authorization of command. You can review it at your leisure, but not now. We're wasting time."

Captain Sarr's wrist pad dinged with a new message as Colonel Li pushed past him and into the control room.

"Bring up the fighters' visuals on this screen here," said Li. "I want to see what every pilot sees. Captain Rackham, Bingwen, you have your orders."

Captain Sarr moved to obey as Mazer pushed off toward the airlock on the far wall, with Bingwen right behind him.

Once Mazer and Bingwen were inside the airlock and Mazer had set the hatch seal and made sure the automatic locking mechanism worked, he asked, "Did you really do two hundred hours in a Tik simulator?"

"It was more like forty hours," said Bingwen. "But I was very good. Better than Nak, anyway. I only crashed three times while docking."

"How reassuring," said Mazer.

Bingwen smiled. "You'll be doing that anyway. I target and give nav support. Piece of cake."

"Kim would kill me if she knew I was I taking you with me," said Mazer.

"Kim would kill you if she knew you had volunteered for this," said Bingwen. "We'll tell her after the war and have a good laugh."

Mazer opened the airlock.

Hangar D3 was empty save for two Tik fighters in their docking harnesses.

They decided on the nearest fighter and launched toward it, into the vacuum of the hangar, soaring across the open space, rotating once as they went to get their feet under them as they had practiced so many times in the Battle Room.

As he flew, Mazer brought up his knees and engaged the NanoGoo on his boot soles. He landed on the roof of the fighter, and his feet locked down and held him firm. Bingwen landed beside him. The hatch was already unscrewed and open. Mazer drifted into the weapons bay and activated power and lights and got everything humming. He did a quick count of the breach weapons and did a cursory sweep of the gear. By then, Bingwen had sealed the hatch and moved into the co-pilot's seat in the cockpit.

Mazer pulled himself into the pilot's seat, buckled up, flipped on targeting and navigation, and initiated the docking arm to move the Tik to the launch tube. "We'll hit nearly six Gs on launch. The simulator doesn't prepare you for that. Considering your size—"

"If I pass out, you'll poke me until I wake up," said Bingwen.

The Tik snapped into place in the launch tube, and the gate before them opened, revealing a circle of black space and stars at the end of a long tube. Mazer hesitated. "Here we go. Try not to throw up."

Mazer flipped the switch, and the slingshot mechanism threw the fighter down the launch tube. The sudden G-force slammed Mazer hard against his seat and he clung to the flight stick with a white-knuckled grip, the tunnel walls blurring past them like a streak of light. A heartbeat later the fighter shot from the launch tube and was free of the space station, rocketing out toward a black canvas of stars.

Mazer put some distance between them and Grav-Camp before he engaged the thrusters, banked to the left, and dove downward, spinning in the direction of the approaching battleship. Mazer's body shifted in the restraints, pushed one way and then another, as he maneuvered the fighter into position and set a course to intercept. Several blips on his HUD indicated the other fighters ahead, already in formation. Mazer accelerated and again felt pressed against the seat.

"This definitely wasn't in the simulation," said Bingwen as he clung to the handholds on the side of his seat. "Or are you intentionally making this a violent ride to teach me a lesson?"

"Close your eyes if you feel nauseous," said Mazer. "The spinning stars outside make it worse."

"I'm fine," said Bingwen. "Just disoriented."

Mazer read the flight data on his HUD and opened a channel. "Green Squad, this is Captain Mazer Rackham and co-pilot Lieutenant Bingwen, come to give you another pair of guns should you need them."

Bingwen muted his comm and sent a direct link to Mazer. "I'm not a lieutenant."

"They don't need to know that," said Mazer.

A woman's voice crackled over the radio. "Colonel Li just informed us you were coming, Captain. Good to have you along."

It was the squad leader. A South African lieutenant named Opperman.

The squad spent a quick moment introducing themselves. There were a total of seven fighters, including Mazer. Far fewer than Mazer had hoped.

"You want to tell us what's going on, Captain?" said Opperman. "Helm is saying this battleship coming in is one of ours."

"That's the story," said Mazer. "Any change in its approach?"

"Negative. Coming in like a barn sparrow, hot and heavy. Did this thing really take out one of our own transports?"

"And the few hundred marines who were on it," said Mazer. "The transport is the Antietam. Lieutenant, with your permission I'd like my co-pilot to check every frequency and see if he can get anyone from the Antietam on radio. Maybe there are survivors."

"I'm looking at the debris field right now on my HUD," said Opperman. "If there are survivors, it would be a miracle. It looks like a few larger pieces were thrown from the attack site, but chances are slim that anyone's alive inside them. But you don't need my permission to do anything, Captain Rackham. Colonel Li has given you this op. We're awaiting your orders."

Li opened a private channel with Mazer. "Don't object to this, Mazer. I know precisely what you're going to say. These pilots don't know you. They haven't trained with you. Putting you in charge will only disrupt whatever rhythm they have. I understand. But I know *you*, not them. And right now, my only concern is every marine on this space station. If you don't stop that battleship, we all might die. That's a scenario I am taking every precaution to avoid. This isn't ideal, but this is the situation we find ourselves in. Your orders are to intercept that battleship and destroy it."

Mazer didn't argue. Li had voiced all of Mazer's objections and dismissed them. There was nothing left to say, only work to be done.

"Sir," said Mazer. "There is a possibility, maybe even a likelihood, that some of the crew members on that ship are hostages. Control of the battleship has obviously been seized by terrorist mutineers, rogue members of the crew, or possibly even a single deranged member of the Fleet. There might be hundreds of innocent people on board who can't reach the helm. If we annihilate that battleship, we kill them all."

"I have already consulted with CentCom on this, Mazer," said Colonel Li. "Your orders are to fire and destroy. That battleship killed some of our own people. Now it's accelerating toward our position. The consensus is that they intend to ram us."

"Ramming the space station would be suicide," said Mazer. "The battleship would disintegrate on impact."

"This isn't an isolated incident, Mazer. I've been informed that it's happening elsewhere in the Fleet. The ships of Operation Sky Siege are under attack as we speak, not by the Formics, but by ships of their own fleet. The battleship on approach is a threat to this facility. I am aware that innocent lives on that ship may be lost, but I'll take that over all of us dying. Now do your job."

"Yes, sir," said Mazer.

He clicked off the channel and began entering data into the ship's flight computer preparing for acceleration and intercept.

"We're going through with this?" said Bingwen. "We're vaporizing one of our own ships?"

"If that proves necessary," said Mazer.

Bingwen frowned. "If? That sounds like you're considering ignoring a lawful order."

"Is it lawful?" said Mazer. "I could probably argue that at my court-martial."

"So you *are* disobeying the order," said Bingwen.

"The colonel told us to destroy the ship," said Mazer. "He didn't tell us how."

"And how, pray tell, do *you* intend to destroy it?"

"We breach the ship," said Mazer. "We infiltrate it at the helm and take out whoever staged this mutiny. We take back control of the battleship and then we stop it or veer it away from GravCamp."

"And if that doesn't work?" said Bingwen.

"We annihilate it." Mazer clicked back to the squad-

ron. "Green Squad. We are ordered to destroy that battle-ship. Lieutenant Opperman, how willing are you to go with me inside and try a less destructive method first?"

"Just say the word, sir."

"Then everyone listen up," said Mazer. "We'll split into two squadrons. These three fighters will stay behind: Borgensen, Porcevic, and Agappe." He tapped the screen in front of him and selected the three fighters, each loaded with a full cache of ordnance and breach missiles. "You're A Squad and our safety net. If the battleship reaches you, destroy it." Mazer tapped at the screen and brought up the schematics of the battleship.

"Lieutenant Opperman," said Mazer, "who's the best navigator in this squad?"

"That would be Nav Officer Sylva, sir. She's sitting right beside me."

"Sylva, map us a path to that ship that gets us there as fast as humanly possible, taking into consideration that we're going in opposite directions and need to intercept. Can you do that in the next ninety seconds?"

"I will certainly try, sir."

"Captain Sarr," said Mazer.

The Senegalese captain back in the control room answered. "Go ahead, Rackham."

"I need you or someone in that room deeply familiar with this class of battleship to identify primary targets on that ship. What should we be hitting? Where are the weaknesses? I want two options. Option one, obliteration. Total destruction. So that every piece of it flies away and nothing hits GravCamp. Option two, scuttle and redirect. I want to know how to put it out of commission without killing everyone inside."

"Give me a minute," said Sarr.

"Sixty seconds and counting," said Mazer, "because that's all we can afford."

Sarr was back in thirty seconds and put another officer on the comms who knew the D-class inside and out. A schematic appeared in Mazer's HUD as the officer went through the targets. Mazer quickly made assignments to A Squad, selecting portions of the schematics for each of the pilots to target.

"It feels wrong targeting one of our own," said Agappe.

"Those are your orders," said Mazer. "We don't know what's going on in that ship, but you will not hesitate to execute your orders if the opportunity arises, even if Opperman and I are still on board and trying to disable it. Are we clear? You will not hesitate to fire."

"Yes, sir."

"Maintain your current velocity," said Mazer. "You should intercept it long before it reaches GravCamp, but there is still a threat of shrapnel and debris striking the space station and pods, so I repeat, do not hesitate. The longer you wait, the greater the risk to every marine at GravCamp."

"Yes, sir. Understood."

"The rest of us are B Squad," said Mazer. "We will shoot forward and intercept the battleship. Mission one is to take out its guns. Here are the assignments."

The schematic lit up again as Mazer doled out targeting assignments to B Squad.

"B Squad, do not breach the hull if it can be avoided," said Mazer. "I want to minimize casualties, if we can. That said, do what's necessary to take out its guns. It decimated the Antietam, so whoever has seized control of the helm controls the guns as well. Once the guns are down, Opperman and I will infiltrate the ship at the helm, if possible. If at any time I give the order or if Opperman and I become casualties and our biometrics go offline, the rest of you in B Squad will incapacitate the ship. Sylva, I've given you about three minutes. What have you got?"

Sylva responded, "I'm sending the flight path now, sir. It's not pretty. But it gets us there."

A crude navigational holo appeared on Mazer's HUD. It showed lines that looped wide and came back toward the center, like the outline of flower petals.

"We need to do a loop," said Sylva. "It's coming toward us at incredible speed. So we've got to reach its speed and match its direction right before it reaches us."

"This says we're going to sustain eight Gs for thirty seconds to accelerate up to that velocity," said Opperman. "That doesn't sound fun."

"It's more than we've practiced in maneuvers," said Sylva. "And far more than safety regs recommend. But it's our best shot."

Mazer muted his comm and turned to Bingwen. "You're small, eight Gs is a lot."

"I'll black out," said Bingwen. "But the suit will continue to feed me oxygen. I'll be fine. Let's go. We don't have a choice."

Mazer hesitated for a microsecond. With Bingwen in the co-pilot seat, it would be safer for Bingwen if Mazer's fighter hung back with A Squad and didn't attempt the acceleration. But Mazer had trained with a breach team. If anyone was qualified to infiltrate the ship, it was him. He couldn't give that assignment to anyone else.

"I'll be fine," said Bingwen. "Every second we wait, we disrupt the flight plan. We go. Now."

Mazer gave the countdown to the pilots as Sylva uploaded the flight instructions into each fighter's navigational system. At zero, the thrusters opened, and Mazer was slammed against his seat again. The pressure grew quickly, and in moments Mazer felt as if he weighed two tons, as if his organs were coalescing inside him into a single blob of tissue, as if an unseen mountain were pressing him against the seat.

After twelve seconds, he didn't think he could take any more of it. He was nearing his breaking point, with eighteen seconds to go.

Seventeen.

Sixteen.

The noise in the cockpit was fading. The console lights, as if seen through a lens losing its focus, began to blend together into a soft soup of color. The biometrics on Mazer's HUD indicated that Bingwen had passed out. Mazer wanted to call out to him, reach for him, turn to him. But Mazer's arms and head were frozen in place. Even speech was impossible. He was stone, lead, immovable, held in the seat by an unseen vice. He watched the numbers for Bingwen's heart rate and oxygen levels slowly dip. Down one digit, down two, down five.

Come on, Bing. Hang in there. A little further now.

The world grew black at the corners of Mazer's vision as the seconds ticked by. He was slipping. Darkness was creeping in, swallowing him, pulling him downward. Bingwen's oxygen dipped farther, then farther still.

Breathe, Bingwen. Breathe.

The numbers for the ship's velocity were a blur of light as they accelerated. Mazer stared at the digits as they raced upward. Would Kim know what happened to him? he wondered. If he succumbed to the darkness, if his heart ruptured, if he suffered an aneurysm, would Kim ever get word? She was whispering in his ear now; Mazer could feel her pressed close against him, lying tangled in the bed, her bare leg wrapped around his, her breath hot on the side of his face, telling him she loved him, telling him she wanted a son or a daughter, it didn't matter so long as it was made from him. A child that was half Maori, half American, half her, half him. She opened her mouth and spoke again, but now the words were silence. Blackness, like a blanket, had smothered the memory.

The pressure released instantly. The velocity numbers stopped spinning. The thrusters had cut. Thirty seconds had expired. Acceleration was over. Target velocity reached.

Mazer blinked, disoriented. Half a minute had felt like a lifetime. A sensation of equal parts euphoria and exhaustion coursed through him. His whole body felt weak and tingly. He shook himself, checked the readouts. They had reached the necessary velocity.

He felt a slight shift as his body slid to the left in the straps. They were moving in the wide loop now. They were circling around, getting into position.

"Report," said Mazer. "Everyone check in."

The pilots all responded. They were shaken but awake.

"Bingwen." Mazer reached over and shook Bingwen but got no response. "Bingwen."

The boy roused, shifted in his seat, his arms floating up in zero G around him. "What did I miss?"

Mazer exhaled in relief. "The easy part. We're in the loop. Battleship is still coming. We intercept in sixty seconds. Opperman, suit up."

Mazer unbuckled from the seat and flew back to the weapons bay. He opened the locker and removed the battle suit, a heat-resistant metal armor engineered by Victor Delgado for asteroid tunnel combat that fit over Mazer's flight suit and oxygen supply. It was bulky and cumbersome, and Mazer felt hindered somewhat in his movements whenever he wore one. But if he was conducting a breach, he'd make that tradeoff for the added protection.

"Who would conduct a coup?" said Bingwen. "How stupid is that? Why cripple the Fleet in the middle of a war? Right when we need a cohesive, unified force against the Formics?"

"Terrorists are willing to burn down the world to promote hateful ideologies," said Mazer. "This is their MO."

"Maybe this isn't terrorists," said Bingwen. "Maybe

these are people who believe they're saving the Fleet and not weakening it."

"It doesn't matter what their position is," said Mazer. "They're killing people."

"All the more reason to be cautious," said Bingwen. "You don't know what you're getting into. This could be the work of a single person or dozens."

"Blowing it up without at least investigating the situation inside feels irresponsible," said Mazer. "There might be innocent people on that ship. We've already lost a lot of marines on the Antietam. I don't want us to lose any more."

"Let's hope they give us good attorneys at our court-martial," said Bingwen.

The console beeped as Mazer snapped on the final piece of armor.

"Here it comes," said Bingwen.

Mazer flew up to the cockpit as the Tik fighters closed back in from their loops to form a wide ring. If the battleship had stayed the course and maintained its velocity, and if the Tik fighters had executed the flight path accurately, the D-class battleship would fly right into the center of the ring of fighters.

"We should be fighting the Formics, not each other," said Opperman. "This is insanity. Marines are giving the bugs hell in the Asteroid and Kuiper Belts, and we're out here chasing down a rogue lunatic."

"Hold your positions," said Mazer. "And stay sharp. This thing annihilated the Antietam. It can pick us off easy if we don't watch ourselves. Opperman, you suited up?"

"Affirmative."

"Bingwen, give me a visual when you have one," said Mazer.

The radio crackled. Colonel Li's voice came through. "Mazer, do you copy?"

Mazer answered, but there was a time delay now. Grav-Camp was an incredible distance behind them.

"Rackham here, go ahead Colonel."

The response was slow. The time delay was maddening. "We've been running the data from our eye," said Li, "backtracking the battleship's and the Antietam's movements. That battleship didn't fire on the Antietam, Mazer. It rammed it. It flew right through it like a comet."

Mazer blinked. "Rammed the Antietam? That's impossible, sir. It couldn't have survived that impact, even with its shields. Both ships would have disintegrated."

And then, like a fog clearing from his mind, Mazer understood.

"What's he talking about?" said Opperman. "What's happening?"

"We're not fighting a coup," said Mazer. "We're fighting Formics."

The battleship came into view, a dark shape advancing in the blackness, moving into the center of the ring of Tik fighters like a leviathan rising out of the deep. There were no lights, no IF markings, no laserline receiver or array or external equipment of any kind on its surface. There was only the hull: red and smooth and glossy, covering the ship from end to end, as if the whole vessel had been dipped in a vat of red molten metal and allowed to cool. A single piece of metal shaped like a D-class battleship. Seamless, immaculate, pristine.

"Hullmat," said Bingwen. "They've taken one of our own ships and covered it with hullmat. That's why it intends to ram GravCamp. They know they'll come through undamaged. They've turned one of our own ships into a spear."

"They didn't cover one of our ships," said Mazer. "They made one of their own to look like ours."

Below them, several doors on the surface of the Formic

ship began to open. The guns underneath, like folded flowers seeking the sun, stretched and extended outward, reaching, rising, turning slightly as they found their targets. Mazer was shouting orders to break formation and scatter when the Formic guns filled the darkness with lethal glowing bursts of green.

CHAPTER 18

Warheads

Perhaps the greatest deception of the Hive Queen was in giving the International Fleet a false sense of security. Or to put it differently, her greatest deception was in creating the perception that her deceptions could be easily discovered.

An example will best illustrate. Shortly after the International Fleet discovered that the Hive Queen was moving some asteroids into clusters and using the raw materials of those asteroids to build large military structures, the International Fleet sent warships to destroy the structures. However, upon arrival, the Fleet discovered that the structures were nothing more than hollow Potemkin bases. Or feints. This simple discovery led the IF to believe that *all* deceptions of the Hive Queen would be similarly easily uncovered.

But in truth, it is likely that the purpose of the structures was not to fool the IF, but rather to lead the IF to believe that they could not be fooled, to fill IF command with vain confidence. Doing so would blind IF command to the Hive Queen's *real* deceptions. This false confidence among IF command allowed the Hive Queen to employ numerous deceptive tactics with devastating effectiveness. The blinds of Operation Deep

Dive is one such example, as is her tactic of building warships shaped like our own.

What is most remarkable about this latter deception is not how accurate the Hive Queen was in copying the shape and structure of our ships, but rather that she was able to produce so many and unleash them on IF targets throughout the system at the same time in a massive coordinated strike, without anyone in the Fleet knowing that she had even built them.

—Demosthenes, *A History of the Formic Wars,* Vol. 3

Inside the cockpit of the Tik fighter, Bingwen's body jerked violently to one side in his restraints as the fighter barrel-rolled to the right and then dropped like a wounded bird in flight. It all happened in an instant, a sudden, hard change in direction. Bingwen's hold on the trigger grip was gone. His arms, now free, slammed into the inner wall of the cockpit, and Bingwen felt an explosion of pain in his right elbow. The projected view in front of him, which only a moment ago featured a calm and steady view of the stars, now showed a spinning, blurred field of red: the hull of the Formic ship coming up fast.

The fighter was falling.

No, that wasn't right, Bingwen realized. They couldn't be falling. They were in space. There was no up or down, no gravity to pull them in one direction. They weren't falling toward the Formic ship; they were diving. Intentionally.

Beside Bingwen in the pilot's seat, Mazer was shouting orders into his commlink, one hand gripped tight to the flight stick, the other hand moving furiously through the small holofield above the console, rearranging a series of shapes to alter the fighter's flight path. Bingwen heard Mazer's orders, heard the shouts of alarm and chatter from the other pilots as they responded in kind and

scrambled to avoid the gamma plasma bursting from the Formic guns beneath them. But the frantic fast-paced dialogue was just noise in Bingwen's ears. As if the voices were a hundred meters away, speaking through a tube.

Bingwen had to get his hands back on the trigger grips. He had to work the guns. Mazer needed him on the guns.

Bingwen's hands wouldn't respond. They shifted one way and then another. Limp and useless and suddenly heavy.

Mazer was shouting again, but the words were even more meaningless. Noise. Screams.

Bingwen's vision couldn't settle. He couldn't find anything to focus on. Nothing held still. The world moved too quickly.

Bingwen knew he needed to use his hands, to get control of his hands, but he couldn't remember why.

Something was wrong, he realized. His mind was muddled.

Blood wasn't flowing to his brain, he realized. They were diving too suddenly, too aggressively. The G-force was too great again. The thrusters had to be screaming.

Mazer banked left hard, and Bingwen's arms struck the inner wall again. Another explosion of pain, this one worse than the first. But it helped. The jolt of instant agony roused Bingwen. Like a bucket of cold water thrown in his face.

"I need you, Bingwen. Get on that gun."

Yes, thought Bingwen. He was the gunner. That's why he had come. To help Mazer.

But his brain wouldn't work. His hands wouldn't hold.

"Bingwen, the guns!"

Mazer's voice. Like a whip cracking. He wants me to target the Formic guns, the large mechanical arms protruding from the red ship. The gun that was firing at them. The gun that would kill them if Bingwen didn't act.

Bingwen's head snapped to one side as Mazer changed direction again, avoiding a wall of gamma plasma that whipped past.

I'm useless, thought Bingwen. This is nothing like the sim.

"Get to the bow of the ship," Mazer said into his radio. "Position your fighters up near the nose. Most of the guns can't reach you there. Use the curvature of the ship to provide cover."

"That gun at 3 o'clock can still pick us off at the nose," said Opperman over the radio. "That's hardly good cover."

"Leave the gun to me and Bingwen," said Mazer. "We'll draw its fire and take it out. Bingwen, look alive."

Bingwen blinked, fighting back the disorientation, his vision swirling. Somehow he grabbed the console in front of him and held tight to the trigger grips.

If only he were stronger, he thought. If only he had Mazer's arms.

"Answer me, Bing."

"I'm here. I'm on it."

Bingwen shook himself, forcing his mind to focus. He flipped on the targeting system, and the boxes of light appeared in front of him. He had done this countless times in the sim. This was easy. These were self-guided lasers. They did eighty percent of the work. He could do this with his eyes closed.

It was pointless training, Bingwen now realized. The sim was nothing compared to this. The fighter weaved and bobbed and rolled so erratically that Bingwen couldn't get his bearings long enough to put the Formic gun in the center of the targeting square. As soon as the Formic gun appeared, it was whipped from view again.

"I can't get a lock," said Bingwen. "Steady us out."

"If I steady us, we die," said Mazer, banking yet again to dodge another burst of fire.

Mazer was not just reacting, Bingwen realized. Mazer

was keeping their movements erratic intentionally, diving downward toward the gun, juking one direction and then cutting elsewhere to prevent the gun from targeting them.

But physics was working against them. Every little tap of a retro put them into a new spin, causing them to drift sideways or rotate in the wrong direction, flying out of control like an errant firework.

They couldn't do this forever, not only because it made targeting the gun impossible, but also because the propellant on the retros wouldn't last, not at the rate Mazer was using it, wide open and nearly constantly.

"Anytime, Bingwen. The closer we get to that gun, the more likely—"

"I know, I know," said Bingwen.

The red glossy hull flew up to meet them. Closer, closer. The Formic gun appeared in Bingwen's targeting square for an instant, and this time he didn't hesitate. A burst of laserfire erupted from the fighter, but the shots were wide by hundreds of meters. The fighter's movements were too erratic, too unpredictable, too fast. Bingwen didn't have a prayer of hitting anything.

He fired again, hoping for random luck, hoping that the Formic gun would pass in front of the targeting square at precisely that instant, but again the fired slasers were nowhere near the target.

"I can't hit it," said Bingwen.

The Formic ship was coming up fast, a vast wall of glossy red metal, filling the projected view in front of them.

Mazer banked hard to the right, pulling away. "We'll get it from another angle. Opperman, status?"

"We're clustered up at the bow," said Opperman over the radio, "but we're cooked if that gun on you turns in our direction."

"Snuggle up next to the nose," said Mazer. "Bring the fighters in tight and push the ship off course. Like a tug guiding a tanker into port."

"You think the fighters can take that kind of structural abuse?"

"They'll hold if you share the burden together," said Mazer. "Wedge the fighters up in the crevices or you'll slide off. Then slowly increase your thrust. It won't take much."

"And if the Formics course-correct their ship?"

"All we need is to push them off course a fraction of a degree," said Mazer. We have to divert them. A Squad doesn't have a prayer of stopping this ship. We knock them off course here and now or there is no GravCamp."

"And that gun?" said Opperman.

"Working on it."

Bingwen felt as if he were going to vomit. Mazer had not stopped his erratic flight pattern, and the fighter now seemed even more out of control and harder to steer, twisting and rolling and spinning in a random fashion. Except now the fighter was skimming along the surface of the ship, flying just a few meters above it, zeroing in on the Formic gun. Twice the fighter struck the surface of the Formic ship and bounced violently upward, like a crazed airplane that couldn't decide if it wanted to land or not. Bingwen screamed in alarm. The fighter couldn't take that kind of abuse. The hullmat beneath them was indestructible. The fighter wasn't. Knocking the two of them together was like a clod of dried mud striking against a rock. Something was going to give, and it wasn't the rock.

Another hard hit.

And another.

What was Mazer doing? They would be ripped in half and ejected into space. Bingwen could feel the hull of the fighter bending inward with every impact.

Another jolt.

Another.

Equipment around Bingwen rattled. Something broke off the wall and hit his helmet and flew off in another direction. A small object, Bingwen didn't know what.

Alarms wailed inside Bingwen's helmet, and for a moment he thought his suit had been breached. But no, it was the fighter. The hull had breached somewhere. The ship *was* breaking apart.

Bingwen looked around frantically, searching for the breach.

Another jolt. This one different from the others. Not an impact. Something else.

Bingwen's targeting display showed him: breach missiles were soaring away from the fighter. Five of them. Mazer had fired them. Mazer had taken command of the weaponry.

Bingwen was no longer holding his firing grips, he realized. He was no longer holding anything. His arms were pulled in tight to his body, as if in a fetal position, or as much of a fetal position as his restraints would allow. Instinctual. Fearful. Like a child.

He had abandoned his guns without even realizing it. He had abandoned everything. For the last few moments, he had done nothing but panic. He could have been targeting the gun, he could have been helping, doing something, anything, but he hadn't. He had frozen and hadn't even realized it.

Mazer had needed him.

And Bingwen had failed him.

It was then that Bingwen realized something else as well. The Formic gun was no longer firing at them. It hadn't fired at all ever since Mazer had come down close to the surface. The gamma plasma was one of the only substances that would cut through hullmat. The Formics were no longer firing because they couldn't risk missing the fighter and damaging their own ship.

Mazer had known that. He had brought them close and crashed them into the hullmat to avoid being shot.

Two of the breach missiles hit the target. Bingwen saw it all on his HUD. The top of the Formic gun exploded

and broke apart into a cloud of shrapnel. The second breach missile hit the gun's scaffolding structure about halfway up. That too broke apart, sending more shrapnel away from the blast.

But Mazer wasn't stopping. He didn't pull the fighter up and away. He stayed the course, soaring toward the remains of the gun tower looming large in front of them.

Bingwen watched, waiting for Mazer to change course and remove them from an impending impact. But the fighter didn't deviate. It streaked forward, heading straight for the ruined scaffolding, a giant twisted metal structure, maybe fifteen meters high, with intricately woven bands of metal that looked unyielding. We're going to hit it, Bingwen realized. Mazer wasn't trying to avoid the scaffolding. He was targeting it.

The bottom of the fighter struck the surface of the Formic ship and bounced upward, but Mazer quickly fired the retros and put them back down to the surface again, back on a collision course. Bingwen called out a warning, but the screaming siren in his helmet from the breach was so loud he couldn't even hear himself.

A message appeared on Bingwen's HUD. Three words. From Mazer, right beside him.

BRACE FOR IMPACT

Bingwen wanted to scream. He wanted to cry out and grab the stick and change their direction and spin off into oblivion. But everything inside him had cinched up in terror and stopped working at once. He was just a ball of mass now, strapped into his harness. Frozen. Helpless. Hurtling toward the inevitable.

Then impact.

The fighter crumpled and spun and buckled and broke as it struck the gun tower. Bingwen felt pulled in a dozen directions at once, as if the cockpit were attacking him

from every side and angle, viciously, ferociously. Shrapnel exploded. A large black something—a beam or bar, perhaps—swooped downward and struck Bingwen's helmet in a microsecond flash of violence, and then all Bingwen saw was . . .

The sun. Bright and burning and golden in the sky above the horizon, its rays filling the whole green valley with a golden glow. He was standing in a rice paddy, basking in the light, shirt unbuttoned and open, skin deeply tanned from months of labor, arms outstretched, welcoming the sun. Like a friend returning. Like a brother come home.

The mud was cold and thick at his feet, oozing up between his toes. The water up past his shins glimmered in the light, sparkling like diamond dust on the surface, reflecting rays back into Bingwen's eyes.

The young rice shoots all around him, in neat, orderly rows, only barely poked up out of the water, each primary leaf barely breaking the surface like a periscope daring to look up out of the deep—or like a tentative toe dipping itself not into water, but out of it and into the world, testing its temperature. They were welcoming the sun too. Every plant, every blade, every cell. Feasting on the light.

A low rumbling sound to Bingwen's left. An animal. Mooing. Father was rubbing the water buffalo behind the ear, like some people did with dogs or cats. Father was strange that way. Doting on it, giving it affection. Why didn't Father ever do that to me? Bingwen wondered. A rub behind the ear. An embrace. A tousle of the hair. Did Father love the water buffalo more than he loved me?

Don't be ridiculous, said Mother. She was beside Bingwen now, arms open, straw hat in one hand, hair pulled back, eyes closed, soaking in the sun, welcoming its blanket of warmth. Father loves you, she said. Just as I do.

But her lips weren't moving.

And she wasn't there. Not really. None of it was there.

Because Mother was dead. Father too. And the water buffalo. And the valley. And the rice and the mud and the water and the straw hat and home and everything.

Was the sun gone too? Did the Formics take the sun as well?

"Can you hear me?" Mother asked.

"Bingwen."

She was calling to him. Her voice loud but gentle. Not a rebuke, but a word that said so much more than his name. Gentle. Warm. Like the sun's blanket. She wanted him to come in for dinner, perhaps. Or to start the fire for the evening, perhaps. Or to get Grandfather his tea. Or to wring out the laundry. Why would she shake him? Mother never shook him.

Bingwen's eyes snapped open.

Mazer was above him, still in his helmet and suit, his face tight with concern. "Bingwen!" His expression relaxed slightly. "Can you hear me?"

It took Bingwen a moment to gather himself. He was still in his harness. The fighter had stopped. The siren had stopped. The spinning had stopped. The harness held him in place, cradling him, holding him.

"We crashed," said Bingwen.

"Had to," said Mazer. "If we had gone any further across the surface of the ship, we'd have found other guns waiting for us, and we weren't in any position to outmaneuver them. I lost two of the retros. The Tik became impossible to maneuver. Had a hell of a time keeping it close to the hullmat to avoid being fired upon. Felt like trying to fly a deflating balloon."

"How did we stop?" said Bingwen.

"Part of the fighter is embedded into the scaffolding. I used the launch hook on the back of the fighter to anchor us. It's not very secure. I don't think it will hold. That's why I need to know immediately if you're hurt. We can't stay here."

Nothing felt broken. Bingwen could see, hear, move. His suit was intact. His helmet visor was clear and uncracked. His body ached where the harness straps were positioned around his chest and waist and legs, but he was in one piece.

Bingwen shook his head. "No. I got whacked pretty hard. But I'm okay."

Mazer pulled a lever to Bingwen's right, and the harness straps loosened and retracted. Bingwen drifted in place, free, still blinking, uneasy, sore.

"These suits are stronger than I thought," said Mazer. "Victor outdid himself." He moved back to the weapons locker and began lifting a bent beam away from the breach missiles.

Bingwen rotated his arm and felt a sharp pain in his elbow. "You crashed on purpose?"

"Maybe a stupid decision," said Mazer, "but I couldn't stop our momentum otherwise. We got lucky."

"You call this lucky?"

Mazer's voice suddenly rose. "No time for snark, Bing. All right? You came on this mission, you act like a soldier."

Bingwen stiffened with surprise.

Mazer exhaled. He stopped pushing on the beam and turned to Bingwen, his shoulders relaxing. "We're in a bad situation, Bingwen. I'm a little on edge. I need you to focus. Please. Otherwise we both die."

The rebuke stung more than the pain in Bingwen's elbow, and he felt his face grow hot with shame. "I choked with the guns. You needed me, and I messed up."

Mazer sighed, looked away, then turned back. "This isn't over," he said. "Opperman has bought us some time. She and the other fighters have pushed this thing off course, but it's only a matter of time before it course-corrects and re-targets GravCamp. You and I have work to do. Help me with this beam."

Bingwen nodded and moved to the back of the ship beside Mazer. The rear of the fighter was crunched inward dramatically. They had struck the scaffolding in the rear with such force that Bingwen was surprised that the fighter had held together in one piece. Had they struck the scaffolding head-on, they wouldn't have been so lucky.

The beam Mazer was trying to move was as thick as Bingwen's arm. It appeared to be aluminum and somewhat pliable, though. Bingwen anchored his boots to the floor for leverage and pushed upward on the beam as Mazer did the same. Whatever contribution Bingwen made was minimal, but the beam slowly bent upward and cleared a path to the locker where the tubes holding the breach missiles were housed.

"We should have ricocheted and bounced off," said Bingwen. "We should be drifting."

"If our ship breaks free, we will," said Mazer. "But not far. I've anchored it to the scaffolding. Here. Buckle this to your suit." He gave Bingwen a D-clamp attached to a wire tether. "This is a precaution. A secondary tether, in case the one holding the ship breaks."

"But if I'm anchored to the ship, and the ship breaks free, what good is that?"

"You're not anchored to the ship," said Mazer. "We're both tethered to the scaffolding outside. Do you still have the NanoCloud paint? Please tell me you still have the NanoCloud paint."

The small bucket of paint and holstered brush were still in Bingwen's pouch. "I have some," said Bingwen. "But not much. I wasn't planning on taking out a huge Formic warship with it."

"If I paint it on the hullmat," said Mazer, "and turn on the nanobots, will the bots unzip the hull forever? Or do they run out of juice? Will they keep going until the entire hull of the ship is gone or do they only work for so long?"

"I don't know," said Bingwen. "I suspect that they keep going, but even if that's true, it would take forever to unzip this entire hull. I have relatively few nanobots in this paint. I mixed it up to break you out of the brig, not for this."

"When you say it will take forever, what does that mean? One hour? One day? One week?"

"You're asking for calculations that I can't possibly make," said Bingwen. "I don't know any more about this tech than you do."

"Best guess," said Mazer. "Considering the size of the ship. You've played with this stuff. Your guess is better than mine."

Bingwen shrugged. "Half a day at least, I'd say. This is a big ship."

Mazer frowned. "We don't have a day."

"And even if we unzip the hull, what's to keep them from putting on pressure suits and flying this thing into GravCamp anyway?"

"We're going with plan B," said Mazer.

"Which is?"

"We use the paint to make a few small holes," said Mazer. "Just big enough to drop in the warheads from the remaining breach missiles. Like a grenade."

Bingwen blinked. "You're going to remove the warhead from a breach missile?"

"We're going to remove *four* warheads from *four* breach missiles. I think that's how many we have left."

Mazer grabbed a drill and began unscrewing the paneling to reach the launch tubes.

"Do you even know how to do that?" said Bingwen.

"It's not rocket science," said Mazer, then winked. "That was a joke."

"I'm glad you find this humorous. I'd laugh along if I thought it was funny. You're going to manhandle a missile?"

The paneling came free. Mazer reached in and opened the first launch tube. It was empty. The next two tubes were empty as well. The fourth tube held a breach missile. Mazer reached in and, with a great deal of grunting and exertion, pulled the missile out of the tube. It was as long as Bingwen and judging by how difficult it was for Mazer to maneuver it in the tight confines of the fighter in zero G, the missile had a lot of mass. The guidance systems at the nose and rear were already blinking.

"You sure you should be touching that?" said Bingwen.

Mazer let the missile hover in the air a moment and handed Bingwen the bag of tools. "We tested all kinds of armaments at WAMRED. Even disassembled a few. It was part of our analysis. Marines have to be able to make repairs. I'm no expert, but it's easier than you think. Each of these segments is self-contained. Like building blocks."

"And you can do this without detonating it and blowing us to smithereens?" Bingwen asked.

Mazer tapped his wrist pad. "I'm not doing this alone. GravCamp, this is Captain Rackham, do you copy, over?"

The time delay was less now. They were close to the station.

Captain Sarr's voice said, "Go ahead, Captain. We read you loud and clear. And we're glad you're still alive. After that wreck, we thought—"

"Shut up and listen," said Mazer. "I need a spacecraft armament systems specialist on the radio immediately to walk me through a warhead disassembly. I'm not certain I can do it solo."

"Warhead disassembly?" said Sarr.

"I need to remove the warhead from a B45 breach missile and detonate it remotely," said Mazer. "Find the crew that loads the breach missiles into the Tik fighters."

"They load the missiles, Rackham. They don't build them."

"Ask them," said Mazer.

Colonel Li's voice took over the commlink. "What's the plan, Mazer?"

Mazer quickly explained his intentions. They would make a few holes in the hullmat, drop in the warheads, and detonate. "If we don't scuttle this ship now, sir, and kill the crew, it's going to course-correct as soon as Lieutenant Opperman and her squad run out of fuel and can no longer push it off course. It might even course-correct before then. I don't know. All the more reason to inflict as much structural damage as we can, as quickly as we can."

"Captain Sarr is telling me that his armament specialists don't know how to disassemble the missiles. He just asked them."

"Then, sir, I need you to get on the ansible and find someone who can," said Mazer.

There was a pause on the line. When Colonel Li's voice returned, it was quiet and subdued, almost angry. "Your security clearance doesn't go that high, Mazer. You're not authorized to know anything about such a device, much less demand its use."

"You can discipline me some other time, sir. Right now, we—as in you and me and every living soul at GravCamp—needs a manufacturer or an armament specialist with intricate knowledge of the B45 to coach me. Unless you have a better idea, sir. Bingwen has already unscrewed the nose on one of these. If someone coaches us, we can move quickly."

By now Mazer had all four remaining missiles out of their tubes and floating in the tight, confined space. It was a miracle that the wreck hadn't damaged them. But the launch tubes were clearly and wisely designed to be especially resilient.

Finally Colonel Li responded. "The ansible transmits text, not voice. Whatever we receive will have to be read to you. Captain Sarr, move this radio conversation to my private quarters."

Mazer didn't wait. There were parts of the casing that he knew how to remove without any coaching. It was a simple matter of removing screws. Bingwen watched him, and then did the same to the others.

Five minutes later Colonel Li was back. "Mazer, whatever you say will be taken as dictation and transmitted instantly. I'm connected with an Officer Bridgewater at CentCom in weapons and armaments. I'll read back to you whatever she types in response."

"Cumbersome," said Mazer. "Is there not a faster way to do this?"

The time delay between each response was only a few seconds, but it infuriated Mazer.

"I've got instantaneous communication across the solar system on my end, Mazer," said Li. "I don't see how we could be any faster than that."

Mazer announced that he was ready, and they began. He soon realized that he didn't need to say much, just a simple confirmation that he had accomplished whatever the tech was ordering him to do. To say more, because of the time delay, would only disrupt Colonel Li's flow as he read directions. Bridgewater understood the urgency and yet was meticulous. Even if Mazer hadn't worked with armaments before, he could have done the task easily with such clear and technical instructions. Whoever Bridgewater was, she was the right person for the job. Li did well also, keeping his diction clear and repeating himself often. Mazer never once wondered if he had misheard.

While Mazer worked, Bingwen made a quick call to the control room with his own radio. "What's our flight status?"

"You're nine minutes out," said Captain Sarr. "You're off course, thanks to the fighters pushing at the nose, but you'll miss GravCamp by only two thousand kilometers if your current trajectory holds."

"I don't know if that's a safe enough distance," said Bingwen. "We only took out one of the ship's guns. Two thousand klicks might still be within range."

"Two thousand klicks is a decent distance," said Sarr. "GravCamp is an *extremely* tiny target at that distance. We've been discussing it here in the control room. That's roughly the distance between Denver, Colorado, and Atlanta, Georgia."

"That means nothing to me," said Bingwen. "I'm from southeast China."

"Means nothing to me, either," said Sarr. "I'm from Senegal, but it put all the Americans in the room at ease. So I'm relieved. As for the Formic guns, the Tik fighters from what Captain Rackham called A Squad are coming in to engage the guns at any moment. If they can take out a few more, our chances increase dramatically."

Bingwen ended the transmission and hurried to keep Mazer's work area clean. Each missile had four main segments, and as Mazer removed them, Bingwen stuffed the unneeded segments back into the tubes to keep them out of the way.

Finally, Mazer said, "Okay, I've got the four warhead segments free. Now what?"

Colonel Li continued to read instructions. "You don't have to remove the warhead from its segment. Don't try. Keep the warhead in the tube. On the inside of the segment on the top side you should see twelve small electronic contacts. Those contacts connect to the detonator found in the segment above it. You'll only need one detonator for the job. It's a green rod. Maybe twelve centimeters long, eight centimeters wide. Gently pull it out of the segment. It should come away relatively easily. It should

have wires protruding from it that connect to the electronic contacts on the warhead."

Bingwen was listening and digging through the segments he had tucked away. He found one of the green detonators and pulled it free.

"I have the detonator," said Mazer.

Bingwen and Mazer then listened as Li read the instructions for how to set a timer on the detonator that would then be transmitted to the warhead. "Once you touch the warhead to the detonator, the warhead is armed and the countdown has begun."

"How will I know that it worked?" said Mazer. "How can I be certain that the warhead is armed? Will it flash a light or anything?"

"You won't know for certain," said Bridgewater, through Li. "The warhead wasn't designed for this type of use and so no mechanism was ever designed to give visual confirmation. But believe me, when it blows, you'll definitely know it."

Mazer emptied the tool bag and stuffed the four warhead segments into it. Then he put the detonator in his front pouch pocket to keep it from touching and prematurely arming the warheads.

"We're moving outside," said Mazer.

Mazer grabbed one of the slaser rifles, gave the other to Bingwen, and moved back toward the hatch. A clustered web of debris and twisted metal blocked his path, so Mazer pulled a few pieces of debris away to make a hole big enough for him and Bingwen to wiggle through. When they reached the hatch, they found the locking wheel bent inward and unmoving. Mazer repositioned himself, anchored his upper body against the wall, and then kicked at the wheel repeatedly until it finally gave and began to turn. When the hatch opened, there was no rush of escaping air. The interior of the fighter was already a vacuum.

Bingwen followed Mazer outside. They gripped the

handholds on the exterior of the fighter, and Bingwen took in the damage. The rear of the fighter was severely crumpled inward, with shards of jagged metal protruding in all directions. Deep abrasions covered the hull, with the paint stripped away entirely in some places. Behind it, on the Formic ship, where the fighter had struck it repeatedly and slid across the surface, Bingwen couldn't see so much as a scratch.

Mazer crawled along the exterior hull of the fighter until he reached the scaffolding to the Formic gun. The alien metal structure loomed over them, a leaning tower of mangled wreckage. The recessed area where the gun was normally housed was a dark black abyss nearly ten meters wide. Bingwen craned his neck to get a better view but couldn't see the bottom.

Mazer checked the strength of the anchor he had made around the scaffolding by pulling on the cable a few times and checking the locking mechanism. Then he swung the slaser rifle over his head and snapped it onto the back of his suit.

"Paint?" he said, holding out a hand.

"I should come with you," said Bingwen. "Provide cover."

Mazer shook his head. "Wouldn't work. Not the way I'm going."

"And what way is that?"

"Nak's trick from the Kandahar. I jump as far as I can and hope the tether cable holds. I need to get as far back toward the thrusters as possible. Wherever I land, that's where I drop the first fire in the hole. After I make the hole. Paint." He gestured urgently with this hand.

Bingwen handed him the bucket of paint, no bigger than a small thermos. "Had I known we'd be doing this, I would have brought a bigger bucket."

"If the hull reacts the same way the glass did, this will be enough. I also need your wrist pad to initiate the nanobots. Show me how this app works."

Bingwen showed him. "This is important," he said. "Once you paint, you've got to reholster the brush in the bucket before you initiate the nanobots with your wrist pad. Otherwise all the nanobots will be turned on, including the ones still in the paint can. And if that happens, then you'll have no more paint to work with and thus no more nanobots to assist you. If you're doing this four times, holster the brush every time. There's a dampener inside the paint bucket that keeps them from receiving the wrist pad's instructions. That way, only the paint on the surface will activate."

"Smart," said Mazer. "Whose idea was that?"

"Nak's. We learned of the need the hard way when we were practicing and making the paint cocktail."

"Got it. Anything else?"

"Don't forget to turn off the nanobots once you have a big enough hole. Otherwise they'll keep unzipping, including the surface of the ship where you're anchored. It will disintegrate beneath you, and then you'll have no purchase or ability to launch away or move. You'll be stuck right where you shouldn't be when the warhead detonates."

"Sound advice. Anything else?"

"If you launch in the air, won't you expose yourself to the other guns?"

"I'll launch off the scaffolding," said Mazer, "and fly as close to the surface as I can."

"That will work only once," said Bingwen. "After you've set the first warhead, you may not have a protrusion to launch from. Your only option may be to jump straight up and let the pendulum swing you."

"Then let's hope A Squad takes out the other guns."

"Is this ship going to break apart beneath us?"

"The nice thing about hullmat," said Mazer, "is that in this instance it will actually keep the explosion contained in the ship. It will shield us from what happens inside."

"Assuming the warheads detonate," said Bingwen.

"Stay here," said Mazer. "Shoot anything that isn't human."

Then he turned around, planted his feet against the scaffolding, bent his body tight like a spring, disengaged his boots, and launched, soaring across the surface of the ship with the slack of the tether cable trailing behind him.

CHAPTER 19

Money

To: lem.jukes@juke.net
From: wilasanee.saowaluk16@freebeltmail.net
Subject: dimming asteroid

Dear Lem,

I have put myself in front of my terminal many times to write you. Sometimes I actually did write a complete email. Other times I wrote only a portion of a message because I would stop halfway through and review what I had written, realize that it sounded childish or unclear or dense, and then despair and abandon the whole enterprise. Other times I noodled with previous drafts I had written only to like them even less once the exercise was through. What I never did, however, was actually send an email.

Why did I agonize over something so simple? Why was it so difficult for me to apologize? I do not know. Part of the reason is obvious. I fear that I set in motion a chain of events that resulted in the company being taken from you. You will almost certainly assure me that this isn't the case, but I will never be able to accept

that I had no hand in you losing what mattered to you most.

It also pains me that I allowed so much time to pass before I mustered the courage to send this. I fear that my silence only added to whatever burden you carried.

There are other reasons why sending you a message was difficult, but they are reasons that I do not understand myself and therefore can't possibly articulate.

And now I am not even certain if you even use this email address. Since it is linked to the company, and you are no longer there, I worry that I have lost my only means of contacting you. I cannot call you. I am no longer on Luna. I am not at liberty to give my location, but I can say I'm not on Earth, either.

I pray that you do receive this message, however, because we have learned of an irregularity that alarms me and all those who travel with me. Eros, the near-Earth asteroid, has disappeared. Its albedo dimmed for three days, and now it has vanished from scopes entirely. This information is not yet classified but only because the paperwork has not yet been completed. By the time you read this, it may be classified and difficult for you to learn more.

A Juke mining vessel is the nearest vessel to Eros at the moment, and arrangements are being made to invite the vessel to investigate. You have many contacts within the company, of course, who can inform you of what is discovered. I know how closely you watch the war, and how being with the company gave you access

to information not available to the public. This is my attempt to keep you informed even now.

For me, this new information, and the link to the Juke vessel, gave me the push I needed to approach my terminal one more time and write an email that I must send.

I pray for your comfort and peace. I pray that this new circumstance of life proves to be the door unopened finally thrust wide, beyond which you see a path untrodden and waiting and full of light.

Wila

The trees at Armstrong Park in Imbrium were real, having been brought up from Earth years ago as saplings and planted in moon soil mixed with organics and fertilizer. A network of nutrient drips kept them alive. Everything else in the park, however, was fake. Lem sat at a park bench under the shade of a maple and marveled at the fake wind generated by the turbines at the park's perimeter; the fake sun overhead, projected on the inner dome of the city to give its inhabitants a false sense of day; and most amusing of all, the fake birdsong broadcast from the tiny speakers hidden somewhere up in the trees.

A city of lies, thought Lem. Not just here, but in the people around him, the people he believed were true, the people who had seemed to show loyalty by their words and comportment. But that loyalty had been a false reality, no more real than the wind on his face and the birdsong in his ears.

No. That wasn't entirely true. One person was real. One person had never given him a false face.

He watched as Noloa Benyawe emerged from her taxi

at the park's edge and approached him. She seemed burdened and tired and trying hard not to show it. She was in casual attire, like something a woman might exercise in: perhaps what she wore on any given Sunday. It surprised Lem because he had never seen her dressed that way. And yet it was obviously what she chose to wear when she was most comfortable, most herself. This was the real her. The unadorned her. The her that Lem had never bothered to get to know. He realized then how little he actually knew about her outside of work. Cold facts were all that came to mind: she had recently remarried, she had three grown children, her first husband was a professor of something at a university somewhere, she was from Nigeria. But . . . that was it. Lem didn't really know her, not at the level that friends were supposed to know each other, that people with any sense of loyalty to one another *should* know each other. Which left him feeling . . . what? Ashamed? Selfish? He hadn't cared enough to know her. He had been so wrapped up in his work, in the company, in himself, that he hadn't shown any real interest in her. Not as a human being, anyway. He had only seen her as an engineer, a builder of ships, a solver of puzzles. Never as a mother or wife or friend.

She reached him and sat beside him on the bench. "You're staring at me with a strange earnestness. Have you gone cuckoo on me, Lem? Have you cracked?"

Lem sighed and leaned back in the bench and let the fake wind blow into his face like a real Earth breeze. "Maybe a little. Maybe a lot. I'm not sure yet. But either way, I think it's a good thing for me."

Benyawe raised an eyebrow. "You sound like one of those guys who decides to go backpacking through Europe to 'find himself.' You're too young for a midlife crisis, Lem. It's not your style. Do I need to slap you out of whatever funk you're in, because believe me, you wouldn't have to ask twice."

He smiled at her. "Eager to slap me, are you?"

Now it was her turn to sigh and lean back into the bench. "There were times. Lord knows there were times. But not today. I'm not feeling particularly slappy. Or would it be slapful?"

"Prone to slap," said Lem.

She nodded.

"How are things at the company?" said Lem.

"Is that why you asked me to come?" said Benyawe. "To have me report on how lost we are without you, how disastrous the company is without your leadership, how directionless we are without your careful guidance? I can say all that if you want me to."

"I don't want you to," said Lem. "Because I know it isn't true."

"No. It isn't true. Everyone is busy. The gears never stopped turning. The Fleet needs supplies, and we're the big supplier. We're as busy now as we've ever been. No one has even mentioned you that I've heard. That's terribly heartless of me to admit, but I'm not going to sugarcoat it for you. The company is doing what it needs to do." She paused. "Now you're sorry you asked me to come, aren't you?"

Lem's smile widened and he put his hands behind his head. "Not at all. You have no idea how happy it makes me to hear you say that. Not the substance of what you said, but that it's truth unfiltered. That's what you always gave me, Benyawe. Truth. I never doubted that."

"You have gone cuckoo on me."

"No question," said Lem. "I'm raving bonkers."

"So why *did* you bring me? To hear how I voted as a member of the board? To know if I cast my vote against you?"

"That doesn't matter," said Lem.

"Of course it matters," said Benyawe. "Or at least it matters to me. You may not want to hear, but I'm going to tell you."

"You always do," said Lem. He turned his body to face her, rested one elbow on the back of the bench, and waited.

"I voted for you to go. Not just to leave as CEO but to get out completely. I didn't want you on the board at all, not under your father. That would be its own circle of hell for you. Your father was coming back regardless of how I voted, but I could at least try and keep you from making the mistake of staying under his thumb. So yes, I made quite a scene and demanded that you go. I put my foot down, more so than I've done in those meetings before. I think I shocked a lot of people. They were expecting me to be an immovable wall, which I was, but it was a different wall than what they were expecting."

"Thank you," said Lem.

"For helping to throw you out of your company?"

"It was never my company," said Lem. "Not really. It was always my father's. I liked to pretend that I had made it mine, that I had built what it's become, but my father was right. The company's growth came from the Hegemony contracts that my father allowed me to have. He was controlling it all along, really. I thought I was a real boy, but I was Pinocchio."

"A habitual liar?" said Benyawe.

"A marionette," said Lem. "Dancing to my father's tugs on the strings."

"Now you're being melodramatic," said Benyawe.

"Grossly," said Lem. "It's rather off-putting, isn't it?"

"Did you call me here to mope?"

"I called you here to offer you a job."

"I have a job," said Benyawe. "One I happen to be very good at, one I've worked very hard to keep."

"You *have* worked hard," said Lem. "And you *are* very good. That's why I want you on my team."

"And what team is that? Community croquet? Ultimate Frisbee? I really only have the strength for bridge these days, Lem. Maybe Go Fish. I'm getting old."

"There aren't teams on Go Fish. It's every man for himself."

"Or every woman," said Benyawe. "But point taken. See? I'm less qualified for teams that I even realized."

"I'm going to miss you," said Lem. "I may not have been a very dedicated friend, for which I'm regretful, but I will miss our banter. You always know what to say."

"First you offer me a job, without explanation, and then you act as if I'll never see you again. I'm getting that Lem-has-gone-wackadoo vibe again."

"I'm not offering you a job so much as a company," said Lem. "I'm starting a nonprofit. I want you to have it."

"I make an exceptional salary at the company, Lem, as you well know. Some people would call it an obnoxious salary. When you say nonprofit, my current salary isn't sure if it should laugh hysterically or cower in the corner and scream."

"Is money all you care about?"

"Retirement is all I care about. Once this war is over, I'm done. Mandu and I go back to Nigeria, and I get some goats."

"Goats?" Lem asked. "You don't strike me as a goat lady."

"I'm not, really," said Benyawe. "Goats are cute. That's about the extent of my goat knowledge. I'd probably enjoy them for an afternoon and then hate them for eating the flowers. But the idea that I can have goats and not have to worry about orbital mechanics or chemical combustion or the schematics of the latest doohickey we're building is what's enticing. I can just focus on me."

"Why not go to Nigeria now?" said Lem. "Leave Juke Limited, with or without goats, and return home while you know there's still a home to return to. If we win, you can remain in Nigeria and make everything of your life that you've imagined. And if we lose, you will at least have lived some of the life you truly wanted. You decide.

I've giving you the company. You can live anywhere in the world so long as you have net access."

"You haven't told me what this company is."

"We're basically a military contractor."

Benyawe laughed. "Yes, nothing says nonprofit like exorbitantly expensive military weaponry. You can't compete against your father, Lem, if that's your plan. If you're doing this to prove to him that you've got chutzpah, it won't work. You'll only prove to him how easily he can crush you. Juke Limited is an unstoppable juggernaut, as resilient as hullmat. The company isn't going anywhere. It will steamroll every competitor in the world, particularly if we win this war and your father gets his wish to build a second fleet with interstellar ships."

"He told you about his little scheme? For us to go to the Formics and wipe them out on their own world?"

She glanced around her. "That's highly classified. Probably not something to be discussed in a public park."

"It isn't a park," said Lem. "It's a phony place pretending to be a park. The real parks are on Earth, in Nigeria, where you should be. This company I'm starting, this nonprofit, it's a military contractor, but not in the traditional sense. My model is what happened with Bingwen and the NanoCloud. He recognized a need for a handheld delivery system, and then you put a team together and gave him a solution for free. No contract. No committees. No red tape. No bureaucracy. No one in finance killing the initiative because the margins were too low. A problem was presented, and a solution was almost instantly provided, one that the marines on site could assemble themselves. You didn't have members of the board putting their nose in it and crunching numbers. You didn't have delays in production and nightmares with distribution. You didn't have any of the normal headaches. None of the parts of your job that you hate. All that went away. You only had to deliver an idea for

the Fleet to build on site, where it was needed, so it got from your brain into a marine's hands immediately. Or nearly immediately, which saves lives because it doesn't leave marines in a lurch, desperate for equipment and solutions. That's the company I'm giving you, Benyawe. One that discards traditional models of military contracting and completely ignores the sluggish quagmire that is Fleet bureaucracy."

"It sounds brilliant," said Benyawe. "But it's missing what such a company requires. Several somethings, in fact."

"Tell me."

"One, the company's objective is to produce ideas," said Benyawe. "Solutions to whatever countermeasures the Formics introduce. But ideas have to come from somewhere, or more specifically, from someone. They can't all come from me. I'm not that smart or that capable. This is a company of engineers. Do you have anyone other than me?"

"Not at the moment," said Lem. "But you'll help me build a team. We'll find them at Juke and its competitors. We'll find them at universities. We'll find them at ten thousand places all over the Earth. Remember when we needed help with the hullmat? What did we do? We reached out to the world. We opened the door and welcomed any and all ideas. And what did we discover? We found Wila, who we wouldn't have found otherwise. And she showed us what the Formics were doing. She opened our minds to a solution that none of us would ever have considered on our own. There are more Wilas out there, Benyawe. More people who have something to contribute, but since they don't work for one of the big players, they don't contribute. I want to enlist the world, Benyawe. I want to throw back the curtains and ask anyone with a brain to help us beat the Hive Queen. We can't compete against her with

only a few members of a select team. We need everyone to help design whatever tool is needed. I call it open-source warfare, and it's our only hope of keeping pace with the Hive Queen."

"What you're suggesting sounds good in principle, Lem, but do you have any idea how difficult it is to manage what you're suggesting? Enlisting that many people? Finding them? Vetting their ideas? This only works if it's fast, if it gets ideas to marines immediately. But what you're suggesting sounds like chaos."

"It will be at first," said Lem. "Finding the right people, collecting the right minds. That won't happen overnight. But once this A-team of engineers is assembled, you're off to the races."

"There's another big problem here," said Benyawe.

"I knew you would spot all the problems," said Lem. "That's why I chose you."

"Open-source warfare only works if we know what the needs are and if there are engineers on the ships ready to implement what we suggest. Every warship of the fleet would need a workshop dedicated to building and implementing new equipment on the fly at the battlefield. That workshop would need to be staffed by mechanical engineers who, like Victor Delgado, can custom-make this equipment to marines' exact specifications as quickly as humanly possible. They'll need equipment like printers that can manufacture any number of different materials, design and drafting software, tools."

"Ships already have most of those things," said Lem. "And we can recommend staffing changes on every ship that will dedicate engineers to these immediate needs. Remember, if we do this, it might save the Fleet tens of billions of credits a year in expensive military contracts. Maybe hundreds of billions. They're going to like this idea. It gets them solutions faster and it costs them next

to nothing, expect perhaps for the expense of materials, which they would be all too happy to provide. They're going to accommodate this. They're going to weep with joy at this idea."

"And they're not going to pay us," said Benyawe. "So where does the money come from? Nonprofits don't operate on air. And people don't dedicate all their brain power and energy for nothing. Even something as noble as saving marines and protecting the human race. People have mortgages. People have to eat."

"Initially I'll fund it," said Lem. "I'll bankroll the whole thing. Then we'll work with people who raise money like this for a living. It saves marines' lives. It expedites the war. It allows people, through their meager contribution, to stick their own hot poker right in the Hive Queen's eye. I'm not worried about money."

"Obviously," said Benyawe. "But I am. How much of an investment are you willing to make initially?"

He gave her an amount.

She stared at him.

"You don't think that's enough?" he said.

"I didn't think it was possible for one person to have that much."

"The last few years have been kind. War has done wonders to my stock options. Yours as well, I suspect."

"That's money on a whole new level from what's in my portfolio, Lem."

"We'll know what's needed," said Lem. "Mazer set up a forum on the IF intranet. We'll access that, and we'll talk to marines directly. No more corporate walls between us and them. It's time engineers went to war."

"You're asking me to leave the company I helped build," said Benyawe.

"And to leave my father."

"I have no loyalty to your father. My loyalty is to my husband and my children and the human race."

"Then I'm making you an offer you can't refuse," said Lem. "Find an office space in Nigeria, something that can accommodate an enormously reliable network and digital infrastructure, someplace the company can call home. My donation is the nonprofit's first grant. You'll have total stewardship. I have a wealth management team. They'll help you assemble a finance team to manage the grant and use it to generate some investment income. That will be your first job, assembling a small team of executives. Decide how many engineers you'll need on permanent staff and how many you'll use via freelance and open-source. I'd like to keep overhead to a minimum. That's the whole point of the model, being as efficient as the Hive Queen. All I need is for you to say yes."

She watched him for a moment. "You *have* lost your mind, haven't you? Not in a deranged sense, but in the sense that you've shed who you once were. The old Lem would think this was lunacy."

"The old Lem is dead. I'm done with the company and this absurd quest to outperform my father. My therapist, if I had one, might call this the great liberation, the moment when I snip away whatever was tying me to that man. I'm free."

He stood.

"Think about it. The money is in the account. I've already given you access. You'll receive a link shortly. You could go home right now, pack your things, and be on the first shuttle to Earth with Mandu, if you wanted. Or you can take a week or two to think about it. Just keep in mind that marines have needs, and that the current model to meet those needs is painfully slow."

He started to walk away.

"Wait," she said. "And you? Where do you fit in this? Before, you acted like I'd never see you again. You're not planning on harming yourself, are you?"

He turned back and smiled. "You're worried about me.

I'm touched. But I'm fine, never been better. I'm glad to have you on the team."

"I didn't say I would do this," said Benyawe.

"No. But you will. Because you have a soul and marines need help."

"I help marines where I currently work," she said. "I help marines every day."

"Others can do your job at Juke, Benyawe. No one else can do this new job."

"Sure they can. Any number of engineers can lead this effort."

"No. They can't. Because if it isn't you, I'm not doing it," said Lem. "You're the only person alive I trust with that kind of money."

She was quiet a moment. "That makes me sad," she said. "That I'm the only one, I mean."

"Don't pity me," said Lem. "Work for me. Save marines. Enlist the world. This is as much a war of logistics as it is a war of violence, and it's time we started winning both. No bureaucracy, no committees, no war profiteering. I know it's what you want. It's what I want too. And it's what the Fleet needs."

He left and didn't turn back. Father would be furious that Benyawe was leaving during a critical transition, right when he needed her the most. The idea of Father raging at the news shouldn't delight Lem—that would be juvenile. But it did delight him. Endlessly.

Meeting number two was in a single-table restaurant in Old Town that was both figuratively and literally underground. A restaurant that only a handful of people used and knew existed. A restaurant that Lem had built and kept a secret from everyone and used only in unique circumstances like this one.

Oliver Crowe arrived on time in a fine black suit and

shirt and tie along with a retinue of grim-faced security personnel, men not unlike the ones who had guarded Father back at the Hegemony offices.

Crowe sat opposite Lem at the table and took in the room. It was decorated in a classical Parisian style, as if plucked from France in the late eighteen hundreds, right at the height of Impressionism. "Those are real Monets, aren't they?" said Crowe, pointing to the two paintings on the wall. "I've heard about art thieves who create copies of priceless art so realistic that even curators can't tell the difference. And then they sneak into museums, steal the originals, and replace them with the counterfeits so that no one even knows the museum is showing a fake. Then the real painting goes on the black market, perhaps sold to wealthy individuals who have secret private restaurants hidden beneath boring municipal buildings."

"I'm afraid I'm not that devious," said Lem. "At least not so far as the humanities are concerned. Skullduggery is more your forte, isn't it?"

Crowe smiled and took a drink of his water.

Louis, the server, came and explained the meal that had been prepared. First a butternut squash soup, followed by a garden salad, then a ravioli with arugula and goat cheese.

"That sounds lovely," said Crowe.

Louis nodded and left.

"You can have one of your bodyguards taste everything beforehand, if you like," said Lem. "In case you think it's poisoned."

Crowe laughed. "And why would I make such a ridiculous assumption?"

Lem shrugged. "You're a spy. Don't you always assume that everyone is trying to kill you?"

"Intelligence work is not as interesting as what you see at the cinema," said Crowe. "I work at a desk. I get my

coffee from a break room. I spend more time worrying about my pension than I do about my food being tainted."

"But certainly all this skulking around and assassination plotting builds up a list of enemies."

"Enemies only exist if they know *you* exist," said Crowe. "That's my first rule: never reveal yourself to anyone."

"You revealed yourself to me," said Lem. "You revealed yourself to Wila."

"Are you angry about Wila?" said Crowe. "That I took her from you?"

"She never belonged to me," said Lem. "And no, I'm not angry. Wila is perfectly capable of taking care of herself. Although I suspect that if she knew what you were doing, if she had any sense of who and what you really are, she might not have jumped into ASH."

"You mean my plans for the Fleet?" said Crowe. "The plans that I hope you will assist me with?"

"Let's call them what they are," said Lem. "Assassinations."

"I prefer the term 'command realignment,'" said Crowe. "Fixing what is broken for the preservation of the species. Did you know that if a coyote gets its leg ensnared in a trap, it will gnaw its own leg off to free itself? Picture that. To survive, it will eat through its own flesh, break its own bones, chew and snap through its own sinew and muscles. All while bleeding profusely. Can you imagine that degree of pain? Not merely cutting your own leg off swiftly with a sharp instrument. But to use your own teeth to tear it away. The International Fleet is a trapped coyote, Lem. And unless the bad commanders are removed, the whole coyote dies. It's not a pleasant business to be in, but that is how nature works. The strong survive, and the weak die. At the moment, the Formics are the strong ones in this scenario. We're the organisms on the brink of extinction."

"Did you come to me because I have money or because you think I'm the kind of person who would condone such atrocities?"

"Both, honestly. You have money. And you fit the profile. We know what we're doing when we profile someone. I wouldn't have revealed myself to you, Lem, if my people weren't absolutely certain that you would come along. I wouldn't have revealed myself to Wila, either. But she fit the profile, too."

"A different profile from my own, I wager," said Lem.

"Starkly," said Crowe. "But keep in mind, Lem, that these are not the only two characteristics that we pursued in seeking our benefactor. There are plenty of men in the world who have a lot of money and would condone extreme measures. But many of them are people we wouldn't want to associate with. Criminals. Warlords. Heads of underground and unseemly organizations."

"But they wouldn't help you," said Lem. "Because they don't care about your cause. They adore their wealth and power. They don't give it away to shady intelligence officers. They keep it for themselves. In fact, I'm willing to bet that I'm not the first person you approached. I'm likely the fourth or fifth, the guy you came to after you approached the wealthiest scum of the Earth."

"I'm disappointed you would think so," said Crowe. "As I told you, we were searching for a very specific profile. Criminals may have some of the attributes, but they don't have the one we needed the most."

"Naiveté?" said Lem.

"Compassion," said Crowe.

Lem laughed quietly. "Yes, all the assassins I know have such big effulgent hearts. They're such tender-hearted honeypots."

Crowe grew serious. "Toxic command is rampant in the Fleet, Lem. Some of these commanders are bad because they're incompetent and idiots and get people killed. But

some of them are bad because they put marines through hell. Not because war is hell, but because these bastards delight in cruelty. They humiliate their marines. Publicly and privately. They shame them. Degrade them. Mock them. Scorn them. Laugh at them. We have marines who have taken their own lives because they can no longer endure the command of a monster. If you think no such commanders exist in the Fleet, then you *are* painfully naive. Sometimes, commanders are both amoral and imbecilic. Those are the especially dangerous ones. To remove them, to put a stop to their abusive power, is an act of compassion, Lem. Every marine deserves to be led honorably, to be treated with dignity, to be given a commander that keeps them alive as they complete their objectives."

"So that's your goal?" said Lem. "For every marine to have a good experience with their commander."

Crowe's expression soured, and he waved the comment away. "Don't be snide, Lem. You and I both know that the survival of our species is what's at stake here. Right now, as we speak, Formic warships disguised as our warships are laying waste to squadrons all over the solar system, the repercussions of which will shatter this Fleet to its core. The Formics have been planning this for the better part of a year, at least. They made warships to look like ours so they could prance right up to our ships without causing alarm and blow our marines to dust. That's what we're up against, Lem. Brilliant military minds who seem to have no end of resources and capabilities. And who do we send to lead and protect us? Clowns. Idiots. Savages."

Lem stared at him, horrified. His network of contacts within the IF and the company had informed him of rumors of a Formic offensive, but Lem hadn't realized the scope and magnitude.

"You picked a hell of a day to meet, Lem," said Crowe. "Because tomorrow everything changes. Tomorrow the

world panics. The casualties of today, the loss of life, the loss of ships, of equipment, of personnel, this will be the greatest war disaster in the history of war. The Formics have been cutting us and bleeding us for a year. Today they severed an arm. Maybe more than that. Most of the world woke up this morning, still clinging to the hope that we could bounce back and turn this war. By this time tomorrow, the world will think differently."

"You're saying we don't have a chance?" said Lem.

"I'm saying this is rock bottom. We need to weed out toxic and incompetent command now more than ever. I'm saying we can't afford to lose anymore."

"This assault would have happened with or without bad commanders," said Lem.

"Maybe," said Crowe. "Or maybe we would have discovered the Formics' plans if not for the commanders who obstructed information and kept intelligence to themselves. Who disregarded warning signs because they were too stupid to notice them, too cowardly to pursue them, or too incompetent to report them. No, we would have been more prepared, Lem. We may not have prevented it, but we would have a lot fewer dead marines to count."

"You'll have your money," said Lem. "But I'm giving it as a grant to the agency. What you do with it is none of my business. I'll not be held responsible for it. I make no demands on its use, other than that it be used legally and ethically for the preservation of the human race. I hope we're clear on that."

Crowe lifted his glass again. "We understand each other perfectly, Lem."

"But if I do you a favor, you do me a favor."

"If it's within my capabilities," said Crowe.

"One, you drop the hypocrisy," said Lem. "You stop professing to hold the moral high ground."

Crowe frowned. "I'm not sure I understand you."

"Then let me be crystal clear so that your keen intelligence-gathering ears will understand. You gave Wila a job in part to manipulate me. She is no doubt brilliant. She has much to offer any study on the enemy. But you could have offered that job a hundred times before and never did. Her work with the grubs is common knowledge now. Has been for six months. You could have swooped in and made an offer at any time."

"We didn't know we needed her until now," said Crowe.

"If you want my money, you don't lie to me," said Lem. "I don't finance liars. I despise liars. I think liars are worse than toxic commanders. You didn't know you needed Wila until you needed leverage. Until you knew you needed my financing and that I was unlikely to give it."

"You think we're holding Wila hostage? You think we took her as a veiled threat to you? That we would kill her if you didn't help us?"

"You're in the business of killing, Crowe. It's your expertise. And before you deny anything and lose your benefactor you should know that I have my own contacts as well."

Crowe was quiet a moment, then sat back in his chair. "We knew that if Wila was in our custody, so to speak, it might encourage you to lean our way. It was discussed, yes. I won't lie to you on that. You can call that leverage, I suppose, but we have no intention of killing Wila if you say no. I happen to like Wila. Maybe not as much as you do, but I legitimately believe she has much to offer. Everything I told her about what we need from her is true. I hope she delivers."

"She is to be given every protection."

"Of course," said Crowe. "I have my fiercest guard at her side constantly. It's a woman, by the way, in case you're wondering. I figured you'd be more comfortable with that."

"I'm not comfortable with any of it. You sent Wila into a war zone."

"We're all in a war zone, Lem. Wila will simply be a little closer. You have my word that she will be given every possible protection. Anything else?"

"Discontinue your association with Sokolov," said Lem.

"The Russian Lunar minister?" said Crowe. "What do you mean?"

"You're lying again," said Lem. "Sokolov is an agent of ASH. He doesn't work for the Russians. Not really. He works for you. You picked him because his connection to the Russians gives him another perceived agenda. Everyone would think he was conniving against my father because of Russia's hope to gain more influence at the Hegemony. Sokolov probably even believed it himself. He's too vain to see himself as a puppet. So when you pitched yourself as an ally, you convinced Sokolov that *you* worked for *him*. You presented him tactics and then convinced him that those ideas were really his own. Humiliating me at the fundraiser, for example. That wasn't Sokolov's idea. That was yours. Some ideas were his, but you were all too happy to encourage him. His dirty promises to the Hegemony Congress. His silent coup among the bureaucracy. That was mostly him. But it has your fingerprints all over it."

Crowe frowned. "That's quite a lengthy list of accusations, Mr. Jukes."

"Not accusations. Facts, Mr. Crowe. Confirmed and validated by my sources. You've taught me a valuable lesson. One that I should probably thank you for. Money can indeed buy you anything. Including information. You have your people, and I have my people, and some of my people are also your people. I know who they are. You don't. You can try to root them out, but I'll only buy more. So you will run your little program of 'command

realignment,' but I will be watching. And in the meantime, your association with men like Sokolov ends here. He's gone. Don't kill him. That's too kind. But you will destroy him all the same and send him back to Russia. You want to root out the worms in the Fleet, I want to root out the worms here, the worms you have infecting your own tower of hypocrisy."

Crowe said, "Our intention was never for Sokolov to gain the Hegemony. It might seem that way, but Sokolov was a tool, an instrument. We used him to make cuts here and there to shift power where it belonged."

"Away from my father?" said Lem.

"Away from your father, yes. The Hegemony does need new leadership, Lem. Not because your father has done a poor job, but because the Hegemony needs someone with military experience who can calm the rising sense of panic throughout the world. There is a war coming after this one, if we win, Lem. I'm trying to prevent that war."

"My father said the same thing."

"Your father and I agree on this front. He can't be the Hegemon when we win."

"So you allied with my father in the shifting of power and yet you also orchestrated his removal by creating an enemy in Sokolov."

"Nation building is a complicated puzzle, Lem. It takes careful coordination."

"You're not building a nation here," said Lem.

"Oh, but we are. Or at least preserving one. The Hegemony itself. It's not technically a nation, but it functions like one. Keeping the right people in power is part of the puzzle."

"And Sharon Solomon. The new Hegemon. Was that your idea or Father's?"

"Does it matter? She needs to be there. She's there."

"Does my father know that Sokolov was your creation?

Does he realize that he was betrayed by you, someone he considered an ally?"

Crowe laughed. "Your father doesn't see me as an ally, Lem. He sees me as a necessity. He and I are like tectonic plates, pushing against each other to move mountains. You're free to tell him, though I suspect he already knows. I suspect he always knew."

"And yet he doesn't fire you," said Lem. "He keeps you close."

"Tectonic plates," repeated Crowe, lifting his glass again before taking a drink.

"Sokolov," said Lem. "Do we have a deal?"

"Consider it done," said Crowe. "He'll be ruined. Which won't be difficult. We merely have to publicly reveal what he is. And in the meantime, I will take a more careful look at my—what did you call it?—tower of hypocrisy. But I'm surprised, Lem. You didn't need me to ruin Sokolov. That's certainly within your own striking distance. Without anyone knowing it was you."

Lem stood and buttoned his jacket. "I have heavier targets than Sokolov, Mr. Crowe. Now if you'll excuse me."

"You're leaving?" said Crowe. "But we haven't eaten."

"Louis will feed you and your guards. I told him to expect at least this many. He'll bring out some chairs. If what you say about the war today is true, tomorrow is a new and darker day. Best enjoy good food while you can."

Meeting number three took place in a honky-tonk down in Old Town, where a sweat-soaked live band in cowboy hats from the United States was squeezed onto a platform not big enough to contain them. They all wore matching leather vests and played various stringed instruments, two of which Lem had never seen before. The songs were all ballads about unrequited love and other sad tales of

misery, but Lem found himself tapping his foot along with the beat despite himself.

A heavyset woman holding sealed containers of alcohol on a tray paused at his booth. "Don't I know you?" she said, eyeing him playfully. "You're some big shot, aren't you?"

"Not anymore," said Lem.

"What can I get you?"

"Privacy," said Lem. He tipped her fifty credits.

She looked half annoyed and half elated, but she left him alone as asked.

Shambhani arrived two minutes early and slid into the booth across from Lem. He offered his hand. "Mr. Jukes. Dalir Shambhani."

He was not unlike the photos Lem had seen of him. Pakistani. Mid-twenties. Stout. The bearing of a soldier. Eyes moving steadily, watchful for threats.

"You were part of Mazer Rackham's breach team," said Lem.

"Until I lost my leg," said Shambhani. He twisted his body, lifted his knee, and pulled up his pant leg just far enough for Lem to see the prosthetic leg underneath.

"That must have been difficult," said Lem.

"I wouldn't recommend it," said Shambhani. "Shall we excuse ourselves to more private quarters? We'll end up shouting ourselves hoarse to be heard in here."

"Please," said Lem.

They squeezed past the stage as one of the performers was tearing into a fiddle solo and made their way toward the back of the building. Once the stage door closed behind them, the deafening roar of the band disappeared. "I'm not a country music fan myself," said Shambhani. "We don't have that in Pakistan. But there's a market for it here, for whatever reason."

They weaved their way through a kitchen, where a half dozen people were cooking, and stepped into a back of-

fice so cluttered with boxes of booze and supplies that
Lem didn't know where to sit. Shambhani moved to a
chair and freed it of the boxes stacked there, then gestured for Lem to make himself comfortable. On the wall
hung a flag of the International Fleet and another of the
Pakistani Special Service Group, the primary special-ops
force of the Pakistan Army. Other remnants of a brief
military career dotted the walls and desktops elsewhere.
A beret, patches, pins, photos of comrades.

"You were with the SSG," said Lem.

"Before the Fleet," said Shambhani.

"Hard men," said Lem.

"They're men like me and you, Mr. Jukes. But they
can be hard. Have to be sometimes. What can I do for
you?"

"I was told you run more than a business here," said
Lem. "I was told you run several businesses."

"I pay my bills," said Shambhani. "What kind of business are you looking for exactly?"

"I need an army," said Lem. "And you're the kind of
man who can assemble one."

Shambhani scratched at his beard as if considering.
"That depends. What kind of army do you need? They
come in all shapes and sizes."

"A platoon. Highly trained. I'm guessing fifty men.
Special ops. Zero G trained. Maneuvers. Formic combat
a plus."

Shambhani whistled. "That's quite a list, Mr. Jukes.
An army like that isn't easy to come by. Men who are
zero G trained and have experience popping Formics are
usually members of a little club called the International
Fleet. They don't hang around in the mercenary aisle
waiting for a shopper to come along."

"But they are out there," said Lem.

"You've set some very narrow parameters," said Shambhani. "If they have to be special ops, you dramatically

lessen your options. Special ops are the best of the best. The Fleet doesn't easily part with those guys."

"They parted with you," said Lem.

Shambhani scratched at his beard again. "Parameters like the ones you're setting are also expensive. As in extremely."

"How expensive?" said Lem.

Shambhani shrugged. "Depends on what you want this army to do. If they need zero G training, I'm assuming this is a space op. Maybe security for a group of people you know. Some bigwig corporate executives, maybe. Or military contractors. You need escorts through the Belt or something? I'm guessing here. What do you have in mind?"

"I want to find and kill the Hive Queen," said Lem.

Shambhani laughed. "You can't be serious."

"I'm quite serious," said Lem. "I need a platoon of highly trained soldiers to board a private military craft that I personally own and help me hunt down the Hive Queen."

"The Hive Queen doesn't exist, Mr. Jukes. That's the official Fleet position."

"And do you believe that position?" said Lem. "Because that will end our conversation."

"Doesn't matter what I believe," said Shambhani. "This is a question of logistics. We don't know where the Hive Queen is. You can't pack fifty men into a ship and go off looking for her like Captain Ahab. The solar system is wide, Mr. Jukes. You're a corporate miner. You know that as well as anyone. We need a destination. A place to target. You have to plan ops like this. We need to know how much food to bring, fuel to load. If we're heading out to the K Belt, that's a year of travel time. Mercs don't jump at those jobs, sir. That's a year of floating in an iron box and doing nothing but riding along and occasionally

trimming your fingernails. Not the kind of work that gets the best men to sign up."

"I have a target," said Lem. "It's not far."

"How far is not far?"

"A near-Earth asteroid," said Lem.

"You think the Hive Queen is parked at an NEA? You better hope the hell not."

"I don't know definitively. But I think it's possible. Maybe likely."

"What's this asteroid called?"

"Eros," said Lem.

CHAPTER 20

Pain

There are several accounts of Formics in the Kuiper
Belt raiding ships and taking human prisoners of war.
Whether these accounts are all tied to a single Formic ship or many ships traveling together is unknown.
What can be concluded, however, is that the abduc-
tions were relatively few in number and that the practice was not reported elsewhere. The recorded dates
and locations of the incidents suggests that the Formics were moving away from the sun and further into
the Kuiper Belt as they collected prisoners. At least
one of these ships—which may in fact be the only
ship that participated in the practice—headed toward
the Formic observer ship out in deep space.

—Demosthenes, *A History of the Formic Wars*, Vol. 3

Alone, inside his dark cell, Khalid held his dead arm tight
against his body as people screamed in terror and agony
all throughout the Formic ship. Most of the screams
belonged to men, he realized, but a few he recognized
as women, their voices higher-pitched and frantic and
piercing. Khalid could only guess what was happening
to them. Torture, perhaps. Or maybe the Formics were
feasting on the humans while the humans were still alive.

He felt like vomiting, but he closed his eyes and tried to calm his stomach. He was in zero G, and the vomit would fill the room and cloud the air. Worse still, vomiting would force him to move and bend his body, and he desperately wanted to remain still. He had struck his shoulder against the cell wall when they had thrown him inside, the same shoulder where his collarbone was broken. His arm was already throbbing before this second injury, but now his entire upper body, from the top of his head down to his groin, was a pulsing mass of pain. Any movement, however slight, was agony.

The snakelike creatures that had bound his wrists and ankles and waist had released him before he was thrown into the room. Khalid was grateful for that, at least, to no longer endure the horror of having a worm or snake or whatever it was squeezing him like a python.

He wondered if that was the source of the screaming. Perhaps people were getting squeezed by the snake creatures. Or perhaps there were other creatures aboard. Maybe *those* creatures feasted on humans. Maybe those were the creatures that controlled the Formics. Or perhaps the creatures were pets to the Formics. Or perhaps the Hive Queen herself was on this ship, and she alone feasted on humans.

He desperately wished the screaming would stop. Khalid found it unbearable. How many people were being tortured and killed? Ten? Twenty? It was impossible to tell. The screams came on so suddenly and overlapped so frequently.

They were his own men. That was the worst of it. They were men who had flown with him, fought for him, killed for him. Were the Formics cutting them open? Was Maja here? Were they cutting her open? Were they taking out his child?

He tried to clear his mind. It did him no good to imagine all of the ways his people were being killed. And

yet, he couldn't focus on anything else. The screaming wouldn't let him. It went on and on and never stopped. Relentless. Agonizing. How could a man or a woman scream that loudly and for that long? That incessantly? Wouldn't a man lose his voice from all that strain? The larynx could only be pushed so far. Sooner or later the tissue in the wall of the throat would tear. The person would go hoarse. Khalid should know. He had heard many such screams over the past year. He had caused many of them as his men took ships and killed those they found inside.

I am no better than the Formics, he thought. I am as evil as the Hive Queen.

This is God's punishment, thought Khalid. God sent the Formics to take me, to avenge what I have done to others. Just as God filled Maydox's heart with mutiny and turned him against me. Just as God filled Maja's heart with jealously. God put it all in motion to punish Khalid for his murders and his raids and his brutality.

But, no. Why would God put murder in the hearts of men? If he did, why would anyone worship such a god? Why would anyone follow someone so vengeful, so full of malice?

Ah, but men *do* follow leaders full of malice, thought Khalid. Did my men not follow me?

No, God was not a vengeful God, for if so, he too, like Khalid, would be no better than the Hive Queen.

A scream right outside his door startled him and made him flinch, which sent a bolt of pain through his body as broken bones shifted in his shoulder. He gently prodded the wound with his fingertips. The broken bone was thankfully not piercing the skin, but the bone had snapped in half, no question.

He was drifting weightless in the darkness and he reached back with his good arm to stop himself. The wall was cold, rough, metallic, and slick with a wet sticky sub-

stance like mucus, as if snails had been using it for traffic all day.

Another scream outside his door, but this one farther away. A brief scream. Not long and sustained like the others.

He wondered if the Formics would come for him next and what they would do to him if he resisted. Rip him in half? Rip his dead arm out of its socket? He imagined all variety of deaths, all of them excruciating and gory and slow. If he did resist, it wouldn't be much. His dead arm was useless, his body aflame with pain. He couldn't scare off a sparrow if one landed on his head.

He steadied himself again as he drifted lazily into the wall. The rough texture surprised him. It was nothing like the smooth polished surface of hullmat that he had heard so much about. This was almost like the surface of stone. Cold and rugged and pitted. And yet when he knocked on it, it had the dull ring of metal.

The only light in the room was a narrow beam of dim blue light that leaked in from the corridor. The door was composed of closed aperture blades that irised open and closed. Two of the blades did not quite connect because of a bend in one of the blades, which created a thin sliver of a hole in the door that Khalid could look through. He drifted to the door and placed his eye close to the hole. He couldn't see much, just a small piece of the wall opposite his cell. The blue light in the corridor was brighter, though it was still far too dim for his liking. He had heard that the Formics were tunnel dwellers and had dug all kinds of paths into the ground when they invaded China. Perhaps they preferred the dark, thought Khalid. Perhaps their massive black eyes, like deep-sea creatures, needed little light to see.

He could not see the source of the blue light in the corridor, but the brightness and hue were similar to the light

produced by the doilies fired from the Formic jar weapons. Perhaps the Formics used the doily creatures for light in their ships. Perhaps the doilies hung on the walls like ornate, web-shaped, bioluminescent nightlights.

He pushed gently on the apertures in the door, but they didn't move. He tried to squeeze his fingertips into the space where the two blades of the door didn't quiet meet, hopeful that he might push down on the blade hard enough to initiate an opening mechanism. But the space was too narrow for his fingers. And what good would it do him if he opened the door anyway? Where would he go? The Formic ship had long since left the Minetek shipbuilding facility behind. There was no chance of Khalid escaping now. His only hope was to kill every Formic aboard, seize control of the ship, and then fly it to some depot without the International Fleet destroying him first. Such a mission was impossible, he knew. He didn't have the strength to button his own shirt, much less attack and kill a ship full of Formics.

No, he thought. I am Khalid. Man of men, the father of fear. No room can hold me. No power can contain me.

But he knew, even as he tried to convince himself, that he could not lie to his own mind. That was foolish. This was his new reality. This cage. He would never get off this ship again. He would never see the Minetek shipyard again. If some of his men had been fortunate enough to evade capture and escape, they weren't coming to rescue him. The men of Khalid were not so loyal as to attempt such a mission. Khalid was dead, as far as they were concerned. If they had reached the Shimbir, Khalid's ship, they were fleeing in the opposite direction now. Khalid had trained them to do so. At the first sight of Formics, they were to run. That had always been Khalid's position. Do not investigate. Do not linger. Flee.

How had Khalid not seen this Formic ship coming? He had put men on watch at Minetek. He had put other

men at the scopes, men whose job it was to scan space for threats and alert him of warnings. Had these men seen nothing?

Maydox's mutiny had distracted them, Khalid realized. The mutiny had made the men on watch abandon their posts. And yet, what were the chances of such a coincidence? How was it that in all the hundreds and maybe thousands of hours that Khalid's men had watched for threats, the Formics had come and attacked during that one single hour when Khalid's men were not paying attention?

No. There was another reason he had not seen the Formics come. A reason he could not guess.

The screams started up again. They had paused momentarily, and Khalid had found the silence a brief mercy. But now they were back again. Loud and long, like sirens.

It was then that Khalid wondered if perhaps the screaming wasn't real. Had the Formics recorded screams? Maybe this was psychological warfare. Maybe they knew that the screams would terrify new prisoners and make them more compliant. Maybe the captives resisted less when they were so disturbed by what they perceived as agony all around them.

But would Formics even understand that concept? Did they comprehend the human psyche enough to create and implement such tactics of fear? Khalid doubted it. The Formics were so alien, so beyond human comprehension that humans must be equally incomprehensible to them.

Perhaps that is what this place is, he thought. Perhaps this was a lab for studying the enemy.

The door irised open. Two Formics were anchored there, shoulder to shoulder. Khalid was right at the door. He recoiled, scrambling to find purchase on the floor and push himself away from them.

One of the Formics reached in casually and grabbed Khalid by the ankle. Khalid screamed because pain

rippled across his shoulder like a thunderbolt as the Formic pulled him into the corridor. Khalid scrabbled with his good hand at the floor to root himself in place and stop them from pulling him away. But his fingertips found nothing, and then he was drifting behind them in zero G like a bag of cargo, helpless.

At first he flailed his good arm about in a desperate attempt to grab at something. There were handholds on the floor. If he could reach one, maybe he could yank himself free of their grasp. But every movement was like a hammer of pain in his shoulder, and he stopped.

What good would resistance do him, anyway? Even if he freed himself momentarily from their grasp, the Formics would only grab him again. They would pull him away, maybe with more force than they were doing now. They could see that his shoulder was in agony. All they had to do was strike it.

A better use of his energy was to learn what he could about the corridor and the ship. To reconnoiter, to observe.

He let his body go limp and took in everything around him as the Formics pulled him along. He had been right about the doilies. They were positioned on the wall and pulsing with light, casting a faint blue glow that brightened and dimmed, as if the light itself were alive.

There were other creatures as well. Worms and grubs on the walls, like slugs on a sidewalk after a rain.

A piercing scream to his immediate right made him recoil. The movement caused another dagger of pain in his shoulder, but he barely noticed, he was so startled by what he saw. It was not a human beside him screaming, but there on the wall was what looked like a human organ, purple and pulpy and breathing. Tube-shaped, with a V-shaped sphincter at the top and folds all along the side that vibrated slightly as air passed by them.

And it was screaming. A woman's scream. A human

woman. Not exactly like a human, though, Khalid realized. There was something slightly off about it, in the pitch or timbre, in the vibration of the air. It throttled too much, the air currents vibrating too sharply, like someone being shaken while they were screaming. He had not noticed it when he had heard it from a distance in his cell, but he noticed it now. It was human but not human. A scream but not a scream. It was an attempt to generate human sound. An organism designed by the Formics to mimic the human voice. But why?

"Hey," he called to it. "Can you speak?"

The screamer didn't respond. It had finished its scream, and now its protuberance was relaxed and no longer fluttering at the ends as it had when it was making its noise.

The Formics pulled Khalid into a cavernlike room with a higher ceiling and walls covered with hundreds of worms and grubs. The Formics turned Khalid over and laid him flat on his back on a stone slab. One Formic held his ankles against the slab, the other put a single hand flat against Khalid's chest to hold him there. Khalid gritted his teeth in agony, forcing himself not to scream. His shoulder was pressed hard against the slab. The pain was excruciating.

They were going to cut him open. This was an altar to their Formic god, a sacrificial table. This was their religion, their worship, vivisecting humans for the Hive Queen's amusement.

A shadow moved to Khalid's right in his peripheral vision. Khalid turned his head and saw a Formic, much smaller than the two who had escorted him in here. This new, smaller Formic was near the far wall, maybe ten meters away, with its back to Khalid. It was examining a dense pack of grubs adhered to the wall, as if searching among them for one specific organism.

Elaborate wings protruded from the creature's back, but they were far too small to provide any lift, suggesting

that they were grossly undeveloped and not nearly as wide and long and majestic as they would one day become. At the moment, they were like pretend wings that a child might wear with a costume, fairy wings.

And then Khalid realized that these *were* a child's wings. *This* creature was a Formic child. A daughter of the Hive Queen. Khalid remembered a report from the ansible maybe seven or eight months ago. A squad of tunnel commandos had killed one of the Hive Queen's daughters, the report said. The description given in the report matched what Khalid saw now. He had found another daughter. Or rather, she had found him.

The tight grip on his ankles loosened slightly, and the Formic holding his ankles began poking and prodding him, not like someone trying to agitate a dangerous animal, but like someone examining a species of animal they had never seen before. Fingers pushed at and squeezed his knee caps, hands, feet. The Formic pulled off one of Khalid's shoes and socks and examined his foot and toes as if they were one of the seven wonders of the world.

Khalid strained his neck to see the Formic positioned behind him at his head. Like the other escort Formic, this one was staring at him with a new unflinching intensity. When they had come for Khalid in his cell, the escort Formics had given him only a passing glance before unceremoniously pulling him down the corridor and flipping him onto the slab, like two unenthusiastic assembly-line workers going about their labor, moving around the stock, doing a rote task in which they were only superficially invested. But now, in this cavern, they both regarded him like he was some prized jewel, as if nothing else in their world had any purpose or meaning. Only him. Only Khalid. Their focus on him was so absolute, so unwavering, so committed that neither of them looked at the winged daughter at the wall. Instead, their eyes were locked on Khalid, as if seeing him for the first

time, as if studying every pockmark in his skin, every hair upon his face.

They were new creatures, as if their previous, disinterested minds had been removed and replaced with new highly intelligent minds dedicated to learning and observation. The daughter is controlling them, Khalid realized. She was examining Khalid through their eyes. These Formics were her instruments, her microscopes, her limbs, her vision, extensions of her own body.

The daughter turned away from the wall. Dozens of worms now clung to her upper arms. She pushed off the floor, and her wings fluttered, not to give her flight, but to propel her forward in the air toward the slab. She was small and hideous, but Khalid recognized, even amid the horror of her features, a certain grandeur, a majesty, an aspect of greatness. This was a future queen. The royalty was already there in her.

She landed beside him, her hind legs grabbing two hooks embedded in the slab, put there for her to perch on, perhaps. She bent forward, bringing her face close to his. Khalid wanted to scream, wanted to cry out in terror, but he could not find his voice. He cowered back from her as much as he could with the two Formics holding him. The movement stretched his shoulder and then he did cry out, now in pain, his mouth opening wide in a scream.

The daughter watched him intently, and when he stopped screaming, she opened her maw as well. Khalid screamed because she was going to eat him now, she would feast upon his face. But she didn't move her head. She merely closed her maw and opened it again.

She's mimicking me, Khalid realized. She's doing what I'm doing.

He opened his mouth wide, though this time he did not scream. He was testing his theory.

The daughter opened her maw again, copying him.

Was she playing with him? Khalid wondered. As a cat plays with a mouse before it sinks in its teeth?

The daughter closed her maw and leaned in closer, her massive black eyes coming right near his face. Khalid saw no pupils or irises in that blackness, but he could sense that her vision was moving all over his face, that her focus was shifting from one feature to the next, taking note of every detail.

Perhaps she rarely sees specimens with skin so dark, thought Khalid. Perhaps I am a new curiosity.

The Formic with a hand against Khalid's chest moved his hands and grabbed Khalid's shoulders instead. The pain was like a mini–atom bomb inside him. Khalid screamed again, and the daughter recoiled slowly from him, not because she was startled but because this was new information that needed examining. The Formic released Khalid's shoulders, and sweet relief washed over Khalid. He still felt pain, but the agony had greatly diminished.

The daughter produced a blade. A knife was suddenly in her hand.

Khalid tensed. She would bury the blade in his chest. She would cut him open, she would disembowel him.

She began cutting his clothes away. First the vest that had once been the jacket of an IF officer. She grabbed the fabric and sliced as expertly as a surgeon, never touching his skin. Next came the undershirt, which she cut straight up the middle. Then cuts from the center to the right and left, slicing through the sleeves, removing it all from him and exposing his chest bare. Some of the fabric she pulled away and tossed to the side, where it floated away. The rest of the fabric remained beneath him on the slab.

Her fingers delicately prodded at his good arm. She was looking for the wound inside him. Like a doctor.

She touched his dead arm and Khalid winced. Her fingers poked again at his collarbone, and Khalid cried out

briefly in agony. Now she focused on that spot. The broken collarbone was her new, central fascination.

She pulled a grub from her arm and placed it on the skin above the break. Khalid tensed. The grub was cold and wet and slimy. He could feel tiny hooks from its underbelly gripping at his skin, holding it in place. Was this a leech? he wondered. Would it suck at his blood? Infect him?

The grub buried a stinger deep into Khalid's shoulder. He hadn't expected it. A sharp needle, like a spear, ejecting downward. Khalid writhed and shook and screamed and tried to thrash and get away, but the Formics held him. The hand was at his chest again. Other hands were holding his own hands against the slab. The hands on his ankles were as strong as an ape's. She was feeding him to her worms. This was his death. She would place the worms upon him and they would stab him repeatedly until he expired.

But then, to his great astonishment, the pain in his shoulder began to diminish. The throbbing, the agony, all dissipated like an ice cube melting in hot water.

The grub had injected him with anesthetic, he realized. The daughter was helping him, silencing his pain.

Her eyes watched his as his face relaxed and his body stopped resisting. He was limp now, and loose, and relaxed, or as relaxed as he could be with three Formics hovering over him.

She prodded the left shoulder again with her finger and waited for his reaction. Khalid could feel the pressure of her touch, but his entire left side, from his neck to the end of his arm, was numb.

Before he knew what was happening, the blade was in her hand again and she was cutting his shoulder open. It happened fast, with a single quick slice of the blade, and it wasn't until her fingers were inside him that he realized what she was doing. He screamed then. There was no

pain, but he could feel her reaching in and rooting around for the bone. A Formic's fingers were inside him, moving things around, pinching pieces of him, shifting them. A feeling of absolute revulsion washed over him, and again he thought he might vomit.

Her small, narrow fingers maneuvered the bone back together again. Then one of her other six appendages plucked a grub from her forearm and handed it to her bloody fingers. The daughter inserted the grub into the open wound and placed it on the spot where the broken bone had been realigned. Khalid couldn't see what was happening now, but he could feel movement inside him. The grub, like the worm that had bound his wrists, was extending inside him and winding itself around the bone, creating a cast around the break, just as the worm-like creature earlier had wrapped around and bound his wrists.

The daughter focused on the wound intently, and then, once the grub stopped moving and was secured, she extracted her bloody fingers from the hole in his shoulder and grabbed a third, larger grub from her forearm and placed it over the wound. The small hooks of the grub buried themselves into Khalid's skin on either side of the wound, and then he could feel the grub pulling the wound closed. This creature was his stitches and bandage, he realized.

She was not going to eat him. She was not going to feed him to her grubs or to some other creature. She was healing him. It would take time for his bone to mend. Six weeks at the earliest. Did she intend to keep him alive that long? Was she getting him well for some other gruesome purpose?

She placed a grub on his right arm on the inside of his elbow. Another grub went to his neck near his carotid artery. Khalid didn't dare move. At once the two grubs buried stingers inside him, only these were not as deep.

Khalid tensed every muscle, but dared not resist. They were taking his blood, he realized. He could feel them sucking in his blood. Twenty seconds passed, then the daughter removed the grubs and placed them back on her arm. She pushed off the slab and twisted in the air, and her wings fluttered again, giving her the slightest push. She moved to the right and back the way she had come, disappearing from Khalid's field of vision.

The escort Formics grabbed him roughly again and pulled him away from the table. They were their original selves now. The absolute control the daughter had seized was now released. They pulled Khalid away, holding on to his ankles, as if he were cargo again.

They did not go back the way they had come. They took him down a different corridor. Khalid twisted in the air to try to take in his surroundings and draw a map of the ship in his mind.

They passed two more screamer organs. One was rooted to the wall and screaming like a man. Another was on the ceiling, its screaming voice also deep and resonant like a male's.

They reached a cell door, and it irised open. The Formics did not roughly throw him in this time. They rotated him so that he was upright and then gently nudged him inside. The room was larger than his cell and dimly lit by two doilies on the wall. With that light Khalid could see people inside, hunkered down in the half darkness. Faces he didn't recognize. Maybe six people total, most of them wearing tattered and filthy uniforms of the International Fleet.

Khalid's body drifted into the room, and at once someone grabbed him.

"Khalid!"

Arms wrapped around his bare chest, clung to him, held him. Maja buried her face in his chest and began to sob. She was alive. She was here. The Formics had taken

her. Khalid took her and gently pulled her away from the others, looking her over in the dim light.

"Maja. Are you hurt?"

She shook her head, then her eyes widened at the grub on his shoulder.

"What is that thing on you?"

"A bandage, I think. For the break in my shoulder. A Formic child has tried to heal me. Who else of our people is here?"

"No one," said Maja. "Or none that I've seen. Only you, Khalid."

He nodded. She was alive. This was good. Seeing Maja was like seeing himself again, reminding him who he was. She was looking to him for leadership, for comfort, for direction.

"Who are you people?" Khalid asked the crowd. He could see now how haggard they looked, how sick and weak and broken. They had been here for some time. They had endured hell aboard this ship. They were shadows of the people they once were.

A strained voice from the back of the room responded. "Who are you?"

Khalid looked to see from whence the voice had come, but he could not fully see the person in the shadows.

"Leave that man," whispered Maja into his ear. "He is sick."

But Khalid didn't heed her. He pushed off the floor and drifted back toward the figure. The pain medicine in Khalid's shoulder was strong, and it gave him a sense of being himself again. He was no longer prisoner to the pain.

Khalid reached the figure back in the shadows and almost recoiled at the sight of him. The man was anchored to the floor, but he was barely a man. His muscles had wasted away to nothing. Grubs and worms covered his body. His left arm was gone. His head was a mat of thin-

ning hair, and yet Khalid could see that he was young. A large organism lay on his bare and filthy stomach.

"I said who are you?" said the man. His voice was weak and strained, as if every word took effort, as if it pained him to speak.

"I am Khalid."

"What's your rank?" said the man. He looked down at the pants Khalid was wearing, pants of an IF officer, pants that Khalid had stolen off a dead marine.

"Lieutenant," said Khalid. "I am Lieutenant Khalid."

"Then welcome aboard the ship to hell, Lieutenant Khalid. We tried to get intel out of this one, but she wouldn't tell us anything." The man looked at Maja.

"She has been through a traumatic experience," said Khalid. "She was part of an asteroid-mining crew attacked by pirates. We rescued her and her crew a few months ago. We were taking them to safety when the Formics attacked us."

"What ship are you from?" asked the sickly man.

"The Bosaso," said Khalid. "It is named for a city from my country of Somalia. That is why I asked to be aboard it, to be connected to my country."

"I'm from the Kandahar," said the sickly man. "Corporal Jackson. From Mississippi in the United States."

"You are a long way from home, Corporal. What have these animals done to you?"

"The same thing they'll do to you. Poke and cut and poke some more. They want to know what we're made of, what makes us tick. You see this thing?" He gestured to the organism on his stomach, a blob of wet purple tissue. "That's my liver. Not the one my body made, but the one they made for me. That's what they do, they take our organs and study them and try to make copies of them."

"Why?" said Khalid.

"None of us know. Maybe they want to make a human. Maybe they want to just understand us. Maybe they want

to figure out the fastest way to kill us. This is a laboratory, Lieutenant. We're the rats."

"Where are they taking us?" said Khalid.

The man made a gesture as if to shake his head, but it was almost imperceptible.

"No one knows that, either. All we know is that we're going out, away from the system, maybe into deep space. They're not taking us to Earth, though. That's for certain."

"How many others are there?" said Khalid. "Like us?"

"There were twelve at one point, but people die quick. We get infections. That's why they took my arm. Gangrene near killed me. I think it still might."

"What happened to your own liver?"

"They took it, gave me this one instead. I think they want to see how long I'll live. They want to know if their replica works or not."

"Are you in pain?" said Khalid.

"If I don't get my pain worms, I'm in constant agony," said the man. He gestured to the others in the cell. "I've asked these people to kill me, but no one will. They don't have the strength themselves. We're all dying."

"I will kill you," said Khalid. "I will give you the mercy you seek."

Relief washed across the man's face and tears came to his eyes. "I've got a mother in Mississippi. If you make it out of here, Lieutenant, you make sure she never hears a word of this. Nothing about this in my file. You tell her my ship blew up or something. Don't let them give her this picture."

"Your mother will hear none of this. And I will kill these Formics for you. Maja and I will kill them all."

The man's eyes went from him to Maja, his expression grateful.

Khalid anchored his foot to a hook in the floor and got down close to the man's face. He pressed his palms to-

gether as in prayer. "Close your eyes and we will pray together. First I will pray to my God and then you will to yours."

The man closed his eyes. And that was when Khalid reached forward quickly with his good arm and his bad one and snapped the man's neck in a quick and violent motion.

The man's body went limp. His chest stopped moving.

There was a shuffling and mumbling of alarm from the others in the room as they backed away from the scene.

Khalid turned and faced them. "I am Khalid, the man of men, the father of fear. If you wish to go to your maker now, I will send you there quickly and end your suffering. Otherwise you will help me. I do not wish to die here. There is a child in this woman's belly that is mine and that will know the Earth. These Formics are strong, and we feel weak. But I am not ready to accept my weakness. Who here can draw me a map of this ship?"

CHAPTER 21

Mothers

Immediately prior to and during the Second Invasion, as tens of thousands of women from Earth, Luna, and the system enlisted, the percentage of female combatants and personnel within the International Fleet far exceeded the percentages theretofore seen in any large-scale military on Earth. By the war's end, slightly more than a third of all IF personnel was female. This trend continued after the war, and the number of females rising to positions of command dramatically rose as well, paving the way for both males and females to be equally considered as candidates for Battle School.

—Demosthenes, *A History of the Formic Wars,* Vol. 3

There were no ships docked at the Minetek facility when Imala and the others aboard the Gagak arrived. "Do we go inside and check it out?" said Imala. They were gathered at the helm, looking at a holo of the Minetek facility. Imala was gently rocking Chee in her arms.

They had seen from a great distance, based on the heat signatures created, that two ships had left the space station recently. Both left at roughly the same time, with one

going outward, further into the Kuiper Belt, and the other launching inward, toward the sun.

"One of those ships had to have been Khalid," said Lieutenant Owanu. "This facility is deserted. Those weren't Minetek ships coming and going."

"Okay," said Captain Mangold, "we'll assume for now that one of them was Khalid. Who was the other one?"

Lieutenant Owanu shrugged. "Another pirate crew, maybe? Or maybe it was Khalid's buyer. These people operate on the black market. They've got to meet and do business somewhere."

"Who's to say Khalid only has one ship?" said Imala. "Maybe he has a fleet of them. Maybe these are two of them. And each is assigned a different sector to raid. Maybe this Minetek facility is the border between their areas, and they meet up to dump their goods, resupply, and have their pirate club meetings."

Captain Mangold still looked uneasy.

"Not having a ship here is a lot safer for us than having a ship here that could decouple from the station and engage us," said Imala. "We should be grateful for that."

"We came all the way out here," said Lieutenant Owanu. "It'd be silly not to investigate."

"Unless the place is crawling with one hundred pirates," said Captain Mangold. "There could be anyone in there. We could be walking right into a trap."

"We call them on the radio," said Imala. "We open a channel and we tell them we're coming in, and if they give us any trouble, we'll blow a hole through the thing and suck them out into space. We know Khalid took four women, and if he doesn't turn them over unharmed, we start doing damage."

"If one of those ships *was* Khalid," said Captain Mangold, "then the women won't be here. They'll be with him, on his ship. And we're not chasing after them anymore.

This is the end of it. We've abandoned our mission for too long already. We did what we could with the resources we had. The miners can't fault us for that."

Mangold had asked the rescued miners to stay in their quarters while he and his officers discussed the situation.

"We won't have to blow a hole in the place," said Rena. "It already has one." She reached into the holo and rotated it so that the group could see the other side of the shipyard, where a small, cleanly cut hole was visible in the hull.

"Why would anyone do that?" said Lieutenant Owanu. "That shipyard is huge. You can do all kinds of things with that much space. Cut a hole in it and expose it to space, and you render it useless."

Captain Mangold turned to Sergeant Lefevre. "Get a recon drone down in the hole. I want to see what's in there before we decide to go in."

Once the equipment was gathered and the drone was launched, Sergeant Lefevre piloted it from inside the helm. He stood in the corner of the room, off to the side, with his visorless flight helmet on, holding the remote controls. The projection inside his helmet was the same view projected onto the surface of the holotable, where Imala and the others were gathered. It showed the drone's main camera feed as it approached the hole in the shipyard, flew inside, and lit up the space with its spotlights. At first they saw what they expected: large shipbuilding equipment, bots, beams, a huge manufacturing complex, with a large segment of a ship in the center that had been abandoned mid-construction. But then Lefevre piloted the drone further into the yard and around the ship segment, and a human arm drifted into view. Not a body, not a person, just the arm.

"Is that what I think it is?" said Rena.

"Bring the drone in closer," said Owanu.

Lefevre piloted the drone right up to the arm, hitting it with its lights.

"Male," said Owanu, "judging by the shape of the hand. Dark skin."

"Could be a member of Khalid's crew," said Rena.

"Could be anybody," said Mangold.

"Look at the wound," said Owanu. "This arm was blown off."

"How can you tell?" said Mangold.

"Slaser cut would be clean and precise. Look at the tissue at the deltoids. Torn, ripped, consistent with blast wounds, and yet no burn marks, no evidence of heat."

"Doilies," said Imala. "We saw this in the Formic scout ship at the end of the First Invasion."

Her theory was confirmed as they kept looking. They found multiple bodies and pieces of bodies near the bottom of the room where it connected with the rest of the station. They found three dead Formics as well, which was all the evidence they needed.

"So one ship was Formics and one was Khalid," said Rena. "Question is, which was which."

"The Formics went further into the Kuiper Belt," said Imala. "Khalid went inward. He was in a mad panic. He was desperate to get away. You don't hurry out into no-man's-land when you're running scared. You hightail it back to where you think you'll find safety. After an experience like this, Khalid would rush into the Fleet's arms, if it meant getting away from the Formics."

"Unless the Formics left first and headed inward," said Rena. "In which case, Khalid would definitely go in the opposite direction, for no other reason than to put distance between him and the Formics."

"We'll find out soon enough," said Imala. "The ship that went further into the Kuiper Belt is going the same direction we are. Once we get moving, we can close the distance and scan and identify."

"I'm not sure I want to close the distance," said Owanu. "Whether it's Khalid or Formics. I don't want to encounter either of those ships."

"This facility is a dead end," said Mangold. "If the women were here, they're gone now. Either dead, or with Khalid on his ship."

"We should sweep the facility to be sure," said Imala. "And at least now we know that there aren't a hundred pirates waiting to ambush us inside."

Sergeant Lefevre and his squad found the women inside. All four of them. Unharmed. They had barricaded themselves in the kitchen when the fighting started. They never saw any Formics, but they heard the survivors from Khalid's group screaming to each other about Formics as they hurried to the ship to escape. None of the surviving pirates had even bothered to come for the women. They simply fled. The women had been eating the supplies in the kitchen for days now, hoping against hope that someone would come. When they learned that members of their original crew were on board the Gagak and waiting for them, one of the women embraced Lefevre and sobbed in his arms.

There were more tears when the women were brought up the docking tube and into the waiting arms of the other miners. The two women who were sisters held each other for minutes and sobbed with gratitude. Rena and Imala waited outside the airlock, giving the miners their privacy. When they emerged and boarded the ship, they all embraced Captain Mangold, both the men and women, which Mangold wasn't particularly sure how to accept.

Then one of the rescued women from the shipyard came over to Imala with her sister. The rescued woman spoke quickly in French through a flood of tears.

"My sister says thank you," the other one translated. "I told her that it was you who made the ship come for her."

"It was all of us," said Imala. "We all came."

"Je vous remercie," the French woman said over and over.

"You're welcome," said Imala. "We're delighted to have you on board."

The woman spoke another flurry of French that Imala couldn't hope to comprehend.

"She says you have a beautiful daughter," translated the sister. "That such a child is fortunate to have a mother so brave and good."

Imala smiled. "You are kind. Thank you."

Lieutenant Owanu directed the women to the examination room where she would give them whatever treatment they required. Mangold returned to the helm to prepare for departure, and Lefevre and his marines hit the lockers to shed their battle gear.

In moments, the area outside the airlock was quiet. Only Rena and Imala and Chee remained.

"You were right," said Rena. "About all of this, about us coming. I was against it."

"You were protecting us," said Imala. "Not just your granddaughter, but me as well."

"There's another depot two months away from here," said Rena. "Out in the direction we're heading. I've already discussed it with Captain Mangold. We'll take the miners there. Then we'll push on to the Formic ship. The miners can either wait out the war at the depot or try and secure a transport to Luna. Either way, they're obviously not coming with us. The question now is, what about you? If we're dropping off the miners at the depot—"

"Maybe Chee and I should go with them?" said Imala.

"Before you object, hear me out, Imala. I'm not advocating one way or the other. I'm only stressing that this is an option. You and Chee can get off at the depot. The rest of us will push on. There's no guarantee that you'll be safe there, but your chances there are much better than where we're going. I know the Fleet has told the world

that they don't believe in the Hive Queen, but we both know that if that were true, our mission orders would have changed."

"I'm a marine of the Fleet," said Imala. "If I leave my post, there are consequences."

"So they court-martial you for going AWOL. So what? What's a military tribunal if it means you and Chee survive?"

"They probably wouldn't even court-martial me," said Imala. "They'd be too delighted by my decision to leave. There would be singing in the halls at CentCom if I jumped ship."

"There you go," said Rena. "You'd be fulfilling the wishes of all the idiots at CentCom. Everyone wins."

Imala smiled.

"I'm not only thinking of you and Chee," said Rena. "I'm also thinking of Victor. My son. I want him to have his wife and daughter after this war. I want him to experience the joy of raising children with you."

"I thought you said you weren't advocating one way or the other," said Imala.

"Mothers-in-law can't remain completely objective. It's not in our DNA. I love you, Imala. I love my granddaughter. And if you choose to get off this ship, I will love you no less."

"I've already considered this, Rena. I've thought of nothing else since Chee was born. I want the same thing you do. I want a life with Victor. I want Chee to have siblings. I want to grow old with my husband. I want to see Chee fall in love and marry a man as good and noble and strong as her father. But if I get off this ship, I'm not fighting for any of that anymore. I forfeit my right to protect everything I want and hold dear. I'd be putting my child's life into someone else's hands. And when it comes to my daughter, I don't trust anyone's hands more than my own. I know I'm not a soldier. I'm not suggesting that

I can win us this war or that we won't win it without me. I'm saying, I think our chances are slightly better with me helping. I can't fire a weapon or beat off a Formic, but I can help get us there. I can help prevent CentCom from mucking up this op. I can help Mangold see a perspective to decisions that he may not have considered. I can help us think strategically. I can keep Owanu company. I can keep you from strangling Mangold and getting your own court-martial."

Rena laughed. "Good luck with that one."

"If we lose, Chee dies, Rena. That is the single truth that hammers into my brain every night as I try to fall asleep. If we lose, this sweet, innocent, beautiful human being will cease to exist. The Formics will hunt her down and kill her along with every human being still alive. I have to do everything I possibly can to prevent that from happening. I have to keep fighting for my child. And in this case that means taking my child into greater danger. I recognize that that defies logic, I recognize that putting my child in danger is the most un-motherly thing any mother can do, but I don't see another road here. And more importantly, I can't think only of Chee. There are millions of children on Earth who are counting on me to do my job. If I get off this boat, I'm abandoning them and all the mothers who are just as desperate to protect their children as I am. So no, I can't get off this ship. I can't be that selfish. I can't only think of keeping my child safe. There are children other than my own."

She stopped talking. It had all spilled out of her in a mad rush because it had been swimming and churning around in her head ever since she had learned that she was pregnant. How could she charge into war with a child? It had taken her this long to realize that the child was precisely the reason why she must.

"Say something," said Imala. "Tell me I'm not a horrible person."

Rena put a hand behind Imala's head, and her words were soft and quiet because emotion made it hard to speak them. "You are not a horrible person, Imala. You are the best of us. I am stronger because of you. And so is Chee. You will not get off this boat. And I will stand beside you until we see it done. The Hive Queen has made the biggest mistake of this war. She has come between a mother and her cub. I almost feel sorry for the Formics."

Then she pulled Imala close and held her for a long time, with baby Chee comfortably held between them. Which is precisely what Imala needed and wanted. A mother, who would fight for her, too.

CHAPTER 22

Hives

Ansible transmission from Oliver Crowe, director of ASH, to Hegemon-Elect Sharon Solomon. File #504736 Office of the Hegemony Sealed Archives, Imbrium, Luna, 2119

CROWE: Madam President, I congratulate you on being elected by the Hegemony Council. Considering the enormous burden now placed upon you as Hegemon, however, and the awful state of the war that now requires your full attention and direction, I also express my condolences. Your new job will not be an easy one.

The device you are holding is called an ansible. As Hegemon, it will be the primary tool of communication between you, the Strategos, the Polemarch, and me. The messages written via ansible are shared instantaneously with other ansibles on a specific network, regardless of the distance between ansibles. This ansible also allows you to have private conversations with any other ansible in the network, as is the case with this message. No one else will see this transmission but you. The Fleet communications officer who delivered this ansible to you will hereafter assist you in its use and in keeping its existence highly secret.

When you arrive here on Luna, the International Fleet will give you a thorough briefing on the state of the war and the immediate challenges we face. The information they share will not comfort you. You will learn that there is much about the Formics, their capabilities, and their military victories that the International Fleet and Hegemony have chosen to conceal from the free people of Earth, Luna, and the system. In addition to this briefing, I propose that you and I hold a separate intelligence briefing as soon as possible wherein we will discuss additional challenges that exist within the IF that they are unlikely to share with you.

There is one matter, however, that cannot wait until those briefings and which we must discuss immediately. There is an asteroid named Eros, provisional designation 1898 DQ, that has recently come to our attention. It is a large object, with a mean diameter of nearly seventeen kilometers, or roughly ten miles. Currently it is only 2.0823 au from Earth. We have recently discovered Formics there, meaning the enemy is dramatically closer to Earth than any of us realized. More alarming still, based on the intelligence we've gathered, it is our belief that the Formics have been on Eros for several years. Maybe for as long as ten years, considering how intricate and involved the tunnel system there appears to be. In other words, their arrival on Eros predates the First Invasion. Our theory is that Formics were sent to Eros to observe Earth and to determine if it was in fact a viable colony planet for their species. Upon discovering the rich abundance of natural resources found on Earth, the Formics on Eros then sent a philotic message to the Formic scout ship to come to Earth and begin preparing

the planet for Formic biota. The Formic colony fleet was not far behind. And now here we are.

My point, Madam President, is that for the better part of a year, we have suspected that the Formics may be building a hive somewhere out beyond the Belt. We now realize to our great horror that the main hive may be much closer than we thought. Eros must be taken, and yet I fear that such a military action will come at an enormous price since that is a battle that can only be fought in the tunnels of that rock. We cannot simply blow it up. Not if we intend to take the fight to them, as I know you and Ukko Jukes have discussed.

There are difficult decisions ahead, and I do not envy you for being the person who must make them.

Mazer stood atop the Formic warship, sweating profusely in his pressure suit, his legs burning, his body aching, grateful to be alive. He had delivered three warheads into the bowels of the Formic warship, throwing them into three different holes he had made in the hullmat at three different sites on the ship. It had required a lot of leaping and running and crawling and soaring across the surface of the ship for as far as his tether cable would allow. And he had not, to his enormous relief, vaporized himself in the process.

His biggest worry during the process had been that the thrown warheads might not stay deep enough inside the ship before they detonated. On Earth, when tossing a grenade, gravity was your best friend. Wherever the grenade landed, it remained until it detonated. But here in zero G you had no such assurance. The warhead would continue to bounce around inside the ship and drift until it

detonated. It might even drift right back out the hole and detonate in front of you, scattering all your molecules in a hot blistering mess. But thankfully, the first three warheads had gone into their holes and stayed there. When they detonated, Mazer had heard nothing, of course, but he had felt the explosions in the subtle vibrations of the hullmat beneath his feet and the slight shifting in the stars overhead as the ship's flight position changed. The ship was no longer flying nose front, but instead was drifting at an angle as it pitched and yawed and spun slowly.

What concerned Mazer now was radiation. He had no idea how much neutron energy the warheads had released. He felt confident that the hullmat had acted as a shield and kept the blast of radiation mostly contained inside the ship. But it was possible that a good of deal of radiation had shot out of the holes he had just made and exposed him to radiation poisoning.

For a moment, Mazer wondered if he needed to deliver the fourth and final warhead. Had he already inflicted enough damage? Was the ship scuttled? He had seen the other Tik fighters zipping around the Formic warship overhead and taking out more of its guns. Perhaps the objective was achieved, and the ship was dead. Perhaps he only needed to wait for someone to extract him and Bingwen and return them to GravCamp.

But then, out of the corner of his field of vision, twenty meters to his right, Mazer saw a piece of hullmat two meters square rise up from the surface and fold backward. A docking door. An egress of some type. A Formic in a pressure suit scurried out the door, crawling across the surface on all six limbs, its back to Mazer. It had not seen him.

Mazer was a good distance from where he had delivered the third warhead. This was as good a place as any to deliver the last one. He bent low and pulled the paintbrush from the bucket and painted a small circle on the

hullmat beneath him. The smaller the hole, the better. It minimized the chances of the warhead drifting out again and the amount of radiation that would leak from the explosion. The downside of a small hole was that air escaped slowly. Mazer couldn't throw in the warhead until the space beyond had lost all pressure and was a vacuum. Otherwise the escaping air would carry the thrown warhead right back to the hole and out again.

Mazer turned on the nanobots, counted to three, and turned them off. That was all the time they needed. A geyser of air shot out from the newly made hole.

By now the Formic had spotted him and was coming in his direction.

The breach continued to silently spew air. Mazer took his slaser, cranked up the setting, and shot the Formic as it scurried toward him. The beam went through the top of the creature's helmet, through its body, and out the bottom of its abdomen, a line straight down its spine. It stopped moving and went limp, with four of its appendages still anchored to the ship.

Two more Formics appeared at the docking door. Then a third.

Mazer cut them in half with the beam of his slaser, and the top halves of their severed bodies drifted lazily away from the ship.

He watched the geyser of air and the docking door. Ten seconds passed. Then twenty. The hole he had made in the hullmat was no wider than a soccer ball. He looked toward the docking door. It remained open, but no more Formics emerged. Mazer lowered himself and placed his hand over the hullmat breach to feel for the slight push of escaping air. He felt nothing. Beyond it was a vacuum now. He removed the final warhead and grabbed the detonator. Just before he armed the warhead, however, a thought struck him. The docking door was only twenty meters away. What if Formics had accessed where he had

made the hole? Might they be waiting just inside to catch the warhead and throw it back out the hole again?

Mazer looked down into the hole but saw only darkness.

He turned on the tactical light on the end of his slaser and shined it into the hole. A pair of massive black eyes inside a helmet stared back at him, less than a meter down. The Formic was not alone, either. A crowd of Formics was clustered at the hole just below the surface, waiting for him.

Mazer turned off his NanoBoots and leaped away. As he did so, he tapped at his wrist pad and turned the nanobots on again. The hole suddenly grew as the nanobots began unzipping the hullmat around the hole in an ever-expanding ring. In seconds, the hullmat hole was two meters wide, then four. The Formics poured out of the hole, leaping upward and out into space, exploding through the dust of disintegrating hullmat. Many of them were armed with jar weapons. Some were already firing.

Mazer was firing as well as he flew backward and away from the site, slicing through the crowd in quick, cutting motions. He had thrown the warhead and detonator aside. He wouldn't risk the blast now. The last of the damage to the ship would be whatever the nanobots could provide. He wasn't sure how long they would run.

Then his tether cable went taut and his pendulum swing initiated. The few surviving Formics he had not sliced were moving farther into space and disappearing from view, well out of slaser targeting range. Mazer ignored them and tapped at his thumb. A slight burst of air expelled from his boots, and his body rotated. He was desperately trying to get his feet under him for the landing, but the hull was coming up quickly. He wasn't going to land right. He tapped another part of his thumb and dispensed some propellant from his shoulders to slow his

rotation, but it wasn't enough. He would still land wrong. But better to break an ankle than to get a doily to the chest.

Strapped into his flight seat in the medical wing of the Vandalorum, Victor felt helpless throughout the entire battle. He had offered to assist the crew multiple times and had even unbuckled himself once to go and find an engineer and volunteer his services. But Lieutenant Rivera, who was buckled into the flight seat beside him, had rather forcefully ordered him to sit back and stay strapped in. "The crew trains extensively for these maneuvers, Victor. You'll only get in their way. Let them do their jobs."

But sitting back and doing nothing while chaos reigned around him went against everything Victor had learned as a member of an asteroid-mining family. On a rock crew, when disaster struck, everyone pulled their weight. Young, old, feeble, strong. It was every able hand on deck. Only younger children sat it out. By the time Victor was ten, he was right there with Father and Mother in the thick of it.

But Rivera gave him a look that could kill every time he moved to get out of his seat, and so Victor had sat back and waited.

It became obvious rather quickly that the three rogue IF ships were not, in fact, rogue ships, but rather hullmat-covered Formic ships built to resemble Fleet ships. The Vandalorum had begun to change course to assist, but it was not the closest vessel to the fighting, and other legitimate IF warships swept in to engage the Formics first.

The NanoCloud missiles that Lem Jukes had provided months before, and which had delayed the fleet's arrival to the rendezvous, proved worth waiting for and critical in the fight. The Fleet counterattack was twofold. After a

NanoCloud missile breached the hullmat, a second chaser missile punched into the hole and destroyed the ship from the inside.

By the time the three Formic ships were destroyed, six ships of the fleet had been destroyed, and three more were badly damaged.

"The Polemarch is dead," Rivera announced to Victor when she returned from an officer debrief after the battle had ended. "The Revenor was one of the ships that was hit first. Admiral Rheine is dead, too."

"What about the quad?" Victor asked. "The instantaneous communication device."

"What about it?"

"Was it destroyed with the Polemarch's ship?"

"It wasn't discussed," said Rivera. "The meeting was mostly about succession. Vice Admiral Connelly and Vice Admiral Duquette are deciding how to divide the fleet between themselves and what to do next."

"We need to find out if someone is retrieving the quad," said Victor.

"If the vice admirals are powwowing on what to do next, then I take that to mean they aren't bothering to ask CentCom's advice on anything. Nobody's going for the quad."

"Then they must know it's destroyed," said Victor. "Because it's asinine not to go and recover our most critical piece of hardware."

"I wouldn't assume they know it's destroyed," said Rivera. "It's no secret that the vice admirals have never been fans of this operation."

"Then they're intentionally not getting the quad because they don't want CentCom giving them orders," said Victor. "This battle and the Polemarch's death are the opportunities they've been waiting for to get out of what they never wanted to do in the first place."

"I'd call that analysis likely accurate," said Rivera.

A different marine was guarding the entrance to Deck Three when Victor and Rivera arrived. A young kid. Male.

"Open the door," said Rivera.

"I'm sorry, Liuetenant," said the marine. "The rear admiral has asked not to be disturbed."

Victor raised an eyebrow. "The rear admiral?"

"Hoebeck," said Rivera. "Battlefield promotion."

"We haven't even tended to the dead, and already we're giving out promotions," said Victor. He turned to the marine. "Please open the door, Corporal."

The marine shook his head. "Sorry. I'm under orders not to open this door."

"Well, I've been given no such order," said Victor, "so I'll open it." He reached past the marine and hit the release button. The door opened.

"Hey!" said the marine.

"If they ask, you can say we overpowered you," said Victor. "Otherwise, you'll have to shoot us."

Victor launched forward and didn't look back. The young marine started to yell after him, but then Victor could hear Lieutenant Rivera getting in his face and giving him a grilling so that Victor could get through.

Most of the helm officers were crowded at the entrance to Hoebeck's office with their backs to the helm. Victor could hear Hoebeck's muffled voice inside, speaking intently. Only two young techs managed the holotable and helm.

Victor approached one of them. His nameplate read Khatri. "Was the Revenor completely destroyed?"

Khatri was a lowly apprentice, according to his insignia. Not a day over nineteen. He looked up from his tablet, faced Victor, and brightened. "Victor Delgado. It's an honor to meet you, sir. Big fan. I read your biography, *Cry of Warning*."

"That's nice. The Revenor. The Polemarch's ship. Was it destroyed completely?"

"The Revenor? Depends on how you would describe completely, sir."

"Were there survivors?"

"Twelve, sir. They were recovered just a few hours ago. All from the rear of the ship. Everyone up at the helm was killed in the assault. Breached hull. Terrible about the Polemarch. I heard he—"

"What about the quad?" said Victor. "Did the rescuers recover the quad?"

Khatri checked his tablet. "Not that I've heard."

A harsh voice interrupted them. "What is this man doing on my helm?"

Victor and Khatri turned to see newly promoted Rear Admiral Hoebeck emerging from his office, red-faced and fuming, flanked by his aides.

"How did you get past the guard?" demanded Hoebeck.

"Request permission to leave the ship," said Victor.

Hoebeck had opened his mouth and raised a finger and looked on the verge of shouting something when the question had derailed him. He blinked. Then his surprise faded and was replaced with a sneer. "You can't run home just yet, Ensign Delgado. I'm sorry if our battle here terrified you, but you're in the Fleet now. You're not going anywhere."

"The quad," said Victor. "Request permission to go to the Revenor and recover the quad."

"You're not authorized to touch the quad," said Hoebeck.

"No living person in this fleet is," said Victor. "I'm assuming the communications officer died in the assault. The quad connects us to CentCom and the Hegemony. We were just attacked by ships shaped like ours. A highly effective deception that allowed the Formics to get in close. Have these Formic ships been traveling with the

Fleet since the Fleet left the ecliptic or did they emerge from behind blinds?"

Hoebeck laughed. "You think they came with us all this way without us knowing?"

Victor shrugged. "It might not be that farfetched of an idea. Our fleet is spread out. With vast distances between each ship. Sometimes thousands of klicks apart. Plus we've been maintaining radio silence. Even the packet system is only used by a small percentage of the ships. Most of our ships don't talk to each other. The idea that Formic ships could remain at our fringes for months on end is quite believable. Maybe not as plausible as the blinds, but if you hadn't already heard about the blinds, I suspect that would be difficult to believe as well."

Hoebeck maintained his grimace but said nothing.

"The Fleet needs to know that the Formics have this capability," said Victor, "that the Formics can shape their ships to look like ours. Without the quad, we can't tell the Fleet anything, and they can't give us instructions, which is what we need right now more than anything."

"We've been given our instructions," said Hoebeck. "Vice Admiral Connelly and Vice Admiral Duquette have ordered us to abandon this operation and return to the ecliptic immediately."

"But is that what CentCom wants?" Victor asked. "Is that what the Strategos wants? The Hegemon? It's possible that they all want us to push on to the motherships."

Hoebeck remained quiet, but Victor could see that he was thinking it over.

"Sir, if the quad can be recovered," said Victor, "shouldn't we at least try to retrieve it and relay this critical intelligence back to the Fleet? Don't we have that duty? If the Formics can mimic Fleet ships here, then they can do so just as easily in the ecliptic. If we don't

warn the Fleet, they might be as caught off guard as we were, which will result in casualties the Fleet could have avoided but didn't. Because of us."

"I have my orders," said Hoebeck.

"Yes. You do. And all of your aides here can vouch under oath if necessary that you strictly forbade me from recovering the quad. You've demonstrated that you are adamant in following your superiors. It's not your fault if I disobey those orders and steal back my zipship. And it's not your fault if your men at the turrets are asleep on the job and don't fire on my zipship as I escape."

Hoebeck was quiet a moment. Finally he said, "In all likelihood the quad has been destroyed. You might be wasting your time."

"Maybe," said Victor. "But the helm was breached. That's how they died. Not from a blast that would destroy equipment, but from loss of air pressure."

Lieutenant Al-Baradouni spoke up. "Sir, if I may, the quad was a tool of the Polemarch. The Hegemon will now need to call a new Polemarch. I'd say it's likely that he would call that new Polemarch among the senior officers of this fleet. Should you have the quad, sir, you could inform the new Polemarch of his new assignment."

Lieutenant Al-Baradouni gave Victor a subtle look as if to cue him. Victor understood at once and felt silly for not seeing the argument immediately.

"I'd go one step further, sir," said Victor. "The senior officer who recovers the quad, and shows great allegiance to the Hegemony by so doing, may even be deemed the frontrunner for the office of Polemarch. Why wouldn't the Hegemony pick you, sir? You would have the quad. You could assume the role without delay."

Hoebeck held up a hand. "You're laying it on thick now. As I've told you, I have orders that I must obey unless I receive orders from a higher authority like, say, the Hegemon or CentCom. But I am not about to be deemed

insubordinate by subverting the commands of my superiors. Do I make myself clear, Ensign Delgado?"

His tone was much more agreeable now. Almost pleasant.

"Crystal clear, sir."

Hoebeck turned to Lieutenant Al-Baradouni. "Lieutenant, I believe it's time for you to do a thorough inspection of the cargo bay, where the zipship is stored. That should keep the loadmasters occupied for quite some time and leave the zipship unattended."

"Agreed, sir."

Climbing back into the zipship in his flight suit felt to Victor like crawling back into his grave.

"This is a terrible idea," said Rivera as she helped pack in the supplies he'd be taking. "Why does it have to be you? You're still recovering from the last time you were in this thing. Now you're going to undo all the progress we've made."

"We haven't made any progress," said Victor. "I still look like a sickly eighty-year-old version of myself."

"You *have* made progress. You used to look eighty. Now you look seventy-eight."

Victor smiled. "Don't let them leave me, okay?"

"Are you kidding? Hoebeck despises you. He'll probably accelerate as soon as you're off the ship."

"Not with the carrot I'm dangling. Not a chance."

"You don't even know what the quad looks like," said Rivera. "How will you know when you find it?"

"It will have a keyboard and be in its own room."

"That's nearly every terminal on the ship."

"I'm pretty sure this won't look like a typical terminal display."

"This ansible belonged to the Polemarch," said Rivera. "He may not have used a communications officer to

operate it. He might have used it himself. More efficient that way. In which case, the ansible might be in his quarters, not at the helm."

"One of the helm officers gave me a map of the Revenor. If the ansible's not at the helm, I'll check the Polemarch's quarters."

"Which might be locked," said Rivera.

"Then I'll break the door down," said Victor. "Anything else?"

"Don't die," said Rivera. "I haven't lost a patient yet. Don't screw up my track record."

It took Victor three days to reach the Revenor since it was still moving in the direction that it had held when it was attacked. Victor was surprised to find the ship mostly intact. The holes were clearly visible, and the damage was catastrophic, but it flew onward like a ghost of its former self.

He had no one to assist with the docking, so he flew the zipship right up into one of the massive holes in the ship and anchored it to structural beams inside. It took several hours for him to reach the helm because the ship no longer had power, and the doors and hatches had to be manually opened with the emergency cranks. By the time he reached the helm, both of his arms ached from all the effort.

The helm had three corpses drifting in the room. The room was large and looked to have held a staff of twenty or more. Perhaps the other marines had been sucked out the large hole near the navigational table. One of the bodies was the Polemarch, Ishmerai Averbach. Victor collected his ankle tag, crossed himself, and collected the other two tags as well.

He found the quad immediately thereafter. The quad room was small and adjacent to the helm. The communications officer was inside. Victor pulled the body out of the room and collected the man's ankle tag. The quad

was smaller than Victor expected. No bigger than a large suitcase. It was simple and boxy. Functional. It wasn't going to win any awards for its design. You typed, you read, you typed some more. A stenographer probably had better-looking equipment.

He had worried ever since setting out from the Vandalorum that he would find the quad intact and undamaged from the battle yet rendered useless by the cold of space. That seemed to be the case now. The machine looked lifeless. He tapped at the keyboard and nothing happened. The small display remained black and devoid of light. He tapped at the keys again, and still nothing.

He noticed a small plate a few centimeters square on the bottom right-hand corner of the display. It was slightly dirty from the greasy residue of a thumbprint. Victor pressed his own gloved thumb to the square, and the square lit up blue momentarily before dimming again. Nothing happened thereafter, which meant it wasn't simply a button. It was a print scan, a form of security. He tried maneuvering the communications officer back into the room, but the corpse was stiff and frozen, and there was no way he would be able to position the man's thumb where it belonged. Victor took his pocket laser, apologized out loud, and cut the man's thumb off. Victor worried that even this wouldn't work, though. The corpses were all severely discolored, and the thumb wasn't as pliable and soft as it needed to be to press flat against the plate to get a thorough scan.

But the quad fired up and the terminal display went from black to a pleasant green. The word "Revenor" followed by a colon appeared. Victor began to type.

REVENOR: Hello
CENTCOM: Revenor, please update. You've been
    silent for almost five days.
REVENOR: this isnt revenor welll it iss but not re-

ally this is victpr delgado the crew of the revenot are dead ship destroyed hard to typee in gloves request permission to take quad to vandalorumm

CENTCOM: Did you say the ship was destroyed? Where is the Polemarch?

REVENOR: deceased

CENTCOM: Who is the commanding officer with you?

REVENOR: Okay, I found the delete and shift key, as well as the punctuation keys. Why would you make those hard to find? There is no commanding officer with me. I came alone from the Vandalorum. I need someone to tell me how to move this thing. Do I need to unplug it? I don't see a plug anywhere. I'm afraid I'm going to break something.

CENTCOM: Name, rank, and serial number.

REVENOR: Serious? I'm typing in gloves. My oxygen is limited. I told you my name. serial # not memorized. Rank=peon.

CENTCOM: Stand by.

REVENOR: Hello? It's been 5 min.

CENTCOM: Stand by.

REVENOR: I'm in a pressure suit. Time's a wasting!!!!

CENTCOM: What happened to the Revenor?

REVENOR: Formic ships shaped like IF ships ambushed us. 6 ships lost. 3 damaged. Need orders. Vice admirals want to abandon op and return. Others, like me, feel we should move on to target. Please advise.

CENTCOM: Stand by.

REVENOR: I've got 40% oxygen. Need to return to zipship. Tell me how to safely move this thing or I'm going to move it without your help.

CENTCOM: Stand by.

CENTCOM: We need to confirm your identity.

CENTCOM: Place your right thumb against the scan plate.

CENTCOM: Please respond.

CENTCOM: Do you copy?

CENTCOM: Do you copy?

CENTCOM: Do you copy?

CENTCOM: Do you copy?

CENTCOM: Please respond.

REVENOR: I told you turkeys that I had to move the thing and that I was going to move it whether you gave me instructions or not. This was a nightmare to navigate through the ship. I am now back in the zipship and moving away from the Revenor. I also brought the communications officer's thumb in case I need it again, which I hope I don't. I am out of my pressure suit and will press my thumb against the plate. Stand by.

UKKO: Victor. It's Ukko Jukes.

REVENOR:—Mr. Jukes. I guess they forwarded my call.

UKKO: We had to verify that you are who you say you are. We've had pirates seize ansibles in the past.

REVENOR: What's an ansible?

UKKO: The device you're using. Quad is the code name. You now have the real name because you are now the designated operator of this device. The only operator. No one else has access. That includes the vice admirals and Captain Hoebeck.

REVENOR: He goes by Rear Admiral Hoebeck now.

UKKO: That hasn't been authorized. And won't be. But we'll deal with that later. I want a full accounting of the battle and all events since. I will be meeting with the Hegemon-Elect soon and want to update her. But first, there is a matter for you. This network you're on is a unique one. It connects to only

a few select ansibles. There is someone you need to speak with because she has information that you may not be aware of. I will disconnect with you and then instruct her on how to connect with you. You'll need to identify yourself. I will connect again with you shortly. Stand by.

GAGAK: Ensign Bootstamp connected. Please identify.

REVENOR: Imala?

GAGAK: Who is this?

REVENOR: It's me. Victor. It's your space born. Is this really happening?

REVENOR: Are you there?

GAGAK: I can't type. I'm sobbing.

GAGAK: Chee, say hello to your daddy.

Bingwen spent the next two weeks practicing maneuvers in the Battle Room at GravCamp, sometimes with Mazer, sometimes with Rat Army, but usually by himself, which was his preference. When alone, he could close his eyes, extend his arms, and drift through the Battle Room like a leaf upon the water. Someone looking in from the outside might see him and think him completely at ease, relaxed, perfectly balanced. But nothing was further from the truth. Bingwen was never at peace. He had never understood how people could take a few deep breaths and clear their minds. Bingwen's mind was never clear. Meditation amplified his worries, not dissolved them. But that was why he loved to drift: It allowed him to focus on his worries, rather than brushing them aside as he usually did to focus on the task or conversation at hand.

Today's worries were many, and at the center of them all was the Hive Queen, still rejected by the Fleet as a theory but more alive in Bingwen's mind than she had ever been. Bingwen had thought that it was all the evi-

dence of her existence that kept his belief in her so strong. But as he drifted and considered, he realized that this wasn't entirely true. He believed because Mazer believed. Because wherever Mazer's roots of logic were planted was where Bingwen wanted his own to grow.

Why was the Hive Queen taking people? That was what weighed on Bingwen's mind the most. Colonel Li had received intel that Formics were taking people in the Kuiper Belt. What was the Hive Queen hoping to accomplish? By all accounts, she had only taken a few, which led Bingwen to speculate that there was a secret strategy here, something she wanted to conceal. Take too many people, and you draw attention to the problem. But take only a few and no one will much notice compared to the number of casualties elsewhere.

By the end of the drift, he was ready to finally confront Colonel Li. He showered, changed back into his jumpsuit, and made his way to Colonel Li's office.

GravCamp was nearly empty now. Colonel Dietrich had been sent off to an administrative position at a supply depot in the Belt, where he would likely writhe in misery until the war ended. The marines who had been training at GravCamp were also sent to the Belt, whether they had finished their training or not. After all the losses from what Nak called the Formic simulacrum ships, reinforcements were desperately needed in the Belt. Twelve IF ships had been lost in a single day. And far too many lives.

Colonel Li removed all of the documents from his holotable when Bingwen entered.

"I've received your orders," said Li. "The transport will pick us up in two weeks."

"Us? You're going with us?"

"How could I not?"

"I thought this was your facility now. You're the CO of GravCamp."

"GravCamp is being abandoned. It's far too costly and time-consuming to bring soldiers here for zero G training."

"I could have told you that a year ago," said Bingwen. "The location of this school is impractical, even considering that it feeds marines to both the Asteroid Belt and the Kuiper Belt. A school like this needs to be close to Earth. Except with better food. And better barracks. And a better Battle Room. And no adults."

"Sounds like *Lord of the Flies* in space," said Li. "Something tells me that wouldn't pass the first committee to consider it."

"Once they see how brilliant Blue Army is, they'll change their tune."

"You're not Blue Army," said Li. "Not really. You only use that name with me. I know you call yourselves Rat Army. Why not just own it?"

"Because you weren't supposed to know. We wanted something to be ours and ours alone. How silly of us to think that we could have any privacy in this universe."

"Silly, yes," said Li. "You're forgetting this is the military."

"What about Mazer?" said Bingwen. "Is he coming with us?"

"He is, but he won't be pleased by the assignment. We'll be under the command of his former CO, Rear Admiral Vaganov."

"You're determined to make Mazer's life a living hell."

"I do what I can," said Li.

"And what will we be doing with Rear Admiral Vaganov? Because if you recall, Rat Army and I aren't technically members of the Fleet. We're at a school."

"We're taking an extended field trip," said Li. "The data cube you brought back from the Kandahar contained photos and information regarding an asteroid the Formics had covered with blinds. We knew the Formics

were moving the asteroid, but we didn't know to where. It wasn't until we got additional information from Victor Delgado that we realized that our one invisible asteroid was actually part of a cluster of nine asteroids that were being gathered out beyond the Belt to provide resources for a Formic superstructure."

"Sounds ominous," said Bingwen. "Any chance it's a theme park?"

"I'm glad you can make light of these revelations. Now's the time to get all the jokes out of your system. Once we reach the structure, any attempt at levity will fall flat."

"That *does* sound ominous. I don't suppose this structure happens to be the place where Mazer and I believe the Hive Queen fled after she ran from Operation Deep Dive?"

"You have no evidence that the escaping ship was carrying the Hive Queen," said Li. "But yes, we believe this structure was the destination of that escaping ship."

"Good. Maybe we'll get our chance to take down the Hive Queen after all."

"There are many Formic structures that could be holding the Hive Queen," said Li. "Both in the ecliptic and in deep space. We have people investigating them all. Someone will find the Hive Queen. Or whatever it is that controls the Formics. And when that someone does find her, he'll kill her. I'm hoping that someone is you."

"I've certainly learned a great deal about killing lately," said Bingwen.

Colonel Li sighed. "Spill it, Bingwen. There's obviously something on your mind. I can see that you're seething. What is it?"

"It *was* you who murdered the captain of the transport. On the way out here to GravCamp. You went in his office, put the laser to his head, shot him, and made it look like a suicide."

"You're making a ridiculous and baseless accusation," said Li. "And to your commanding officer, no less. Why, great detective, would I kill a stranger and risk my career and livelihood?"

"He was about to be promoted again," said Bingwen. "His friends at CentCom had arranged to move him from his post on the transport to a new warship, where he would serve as captain. A crew of nearly three hundred marines. You and the intelligence agency knew that he was incompetent and dangerous and thus a risk to his subordinates. It took me a long time to find that information. The plans to promote the captain were never publicly known. He didn't even know it himself, which would have thrown a wrench into the suicide narrative, if he had known. But you also did it because it was a test of a new program, identifying incompetent and high-risk commanders and then removing them. Sometimes non-lethally. Sometimes not. You and your superiors wanted to know if it would work, if you could stage a demise like his in plain sight without anyone suspecting anything. And then you had Rat Army serve as analysts identifying the other targets. What's sad is that I knew all along that that's what we were doing, giving you people to remove, helping you kill people."

"A fascinating story, Bingwen. Sadly, it's one that all the evidence disproves. I know you think I'm an evil human being. But when this war is over, and we've won, and you see how we've won, and how we would've lost if hard people had not done hard things, you'll thank me. Because you'll still be alive, and you'll still have a world. You're dismissed."

Bingwen left. He had said his piece, and he would never bring it up again. Not until after the war, perhaps. And maybe not even then.

He returned to the Battle Room and was surprised to find that it was no longer empty. Mazer was launching

back and forth, twisting in the air, landing somewhat awkwardly.

"I thought you were supposed to stay off that ankle for a while," said Bingwen.

"I have been. I'm bored."

Bingwen didn't mention the superstructure or Vaganov. Mazer would find out soon enough. He didn't mention the dead transport captain, either. He probably never would. Instead he called Rat Army to the Battle Room. "We've got two weeks to live it up here," he told them. "Then we're off to places with far less leisure."

"That stinks," said Nak. "Just when I was starting to like this place."

"Let's divide up," said Bingwen. "Mazer counts as three people."

"Are you saying I'm fat?" said Mazer.

"I'm saying you've got three times the skills that we do."

"Speak for yourself," said Chati. "I can take this old man."

"What are we playing?" asked Jianjun.

"I don't care," said Bingwen. "So long as it's just a game."

ACKNOWLEDGMENTS

The talents and assistance of many people made this book possible. The authors would like to give special thanks to our editor, Beth Meacham, who is such a wise and careful reader and always kind. Thank you, Beth, for your patience and suggestions. Thanks also to Jen Gunnels at Tor for all her assistance. Liana Krissoff caught and corrected errors you will thankfully never see. Bless you, Liana. Cyndie Swindlehurst caught even more errors and greatly improved this novel with her careful reading and meticulous notes. She is the type of beta reader every writer dreams of, attentive and thorough and always right. Our deep gratitude also goes to the brilliant John Harris, whose art graces the cover of this book. John has created the art for all of the Formic Wars novels, and we could not be more delighted and honored. We would be remiss if we didn't also thank our wives, Kristine Card and Lauren Johnston, who are always our first readers, and who gently nudge us along with loving encouragement. Lastly, thank you, dear reader, for believing in this universe and in these characters. We appreciate your support. May your dreams be free of Formics and your slasers always charged.

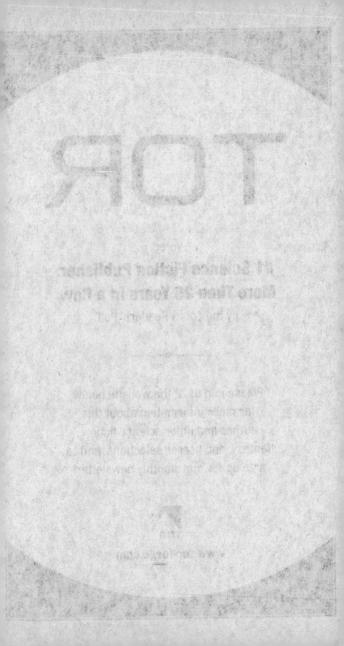